THE GROVE OF
THE CAESARS

Also by Lindsey Davis

The Course of Honour
Rebels and Traitors
Master and God
A Cruel Fate

The Falco Series

The Silver Pigs
Shadows in Bronze
Venus in Copper
The Iron Hand of Mars
Poseidon's Gold
Last Act in Palmyra
Time to Depart
A Dying Light in Corduba
Three Hands in the Fountain
Two for the Lions
One Virgin Too Many
Ode to a Banker
A Body in the Bath House
The Jupiter Myth
The Accusers
Scandal Takes a Holiday
See Delphi and Die
Saturnalia
Alexandria
Nemesis

The Flavia Albia Series

The Ides of April
Enemies at Home
Deadly Election
The Graveyard of the Hesperides
The Third Nero
Pandora's Boy
A Capitol Death

The Spook Who Spoke Again
Vesuvius by Night
Invitation to Die
Falco: The Official Companion

THE GROVE OF THE CAESARS

MINOTAUR BOOKS
NEW YORK

Lindsey Davis

First published in the United States by Minotaur Books, an imprint of St. Martin's Publishing Group

THE GROVE OF THE CAESARS. Copyright © 2020 by Lindsey Davis. All rights reserved. Printed in the United States of America. For information, address St. Martin's Publishing Group, 120 Broadway, New York, NY 10271.

www.minotaurbooks.com

Map by Rodney Paull

The Library of Congress Cataloging-in-Publication Data is available upon request.

ISBN 978-1-250-24156-6 (hardcover)
ISBN 978-1-250-24157-3 (ebook)

Our books may be purchased in bulk for promotional, educational, or business use. Please contact your local bookseller or the Macmillan Corporate and Premium Sales Department at 1-800-221-7945, extension 5442, or by email at MacmillanSpecialMarkets@macmillan.com.

Originally published in Great Britain by Hodder & Stoughton, an Hachette UK Company

First U.S. Edition: 2020

10 9 8 7 6 5 4 3 2 1

THE GROVE OF
THE CAESARS

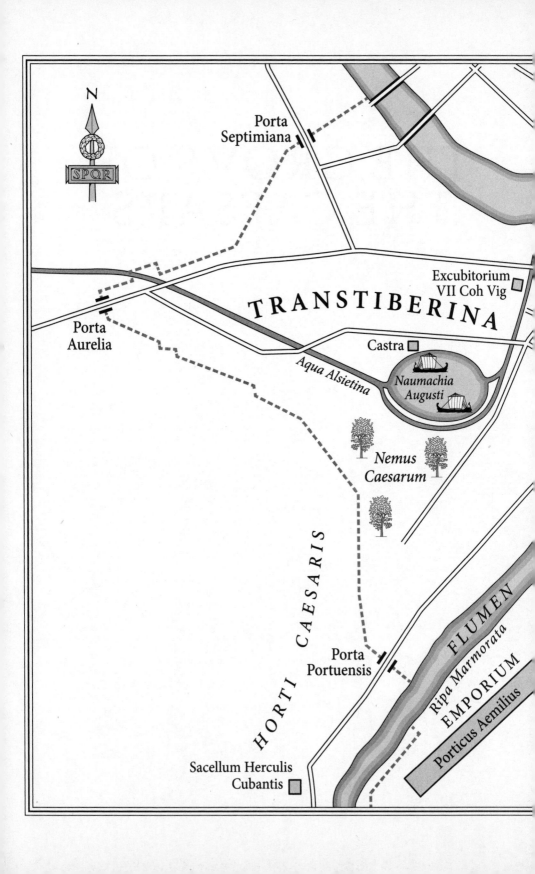

N

SPQR

Porta
Septimiana

Excubitorium
VII Coh Vig

TRANSTIBERINA

Castra

Porta
Aurelia

Aqua Alsietina

Naumachia
Augusti

Nemus
Caesarum

HORTI CAESARIS

Porta
Portuensis

FLUMEN

Ripa Marmorata

EMPORIUM

Porticus Aemilius

Sacellum Herculis
Cubantis

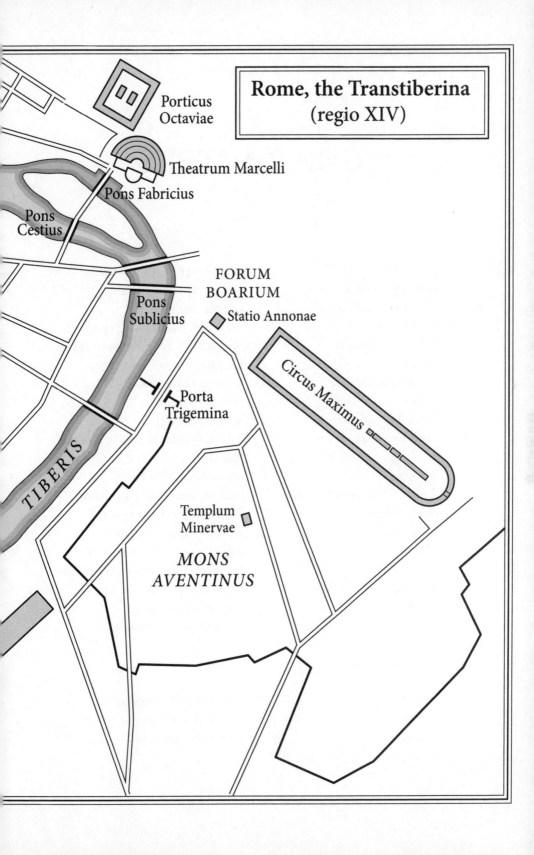

Rome, the Transtiberina
(regio XIV)

Porticus
Octaviae

Theatrum Marcelli

Pons Fabricius

Pons
Cestius

FORUM
BOARIUM

Pons
Sublicius

Statio Annonae

Porta
Trigemina

Circus Maximus

TIBERIS

Templum
Minervae

*MONS
AVENTINUS*

CHARACTERS

Flavia Albia	an investigator, stuck at home
Falco and Helena	off the scene, her parents
Julia, Favonia, Postumus	on form, her siblings
Suza	her stylist, on a learning curve
T. Manlius Faustus	her husband, away for family reasons
Dromo	his slave, who will never learn
Gratus, Fornix, Paris	their expanding household
Barley	their nervous dog
Galanthus and Primulus	new helpers, a gift
Fania Faustina	Tiberius's sister, hoping to save her marriage
Antistius	her husband, a no-hoper
Aellius, Daellius and Laellius	their hopeless sons, poor ducks
Uncle Tullius	Tiberius's uncle, a pragmatist
Aunt Valeria	Tiberius's aunt, a fatalist
Marcia	Albia's cousin, a drama queen
Corellius	her lover, absent on a secret mission
Stertinius	the Fabulous citharode, a purist
Fluentius	his flirtatious flautist
Pamphyllus	his peckish percussionist

In the building trade

Larcius	a reliable clerk of works
Serenus	a satirical workman
Sparsus	a put-upon errand boy

Trypho	a jumpy night watchman
Spendo	a lopsided surveyor, dead-straight estimates
Sosthenes	a water-features expert, bit of a drip
Two painters	hired by somebody to paint something

In the Saepta Julia

Gornia	an ancient auction porter
Cornelius	a young auctioneer

In Caesar's Gardens and the sacred Grove

Berytus	a plant-loving supervisor
Blandus	a rough-sleeping gang leader
Rullius	a home-loving path-sweeper
Quietus	a prime suspect, says he didn't do it
Gaius	an apprentice, says he saw something
Alina	a wife, dreaming of love: no chance
Cluventius	enjoying his birthday party
Victoria Tertia	putting up with it for his sake
Cluvia	their daughter, taking on burdens
Engeles	a shocked retainer
Vatia and Paecentius	trusted family friends
Romilia	a sensible woman
Satia	just another missing victim
Methe	yet another, never forgotten
Seius	her husband, a decent fellow
A tomb curator	his kindly friend
A shrine guardian	blind to the truth

In the untrustworthy Seventh Cohort of Vigiles

Ursus	a diligent inquiry chief
Julius Karus	on a mission, beefing up Ursus
Arctus	a nude

In the exciting world of books

Mysticus	an admired scroll-seller
Tuccia	now running the shop
Tartus	a scroll-mender, glued to his task
Diocles	a principled scribe
Marcus Ovidius	a reclusive collector, an obsessive
Donatus	supplier of rare works, a benefactor
Xerxes	his partner, hard to find
Callista	a disappearing widow
Epitynchanus the Dialectician	"the Controversialist," a cosmologist
Philadespoticus of Skopelos	a materialist fragmentalist
Didymus Dodomos	a ghastly horticulturalist, ghost-written
Thallusa	an underrated poet
Obfusculans the Obscure	a very obscure author

ROME:
THE TRANSTIBERINA
December AD 89

———————

I

I want to make a complaint. Poets are wrong about gardens.

Your average poet, scratching away to impress his peers in the Writers' Guild at their dusty haunt on the Aventine, the Temple of Minerva, will portray a garden as a metaphor for productive peace and quiet. In such secluded places, poets will say, men who own multiple estates engage in happy contemplation of weighty intellectual matters, while acquiring a glow of health. These landowners, idiot patrons of ridiculous authors, take pleasure from topiary cut in the shape of their own names, yet they avoid the slur of self-indulgence, simply because their box-tree autographs have roots in the earth.

When garden-owners step indoors, it is no better. Every wall in their houses adds to the lie, with pictorial herbage cluttering up frieze and dado; sometimes branches and garden ornaments even dangle from ceilings. For most Romans, growing a shrub in an urn reminds them of their agricultural forebears quite enough, while the landscaped panoramas they gaze upon indoors are a symbol of the leisured life in a civilised city, where the natural world can be permanently tamed without the intervention of worms.

Both poets and landowners live in a dream. These fellows couldn't plant a seed, or if they did it would damp off.

Art and literature are wrong. A gardener keeps his grounds tidy by inflicting death; he sees living things as weeds and pests, so he kills them. Horticulture calls for a shed that is cram-full of poisons and very sharp tools. Do not be fooled. Any walk through a garden will take you past amputated branches, torn-up beds, desiccated trees, mould, blight, fungi, smells, and dead rodents with bedraggled fur that expired last night in the middle of your path. Crows flying overhead will have dropped bloody entrails they snatched at the meat market. The elegant ivy winding itself up that tree is strangling it.

You yourself are in danger. As you recoil from the carnage that greets you on all sides, take care: you may slip over, tumble down a slope or turn your ankle in a hole. Watch out for wasps. Make sure you do not step on a rake. That's a common route to a cracked skull and sepsis. You may enter a garden on foot, but you will probably leave it in a barrow, carried like a sack of trimmings. The man wheeling you is whistling, while you are moaning with pain.

Gardens are regarded as places to be solitary. Don't believe it. Naiads are raped by randy satyrs. Gods chase after girls, who must be turned into trees for their own good. People you wouldn't want as neighbours bring obscenely stuffed bread rolls, then play shrieking games at picnics. Grass-mowers who look as if they are planning to stab someone edge too close then if you dare to catch their eye, they talk to you interminably. Everywhere there are isolated spots where bad things happen. That predator rustling unseen in the undergrowth may not be a snake, but something much worse. Public gardens are favourite places to dispose of murdered corpses.

In all of this, the sacred Grove of the Caesars was no different. I would never have ventured within its pesky railings, except that my husband had had to rush away to the country because a relative was dangerously ill.

II

When the letter arrived, Tiberius was feeling tired. Everyone in our house was the same that morning, because yesterday had been the Emperor's triumph. Last night my family had decided a feast must be hosted by Tiberius and me. We were newly wed: we hadn't yet quarrelled with enough people to be off limits. Besides, since we owned a building firm, we had a big yard. My family welcomed that with glee. So, a firepit for roasting meats was dug there, men knocked together trestle tables, women decorated our courtyard with garlands, then scads of relatives turned up, led by dippy aunts with trays of suspiciously dog-eared pastries. The words "Don't worry, we'll bring food" can be a double-edged promise.

Today, as the aunts came to ask for their trays back, even our cook was tired. Anyone who could face breakfast had to fend for themselves. My elegant new steward was wandering about like a man who had tidied up the wine flagons last night by drinking all the dregs in the bottom. Dromo, the slave who looked after Tiberius, was sound asleep; Suza, my maid, ditto. The dog was hiding. My husband could be seen sitting in the courtyard, as motionless and silent as a man who was wondering how the universe began; a beaker of herb tea had gone cold on the bench beside him.

I was awake. Someone must stay on duty. The place was a wreck. I tried some gentle clearing up. Soon I stopped bothering.

Two messengers came that morning and were admitted by me when everyone else ignored their knocks. The first was a soldier bringing an invitation for Tiberius to attend what would subsequently be known as the Emperor's Black Banquet. I quickly penned regrets: my husband the aedile had recently survived a lightning strike; on medical advice he could not yet socialise. I added "as reported in the *Daily Gazette*," because when you are refusing a chance to be poisoned by your emperor, it is best to sound factual.

Next came a worrying letter from his aunt Valeria about his sister. I nearly kept that until Tiberius was feeling more himself, but he called out to ask what it was. The aunt, poor old dearie, liked to steep herself in misery, but I could tell as he read it that her news was worse than normal.

She thought Tiberius ought to come urgently to Fidenae. That was where he grew up and a few family members still lived. Valeria warned darkly it might be his last chance to see his sister.

We knew Fania Faustina was pregnant. She was married to a Fidenae man called Antistius; they already had three young sons. Tiberius and I found Antistius uncouth: we had witnessed him trying to be unfaithful with a barmaid, although even that grubby working girl rebuffed him. Fania must always have realised what he was like, but when they visited Rome for our wedding this autumn, she began to admit his inadequacy. She wept and spoke of leaving him. That plan failed because she was having a new baby—perhaps it was an attempt to save their marriage. Misguided, we thought privately. Aunt Valeria agreed in principle but reckoned that, after three sons, her niece wanted a daughter.

Valeria, who lived near the couple, had been keeping a sharp eye out. She so much enjoyed being a snoop she could have spied for the Emperor. Fania was typical of the clients I worked for as an informer: a pleasant, sad soul who felt her life might be better. Too right, unhappy sister-in-law! She needed to shed the louche louse she was shackled to. I had attempted guidance, but Fania was soft dough. She believed she must stay married for the children's sake. I last encountered those little boys holding my hands with sticky fingers in my bridal procession: not my favourite nuptial memory. Fania really ought to have told Antistius that legally the boys were his problem, then left him with it.

Despite their difficulties, now Fania was bringing another unfortunate into the world. But the aunt wrote that Fania was experiencing terrible pain. I had no idea whether Valeria herself had ever borne children, but Fania would know if this pregnancy was going wrong. The husband was useless; the rat just went out and left her to suffer.

Valeria, who had brought up Fania Faustina after she and Tiberius were orphaned, told us she had stepped in. She took Fania back into her own house, with her own doctor looking after her. But the doctor looked grim and Valeria was so nervous she wanted Tiberius to come.

When I read this letter, I thought he should take it seriously. Aunt Valeria liked to exaggerate, but she had a kindly nature and was no fool. She loved her niece. I even detected anxiety for her nephew; if anything happened to Fania and he hadn't reacted soon enough, he would blame himself. They lost their parents in their teens, so given her husband's conduct, Tiberius felt he still had head-of-household responsibilities.

Tiberius wanted to believe that his sister was in no real danger, but he decided to see for himself. He sent Dromo to hire a horse, which would be the fastest way to get there.

"I hope nobody expects me to ride him, Master!"

"That would be too unkind to the horse. I'm travelling light, Dromo. If I need to stay for long, you can bring more stuff for me in a cart."

"I can't go in a cart all by myself."

"Noted. Now shut up, please."

Even Dromo finally saw that Tiberius was worried.

The plan was for me to stay in Rome. I never said it but, like Dromo, nothing would entice me onto a hired horse for a ten- or twelve-mile journey. But there was no need to stress. With his magistracy due to end, my man had bought a moribund building firm to keep him occupied. Its revival was still in the start-up phase, with Tiberius wanting to branch out from remodelling backstreet food shops to more ambitious projects where he wouldn't keep finding rats in old food bins and skeletons in back gardens. He had a clerk of works, who verged on fairly reliable, plus workmen who had sometimes been known to build a wall that stayed up. He could safely leave them, but he liked the idea of me acting as his deputy. His team were scared of me. That might be because of what I had said to them last night, when their fooling in the roasting pit had nearly set the yard on fire.

Just words. Those men were wimps.

Tiberius threw a few things into a luggage roll, while giving me details of projects to monitor. I nodded. He was too upset about his sister for me to say, "Don't fuss." I gravely promised to make sure all the snagging at the Triton was finished this week, then send an invoice. Yes, I would chase up the marble order for Fullo's. *I love you, darling, fear not, I know how you like to do things. Yes, if I am unsure about anything at all, I shall put it on hold until you come back* . . . Tiberius reckoned I could trust Larcius, the clerk of works, to progress their big nymphaeum rebuild in the Nemus Caesarum. When he mentioned that scheme, I barely noticed how—as if simply to save me any trouble—he murmured, "Don't go to the Grove."

Of course, if I had noticed, it would have been a certain way to send me scurrying over there.

III

In his absence I would have my hands full.

Most informers live alone. It's advisable. Our hours are uncertain, our breath stinks of street food, we frequently come home in a foul mood. To share an apartment with one of us is worse than living with a sozzled old stevedore, who keeps telling you he wishes Rome still had Nero, while he scratches his scurvy. Informers, as we are the first to admit, are rough. Apart from our personal habits and those seedy clients who call to discuss taking revenge on their revolting acquaintances, it's a rare month when one of us can pay the rent.

Solo living was what I was used to, though I had been a wife for a short time when I was young. After that, until I remarried recently, I lived by myself for years. I used to have the best apartment in the Eagle Building, Fountain Court; it was a terrible tenement near the Street of the Armilustrium, where "best" only meant there were four floors above me to soak up the deluge when the roof leaked. From my prestige rooms, I could dodge the landlord by nipping down a balcony staircase. Since the landlord was my father, he normally arrived by the back way in any case, though, to be fair, he wasn't coming for money from me because the softhearted sop never charged me any rent. He simply wanted to avoid his other tenants.

The independent life had suited me so, these days, I was having to adjust. When you fall for a fine man, who is mad enough to fall for you, there are gains and losses. Once, my world was cheap to run and, whatever I did or didn't do, nobody complained. If I grumbled about life, nobody heard. Most times, other people never even knew where I was.

Now I had to budget for a household, help with a business, entertain all kinds of visitors and be right here the moment anyone wanted me.

We lived in a house that would be beautiful one day, though we might be eating gruel in the care of nurses by the time it happened. Our home was under constant renovation, which only moved on slowly because we had to give precedence to our paying customers. Even so, we always had a pair of painters on the premises, two odd men who kept arguing. They never seemed to paint much. Tiberius thought I had hired them; I thought he did. As well as wondering about these loud louts who were dripping red ochre on my staircase, I seemed to spend a lot of time soothing overwrought domestic staff. Callers dropped in without warning. Nobody here ever saw it as their job to answer the door.

Tiberius believed I could handle all this. Fortunately, he was intelligent enough to see it might be a challenge, then affectionate enough to keep asking whether I was happy. I said yes. Even I could not decide whether it was true. That's marriage. I had known what I was taking on. In return I got him. Well, I had him when he wasn't being dragged away by his family.

As soon as he left for Fidenae, I tackled my task list because once I began to miss him, I might end up moping uselessly. Besides, it was possible clients of my own would come along to commission me. The imperial triumph might work in my favour: festivals always lead to upsets because too much drink is consumed and, traditionally, mothers-in-law are at their worst while feasting. Then nightmares happen: unwise confessions, running away from home, or even suspicious deaths. No one had turned up for help yet, but perhaps they were checking my references.

While I waited for hypothetical clients, I nipped out to the Triton. This was a bar where the owner foolishly believed that after you have building works you can demand that the contractor comes back to fix any cracks, missing tesserae, bent hinges or bumpy grout. How do these myths start?

"Will your husband be away for long?"

"We are a working partnership. He sent me."

"Oh, bugger."

The place was a backstreet soup counter, newly spruced up with perfectly smart results. The owner had broth stains down his apron, a permanent odour of chopped onion and no judgement. I pretended to sympathise over the standard of work we had done for him, after which I pointed out that Tiberius had sent a man yesterday for remedial touch-ups. Next I set him straight. I placed a neat bill on his new counter, saying someone would collect the money tomorrow.

I wasn't an auctioneer's daughter for nothing. I knew how to gather in payments. I mentioned that our terms were cash on the nail, or we would have him chained to a trireme oar. "No, no, I'm joking. Really, if you don't cough up, Tiberius Manlius will send the boys. The reason you haven't heard about them is that once they make a payment call any debtor is too shocked to speak . . ." I breezed off home while the bar owner was still blinking nervously.

Tiberius had no enforcement team. He used to saunter along himself and charm people.

I never bother with charm.

Back at the house, I found a woman who looked like a potential client for me. She came on her own, a middle-aged, middle-income type, with a tentative air. That fitted my customer base. She might want me to find her long-abandoned baby or the lover who had skipped off after helping himself to her jewel box. I mentally placed her as able to afford a records search, though unlikely to fund a full-scale surveillance. I was all set to explain my terms when I learned she had a problem of a different kind. She wanted to know if Tiberius Manlius would come and look at her drainpipe.

I sized her up with new eyes. My husband was a virile, handsome man in his prime; she must have seen him out and about on the Aventine. As aediles do, he was still extracting fines from dodgily run bathhouses and telling householders to sweep donkey droppings off their pavements, but his term was due to end next month. He would then revert to being an amiable neighbour who had renovation knowledge and supposedly spare time. He would be very attractive to any woman who wanted a free maintenance job—or whose drainpipe did not leak at all, but she had other ideas.

I was going to see a lot of this.

I smiled and said I was his wife. Would she like me to inspect her drainpipe? I could assess leaks and price up renovations . . Then I set her straight too.

IV

Next morning, before Larcius led the workmen out with their barrows of tools, I went through to the yard. I was hunting our order for the marble at Fullo's Nook, so I could chase up the late delivery for Tiberius.

"Good luck!" chortled Larcius, through whistly gums, when I invaded the office. The clerk of works was forty-five and must have lost his teeth ten years ago. From the challenge in his tone, I deduced that the marble importers were being their unhelpful selves.

Fullo was the usual kind of proprietor, who was sure he knew how to organise catering. His Nook was a hot-scoff popina in the portico outside the Circus. Smartening it up would hardly impress its customers, who ignored everything but their obsession with racing form. Still, Fullo was impatient. He had been thinking about exotic improvements for thirty years, so now he wanted it done by next week.

I told Larcius I would chivvy the suppliers but could make no promises. "Tiberius Manlius gets annoyed because his grandfather was in marble. He says it can be done perfectly well, without messing clients about."

"He's right. They're crap. We only want a few off-cuts," agreed Larcius. "We're not surfacing an imperial bath-house, it's a patchwork counter . . . Problem with his sister, is it?"

Without going into details, I said enough to let Larcius feel I had confided family secrets. To change the subject, I mentioned the woman with the alleged leaky drainpipe. "I think it's her story that has holes in it."

Larcius grinned. "One of those! We know the type. When they plead for Faustus to look at their bedroom cove, he sends along our lopsided dwarf to do an estimate—that's usually the last we hear."

"Which high-class specialist is this?"

"Spendo. Face like melting rock. That scares them before he's got a foot in the door—and his feet are a bit gnarled too. He's three foot high on his good side, and his pricing-up makes punters wince. We use him to survey all the jobs we don't want."

I said I was glad Tiberius Manlius was so savvy. Larcius promised that if there was ever one of these women I really ought to know about he would tell me.

Probably he would. The workmen knew they had been rescued from a dying concern, so they welcomed having more secure employment now that we owned the firm. I was seeing how family businesses work. The wife matters. They would ensure the master had peace at home.

Larcius assured me that nothing else on the stocks needed my attention. He and the lads would be at the nymphaeum job. It was right over in the Transtiberina, so they were off there now. He would check in with me here tomorrow.

He didn't specifically tell me not to come to the Grove. In retrospect, his distraction technique had a very light touch.

I was called away, back into the house. A new crisis had arisen. Everyone at home had turned out to stare: Dromo, Suza, Fornix the cook, Paris the runabout, both quarrelsome painters, even Barley the dog. Barley was too curious to growl. My steward, Gratus, was stalling, for once unwilling to second-guess my opinion.

I wasn't happy. "Eurgh. Gratus, what foul eruption from Hades is this?"

A facer. Two aunts on my mother's side had given me a "present." Unlike Tiberius, who only possessed one, I had aunts the way some people have warts. All over.

Claudia and Meline's present was certainly not a cornucopia overflowing with sweet grapes. The aunts knew better than to come themselves: they sent their delivery slave. He intoned a sorry tale.

Last night my two uncles, Aulus and Quintus Camillus, who were senators, had been invited to an imperial banquet—the same one Tiberius had ducked out of. Domitian, our maverick ruler, had a low regard for the senate, so most were prepared for an unhappy occasion and this particular banquet was to become notorious. The feast was supposed to be in honour of fallen soldiers. After terrifying everyone with fears that he might be intending executions, Domitian had his guests solemnly led into a pitch-black room that was arranged with funeral couches, where the place-markers were tombstones inscribed with their names. He served up funeral meats and talked all night about death. This, and the sinister decor, made them certain he was going to kill them.

During the awkward dinner, black-painted naked boys had pranced in, acting as servers. When the bilious guests escaped and were back at home, shuddering in their beds, they were woken by thunderous knocking; the clamour was to make them believe their executioners had arrived, after all. But Domitian, that macabre joker, had merely sent them gifts: their "tombstones," which turned out to be slabs of silver—very nice, thank you, godlike Augustus—and their cleaned-up serving boys. No thanks for that. Even with their paint scrubbed off and tunics on, the sly-eyed entertainers looked like brothel bunnies.

It would be mad to refuse a gift from the Emperor. Nor could the family quietly sell these creatures in a slave market. Domitian was bound to find out.

My aunts, both prudish, cringed from taking ex-imperial floor-show floozies into their nice homes. For one thing, Claudia had six young children whom the dancing boys might corrupt. Instead, since I was setting up a household, the aunts sweetly sent word that *I* could have this pair "to carry snack trays."

The messenger grinned. He was an old family slave with bushy eyebrows who took delight in telling me that the freebies' language was lavatorial and their habits matched. But Claudia and Meline thought I was so scary they would run away.

I huffed. I thought if Domitian heard that his gifts had scrammed, he would just annoyingly send replacements. Somehow we had to live with this.

"Oh, really?" asked the urbane Gratus, my steward, for once sounding strained. "I can train them to serve dinner, madam, but moral guidance is not in my remit."

I gazed at the boys. They brazenly stared back with limpid eyes, below brows that had been more exquisitely plucked than mine. They were about twelve. They looked like brothers, possibly even twins. Their beautiful features were sullied with foul thoughts. Puberty was looming. It would be dire.

"What are your skills, lads?" I snapped out.

"Erotic dancing," one boasted. Claudia's slave had told me that their behaviour at the dinner last night was blatant enticement; Uncle Quintus said they even served platters suggestively.

"No call for it. But can you hand around appetisers nicely?"

"With a bum-wriggle!"

"Wrong answer. Your clothes will stay on at all times, am I understood? Do not shimmy your horrible rear ends in my house—not ever."

"That's what we do." The second boy was daring me to react badly. He sneered. "Is it true you're a druid?"

"You want to be strung up among the mistletoe while your head sits on an altar three feet away? I am not a druid, but it can be done . . . You may live here temporarily." I made it cool. "On trial. See it as an opportunity. My husband is a magistrate, a stern man and extremely pious. You can choose to behave yourselves and be accepted in our home. But one dirty move, one complaint from my people here, or the neighbours, and you will find yourselves cleaning temple steps with toothpicks."

While I went to find a tip for the old slave who had delivered them, the boys hung their heads and muttered. They sounded rebellious. I could already sense a swell of dispute between these incomers and my existing staff.

Behind me, Gratus stepped forward. Tall and elegant, my steward looked as if he had only ever spent his life twirling honey on swizzle sticks to flavour drinks for masters who had pure good taste. He was such a refined factotum, people in the Aventine alleys sometimes apologised to him for the state of their streets—and meant it.

"What's up, Your Majesty?" one of the boys jeered.

Big mistake.

Gratus addressed them in his clean accent. "Listen to me." He looked as if he might be Greek-speaking, though his Latin was classy. He then reiterated what I had already said, but with vivid detail: "I don't like punks. This is what will happen: I make the rules, you follow them. No wanking, no thieving, no bad-mouthing the family. Don't curse, don't flirt, don't bugger the dog, and never answer back to me. One jiggle, and I shall pull your lungs out through your miserable throats."

They were stunned. I was rather surprised myself.

I saw Dromo stick his head around a colonnade pillar, gurning triumphantly. At last somebody in our household was in more trouble than him.

They hadn't even done anything yet.

They would. I might not be a druid, but I could prophesy.

V

I fled the house, taking only the dog. I hoped to teach the dancers that the owners went out a lot but would return unexpectedly; if anyone was up to something, we would catch them at it.

Gratus remained in charge. Today I had discovered he must have spent useful time slumming. Now I felt even more confidence in him. I had hired him specifically to cope, so I told him to enjoy his day. He gave me a wry nod.

I was headed to the marble Emporium. I dropped down to the river via the Steps of Cassius, calling first at my parents' house. Only my sisters were in, two richly clad teenagers, slathered in necklaces and startling perfume. "Where's little brother?"

"Oratory lessons."

"Does he like it?" Did my strangely self-assured brother *need* lessons in public speaking?

"He likes bossing the other boys."

"And the teacher, I suppose? Listen, girls . . ." I explained how and why Tiberius had gone so suddenly to Fidenae. "Tell the parents. Don't forget."

"We won't." They would.

"Just do it, scatterbrains. Where are the oldies, incidentally?"

Julia looked up from smothering my dog with cuddles. Barley took her chance to wriggle free. "Mama came home late from the Capena Gate relatives. She's full of horrible details about that banquet. It sounds absolutely brilliant. Why wasn't your triumph party like that, Albia?"

"Tiberius and I are too clever. When we decide to murder people, no one will see us coming."

"Ooh!" For daughters of an informer, my sisters were oddly innocent.

"What's up with Helena and Falco?"

"The dinner. They were all stirred up by hearing about Aulus and Quintus going—and *not* being murdered, which would have been *so* distinguished. They started stressing about some secret old plot, then stormed off in two directions today."

"Well, if they never come home, bring Postumus and pop up to mine. With Tiberius away, I can look after you." I was never maternal but I had looked after my siblings many times and had even grown fond of them.

"Oh, they'll be here again once they've thought up more wit to snarl at each other. We'll wait until after Tiberius is home. We like him. When's he coming back?"

"He can't say."

"When do you think?"

"It's medical. If he can't say, how can I know?"

They considered that.

My sisters exclaimed that Fania Faustina having pregnancy problems was terrible; they believed this, yet I knew they could not imagine it. For Julia and Favonia, babies were sweet bundles to play with, then to hand back as soon as they pooed or began crying.

"Are you and Tiberius going to have any?"

"Not if I can help it."

This giddy pair might soon start their own families. They were beautiful and had wealthy parents; chancers would snap them up. Then they would learn fast: the fears and misery of pregnancy, the danger of birth, the lifelong trials that followed . . . They swiftly lost interest in Fania and wanted to come out with me, shopping. They dropped it once they knew where I had to go. Building materials held no appeal.

I liked the Embankment for its busy interest, but I braced myself because it was thronged with hazards. Our family house stood in a part where the space between the Aventine cliff and the Tiber was so narrow that little happened nowadays. I turned left. As I moved downriver, the jetties widened into a mile of commercial activity that was ever changing and expanding. Barges from Ostia and light ships that could manoeuvre the sludgy currents drew up at long wharves where big stone bosses, some formed as lions' heads, allowed mooring by low-in-the-water transports. Making hurried stops while a procession of others queued for the unloading bays, the boats disgorged every kind of raw material. To receive the incoming goods there were ramps or block-faced revetments, with storage bins carved into the hillside and open areas.

The riverbank was no place to stroll. Winches and cranes posed a constant danger. Pedestrians were cursed and buffeted. Some dock labourers viewed knocking over other people as a hereditary right, passed on by their bale-toting ancestors. They probably had a points system and could claim a free drink for each casualty.

Pride of place in the Emporium area went to the enormous building called the Porticus Aemilius, where I was going. It had to be over fifteen hundred feet long, divided into bays that were themselves the size of meeting halls. It stood in front of the massive Granary of Galba, which fed the city and had military guards who, if not much else, liked to chuck stones at rats. Only very bold rats invaded the Emporium, which was a deafening hive of entrepreneurs. These days, especially with a huge imperial building programme, it mainly received marble. Most other commodities had been diverted elsewhere, though there were plenty of exotic smells: spices, leather, rich woods, incense. You could buy glass, carpets or ivory. Endless barrels of wine, oil and seafood arrived there daily, along with straw-layered towers of glossy red pottery so Rome could eat and drink the imported produce.

Only a banquet like the Emperor's would have tableware bought wholesale at the Emporium. Normally, goods came in, then were swiftly moved out to retailers. The Emporium was crammed with negotiators who would earn fees by facilitating this. No city in the world had such slick supply-lines as Rome. Nowhere had such a grasp of economic truth too: if it's cheap, people feel suspicious. Beef up your price. End users are such idiots they expect multiple layers of on-cost to accrue, before the one-man pedlar brings his tray to their gate or the rude stall-holder fiddles their change.

Importers tended to band together in one area, according to the material in which they specialised. This might be camaraderie but was probably so each firm could spy on the others' methods of sharp practice.

There were so many marble importers it took time to find the right ones. I introduced myself politely. Impatient men paused, inquisitive because I was a woman. I had dressed carefully for them. My new maid Suza deplored the way I presented myself on business occasions, but I liked to strike a balance: a glint of gold in my earrings to hint at status, yet a battered leather satchel where I had stowed the marble order, plus shoes that were sturdy enough to kick pigeons out of my way. I was in blue, with a moderate flutter of light ultramarine stole. I must have looked easily dismissable, especially if the men were aggressive—as they tried to be. "No sign of yours yet."

Not so fast, laggards! I looked unfazed. With a sweet smile, I hid my stern intentions. The marble dealers lapped it up. I spoke. The men recoiled, as I encouraged them to remove whatever digit they had stuck somewhere so intractably that our order for Fullo's Nook was paralysed. They became stroppy. I was unmoved.

Finally impressed, they admitted the marble had been there all along. They pointed out the corner where they had stacked our goods. I went and looked. I dragged the order out of my satchel to consult. I admired thickness, colour and patterning. The men were flattered and came to talk about quality. We all calmed down.

The problem was delivery. Our requirement for Fullo's was too modest compared with the massive slabs they usually shifted; they had simply never bothered to stick our stuff on a cart.

Would it be all right if I sent Larcius and our team with their sack-truck to pick up the goods? I asked. Nobody had thought of that; it would be more than acceptable. As a courtesy of their trade, the men apologised for any inconvenience. Even though they did not mean it, I replied it had been very pleasant dealing with them; like any informer, I could be wildly insincere. No matter. This was Rome, city of a thousand daily adjustments; we had successfully made one. They winked, telling me to ask Tiberius to send me along any time.

All sorted. Easy. The worst part was having to dodge predictable offers to take me for lunch at a place they knew. I made my excuses, saying I had to rush off to tell our workmen to pick up Fullo's marble.

Then, since I was down by the river, I walked the long way back to the Sublician Bridge and went over to do just that.

If I had known that a curious adventure was about to begin, would I have gone? No question, legate!

The fragile old bridge is the first Tiber crossing point, coming up from the coast. I had to walk right back past my parents' house almost as far as the Trigeminal Gate. Beyond, between the Pons Sublicius and the Pons Aemilius below Tiber Island, were open-air riverside porticos, a couple of small ancient temples, the meat and vegetable markets and a building with a fancy entrance where subsidised corn was handed out to the poor. Given the importance of this area, it was amazing that the Sublician Bridge had never been improved, yet it still stood as a part-wooden structure on rickety piles. I think it was the bridge that Horatius defended single-handed, so it was always kept narrow and easy to dismantle, just in case Lars Porsena of Clusium and his army came back. It formed a vital route to the Transtiberina, but emperors lavished all their attention upstream. This corner of the Aventine was typically neglected.

Over the river had once been an escape for the aristocracy. Much is always made of the fact that when Julius Caesar was murdered he bequeathed his extensive gardens to the people of Rome. A cynic might say, if the Pons Sublicius had been upgraded afterwards, more people of Rome might have gone to enjoy Caesar's Gardens. Its rickety nature discouraged visitors.

When Cleopatra came to Rome to visit Caesar, she was put there beside the Tiber. In those days, the right bank was *outside* the city. Julius Caesar cannot have wanted his mistress, a maverick young queen of extraordinary character and beauty, coming close. Not when he had a wife in Rome. Ooh, never mind her, perhaps, but Calpurnia's father was a stern traditionalist. "Let justice be done, even if the heavens fall," was said to be a motto in their family. Breakfast must have been gloomy. Time to ask for a tray in your room.

It was the father-in-law who stipulated that Caesar's will should be carried out to the last detail, thereby giving all Roman citizens the perpetual right to totter across the Sublician Bridge for a stroll in their handsome inheritance. Thanks, mighty Julius. Even though you wanted to be king over us, we yammering republicans will always adore you.

Augustus took over the gardens, as he interfered in everything. He brought the whole Transtiberina into his new district system as the Fourteenth Region. It became a different kind of bolthole. Runaway slaves, displaced foreigners, workers in antisocial industries and straightforward criminals burrowed in the northernmost ghettos. But in the southern part, for more than a hundred years the extensive gardens remained. Augustus and his descendants never improved the bridge though they added new amenities. There was space; they used it. Caligula started a racetrack, completed by Nero. Augustus built an aqueduct to supply a new arena that could be flooded for mock-naval battles. That had been used again recently by Titus.

The aqueduct also watered Caesar's Gardens. There, Augustus created a special area he called the Grove of the Caesars. This sacred arboretum was dedicated not to the people's benefactor Julius, hungry for reputation even in death, but to the imperial grandsons, Gaius and Lucius, whom Augustus had nominated as his own heirs. You can see them as toddlers on the Altar of Peace; one has pulled up his tunic hem, so he can scratch his chubby buttock.

Carrying the hopes of the Princeps proved too much for his noble young relatives. They both died in their twenties, which at least stopped them turning into power-crazed tyrants. Some said the Empress Livia killed them. Never trust a step-grandmama with a son of her own to promote, especially not if her best friend is the Palace poisoner.

In the Caesars' Grove stood a rocky grotto. Puddled by seepage from the aqueduct, it had turned into an unpleasant haunt of slimy green crags filled with litter. If anyone tried its echo, it was bound to reply obscenely. The smell was bad. The atmosphere was clammy. Its time was up.

My husband had won himself a minor works contract to dismantle this old grot. His men thought green slime was not much fun, but he was convinced the job would position him well to tender for the next renovation stage. This, he had heard, would be a lucrative project to build a monumental nymphaeum. The full deal: splashing fountains, marble basins, mosaics, shells, statuary and, best of all, treasury funding.

Tiberius was an optimist. Also, for some reason, he enjoyed dealing with water features.

This, therefore, was our current building site. Although I did have a memory of being advised not to go, I made my way to the Grove. There, I wandered about for ages, trying to find our workmen.

VI

The Transtiberina was a curious mix. Not only was it colonised by in-comers and undesirables, but after Julius Caesar a large swathe had been commandeered as the private domain of imperial in-laws, starting with Agrippa, Augustus' henchman, then his daughter Agrippina, Nero's mother. In those days this must have been a Julio-Claudian family compound, with one swaggering owner crushed up against another. Even now the right bank made a bolthole for the Emperor's family: upstream, Domitian's wife had a large garden, which must help her avoid him, and vice versa.

As I wandered about, lost, I found changes afoot. Down where Julius Caesar once stomped around his arbours, dreaming of world domination, a verge of warehouses was creeping into existence beside the water; many of these had been built as secure cellars for receiving wine imports. Away from the river lay the Naumachia, which I tried to avoid. This enormous man-made lake, with spectator seats, had a large barracks adjacent, to house sailors from the Ravenna fleet. They had always worked at the lake when a sham sea-battle was staged, though nowadays they regularly came across to the Flavian Amphitheatre to operate shading veils that were unfurled from the top.

Large numbers of bored sailors are a disaster. My younger siblings were barred from coming over here because our parents viewed the barnacles as worse than any horrors on the Aventine. A vigiles station-house existed, but not in my direction today; besides, the Seventh Cohort was notorious for lack of diligence.

Fortunately, in the public spaces I met few people. I walked briskly, circling the Naumachia on the opposite side from the barracks. Beyond, the Grove of the Caesars spread towards the district's boundary. I wondered how many drunken sailors had been sick in its sacred shade. There was no mistaking this large dark arboretum, quite different from the formal terraces and airy walks of the main gardens. The gardens were open tapestries of different greens, punctuated with slim cypresses and burdened with statuary because the people who had founded such places had access to stupendous foreign plunder. The Grove was different. Even before I went among its enclosing trees, I was struck by its sombre atmosphere.

In their eighty years since planting, the plane trees had grown tall, with wide horizontal boughs, which provided their characteristic shade. Greek intellectuals had founded schools of learning under trees like these. Augustus would not have settled for mere slips or half-standards to honour his grandsons, so a dense overhead canopy must have formed from early on. Now they were impressive. Even in December, even after leaf fall, they kept out light. Their huge trunks, mottled with peeling bark, made an impressive stand, almost a small forest. They must always have been tended by imperial tree surgeons, but with a tangle of brushwood underneath, they kept an overgrown, wild air.

This grove was certainly big enough for an untrained dog to lose her owner. Happy at our long walk, Barley kept running off in crazy loops, a pale beige streak that I glimpsed sometimes as I tried to find our site. She was a stray who had adopted me. I had not been hers for long, though long enough to want to keep her. At home, she slept in a fine kennel that Tiberius had made. He knew I loved dogs, though for an informer any pet is a tie. Still, so is a husband: since I had acquired him I had decided come one, come all.

"Barley!" I stood, listening.

The Grove was supposed to be sacred. I wondered how Augustus organised that when he planted up. Did he advertise? *New workplace for discerning operatives: dryads apply with full curriculum vitae and refs, must love trees* . . . Nymphs are not always reliable. They cavort. They mate with demigods, or their own brothers. Their offspring are monsters, or the more unreliable heroes. The Emperor would not have wanted supernatural squatters of the wrong sort to take up residence: that stickler for morality (other people's) would have checked them out.

"Oh, Barley, come back to me, you daft creature!"

I had accepted this dog when she followed me home, partly because she was persistent but mainly because she was shy. She liked to sit quietly beside me, which would work as good cover on surveillance. In the streets, nobody looks twice at a dog-walker. I could gaze around as if I was in a neighbourhood solely to exercise Barley, not in pursuit of suspects.

She needed a home. She had known trouble. She flinched from noises, unexpected movements, even sometimes from men. With my past life, I related to her insecurity.

I heard a noise close by, something alive, a discreet, restless schmooving among the dense undergrowth. Something quite large, surely. When I listened, all movement stopped.

Without thinking, I began to go in deeper, supposing this was my dog, busy with a discovery. If it was smelly, I would need to part her from it . . . Then a yap from afar told me Barley was elsewhere, looking for me. I turned to emerge from the trees. She ran up to me eagerly. Then she stood for a moment, staring past. I heard a faint growl, more curious than aggressive. Perhaps she was aware of shy dryads, spirits of the Grove, watching us from their hiding places.

There was nothing to see. I bent to stroke her head. Barley forgot her interest in the Grove, licked me, tensed to dash away again. I hauled her leash from my satchel, to keep her with me. We walked on together. I felt tired and she was docile. Off guard, we would have been prey for muggers, though these were empty paths, with only us in evidence.

Still unable to find the grotto, eventually I had to double back. Luckily, I came upon a man with a broom, sweeping a path. He had appeared there since we walked past before. He worked at the usual tentative pace, because the beaten earth of garden walks is easily destroyed. He was by no means subservient but told me quite politely how to find what I wanted. The site was quite close. I had simply missed it.

Larcius and our workmen were pottering in an excuse for a cave. Grottos are best dug out of a hillside. This fake "natural" feature was too far from the end of the Janiculan to be craggy; the reason for its siting was that the Alsietina aqueduct ended there, built to supply water for the Naumachia. Once you connect an aqueduct, it keeps going. Since the arena was hardly ever used, there was plenty of water to spare. The plentiful run-off was used for gardens, and to dampen this sorry pile of mock hillside.

The man-made cavern was a high pile of jumbled rock that had to be entered under a worrying overhang. I only peered in. Scattered around were flat ledges, once bases for statues, no doubt intended to show a contrast between their smooth marble and the jagged limestone of the main feature.

"Your pa came down to look them over," Larcius told me.

"I see they have gone. Does that mean Falco made a good offer?" I was sceptical.

"Well, he decided how much your husband could pay him to carry them away."

"And?"

"Faustus replied, 'That must be a leg-pull.' They were fifty each as salvage, buyer collects, as seen, with no comeback if they fell to pieces. The statues were rubbish, but Falco still took them."

"At fifty?"

"No, they shook on thirty-five."

I was surprised Pa had given in, but I liked this glimpse of my father and my husband each doing his work, while getting to grips as in-laws.

Water splished unconvincingly. Puddles festered where no puddlery was designed to be. I breathed, then regretted it. "As a feature, this is dismal!"

"Oh, we rather admire its free-form charm," Larcius joked. He stuck out a leg to stop a large chunk of pick-axed rubble, suddenly freed, that came bounding towards my weary feet. Nasty water oozed in the hole it had left behind. A tuft of slimy foliage, with long tubular fronds, was anchored to the rock, looking as if it would turn to green goo if you touched it. I stepped back.

"Sorry!" Serenus called to me. He had been concentrating on the effort needed to hack out the boulder; he had not properly taken in my arrival until he straightened up.

I turned over a bucket to sit on. Barley went around the men, sniffing and hoping they had crumbs to share. Once the softies started feeding her, they decided to feed themselves too, so they stopped work and lolled against handcarts. With practised ease, picnic snacks appeared. They had probably taken several breaks already today, but I made no comment after they handed me cheese and broke off a spare segment from their loaf.

In addition to Larcius, in our team were Serenus and Sparsus—the heavy-duty muscle man and the boy who did all the jobs no one else wanted—plus Trypho, who carried out general tasks and acted as night watchman. I said I was sorry they had to work out of doors in winter, but they claimed they liked it.

I explained about the marble for Fullo's Nook. They seemed impressed by my wheeze of picking it up ourselves. For one thing, it was a good excuse to knock off early from here and go to the Emporium right now. Young Sparsus was told to take all the rock they had dismantled today to the gardeners' compound; apparently our men were dumping grotto rubble in a big cart whose official purpose was removing weeds.

"Have you cleared it with the gardeners?" I asked, as Tiberius's representative. Pious in his role as an aedile, he was hot on any unregulated usage of public amenities. Even I knew enough to mention that site clearance was normally a contractor's responsibility. That's why so much abandoned building material turns up in the street. "Isn't removal of rubbish listed as standard in your spec?" I also knew this is always a contentious item.

"Well, the carter has seen us doing it." Larcius grinned. "Seius has never complained."

Sparsus whined about having to manhandle all the barrows himself, but the others explained how young arms fitted barrow handles better.

He accepted this, as if he believed it was also the role of an apprentice to be very dim. They watched him set off with the first load, all gently smiling. Larcius said they couldn't even bring themselves to send him to the store for a post-hole, in case he had a nervous breakdown when he couldn't find any.

"Rainbow paint," murmured Serenus, thoughtfully. "Next time we do a bar renovation. We'll get him easily."

"Took him all morning when we asked him to go for a left-handed spade," Trypho told me.

We continued snacking.

"Did you come by yourself to the Transtib, Flavia Albia?" asked Serenus, as if in surprise.

"I had the dog. No one bothered us."

They accepted this, though I felt they were exchanging glances.

Eventually I revived enough to feel ready to go home. A sudden scramble among the workmen took place. Serenus and Trypho jumped up to complete the barrowing task with Sparsus, while Larcius quickly gathered up tools as he tidied the site for departure. "We won't leave anything, then Trypho doesn't have to stay on guard. It's just rock—nobody's going to come and steal a grotto. Actually, we wish they would . . . Trypho hates it; this grove spooks him."

I still wanted to start for home before them, but they nagged me to wait, saying they would see me safe through the Transtiberina. To me, this was a very old-fashioned attitude. I supposed they were conscious of Tiberius being away; they seemed to feel they had a duty to stop me romping around unchaperoned. But I had been a lone informer for a decade and was used to it.

To deter me from buzzing off by myself, Larcius thought of something: "Flavia Albia, I don't suppose you want to look at something peculiar the lads dug up?"

The pressure was on. I dutifully gave in and stayed longer. I even pretended that seeing some mystery unearthed from a damp grotto was the best offer I had had since my husband left.

VII

It was a dirty bundle of old scrolls.

"Normally you find me human bones," I complained. "Much more thrilling. I shall never forget the time you dug out six skeletons." We all winced. "Plus a bar landlord's dog."

"Oh, go on, try to be more excited!" Larcius was being ironic; he seemed to sympathise with my lack of interest. Held between his grimy hands were several tattered items, still rolled up. As buried treasure, they were unappealing. "We can just chuck them out if you think so, Albia. They would already have gone on a bonfire but they are so damp and mouldy they will never burn."

I pulled the knowing face of a woman who understood that when men curate a bonfire, they want it to look spectacular. Whatever blaze they build is a measure of their masculinity. I could accept that this collection would never make good kindling, though I was minded to tell them to persevere. Nevertheless, I paused. "Larcius, you don't normally make a fuss about finds."

"Just seemed a bit funny."

"Since the grotto's decline, I imagine this cave has been used for nefarious purposes quite often. Lovers. Crooks. Young boys doing hideous things, while telling filthy jokes . . . This bundle looks to me like some very careful degenerate's private stash of bum-wipes."

"Oh yes, there were signs of lavatory use!" Larcius agreed. "We trod carefully when we first got started. But plenty of ferns were growing around in the rocks, nature's own for shit-cleaning. I don't think this papyrus was here for hygiene purposes."

I didn't suppose people who came to a cave would be that fussy in any case. "Let's not be prejudiced, Larcius. There may be an explanation: people do use gardens to work in. Some high-minded scholarly person might have been visiting this quiet spot to read and do correspondence, so this could be his private library."

"Well, he's lost it now!" cackled Serenus. "We've got it."

"True. But you could put his scrolls on one side in case he comes to ask for them back," I suggested.

The men stood around looking helpless.

I tried again to be sensible. "What made you think these old things might be special?"

Larcius gave it fair consideration. "Well, Albia. They weren't strewn on the ground, like all the other mess we found. These were laid in a hole. Someone had specially dug it out, made a neat job, set the scrolls there in a line, then backfilled nicely."

I tipped my head on one side. I saw their point. "They brought a spade. Sounds deliberate. Might it be a votive deposit, made to honour the nymphs of the sacred Grove?" We all sniggered. "I never heard of nymphs being great readers, though perhaps there are quiet times during their tree-fondling . . ." None of us believed it. "All right. Never mind nymphs. It seems more likely someone interred these things for a reason and is intending to come back for them. Where did you find them?" They showed me a place to one side of the cave, close to the overhung entrance. "Was there any form of marker at the spot?"

Now everyone looked shifty. Larcius said there might have been a stone or stick, but since they had not expected to find anything, it must have been thrown aside during the work. The men glared sternly at Sparsus. This was their customary reaction when anything went wrong on site.

"You should of told me to look," he muttered, on the defensive.

"Always look. Look, before you start to demolish!" intoned Larcius, an instructional talisman like *Don't step off your ladder until you reach the ground*.

Sparsus refused to be blamed. "It wasn't me. Why do I always cop for it? I'm getting my mother to come and have a word with you lot!"

The others turned away, uttering loud stage groans. So, the apprentice's mother had a way with words and was no stranger to the crew. Sparsus was biddable and good-natured; I was happy he had somebody defending him.

I volunteered that if they didn't want to shove the scrolls in a fissure so their owner could reclaim them, I would take them home with me. With Tiberius away, I might welcome light reading material. However, when I gingerly unravelled the beginning of one, its frontispiece had Greek lettering with long words of an abstract intellectual kind. I can read Greek if I have to, but at that I lost interest even more.

Trypho was grateful not to have to stay overnight at this isolated spot. Encouraging a quick departure, he considerately wrapped the filthy finds in a napkin from their picnic basket. Normally used to keep around their loaf, the cloth looked cleanish. This gave some protection to my satchel when they rammed the scrolls into it.

Barley looked up with a small tail wag. The bundle's mustiness made her hopeful it contained a well-aged marrowbone. "I see that look, doggie. I'll get you one at the meat market."

Collecting up tools and barrows, we set off away from the Grove and across the gardens. The men escorted me all the way back to the Sublician Bridge.

"You don't want to go wandering by yourself in the Transtiberina," Serenus admonished me, as we crossed the river. "There's no need for you to bother coming to see us, anyway. We'll check in with you when we need to."

"Or at least bring that runabout with you," added Larcius. The clerk of works knew what I was like. I would come if I wanted to. "That Paris."

I held off from saying I could handle match-salesgirls or leatherworkers without Paris. I might give any sailors a wide berth, but the immigrants would not faze me. Trypho patted Barley goodbye, telling her to look after me. Then they turned up the Marble Embankment, going to collect the order for Fullo's Nook, while I was allowed to make my own way home up the Aventine.

VIII

On my way, I stopped off at Prisca's baths. I tried leaving Barley to guard my clothes, though she was too preoccupied with her new bone from the Forum Boarium. She liked to lie in the clothes-manger while she waited in the changing room, but I refused to lift her up today. I had no spare garments with me and didn't want what I had on to end up covered with blood and bone splinters.

From what I said about Fania Faustina, Prisca reckoned Tiberius would be away at Fidenae for several days. "He'll have to comfort her. Sounds as if the ratty husband is no use. Pamper yourself while yours is off. Take your time," she advised, hoping to sell me beauty products. Without him, I wasn't in the mood. Knowing me of old, Prisca bounced off sulkily to some other client.

Once clean, I would have opted for a massage but Serena was not working today. Instead, before going home I took myself over the Aventine to see Uncle Tullius in his quietly elegant house above the Lavernal Gate. Heavily built and dogmatic, he was a typical Rome businessman. He was suspicious of me and I didn't trust him, but we had buried our differences; we shared enough affection for Tiberius to coexist.

I knew Tullius had never had much to do with Fania, but she was his sister's daughter. At our wedding, he had been polite to her, though he ignored Antistius and he openly drew the line at their whiny boys. A lifelong bachelor, now in his sixties and rooted in his way of life, Tullius avoided children. But he went so far as to thank me for telling him, then even asked to be kept informed. I would wait a long time to be served visitor snacks at that house, so I went home.

There, things were quieter than I had feared. A nicknackaroony plat-ter of tasties appeared as I entered, magically followed by a restorative cordial in my favourite glass.

Gratus had found out that the dancing boys were called Primulus and Galanthus. "Primrose and Snowdrop!" I chortled. "Want to change them to Vilis and Impurus?"

"Unlikely to help. My system," Gratus suggested grimly, "will be to separate our two little spring flowers whenever possible. Then they may get up to mischief but won't worsen the problem by giving each other ideas. If you go out, madam, please take one with you. If it is not too much trouble," he decided to add.

I meekly agreed to be lumbered. The disadvantage of a smooth steward was that as well as beguiling everyone else he could win me around too.

Not much happened that evening. It was too soon to hear anything from Tiberius. I decided that, even if the news was good, he would probably stay a few days to settle his old aunt and his sister.

Disconsolate, I cleared out my work satchel. I took a bored look at the bundle of scrolls. Rooting through ancient Greek philosophy is not a job for when you are tired, even though I found many of them had at least been translated into Latin. To be frank, after a day in which my husband had left and horrible youths had been dumped on me, after long walks and much dealing with men in dusty tunics, I could not be bothered with the ideas of an obscure old fellow from Miletus who was struggling to define Chaos.

Hell! Refute him, Flavia Albia. I knew all about chaos. It happened in my house on a daily basis. The five elements of it are: mismatched people, the aftereffects of a party, an absent master, a weary mistress and newcomers being picky.

That night I went to bed early.

IX

Whatever my sisters had passed on about Tiberius and Fania must have been so vague that my father was sent up to our house next morning to learn the true story. He took one look at Primulus and Galanthus, then said even breakfast at the Stargazer would be preferable to eating rolls with a pair of Palace catamites.

As a family we owned the Stargazer. Tiberius and I had even carried out some of our courting there. My father's sister Junia, who managed the spider-infested place, thought anybody could run a caupona and deemed herself especially good at it; Junia had no idea about food and was equally bad with people. Still, she was family. First Grandfather and now Father felt it would cause more trouble to stop her than to let her carry on.

I believe rude people said the Stargazer was the lousiest bar on the Aventine. That's unkind. The Winged Pig once caused an epidemic in which seven people died, whereas the worst anyone picked up at our place was colic and a black depression. Well, I picked up my husband there, though I had reason to think he had noticed me first and would have made his presence felt anyway.

I agreed to go, but before we set off, I showed Falco the dirty scrolls. He sneered, dismissing them as rubbish. With an auctioneer, you always need to decide whether his verdict can be trusted, or if he knows this is special and secretly intends to profit. I asked if he thought he could sell them. He boasted that now he was in charge, instead of my wide-eyed grandfather, the Didius auction house could sell anything.

At the Stargazer, I spent some time laughing over this with Junillus, my cousin the caupona waiter; we agreed that my father and our grandfather were as devious as one another. Junillus, who was deaf, mimed that if they weren't his relations, who owned the snack bar anyway, he would double-check their payment because they were bound to diddle him.

Father snarled, "Do not expect a tip, you rascal." With his good-natured silent grin, Junillus mouthed back that he never had tips from family members anyway.

Later, as Pa and I desperately chewed on the hard bread crusts my cousin served us, Falco backed off slightly. He was willing to put the scrolls into auction, but they must first be sorted into sets and cata-logued. He had no time, so I would have to get my hands dirty. In case I felt they might have literary merit, he told me the name of an expert the auction house sometimes consulted.

After I had answered through a mouthful of olives, oh, thank you for letting me do your work, Father dear, I asked to borrow Patchy, the auction-house donkey. I wanted Paris, my runabout, to ride out to Fide-nae and report back what was going on. Father said no. I did a teenage whine of "I hate you" and "Mother would let me." He growled all right then, as we had both known he would. I won't say my father was scared of my mother. Helena Justina was the elder sister of brothers. Falco grew up with five sisters, four older than him. When they first met, Helena must have treated him like Aulus and Quintus; he played along because being scoffed at and bossed felt natural.

Actually, he once told me that meeting Helena Justina "was like coming home." She chuckled at this but looked misty-eyed. My parents were the most romantic people I had ever known.

I went back to my house. I helped Dromo pack a few more things for his master, then told Paris to take him to the Saepta Julia and collect Patchy; he and Dromo could both ride on the donkey to Fidenae. The runabout was sensible, but I prescribed a route. Paris should then come back, bringing news from Tiberius. Depending on how long Tiberius wanted to stay with his sister, I would send Paris on further trips. Dromo could stay there. It meant one less worrisome boy in the house.

I was at a loose end, so I threw the excavated scrolls on a table and sorted through them. Some were in Greek, others were Latin translations. They were an unappealing clutch. I had never heard of a philosopher called Epitynchanus the Dialectician. He had a whole set of theories, elaborating his vision of the cosmos; skimmed over fast, they all seemed stratospherically unlikely. Even Philadespoticus of Skopelos was new to me; he had one fragment, which did not make me wish for more. I could not help viewing these works as an auctioneer's daughter: somebody might buy them—if he or she wanted a library containing all the books in the world. I would never bid, not even to get a cheap present for my husband; I didn't want him reading twaddle like this aloud to me. Tiberius liked to share; he would love to amaze me with such barminess.

Nevertheless, somebody had buried these scrolls for a purpose. Having them checked out seemed a good idea. I whistled up Barley, but she was lying half out of her kennel, still manically gnawing the marrowbone I had bought her yesterday, and would not budge. To please Gratus, I split Galanthus off from Primulus and took him with me. I could have made him carry the scroll bundle, but I was hoping he would run away.

He lacked the gumption to escape. In fact, as I watched him sashay along on his little dancer's feet, I reached the conclusion that during his short life as a Palace slave, he had never developed any independence. Gratus had handed him over to me, complaining the boys were lazy. They could answer back, but that was all. I deduced that Galanthus and his brother really had a lot to learn. Degenerate dancing, with its sinuous moves and enticing gestures, made them seem experienced, yet in many ways even Dromo knew more. On their own, they would be helpless.

I wasted no time thinking it was sad. I had once looked after a puppy that had been tied up alone in a shack all its short life; I had to teach it how to play. I felt more sympathy with that creature than with the dancing boys. The puppy asked nothing of me; the boys saw my family as prey.

We walked down to the end of the Circus, around the Palatine on the meat market side, then towards the Forum Romanum. We were in the Vicus Tuscus, a well-trodden throughway that had a busy commercial life.

"Stay close, Galanthus." I decided not to mention that this street was famous for men selling themselves. His beauty and long hair were attracting attention. Galanthus found this normal; fortunately, he made no response when anyone called out to him. At one point he did start to chassé instead of walking straight, but I gave him my look. Albia's death stare, my family call it. He stopped.

My father's directions were so casual, I could not find the stall he had mentioned. Since we were close to the baths run by Glaucus, I went to ask him.

Old Glaucus had trained my father so that Falco could handle himself in a fight when he had to. Now Young Glaucus, a massive ex-Olympian, still kept Father fit and also set me an exercise routine to overcome weak muscles and bones after my deprived childhood in Britain. As soon as he saw me, he moaned that I had been neglecting my workouts, so he grabbed me for a session. At the same time, he eyeballed Galanthus.

I anticipated. "Imperial gift. Isn't he pretty? We have a matched pair. If they were vases they would be more valuable."

"Shame they aren't!" scoffed Glaucus. "You could hide them at the back of a shelf." He let Galanthus posture around with some weights while I was put through stretching, pushing and balancing. I only did it because he was right: it worked.

Glaucus worried over me in the same way that his father used to worry over mine. He knew I sometimes ventured into dangerous situations in my work. While I was not supposed to engage in any form of combat, he wanted me to be able to slip out of trouble safely. The gentlest of men, he had taught me to be aware of what other people were planning, to duck, to dodge, to pull people off balance using their own weight—and, if absolutely stuck, to use the trick that athletes in Greek pankration keep as a last resort. Pankration is a filthy sport. It has almost no rules. Gouging your opponent's eyes is not allowed, though that never stops participants. "You have to claim they cheated first, Albia."

"What do they say about that?"

"If you poke them hard enough in the eyeball, they are in too much pain to speak."

"I thought a woman is supposed to knee an attacker in the balls?"

"That's what he'll expect. While he's guarding his jewellery, just blind him," instructed Glaucus, cheerily.

I explained about the scroll expert. "Pa told me to find someone called Mysticus, here in the Vicus Tuscus. Apparently, it's been a haunt of scroll-sellers since Horace was flogging off elegant odes."

Glaucus nodded. Many athletes are so obsessed with their sport they have no idea what goes on around them. This low-profile gym was lodged at the back of the Temple of Castor, only ten steps from the Forum although few outsiders noticed it. Clients here were business professionals, not self-absorbed bodybuilding show-offs. Young Glaucus tried to make his place discreet, while he kept aware of what happened outside so he could forestall problems. No thieves got in. No busybodies made complaints. He rarely mixed with his neighbours, but he knew who they were.

"Mysticus. He used to offer scrolls by the Temple of Janus. He laid out a table. There's a good footfall in the vicus, but he never appeared to sell much. He must have made a living, though, because he was at it for years. I hadn't seen him for a while. Then about six months ago someone told me he had passed away."

"Father can't know that. I'll have to tell him. Was Mysticus old?"

Glaucus paused to stop Galanthus swinging weights too wildly. He gave him a feather-stuffed ball to pat instead. The boy looked disgusted, but Glaucus's large size and quiet authority quelled him. He could easily have rolled up the dancer and let clients use him as a balance ball.

"Mysticus? Probably not old," he said in due course. "He was one of those weather-beaten chaps who turn out to be further from retirement than you might think. I believe he had quite a young family, so that was sad. Everyone who knew him said he died too soon."

"What got him?"

"Usual story." While we talked, Glaucus was still watching Galanthus fooling about. "A short illness, then he died in his sleep. But if you want advice about some scrolls, Albia, the business has been kept going.

Someone inherited the stock and premises. It was never only the table outdoors by the Temple of Janus. There's a hole-in-the-wall quite near you, at the foot of the Aventine. You should find it to your liking. It's now in the hands of a woman, I believe."

As soon as I'd stopped Galanthus spraying exercise oils about, and made him apologise, we went to see her.

X

The scroll shop was dangerously close to the corn dole station, so although no free grain was being handed out to the public today, beggars were hanging around the corner. I rebuffed them cheerily.

I found the shop, tucked in behind. I made Galanthus wait outside, telling him to squat on the kerb. He moaned that he was exhausted; I scoffed that that was because he had been mucking about. I could see he was used to answering back, but not to put-downs aimed at him.

Glaucus had underestimated the size of this place, mainly because for him no building counted unless it housed a Greek-style palaestra in handsome colonnades. This was so close to the Circus starting-gates that the race-day racket would deafen customers as they browsed. There was a counter at the front where purchases could be arranged, if it ever happened. Customers could wander through.

Inside there were book cupboards, like those in libraries, where stock lay ends-out in pigeonholes. Labels dangled off. A couple of stools had been supplied, perhaps for staff, but the regulars took them as if by right. Some clearly intended to stay all day; they looked annoyed when my enquiries disturbed their reading. I had already discovered when working in libraries that the pursuit of knowledge does not include acquiring tolerance. Those researching ideal human behaviour are the rudest men on earth.

The ones I saw here looked grubby and peculiar, misfits who came for a free read. They were unrolling samples vaguely, as if waiting for a chance to tuck scrolls under their tunics and make off. I felt guilty that distracting the manager with my questions might aid pilfering. Still, to judge by the customers, failure to buy would be nothing new.

There seemed to be an area at the back where I could see work on scrolls being carried out, though it was not a full-scale scriptorium, so I guessed they offered repairs more often than copying. Papyrus is durable; if it's handled right, it lasts for years. But rough treatment has left many a scroll with its batons ripped off or tattered on its long edges, like the ones I was carrying.

A woman was the front-of-house representative, presumably the person who had taken over. She was a few years older than me, though with small, mimsy features, untouched by the stresses of life. She was ordinary-looking, neat enough in her long tunic, though its green dye was fading in streaks and her red stole, with bleary pink patches, was not a good pairing. Her hair had been pinned in a tufty roll; it looked ready to uncoil at any moment. She wore neither jewellery nor cosmetics. My maid would have had no time for her.

Suza despaired of me too, but today she had managed to pounce. An informer normally looks rougher than their suspects, but I was over-tidy for this shop. My own hair was securely fixed with long bone pins that had fancy heads. Suza had chosen my oatmeal tunic to contrast subtly with a browner wrap. I had on seed-pearl earrings that I brazenly enjoyed wearing. Here, I felt like a piece of patisserie with very rare cherries that had strayed into a stokers' chophouse.

Tuccia seemed unfazed, even when I admitted I was not a prospective customer. I told her my name, mentioning my father. She knew who he was and even managed not to call him a "lovable rogue." I explained our need for advice about goods that had come to us with no provenance. Afterwards I realised I had sounded like a family member from the auction house; I had not mentioned my informing work.

When I fetched out the scrolls, Tuccia did look surprised. I talked them up as best I could. "I am sorry, they are a bit dirty. They were dug out of an abandoned cave." I had brushed off some of the earth at home, but I shook them to loosen any that remained.

Still in silence, Tuccia unrolled the frontispiece of one, using her index finger gingerly. She was reading the author's name and the subject matter.

I admitted that there was a chance these had been stolen from a library by a slave who had hidden them in a hole, then done a runner.

"Or a furious wife in the throes of a bad divorce," suggested Tuccia, looking up with a sudden giggle. It was the kind of thing I would say myself. "From an old swine who loves his books more than his marriage! The desperate woman did this because she knew it was one way to make him *absolutely furious*."

At which point I happily grinned with her.

Tuccia unrolled more of that scroll, spreading the papyrus along her counter, then smoothing it gently with her small fingers. A love of documents was evident. She seemed to be examining its colour, which, away from the end, was much cleaner than on the outside. I said it was pale as new straw. "Or a healthy urine sample!" As Tuccia pursed her lips in thought, I pointed out the author: "Epitynchanus the Dialectician. An original in Greek though most of the rest we found seem to be copies in Latin translation."

She nodded. "Known as a Controversialist," she told me. "So I always think he cannot have had many friends."

I received the information with a smile. "Some people love an argument . . . Clearly you are better-read than I am, but I see no point in pretending I was enthralled when I dipped in." I brandished one of the other scrolls. "Nor, from a quick glance, would I want to waste lamp oil on the verbiage of Philadespoticus of Skopelos."

Tuccia stifled a burst of laughter. "Philadespoticus! Not everybody's taste."

"Lucky this is only a fragment. He's excruciating. These writers are old fellows?"

"The famous School of Miletus. Thales, Anaximander and Anaximenes were its founding intellects."

"Very pre-Socratic!" I can talk the talk.

"These are the 'materialists,'" explained Tuccia. "They believe all things that exist are derived from one primal substance."

"Hot air?" I supposed, still determined to be satirical. "Anyone from Miletus with a long Greek beard can join the club? Who started this babble?"

Tuccia answered gravely, though I could still see a wry twinkle: "Thales came first, and his choice for the ethereal medium was water. I

myself like Anaximenes, who suggests air as the beginning of matter."
Her manner had become respectful. "We sell a lot of him—his ideas are
very popular with my customers. Anaximenes tells us that when air be-
comes finer, it turns into fire, or when it condenses, it is first wind, then
cloud, then water, then earth, then stone."

"Holy erudition!" I grunted. "I gather, Tuccia, you actually read your
stock?"

"I need to know what to recommend."

"I admire your dedication. So, you can talk up the well known Milesians,
but how about my scroll scribblers, Epitynchanus and Philadespoticus—
have you studied those ancient authors?"

She looked guarded. "Good men, I am sure, Flavia Albia, and no
doubt with very plush Greek beards."

"But?"

"Rather hard to read," Tuccia concluded sadly.

Just as I thought. Unlike Tuccia, I felt no need to admire masters of
tedium. In representing the Didius auction house only one thing mattered: "So, if 'hard to read' means they haven't attracted fans, my thought
as an auctioneer's daughter is: has their work almost vanished? Are their
scrolls extremely rare—so therefore highly sought after? Will people at
an auction pay through the nose for these grubby pieces?"

Tuccia answered with stylish simplicity. "You should make a killing,"
was her sweet reply.

Larcius had nearly tossed out these beauties and I still despised
them. But now I saw why Father used the Mysticus emporium for expert
advice.

XI

Tuccia decided it was time we moved deeper into the shop. Laying a finger to her lips, she led me to the back workshop area. It was more private, away from customers.

As we reached the benches where slaves were hunched over tools, she cried out to them cheerily, "Somebody found some buried scrolls!" I heard warning in her tone; I took it as a hint to them that a tricky renovation task might be looming. They managed not to wince in anticipation but a couple left their work and collected politely to look.

Tuccia cleared a space and laid out my offerings. "See—the highly esteemed Epitynchanus the Dialectician! What customer asks for him nowadays, or when did we last see his outpourings on sale? And here's a substantial fragment of Philadespoticus of Skopelos, whose opus was thought entirely lost. How tasty is that?"

"You never told me the Skopolan opus had vanished!" I reproved her, though gently.

"I would have." Tuccia was unapologetic. "We never expected anyone to bring in an original Philadespoticus, did we?" she marvelled with her staff, as if it was an in-joke. They looked diffident, nodding slowly. "The handwriting style is right for the period . . ." Tuccia picked up a few other scrolls to check. "These others are Latinised but they do appear to come from ancient sources . . . Primarily, it's the Philadespoticus I like . . ."

Father's training took over. While auctions are fine occasions for testing the market, if it's ever possible, you should grab an on-the-spot deal. Clients want to believe that bidding ensures the best possible price, but when you yourself possess the goods, don't waste time; take cash in hand. For one thing, that way you don't pay sales tax. You're not going to volunteer it, are you? "If this fragment is unique," I suggested swiftly, "do you want to make me a private offer?"

I thought Tuccia jumped slightly.

One of her slaves, a crusty elderly character who was holding a glue-pot, broke into a grin. He hid it, but another said, "Go on, Tuccia! This is a previously unknown work!" It was obvious teasing.

Tuccia pulled her blotchy red stole with its washed-out dye tighter around her, almost writhing in her awkwardness. I tried fellow-feeling: "Don't let them rag you! You're a young woman in a family firm. These fellows think they know everything, but I can tell you have mastered your subject."

"It is a tricky market. I am wary of making mistakes." Tuccia excused herself.

It seemed the moment to ask about the history of the business. "My father used to deal with Mysticus and believes he is still alive. Can you tell me what happened to him?"

Tuccia seemed more comfortable with this question. She looked solemn, but answered easily, not allowing the scribes to muscle in: "It was sad. The poor man had a short illness. He seemed to be rallying, but then without warning, just as he was getting well, he was found dead in bed." It was the same story Glaucus told me. I could tell that plenty of people had asked, probably all surprised to hear that Mysticus was gone: Tuccia's answer was well-practised. "Vague questions were asked about the drains, but nothing came of it." Vague questions about drains never work; people just sniff and wander off.

"Did he have family?" Politeness requires you to drag out every gloomy detail.

Tuccia shook her head. "None to speak of."

The slave with the gluepot suddenly turned away to resume what he had been doing, as if he couldn't bear to remember. He had light, fading hair and not much to say for himself. He was probably a good worker.

I asked the one who remained near. "Mysticus seems to have been a popular figure. Did you like your old master?"

This one had a pointed nose set in a forward-pushing face, so when he turned sideways his profile was almost an isosceles triangle. He had previously been using small tools to smooth down papyrus wrinkles and snippers to cut out bad tears; once he had done that, he pieced in more papyrus, ready for gaps in the written work to be filled. An ink-stained scribe, hunched over on a stool, was already working on another scroll, carefully replacing missing words. He used a half-unravelled one to copy from.

"Mysticus was good to work with," the mender told me. "And knowledgeable. This was his life. He loved what he did—the interface with customers, making suggestions, finding things he thought they would enjoy. He would be out in all weathers in the Vicus Tuscus, busily chatting about what he had taken to the stall. All the collectors adored him. His regulars knew he would go out of his way for them. If they wanted something unusual, he went to any lengths to hunt it down for them."

"Still, Tuccia seems to have made herself very familiar with what you stock." She was standing right beside us; I felt I should give her some credit.

"Oh yes, our Tuccia knows how to carry it off!" He grinned, teasing her again.

"Careful, Tartus!" Tuccia warned him quietly.

I liked the way she was standing up to the staff, despite their strong loyalty to her predecessor. Was there real tension? Probably not. No doubt they accepted she was a permanent fixture now. "Did you work here before, Tuccia? How did you come into the business?"

"I was a relative, his cousin's daughter. I had known the shop since my childhood—I worked here if Mysticus was short-handed. Afterwards, his wife wasn't interested in the shop. I just naturally moved in."

"What happened to her?"

"Quietly disappeared. We think she went home to her own people. Too distressed to stay in Rome. She was a country girl, so there was nothing to keep her."

Still making conversation, I said it was good that the business had been able to continue. But I needed to press Tuccia about the excavated scrolls, so I went back to discussing them.

She told me she thought that if we put them into auction, on a good day, with specialist dealers in the crowd, they would sell. She could tell Father which dealers to invite; Mysticus used to give him that kind of steer. Otherwise, she herself would be happy to buy them for a low price on spec, keeping them until the right customer came by. She had contacts who might show interest.

Before she would make an offer herself, she wanted to do more research; once she was sure of the scrolls' exact rarity, she would have more idea of demand. She asked if I would consider leaving them with her, but I became protective and chose to keep them myself. Father never lets goods go off the premises before a sale, not unless he thinks they are such utter rubbish he hopes they won't come back.

These scrolls, it seemed, had value. I rewrapped them and put them safe in my satchel, before taking my leave.

XII

I called up Galanthus, who had been lolling against a wall, half asleep. People were good-naturedly stepping around him. If I could have trusted him, I would have sent him home, but I was certainly not setting him loose alone on the Aventine; he would never find his way. He was a slave. It was not his fault no one had taught him life skills. I had been brought up to take responsibility for people like him.

Yes, he was a slave, so I had to listen to the ungrateful lummox moaning again, because I now walked over to the Saepta Julia to tell Father about Mysticus. After the triumph, which had started close by, the Saepta was settling down again. We found it unusually quiet. Not seeing Falco at his ground-floor antiques showroom, I hauled Galanthus with me upstairs to the office.

This sanctum, overloaded with a gallimaufry of real specials and complete tat, had always been a seedy refuge for my male relatives. It made a discreet snug in which to entertain favoured clients, serving tots of fortified peppermint tea to weaken their resistance, while expensive goods were paraded. Perhaps these bazaar tactics sometimes worked, but mostly the Didius boys just hid out there.

Father was missing. He had gone to view items he hoped to grab for an estate sale. These can be mixed opportunities. Heirs talk up the stuff, accountants talk it down again. Long-treasured items turn out to be worthless, while other things hidden at the back of a cupboard may be priceless rarities. Falco usually went to make sure for himself. He also enjoyed poking around strangers' houses.

Gornia, the ancient head porter, was left in charge. Now papery to look at and so frail a breeze could have knocked him over, other members of staff had put him outside on a daybed on the balcony that ran around the upstairs interior. They had wrapped him in a blanket so thoroughly I told him he looked like a swathed Egyptian mummy.

"Yes, I'm waiting to die!" Gornia could still pipe up with the wit that had made him an unexpected hit at auctions. "But I'll go when I'm ready and the lads are fetching Xero's pies. I'm hanging on today, in case they bring pork-and-pickle."

"Eat one of those and you'll go off pop this very afternoon!" I joked back. "Last I heard, Xero was using up a pig that was slaughtered in Campania a year ago. He claims he got a special deal because the scratchings had gone a bit mouldy."

I ordered Galanthus to fetch me a stool from indoors. He looked surprised at having tasks, on top of being route-marched around Rome. I ignored him. Then I sat down to chat with Gornia, who nowadays seemed older than some of the antiques we sold. Gornia asked about the boy, who was hanging over the balcony rail as far as he dared, wondering at which point he might fall. I told the tale, then Gornia said Galanthus could be auctioned if I wanted. We disliked handling human lots. "But if he can stand still long enough, we can pretend he is a statue."

"I'm sure Galanthus would prefer a new home," I answered, "but I cannot risk Domitian finding out that the family don't cherish his gift."

"Want to learn about antiques, son?" Gornia demanded. He was always on the lookout for staff. If he didn't find his own vase-lifters, he got stuck with spotty young Didii—truculent punk nephews who were going through a difficult phase. Which is to say, nephews who were just being members of our family.

Galanthus looked happy that someone was taking an interest in him, but I threw cold water over any fancy ideas. "Better warn him, Gornia. You won't just let him dress himself up in jewellery that clients want to liquidate. You need all-day heavy lifting. Have you ever moved a huge cedarwood armoire, Galanthus—or transported a deadweight, twice-life-size marble Hercules?"

"Down a narrow flight of stairs!" Gornia chimed in. "What about that time we had to shift the huge chest with the horrible smell, young Albia—and we found the lads were hauling along a half-decayed corpse inside it?"

"I certainly remember. He was a burly man, he'd been in it for days—and it was hot weather. He was very ripe. Your lads knew he was in there, but they still lifted up the lid and made me come close for a look."

"She wasn't sick," Gornia told the slave. "We were proud of her."

This gossip appealed to Galanthus, who beneath his training in sexual enticement was a normal boy. He might not view me with greater respect as a result, but he stopped hanging over the rail. Gornia, who had had a lot of youths through his hands over the decades, gestured him to sit down out of harm's way. Probably to his own surprise, Galanthus obeyed. He even stayed quiet while I asked the ancient porter about the scrolls.

Gornia took on board that I was not entirely at ease with Tuccia.

"You have to be fair. The thing is, Albia, she must make up her mind first that your scrolls are genuine."

"Genuine? How come? Most scrolls are copies made by scribes, Gornia, so what's this?"

"Well, first, are they bad copies—not properly transcribed, all gaps and wrong words or altered phrases?"

I did know that many very poor versions existed for all types of writing. I had once been taken on a trip to Greece and Egypt. Falco and Helena had conducted an investigation at the Great Library of Alexandria; I remembered much discussion of ideal scholarship, and the hunt for accuracy instead of mangled texts.

Was that what Gornia meant? Impure copies? Rather, he had picked up from me that the philosophers in question purportedly existed in remote times, with much of their work supposedly lost. So, he reckoned Tuccia's next question would be, were these scrolls genuine missing texts from centuries ago—or were they deliberate fakes?

"Fakes?" I was amazed. "Do people invent philosophical scribbles?"

"People fake anything. There is a lively market for rare works," Gornia assured me. "Scrolls that are said to be 'missing' command a premium. You know what collectors are like about the chance to own something nobody else has. News of a lost scroll drives them into a frenzy. They drool, they need to gloat over it alone at home, they want to be the first to have it on a shelf."

"So . . ." This was a new thought. "Falco might be very keen to advertise a sale that includes sought-after scripts by Epitynchanus, the hilarious Controversialist—not to mention a completely new fragment from the crackpot Philadespoticus of Skopelos?"

"Oh, he'd make a few jokes, but he would be."

"Then, Gornia, might Tuccia try to play down their significance, so she can wheedle them off us for less than top value and sell them on herself?"

"She certainly would try, young Albia."

"Right. I'm on to her! But let's set up an auction. I suppose Father knows some collectors, but the late Mysticus and his shop's new owner will have better contacts? We need Tuccia, and she knows this, to bring in the right maniacal collector. Better still, at least two rivals to force up the price."

"Correct."

"It's happened before? So, Father and Tuccia will play a delicate game, dancing around one another to grab the profit?"

"An accommodation will be reached," Gornia assured me.

"How lucky that I clung onto the goods, then! Tuccia wanted to borrow them to show to people."

"Your father has taught you well," said the trusty auction porter, revelling in our family's guile.

He drifted off into a world of his own. I waved to Galanthus and was about to tiptoe away, leaving Gornia to sleep out the afternoon, when the old man rasped, "And if these scrolls are fakes, you can bet there will be others. Fooling collectors into paying through the nose for 'new discoveries' is big business. Albia, have a poke around that site with a spade!"

Hard luck, Galanthus! The pretty boy and I were off on another route-march. Now I wanted to go back to the Grove of the Caesars, to tell Larcius and the team to dig for more buried treasure at the nymphaeum.

"Fake scrolls at the fake cave!" Wonderful.

XIII

A big meatball called Cluventius was about to hold his birthday party in Caesar's Gardens. Contractors were swarming everywhere, preparing fancy bowers and draping awnings from existing structures. Despite the vehicle curfew that applies throughout Rome in daytime, carts trundled in from all directions, laden with seats, serving tables, garlands, comports and goblets. The wagon bringing platforms for entertainers nearly broke an axle under its load, while there was enough portable cooking equipment to feed cavalry after all-day manoeuvres. Even statues were supplied, though plenty of ivy-twined figures already stood proud among the box hedges or posed in arches.

I wondered if you had to obtain permission for a private function in a public space. If so, that did not stop Cluventius. He was intent on holding his pop-up orgy that evening, regardless of protocol. By the time the park-keepers could round up a magistrate to expel him and his paraphernalia from their walks, Cluventius would have disappeared, leaving behind only unwanted pavilions, folding up on themselves, and festering mounds of food rubbish, attracting crows. In the meantime, he had taken over half the gardens.

I found out who he was, and his view of his own importance, when I finally forced a passage through his teeming contractors to reach our site. Hired caterers were diverting the aqueduct to service their cookery and washing-up—assuming hygiene was part of their remit, which is not always the case at functions. A few of them were fixing a temporary pipe to the Alsietina, illegal, of course, but they seemed to have done it before, judging by the tools they had brought with them. Others just stood and watched Larcius and our team dismantling the cave.

I asked sharp questions. Cluventius wasn't a senator, he was much more impressive. Politics lay beneath his notice. He was a very big force in transportation. He moved mass consignments of heavy goods to and fro across the Empire. If anyone wanted something shifted, he could do it. This was on a scale that enabled him to celebrate his fiftieth year with a night that his friends and family would long remember.

"Though tasteful," the preparation team assured me. "Everything high class." This option was apparently the most superior level of event their company offered.

"No nudity?" I guessed.

"Nor groping, nor nipping behind a marquee. If anyone wants a leg-over, they have to go home for it. The party is expected to go on so long, they can always come back afterwards. The client has chosen a recital of lyric poetry by actual poets—" I openly groaned. "Then a display of proper Greek dancing, the kind they have at festivals—" Dear heavens, the utterly boring kind. "— and respectable music."

"Respectable?"

"Again, clothes on, everyone stops nattering and listens to it, lots of really lovely lyre tunes."

That sounded familiar. "So, don't tell me—your client has hired the Fabulous Stertinius?"

"You have heard of him?" Stertinius was a much sought-after celebrity player. Judging me as a builder's wife, the contract party-planners looked surprised.

"He played at my wedding." He and his backing musicians had taken to us; now they even came to our house to practise sometimes. I did not boast, though getting Stertinius at home was a coup. Tiberius and I are modest.

The party-planners found it hard to believe me, but now I had shaken their ideas they did wander away, leaving my workmen space to do their jobs. Once he could speak freely about them, Larcius started going spare. "We can't move for their bloody transports. They keep loafing here, asking daft questions. Anything to avoid doing their own work—if you call handing out appetisers work."

"Squid parcels call for special skills," I said, smiling. "Look, it sounds like just one night and they will disappear. Do you want to call a halt today?"

"What do you think the master would say?"

"I think he'd be realistic, don't you?"

"So long as the final decision is yours, then!"

Being Tiberius's stand-in had its complexities, but I felt safe to say our men could leave the grotto temporarily. I told them to go and start on the marble at Fullo's Nook. Our next work here required discretion. I did not want a bunch of party-primpers watching us unearthing rare scrolls.

I told the clerk of works in an undertone what Gornia had said. Larcius agreed to have the boys start an exploration dig tomorrow, when the Cluventius event was over. "Let the cooks scram. If there are spare drunks lying on garden paths in the morning, they won't be thinking about us. Forgive me, though, there is a catch and it's bad news for Trypho. We do need to keep a watchman on site this evening while this big carry-on happens. I'm worried about the state of the works—what's left of the grotto is unsafe. Putting barricades around it will never be enough. Those caterers telling me their party will be 'respectable' only suggests one thing—it won't be. Once guests get bored with Greek dancing and poets, they will come swarming all around the gardens, with wine inside them, looking for mischief. We don't want merrymakers clambering over the rocks until they fall off and break their necks."

Trypho looked amenable to guarding the works. He would like to watch the party as his evening treat. Maybe the caterers would even give him a drink. Serenus thought that was such an attractive idea, he would stay as well. Since the grotto spooked Trypho, young Sparsus offered to overnight with them: he, too, wanted to gawp at the event. We said he could, provided he kept Trypho sober.

I muttered to Larcius that I did know having a sober night-watchman was as impossible as sending your apprentice to buy rainbow paint. Larcius said not to worry: Trypho was used to drinking.

"What about young Sparsus, though?"

"We're giving him the right education."

"How does that square with his mother? Isn't she formidable?"

"She believes Sparsus is safe with us. I told her Faustus only allows goat's milk on site."

We left Sparsus behind to keep an eye on things now, while the others went to Fullo's. Galanthus was complaining about another walk, so I told him to stop with Sparsus.

Of course, by evening all the men had built up the Cluventius birthday party in their heads until it was potentially an epic carnival. Larcius was too sensible to bother, but when they finished at Fullo's Nook, Serenus and Trypho came back to the yard to clean up. Then, after assembling vast provisions for supper, they eagerly started back to the Grove. Once Primulus heard that his brother had been allowed this exotic sleepover, he was so jealous that I let him go with them.

My steward could not decide whether to purse his lips at my granting the boys favours or to accept the temporary peace. "Trust me, Gratus, this is not going to be the treat they think. It will be dark, in a garden in December. Cluventius is having a private party, so I doubt there will really be much chance for outsiders to ogle. Besides, if the dancers disappear in the Transtiberina, that solves our problem."

Gratus had had such a day with Primulus, he admitted he would be happy to lose them.

In fact, we did lose them. The relief was temporary, worse luck. But it would change their young lives unexpectedly. What happened to the dancing boys was too exciting even for them.

The party that night was memorable in ways I had never expected. During it, someone disappeared. When he realised her absence, Cluventius created a major fuss. Nobody could blame him. The woman who went missing was his wife.

XIV

At our house the alarm was raised by Sparsus. Builders start work early. With all of Caesar's Gardens now further disrupted because of the vanished partygoer, Serenus sent the apprentice to ask Larcius what they ought to do. Since they had no Tiberius, Larcius came to ask me. Muttering, I got out of bed to see to it.

I was soon curious. Birthdays can be good occasions for misery. If there was already trouble in the Cluventius household, holding a big party was quite likely to stir up a hysterical climax. Many wives who finally snapped would make a theatrical performance of it, but this one had apparently caught everyone by surprise. Maybe she was a nice woman (they do exist) or else she simply thought a quiet exit was best. Maybe she could not face telling her husband she intended to leave him. Perhaps he would not want her to go, because he cared, or else he was a tyrant who would not allow himself to lose face. Perhaps she wanted time to escape with her lover before her husband noticed. One way or another, this had the makings of intrigue and scandal.

I had been edgy about Tiberius and his sister, so this would be a distraction. I hoped Paris would return today with news, but the runabout could not be expected until after midday. While I waited, I could trot over the Sublician Bridge to find out what was happening. Larcius seemed strangely reluctant for me to go, but once I had made up my mind he gave in and came with me.

By the time we reached the Grove of the Caesars, search teams had found a body.

XV

To the family concerned this must have been a highly unusual situation, though I had seen similar too many times. To me the woman's disappearance now had horrid inevitability. I knew it would not have been an accident: she had met a bad end.

In the gardens and on the edge of the Grove, unhappy groups of men were standing in silence. The find had only just been made, where the plane trees started. No one was sure who should break the news to Cluventius. No one wanted to volunteer. Most of those who had been brought to search were slaves, perhaps afraid of his reaction.

Even at that early point, I felt the draw for me to offer help. I picked out a possible overseer. "What have you found?"

"She's there, lying in the undergrowth."

"Alive or dead?"

"Dead. Naked. Obviously murdered. And . . ." He could not say it. My heart sank. The woman must have been violated.

"Yes, I see. You are certain it's the wife?"

"I work for them. It's definitely her."

"Does he know?"

"Not yet."

"Then that must be dealt with, and it's urgent. Would you like me to tell him?"

"Who are you?" asked the man, rather late in the day.

I had only offered out of sympathy, wanting the husband to be told as kindly as possible, but I dressed it up with official status. "Flavia Albia, wife to the aedile Faustus. He had to travel out of Rome but has given me his seal." If anyone challenged that, I could pretend I had left his hippocampus ring behind at home. I spoke with the quiet gravity he would have used. "Let me do it. The bad news may seem gentler coming from a woman. Bring me to your master—he's called Cluventius, isn't he? Come with me, then once he knows, you can confirm the details."

Simply to sound as if you know what to do often works. From then on, I was accepted as a person of authority. It seemed easiest for me to take over. And it saved anyone else having to assume a role that made them nervous.

I gave instructions not to touch the body. No one had been sent for the vigiles; I still had the reliable Larcius with me, so I despatched him. "From here, go right around the Naumachia, then if you come to the Via Aurelia, you've gone too far. You need the duty officer. Mention Faustus. Say the victim is the wife of a man of consequence. They need to send their top investigator immediately—if he has gone off duty, they must call him in again—and my advice is to let their tribune know, because he will want to inform the Prefect before anything leaks out." Once he had done that, I told Larcius to come back to our site and look after our men.

Then I did not hang around. My investigative mode was automatically kicking in. I could not help mentally asking the usual questions. I wanted to announce the news to Cluventius myself, so I could observe his first reaction. In a case with a dead wife the first rule is: assume the husband did it.

On the other hand, I would not have expected a spouse to leave his wife stripped naked in the middle of a wood. Men who kill their womenfolk use other methods, in different locations. Quite often they do it at home. They may make it look like a burglary gone wrong, rarely a sex crime. Most like to finish off their victims when no one else is there.

Cluventius's overseer walked with me as I had suggested. In shock, he was still carrying the big hoe he had been using to bash down undergrowth; he gripped it without knowing he did so. I ascertained that his name was Engeles. He was a steady, capable type, about forty, looking like a house slave, though some of the others were from the transportation business. Teams of their own men had been summoned early this morning to look for the woman.

Her name, Engeles said, was Victoria Tertia. I kept him talking to settle him. She was a second wife, the first having died of natural causes a long time back. This marriage was around ten years old, generally seen as a strong partnership. Victoria came from a similar background, another family in haulage, so she and Cluventius had everything in common. There were two almost adult children from his first marriage, who had been at the party; they had gone home to comfort the three much younger offspring of Victoria Tertia.

Cluventius had become uncontrollable last night when he found that Victoria had disappeared. Fired up by adrenalin, he went crazy, sending for help, for men with tools and lights, even for dogs. At first he supervised in person. It had been dark then, so the searchers could do little except walk about with torches, calling her name. Once the husband had people looking, he seemed to run out of energy—well, said Engeles, the man had spent an evening whacking down the wine. It was his big celebration. Until then, he had enjoyed himself, never imagining what was about to happen.

Even now, he would be unprepared for the full horror, I thought bleakly.

"Were you at the party, Engeles?"

"Yes, quite a few staff had been invited. Most of us have worked with them for many years. They are good people. They treat us like family."

He stopped in his tracks, overcome, covering his face with his free hand. I might have tried to take the long hoe but did not want to be lumbered with it. As tactfully as possible, I ascertained that in the period before Victoria Tertia's absence was noticed, Cluventius had always been in the middle of everything. Playing the attentive host, he was always visible to his guests.

Right. Even before I met him, I had established his alibi.

Who did it, then? Hired assassin? Loyal henchman? Somehow the family details were making that seem unlikely. What I had been told about the body suggested an attack by an outsider.

They had put Cluventius in a tented bower from the party, some distance from the Grove. Two men his own age sat with him, old friends or colleagues, sensible and sympathetic. They were keeping him calm. They had had the nous not to give him more wine, but a large beaker of water. If he had been drunk from last night, he was now coming out of it, though heavily.

I met their eyes quickly, enough to signal what news I brought. I left them to cluster to one side with Engeles while I went straight to Cluventius. He was a big man, broad, though not gross. It was probably years since he had done it himself, but he looked as if manhandling a stroppy draught-ox would come easy.

I introduced myself in a few swift words, using the story about acting for my husband. Cluventius made no objection. Still seated, he gazed up at me, pleading not to hear the words he knew were coming.

"Sir, you have to be brave. Think of your children. A body has been found, hidden deep in undergrowth. People who knew her have confirmed it is your wife."

He slumped. He could not speak. I noticed his birthday haircut still looked neat, though his birthday shave was already starting to show purple jaw.

"Cluventius, I did not stay to look, because I wanted to let you know that at least she has been found. I am desperately sorry, but I was told by the searchers it is evident she was murdered." I did not tell him the rest. Not yet.

He spoke her name. It was forced out of him by the torment of knowing she must have been afraid and had suffered, out there alone in the dark. "Victoria," he said, almost to himself. "Oh, darling." I knew straightaway that this time it was not the husband. Cluventius would never have killed Victoria Tertia. He genuinely cared for her.

XVI

He wanted to see her. Almost at once, he jumped up demanding to go to where she lay. I knew better than to try to deter him.

Engeles led us back. I went too. I knew something about murder scenes and thought I might be useful. The two friends walked either side of Cluventius, each taking an arm, slowing his mad dash, speaking in low voices to calm him. I had the sense they were men of the world who already had a good idea what we were walking into. It must have disturbed them, too, but they put it aside so they could look after Cluventius. This was a man people liked. A family who would have people grieving for them. A death that would hurt.

I managed to ask briefly, "Cluventius, do you know why your wife left the party?"

"She was a modest woman, very quiet. All the celebrating was too much for her. She needed to take a break. She told me she would not be long."

"It was like her to do that?"

"It was like her. Just like her."

I had a brief vision: birthday boy throwing himself into his big evening with joyous gusto, a happy occasion but interminable rowdiness and noise, then a shy wife who was so exhausted she had to step away . . . She never enjoyed big occasions as much as he did. She let him have his pleasure, though; she probably enjoyed seeing him so happy. A good wife—and her qualities were appreciated by her loyal husband. This was going to be hard.

We walked from the gardens where the party had been, leaving the trim hedges and symmetrical plantings, the tenting that was still bedecked with bunting and garlands. When we approached the Grove of the Caesars, we saw the searchers had all bunched close to the location of the find, though they were still simply standing on a path, waiting for someone else to decide what next. At the edge of the wood, we paused to brace ourselves.

We entered the thicket. The big plane trees cast a grim shade. After the trim beds of Caesar's Gardens, we were now in wilderness. Wet leaves were underfoot, dampening the hems of long garments. After we left the pathway, I took care not to slither and lose balance.

Cluventius groaned. "What a terrible place!" Floundering through tangled bushes, he made an error of judgement. "My children must be brought. They have to know where this happened to their mother."

"No, sir!" I was crisp. "Don't do that. They should not visit the scene while the body is present, or they will never recover. I wish you would not do it yourself. If you insist on going on, prepare yourself. She was assaulted."

"I have to be with her." He realised what was about to come. It would still be shocking, but he understood. He was starting to suffer already, but he made himself continue.

Then we reached the body.

I took one look, then knew she had been raped and strangled.

The bastard had posed her. It happens. Having violated his victim, a pervert then also assaults the people who find her; he leaves the corpse in a position that is deliberately appalling. This vile man had stretched the woman on her back, arms wide, legs wide, staring up at us. In a swift move, I unwound my stole and dropped the light material across her, saving as much of her modesty as possible.

Cluventius choked. I ordered the crowding searchers to move back, well away. The husband dropped on his heels beside the remains. I leaned down to hold his shoulder, mainly to prevent him touching her.

One of his friends gradually pulled him upright. "Come. She is gone. This is not the wife you knew. There is nothing you can do for her here."

Good men, they were safe in charge. "We shall take him home." They were called Vatia and Paecentius, work colleagues and friends of the family.

I was angry for the woman and my heart ached for her husband. Before his friends led Cluventius from the scene, I told him, "I will stay with her. I shall make sure everything is done properly, by professionals, who will handle her gently. Go home to your children now."

"I want to know who did this!"

"That will be a priority."

I hoped what I said was true. Once the vigiles were brought to this unholy spot, I must take it upon myself to persuade them they had to be thorough. Sometimes it was all too easy for them to say no clues, no witnesses, so no solution.

Vatia had enough sense to make sure he told me where the family lived. His own address too: "Anyone investigating should ask us any questions first, in case we can spare the family." The other friend nodded.

I was left alone with her.

The wait for officials seemed unbearably long. Everyone else had withdrawn from the immediate scene. They must still be congregating on the pathway, so I heard their voices intermittently, but she and I were in solitude here under the trees. As I had promised, I stayed with her as long as necessary. It was a hard thing to do. I could easily have been very nervous.

It gave me time to look at her. Victoria Tertia had been in her thirties. She had a round face that must have been pleasant, with equal features and a small chin. Latin colouring. Brown eyes. She was slim, not undernourished, yet slightly built so she would have been easily overpowered. I could not see clothing in the immediate vicinity, but she still wore rings on several fingers and had an elaborate multi-curled hairstyle that looked too formal for her face. Presumably that was special for the party. She had been painted with cosmetics, though lightly, as if she had waved away the beautician, as my mother always did. Her dangling gemstone earrings looked like a gift from Cluventius to mark a special occasion.

Fairly soon in my vigil, I defied protocol. I stooped down and closed her eyes.

I forced myself to lift the stole I had placed on her, in order to check her injuries by eye. The vigiles would do this, but their scrutiny would be prurient. Fellow-feeling with Victoria made me unwilling to stay once they were involved, so I had to make my own examination while I could. I had already glimpsed scratches and sexual bruising. Now I reviewed these, though learned nothing further; rape is rape. It had clearly happened. She had tried resisting but must have been in the grip of someone very much stronger.

I saw obvious finger-marks from the strangulation, crossing another wound: a long thin line of reddened flesh, partially bloodied, a scratch that told me a necklace must have been torn from her throat. It was nowhere to be seen.

I stood under the plane trees, alone with what was left of Victoria Tertia, waiting. I heard the slight sounds of a forest and undergrowth, the rasp of dry branch on branch, the natural twitch of a stem or uncoiling of a seedpod, a few tentative bird calls, perhaps the scamper of a wood mouse. I could smell the worrying dampness that hugs the ground in forests.

Everywhere seemed completely still. It never struck me that anyone might come to attack me too. However, I would not have been surprised to find someone had been watching.

XVII

In my family, the Seventh were always a byword for untrustworthiness or even corruption. There had been some past encounter, a shared mission that ended badly. My uncle, Petronius Longus, long-time stalwart of the Fourth, routinely decried the Seventh as the worst cohort. I had low hopes of their investigator.

Ursus surprised me, however. I had heard an official clear, dry voice give instructions to whichever of the vigiles had come to the grove, telling them to start interviewing bystanders. A man then approached through the undergrowth. He was heavy-footed but sure, not blundering into ruts nor tearing at long whips of growth to keep his balance. He arrived alone. That is, he had a clerk to take his crime-scene notes, but stylus-pushers are like ghosts. Until someone in an office wants to send out for flatbreads, his clerk counts as invisible.

The man who appeared through the trees was close to fifty, rat-mean, mint-clean. I could tell he had a military background. That was normal. He was one of those types who keep fastidious army habits for ever after discharge. It would affect everything in his daily life: food, personal hygiene, timekeeping, even relationships. Large ears stuck out sideways from a close-cropped head. He wore a red tunic, which was not required in officers, under a cloak against the winter weather. He looked to be unarmed. That was the rule in Rome. Never be too sure, though.

Someone had told him I was there, so he showed no surprise, giving me an indifferent nod. I wished I knew what had been said. He would probably have ordered me to move, but I stepped aside anyway. I expected his methods to annoy me, so was intending to return to the more open part of the Grove. Once he began to appraise the location, I stayed, feeling intrigued.

Without speaking, Ursus positioned the clerk, a youthful slave. He did that by taking the lanky lad's shoulders. He placed him exactly where he required him to stand, on the edge of what passed for a clearing, where he was unlikely to damage evidence.

First, Ursus simply stood. He looked down at the body, gazed around at the brushwood surrounding her, moved a couple of large twigs with one hand as if inspecting them for snagged fibres. He took note of the ground condition. Talking as if to himself, he decided the condition of foliage where she was lying meant that Victoria Tertia had been snatched elsewhere, assaulted, killed, and then her corpse carried here. His voice was medium-low; his Latin accent all-purpose, army-educated junior officer.

He was sure: there was insufficient disturbance for the attack to have happened here. Nor could she have been alive and struggling as she was brought through the woods. That would have battered bushes all along their route.

Though I had not been included, I joined in, saying, yes, this place was a distance from the event's pavilions, where I thought she would most likely have been snatched. A respectable woman, merely taking a short break from the party, would hardly have walked so far, especially since it was dark at the time; neither would she have strayed from a path into undergrowth. If the perpetrator had dragged her there alive, we would see much more disturbance.

Ursus took no notice of me. "Naked, suggestive pose, affront intended." He was now slightly raising his voice for the clerk. The youth wrote it down impassively, as if nothing said was unusual enough to shock him. Ursus called out points he wanted noted. The lad seemed to know procedure, and his role in it. "Classic shaming. Aggression aimed at finders." Ursus lowered his voice again: "Stripped elsewhere, or undressed here and her clothes taken. This?"

As he looked curious about the modesty stole, I admitted it was mine. Ursus shook his head reprovingly. He picked it up with two fingers, then flicked it well aside. I moved back carefully to retrieve it.

My fears about how a vigiles investigator would treat the body were unfounded. On uncovering the corpse, Ursus winced to himself. His subsequent comments were factual.

I saw the clerk write briefly as Ursus listed that the individual had had to silence her, then carry out his assault very fast because of people in the vicinity. There would be no question of making his victim take her own clothes off. He probably kept a hand over her mouth throughout. He must have stripped her after death.

"Her clothes will be near the path . . . She struggled as much as she could. He would enjoy that."

"Power," I said, sounding bleak.

"All about power," the officer agreed, less moved by it than I was.

Suddenly he asked, as if he had guessed the answer, "When she was found, were her eyes closed?"

"I closed them." Our stares clashed, but he said nothing.

He squatted close to the body. He stared at the finger pattern of bruises that showed the manual strangulation. He even took her head between his hands, turning it. I wanted to protest, but he was neutral, professional. He removed a rule from a pouch on his belt, then even measured the fingerprints, gauging the size of the hand they belonged to—he called out the inches to his clerk. After that, he spread his own hands above the marks until he decided from their position that the perpetrator had seized his victim and strangled her from behind. "Rape was frontal." Happening to catch my eye, he added, "She was probably dead."

"Don't such men like to look into their victims' eyes, to watch them go?"

For a moment Ursus assessed me, wondering how a magistrate's young wife could know such details, speaking of them with quiet experience. I let him wonder. "Some do that," he said. "Some enjoy the experience of causing death, but some only want sex, with no argument."

Returning to his task, he gave the clerk a jewellery list, mentioning that one of the rings was a wedding ring. He looked intently at the second mark on her throat, the long, thin abrasion. Though probably unnecessary, I spelled out that it must have been from a necklace chain, violently removed. He keenly agreed: the killer had taken a trophy. If we found him, we might find the trophy, which could be used to prove his guilt.

I said, "I imagine the man who did this may well have a whole casket of personal items—taken from other victims."

"Yes," answered Ursus, looking dour. After a moment he added, still staring at the corpse, "Yes, he has done it before."

The way he spoke caught my attention. I asked bluntly, "Have there been similar attacks around here?"

"Yes and no." He was being cagey. He saw me considering why that should be, so tried to dismiss any idea he had given me: "There will always be attacks in public places. Over the years. Now and again an incident."

"I see," I said, showing what I thought of that.

Ursus straightened up from his crouch by the body, easing his back. He continued to minimise the situation. "There is a large barracks, crammed with sailors. The Transtiberina is awash with women. Night moths. In that situation, some are bound to get knocked off occasionally. Incidents happen."

Too bland. Too easy. I refused to accept it. "You are implying such incidents are always random acts. A sailor gets drunk, knifes another sailor. You take that as natural. A sailor, who may or may not be drunk, falls out with a woman—he can't do it, or can't get her to perform what he asks, or else he hates women who laugh at him, or he thinks they are laughing—so he retaliates. Ruins her face. Smashes her. Wipes her out . . . I know this, I accept it happens. But two things today, Ursus: first, this woman was no night moth plying a trade; she was respectable. Married. A matron, in the gardens with her husband, his friends, their family. If this man had hidden in the bushes, watching, he knew that. Then you say, 'He has done it before.' Those are the words of a professional who has recognised a method."

The investigator pursed his lips hard. He refused to comment.

"Are others like this already on your case list?" I persisted.

"This is unique." He was lying.

"So, you are not saying, 'Here we go again. This is another of his'?"

"I'm not saying anything at all to you!" Suddenly things changed. A complete breach abruptly opened between us. It might have startled me, but I had dealt with the vigiles before. "You are a woman. You have no right to interfere with due process. This is my crime scene," declared Ursus. "Leave it now."

I stood my ground. "I told the husband I would ensure his wife's body was treated with respect." Seeing no reason to antagonise the vigiles, I added, "I know you are professionals. But Cluventius was agitated and I made that promise."

"I won't throw her on the back of a cart!" Ursus snarled. I waited. "We will cover her and carry her gently. No ghouls will get to gawp at her. I'll have our cohort medic see if he can tidy up the obvious before she goes back to her family."

I tossed my head, but he saw I would trust him to do that. Now I would leave.

My relatives were right. The Seventh were hard-core, stubbornly un-helpful bastards. I believed everything my uncle had told me: the Seventh put themselves too close to the wrong elements in the local community, they took bribes to look the other way, they ignored any suspicious acts that would cause them real work. None of them was reliable, so I had better not tangle with this one, let alone trust him.

Of course, Ursus would decry me too. I was an interfering menace, a female, an amateur whose interest was dangerous. No one had asked me to be here. I needed to be kicked out and kept out.

To me, that only proved the Seventh Cohort's lack of judgement.

Without another word, I turned away, beginning to walk back to the gravel path. When I heard Ursus and his clerk following, I quickened my step. I passed through the remaining searchers and the vigiles who were asking them questions. I could tell the conversations were useless, as casual as caupona gossip. No one was pressing. No one was volunteering facts. No one took notes or details of whom they spoke to. The search team Cluventius had brought out here wanted to go home to recover. The red-tunics looked half-hearted, as if determined not to inconvenience themselves with finding answers.

I spoke to nobody. I went around the area where the party had taken place, moving steadily though I refused to rush. I felt thoughtful but sour, full of bitterness. I was angry for Victoria Tertia. When women were destroyed by men, it had that effect on me.

As I went, I folded up my stole into a small square, then shut away the light material in my satchel. I had remembered that Fania Faustina, Tiberius's sister, had given it to me, when she came to Rome for our wedding: someone else who was suffering for being a woman. Miscarriage was the best we could hope for there, if not already too late. I would keep the stole, though probably never wear it again.

I was upset. That need not be bad. You need to react. You need to care. Then you do things right.

I was already intending not to let this go.

At our site, Larcius had the men on light tasks, things that did not involve strenuous demolition or noise. They were all subdued. In part this was because of what had happened to Victoria Tertia. But there was another reason.

Now we had a mystery of our own. The men nervously owned up to me: they said that during the night Primulus and Galanthus had disappeared.

XVIII

"Both gone? How did this happen?"

Serenus, Sparsus and Trypho looked uncomfortable. Some masters' wives, worse women than me, would have blamed them for losing our madcap newcomers. I yet might, but I wanted to hear the story first.

The beginning made sense. As I had prophesied to Gratus, the Cluventius party was a private affair, with little visible to the public. A procession of litters had disgorged well-heeled guests, then parked up in a temporary enclosure that no one else could access. Our lads had been able to hear a hum of activity that lasted all evening, with music, declamations and much happy laughter. The caterers had probably taken their own share of food and drink, but never siphoned off any to outsiders. Anyone who tried to approach was firmly shooed away.

In the end, bored and disconsolate, the workmen had retired to the grotto site, where they dived into their own feast while they sat around gossiping. The two dancing boys had become even more disappointed than the builders and, soon, even more bored. When new music started up, they improvised a few steps together. The men stared at first, then found the lads' antics too lewd.

"Juno, I hope they kept their clothes on." I knew that at the Emperor's banquet the serving boys who writhed among the guests had been painted black but otherwise were naked.

"It was bad enough as it was. They didn't need to strip!"

"Oh, go on, Trypho, surely you've seen it at the baths."

Instructed to stop their wriggling, Primulus and Galanthus had left the work site, saying they wanted to practise their moves. They would go among the trees to see if they could dance with wood nymphs.

That went down with a bunch of builders the way you would expect.

Nobody knew how far along the grove's paths the boys had wandered, or how long they cavorted under the trees. The others forgot about them.

Once the commotion over Victoria Tertia's disappearance started, our dancing sprites were guiltily remembered. Thinking that if trouble was abroad, they had better be fetched back, the workmen had searched for them as best they could, given the darkness and other people looking for the woman.

I sighed. "Did you think Primulus and Galanthus intended to do a runner?"

"Oh, no!" Serenus assured me, self-righteous as a teenager. "We would never have let them go off by themselves if we'd thought they was up to something. We could see their little feet twitching as soon as the music started, so we just let them go and play, like a pair of nagging kiddiewinkles."

"Maybe they honestly got lost," I said, while thinking anxiously that maybe the same man who grabbed Victoria Tertia had grabbed them.

Larcius decided to discipline the others. "You were wrong there. You should have kept an eye on them. Those boys are not used to being out alone, especially at night."

"They have no sense of geography," I said more soothingly. "Let's presume they simply went too far and could not find our site again."

"That was what we thought," said Trypho, sounding relieved. "We kept telling ourselves they would turn up again soon." After a moment, he added gloomily, "I never liked it here."

"Well, bear up!" I answered heartlessly. "The boys might have made friends with a ghastly ghost or two who would scare you, Trypho. Or perhaps they are cuddling the plane trees, and leading dryads into terrible habits."

"We thought you wanted to lose them," Larcius hinted.

"Sort of."

But the dark pall of responsibility wound itself around me. I made the men conduct a daylight search, calling the boys' names loudly. With a bad conscience, I joined in. We told a group of gardeners to watch for them. I had visions of the pair falling asleep in a rubbish cart, being carried way into the countryside before they woke up, then ending their days smothered under mounds of compost or even burned alive on a bonfire . . . Most of the vigiles had already returned to their station-house, but we found a couple loitering, so I asked them to keep an eye open.

We could not find them. We did our best.

My concern was genuine. I really did hope no harm had befallen Galanthus and Primulus. The longer they were missing, the more it looked as if they had run away. Still, if they did flit off on purpose, I was sorry they had only given us such a short trial first.

The dark worry stayed with me. I was too wise to hope we might ever have changed them for the better. I knew if we had been more welcoming, they would only have taken advantage. They would have been as light-fingered as they were light-footed, not amoral but positively immoral. They were impossible to like; they would never have liked us.

All the same, Primulus and Galanthus had been given to me, so they now felt like unfinished business. I had the workmen put up notices, asking for sightings. Then I abandoned the hunt for them, though I did so with regret.

After that, I had no reason to stay in the Transtiberina. I wanted to be at home if Paris came with news from Tiberius. I said I was leaving, so Larcius told Sparsus, the apprentice, to escort me to the river; then he changed his mind and decided to send Trypho as my guard. Trypho was bigger, more experienced, and known to weigh in with his fists if faced with any kind of bother.

I squared up to the clerk of works. "Come on, Larcius. Truth time. A woman was murdered in the Grove last night—but even before it happened you and the lads were obviously being careful. The vigiles agent said there have been previous attacks." I was stretching what Ursus had told me because I had drawn my own conclusions. "Own up, Larcius. You'd already heard that women disappear in the Grove, hadn't you?"

They all looked shifty. To some extent this was normal. They were builders. Builders on principle tend to look as if they are hiding something. Given how much can go wrong in construction work, this is wise.

"Now then, Flavia Albia." Larcius tried to defend their position. "That fellow of yours told us you would be like this! Faustus said he wouldn't even let you come across with any lunch baskets, like you sometimes bring for him. To tell the truth, we didn't know how we ought to play it when you turned up of your own accord the other day."

"You and Faustus *discussed* what goes on?" I was furious.

Larcius looked nervous. "It came up in conversation. We had checked around. When we first started here, people in the area told us what happens. You know how he is about protecting you. Faustus decided he wasn't going to let you come because it's too dangerous, but if you knew you would be straight in, wanting to get justice."

"Justice for what? For whom? What exactly happens here? Cough, Larcius!"

"Bodies of murdered women have been turning up in the Grove of the Caesars for years."

XIX

By now the situation they described came as no surprise. I made the workmen all sit down and tell me. "You may as well talk to me. You are not going to do much work today—and don't worry, I'll convince Faustus I learned about it from the vigiles."

They were relieved the secret was out in the open. Typical men, they were yearning to gossip.

They had been working at the grotto for a couple of weeks now. They had spent the usual time talking to gardeners, snack-sellers, water-carriers, even scavengers, who wanted to pick over the loose rubble. Passers-by came to stare at the site, because people always like to watch. Even though no big hole was involved, knocking down a large pile of rocks was fascinating. "You always get some know-all who tells you your job," Larcius grumbled. "Never mind that an architect has spent time and effort drawing up a set of plans, then a surveyor set him straight, redoing his nonsense with proper working drawings."

"And the building inspector tries to change it all," I sympathised.

"There is a wealth of professional knowledge out there, Albia," Serenus supplied drily. "You wouldn't believe how the most unlikely-looking people know all about how to build a wall, how deep your footings need to be, what mix you ought to use for the mortar, where to buy the best bricks and so forth."

I smiled, leading them on again. "Or sometimes you even have a client who actually knows what he wants."

"Yes, but he's only the person paying for it. What's he doing having an opinion? The man in the street knows better!" chortled Larcius.

"So, good try, lads—but let's drag the subject back on track, shall we? You have talked to these folk, even the idiots who say where you are going wrong. And what have they told you?"

The workmen all pretended to be mystified as to why I was carping—but then they did stop messing about and told me.

Attacks had been occurring not merely for years but for decades. Bodies of women who had been assaulted and murdered turned up, usually in dense undergrowth in the Grove of the Caesars, but sometimes in plain sight in the formal gardens. Normally gardeners found them, or someone walking a dog or otherwise taking the air had a nasty shock. Some corpses were fresh when found. Others had remained hidden until they were decomposing.

"Are they buried?" If they were, the graves were so shallow, it counted for little. Animals frequented the area, so bones sometimes turned up far from original dump sites.

It was assumed the women concerned were prostitutes. Most victims had never been reported missing. Only a proportion were ever identified. No one had ever been arrested for the crime.

"Let me guess," I growled. "A naked female corpse is reported, but the Seventh Cohort of Vigiles, publicly paid shysters, don't try very hard to solve the case?"

Larcius defended the Seventh. "I expect it's almost impossible, if they don't even know who the victim is. People told us that these bodies turn up out of the blue, unknown women, sometimes looking like immigrants. No one knows who put them there, of course, so nobody can say how they ended up in that situation—being done in, I mean."

"Well, if they were good-time girls, it is obvious," corrected Serenus, the literalist.

"Thank you, Serenus! The vigiles could try harder," I said. "The man I saw today was so tight-lipped he would not even admit that it had ever happened before. From what you say that's nonsense."

"Well, it does reflect poorly on him, I suppose." Larcius was still being generous. "If he can't ever catch the killer."

"He might do, if he thought it was worth bothering!"

"Oh, go on, Flavia Albia, you know they try their best," Larcius reproved me. I wondered if he had family in the vigiles, or they had once saved his house from burning down. "They don't like it any more than we do. They have hearts. Anyway, the officers all want to be known as the man who solved a famous set of crimes."

At that I did nod agreement. I can be fair too.

I made the mistake of mentioning that I might venture to the Seventh's station-house to ask more questions. The workmen thought I should not go so gathered themselves together, intent on shepherding me home. "You stay in the house," said Larcius. "You don't need to keep coming into the Transtib to see us. I can let you know what's going on."

So much for Tiberius leaving me in charge of his men; they thought they were looking after me. They were wrong. I gave Larcius a look, so he sent me a wise one back, almost admitting the situation.

"I'll go home," I said, sounding meek enough. "Trypho can take me. The rest of you can abandon the nymphaeum for today. Go and finish Fullo's snack counter so at least that's done. You can start afresh here tomorrow, when the disturbance has died down."

They were wasting their effort, trying to protect me; I could feel myself being drawn in to investigate. I was sure Tiberius would support me eventually. Since we had first known one another, he and I had solved intriguing crimes together. But the men were right; he would be anxious about me investigating a serial murderer on my own. If I took it on, I would need to find the answer before he knew I was doing it.

I let Trypho march me back to the Aventine. There, I went indoors to report to Gratus that we had lost Galanthus and Primulus.

To Larcius and the lads, I might look like an obedient wife, but if there was still no news from Fidenae, I would assess what I had learned today. Being alone always leaves you free to think.

XX

Glumly, I described to Gratus how we had lost the dancing boys. My sharp steward immediately shared my own thoughts: "If there was a murder last night, they may have seen something."

"Yes, and I hope ran off scared." I could easily imagine those two watching, wide-eyed and fascinated, while a woman was attacked. I doubted they would have called for help. And if they were excited, they might have given away their presence to the killer. "I hope they did run off," I said frankly. "I wouldn't wish the alternative upon them. A man who is angry at women may become just as angry at beautiful long-haired lads who prance around in suggestive poses."

I would not make a second journey today; the Transtiberina was too far. I confided in Gratus I would hide until the workmen left tomorrow, then sneak over the river. Gratus said, since we were running out of helpers, he would come with me. I was fretting to be on my own, the way I used to be. I pretended I wanted Gratus to sort bed linen. He said Suza would have to do it. I expressed doubts as to whether Suza knew the difference between a sheet and a bolster case. He said, time to learn, then.

Suza appeared, so Gratus and I buttoned our lips before he served lunch. There was still no sign of Paris.

After I had picked at a few olives to keep the cook happy, I went to my room. I kicked off my shoes as I made it plain to the dog I was staying; Barley grumbled but moved over and let me have a narrow space on the bed. I lay down, absorbing what had happened that morning.

I could not ignore this. A long series of women had been assaulted over the years while men simply convinced themselves a solution was impossible. If there had been only one perpetrator, he must now feel invincible. He would not stop. He would attack more boldly, as if the gardens and the Grove were now his by right, those quiet walks becoming his own loathsome playground and graveyard. Nobody had yet suggested he might be showing off or taunting the authorities, but Ursus had given the impression this was a man who enjoyed the act of killing. So, as long as he was left free to continue, women would remain at risk.

Now I, Flavia Albia, had learned he existed. Could it be a turning point? I was not vain, but I knew I had skills. Nobody wanted me to be involved. That, naturally, convinced me that I should be.

I was close enough to Tiberius to wish that I could talk to him, and I don't only mean talk him around. But I was also remembering my life as a solo informer before I was married: I made my own decisions. I chose what to take on. I rarely avoided any task where I felt I had the right experience, or simply the tenacity to do what other investigators failed to achieve.

I could ask my father about it. Hell, no.

Falco would tell me not to touch this. He would threaten to tell my mother (who would herself tell me not to do it) and if it seemed an interesting puzzle, he would steal it.

Wrong. Falco and Helena were a long-standing detection partnership. If it was *really* interesting, *they* would pinch it.

I loved my parents. Like any daughter, I loved keeping them out of things.

After a rest, I confirmed my decision not to go back to the Transtiberina now, though I had an idea to follow up nearer home. I took Suza, so Gratus was satisfied. Respectable matrons always have a maid present when they are about dubious business. Then nobody questions them, do they? In any other household, with the master away, Gratus would have assumed I was tripping out to visit my lover, using Suza as disguise. Or she was being brought to whistle if an angry wife appeared . . .

Suza had adopted me in the same way that my dog had, at around the same time. She was a dark-haired, big-bodied young girl, who managed to be both a dreamer and a surprisingly practical schemer too. Her personal goal was to be trained in my service in the creative arts of fashion. She had told me this openly. As her helpless model, I would be used for experiments in dress, jewellery and cosmetics, while she sneered at my own incompetence and lack of interest, as she saw it. I suspected that, once training at my house had made her proficient, she would abandon me for somebody more beautiful, rich and social.

Meanwhile, she had come from a seashore shell factory, so there was much to do before she met metropolitan standards. I would not yet trust her with a hot hair-curling rod. However, she might pass muster as a chaperone, since in Rome no one looks twice at your maid. I was often so plainly turned out that few people looked twice at me either. For work, that was how I liked it.

Trailed by this young girl, I went to see Vatia, Cluventius's friend, who had given me his own address and told me questions could be asked there first, before I bothered the stricken family. He lived in a comfortable apartment on the first floor of a building on the Aventine, though on the other peak, which thought itself the more exclusive. More and more self-made people of wealth were coming to live there. It was a short walk from Lesser Laurel Street.

We were admitted at once, almost as though I was expected. While we waited in a small salon with couches and floor rugs, I instructed Suza to sit still, not to fiddle, and never to speak. "What if I need the lavatory?"

"Go now. Ask the porter to show you. Don't chat to him. Look demure while you're walking through the apartment. Be quick, then come straight back. If I'm talking to somebody, just sit down, silent."

Of course, now she had mentioned it, I felt I wanted the facilities myself, but I had learned to ignore that while on duty. Suza just managed to slip out before I heard someone coming.

XXI

Vatia was older than his friend Cluventius, though still working in the transportation business. A man who thought himself too shrewd to be bamboozled, he looked his age after last night's event; he might be less tough than he had been in his prime.

He called me a pretty little thing more than once. It was just his way of speaking, which was good because if he had been the type to turn frisky Suza might have socked him. She had no time for men who were dangerous on couches. But he and I held a perfectly sensible conversation, except that it was based on the premise that I was speaking for my husband.

I did explain that I worked as a professional informer, operating my own business for my own clients. Vatia seemed not to understand this concept. We carried on anyway. At heart he was a kindly old cove. If he believed that everything I wrote on my note-tablet was for the absent aedile, I could live with it.

Sometimes I tell people I come from Britain; they find this exotic, which explains me having an unusual role. British women are mystical empire-bashers, everybody knows that; all I needed was a queenly stance and wild red hair . . . Here, that would not work. Among the hard-working, hard-headed world of trade logistics, anything "exotic" reeks of bad faith and bad debt. Better to make myself look as if I could do neat shorthand and report faithfully to my head of household.

Vatia repeated what I had already been told about the Cluventius family. Although he let me delicately probe the state of Victoria Tertia's marriage, he could not understand why I needed to ask, since to friends the domestic relationship looked so stable. I explained that unfortunately, when women disappeared or were murdered, an inevitable question was whether they or their husbands had lovers; Vatia and I then solemnly agreed there was nothing like that here. I told him the vigiles were seeing it as a plain case of predatory assault, which seemed to have happened before in that neighbourhood.

Vatia was disgusted. His friend's birthday party had been arranged there because nobody would imagine anything untoward at Caesar's Gardens, let alone in the sacred precincts of the Grove. He seemed worldly enough, so I mentioned that previous victims were thought to be prostitutes—I clued him up on the marine barracks. I thought that in Victoria Tertia's sad case, we should assume the killer mistook why she was walking alone.

Vatia was shrewd, because he immediately demanded, "And *were* the others all prostitutes?"

"To be honest, I don't know. From what I have heard, many corpses were never identified. Certainly, they would have been women from a poor background, possibly foreigners in the Transtiberina, whose associates might not have wanted to alert the authorities. Or they might not have known how to report a disappearance. Perhaps they believed no one would care, no one would bother to investigate. I'm afraid the authorities have some explaining to do. Very few people have *nobody* who will miss them if they suddenly disappear."

"Time to find out!" snapped Vatia.

"I would agree."

"Will it be the vigiles looking into what happened last night?"

"It will."

"You spoke to them?"

"I met their investigator."

"What did you think?"

"He seemed competent."

"Seemed? Was he too casual?

"He did his job. None of them were rushing into action, but for the time being I suggest giving them a chance."

"It cannot wait. They need to be shaken up. Cluventius will raise hell. Paecentius and I will support him in any way he needs. This should never have happened. The perpetrator must be brought to justice. Such things have to stop."

I looked sympathetic, but my intuition told me it was too soon to offer my professional services. Let them agitate. That was, assuming complaints happened: some people make wild claims yet never do anything about it. I merely said I would be happy to give advice. Vatia did not take it up.

My one suggestion was that if friends were able to act on behalf of the family, Vatia and Paecentius should organise an undertaker as soon as possible. Victoria Tertia's body should not be left at the vigiles' station-house. I had been promised that her corpse would be treated with respect, but she ought to be reclaimed.

"In terrible circumstances like this, it can help the relatives to bring her home," I told Vatia. "Of course, they have lost her, but in some strange way they will feel she is safe again among her own. When they give her a funeral and put up a memorial, they take back control. Those who love her are making her theirs again."

Vatia listened. He nodded. "You seem to know about terrible situations."

"I have seen grief."

"You know what to do."

"Unhappily, yes."

It was significant that before I left, Vatia led me to another room, where he introduced me to his wife, Romilia. She was a grey-haired, weeping woman of sixty or so, who could not bring herself to say much. I expressed my condolences quietly then we kissed cheeks.

The Cluventius home was also on the Aventine, farther over, on the street down to the Raudusculana Gate. Another comfortable apartment, another tidy reception room. There, I found him in shock, muttering over and over, *"Why?"* He was among his children, a boy and girl both approaching twenty, who were white-faced, tired and overcome, plus another tear-stained little trio of around four, six and seven, who sat in silent distress. The older pair had been at their father's party, while the little ones still had not grasped that their mother, who had tucked them into their beds last night, kissing them goodbye and promising to tell them all about it, was never coming home.

I told him that Vatia was calling in a funeral director, so Victoria Tertia's body could be returned. Today this gave no comfort, though eventually it would.

I knew it was useless, but I assured Cluventius that what had happened was in no way his fault. I could see how things were. He blamed himself. He felt guilty about his choice of venue, then berated himself for having enjoyed his party so much, leaving Victoria Tertia to talk to people by herself, letting her wander away for respite, sending her alone into the clutches of her killer. He ought to have noticed much sooner that she had gone missing. He should have tried harder to find her . . . There was no point in telling him she had been taken and was already dead before he even started.

Ursus from the vigiles had already been to see him. I probed gently. As far as I could gather, everything said had been proper, though conventionally routine. Following the interview, Cluventius now knew that his wife might not have been the man's first victim. Nothing was being kept from him, though I guessed the Seventh Cohort were doing their best to play down the historical situation. It was too soon to stir up Cluventius by criticising their past actions. He needed to rally, then start asking questions himself. As I had with Vatia, I left the widower to react when he was ready.

Tomorrow or soon afterwards, it was likely that Cluventius would recover enough to want revenge. He would need to pass on his guilt, need to place blame elsewhere. Then he would throw himself into demanding more activity from the authorities. Ursus, poor dog, would be expecting this. I did not waste time shedding pity on him and his beleaguered men. They were calling the repeated deaths those of mainly unknown women in a worthless trade, even though there might have been other occasions when the victim's identity was certain and her lost life mourned by angry relatives with social voices.

If Cluventius ever found out that his wife was not the only respectable victim, the Seventh would be for it. Then would be the time for me to put myself forward professionally.

XXII

I s your work always sad like that?" asked Suza, as we trudged home. At the end of a winter afternoon, the Aventine heights became dark and chilly. We huddled in cloaks. Our mood was ever more sombre.

"That is why I do it. People in trouble need help."

"But you were just visiting. They are not going to pay you."

"Patience. They may do."

I thought they probably would. Cluventius would consult his friends. Vatia and Paecentius, already horrified, would lean on the troubled man to initiate his own enquiries. They might not know any other informers, but they had met me. Vatia's wife had liked me. His taking me to meet her showed the respect he had for her. She must be a force in the household, one of so many Roman women who contributed to daily life without ever being given much notice. Barely acknowledged by the law or mentioned in literature, they gave vital support to the men who thought they ran the Empire. In that long-standing partnership, Rome's existence was grounded.

Thinking about these good family friends made me sure of domestic parallels. Victoria Tertia must have held a similar strong position to Romilia in her home. A terrible gap there would quickly become apparent. As the days passed, Cluventius would realise over and over again how much his wife had done, how bereft he and his children were going to be.

I was certain my being commissioned was guaranteed.

———

At my own home, Paris had returned. He brought our own troubles. Tiberius's sister, Fania Faustina, had died. Tiberius had not reached her in time.

Paris slumped and rubbed his eyes, worn out by his journey and depressed by carrying bad news. He had served his previous master as a runabout so was familiar with travel. Since his old master had been murdered, he knew tragedy too. That was how he had come to us; Tiberius and I were friends with his old master so taking him on after the loss had suited all of us.

Paris would recover but was temporarily deflated. Fornix, our cook, brought him something to eat and mulsum, the sweet fortified drink that serves as a restorative. Then Fornix turned out to be unexpectedly good with live animals as well as a master of meat; it was he who he persuaded Patchy, the borrowed donkey, to step into the yard where he could be fed, watered, and kept safe from thieves. It took some effort. Paris mentioned glumly that Patchy was hopeless.

"His normal job is carrying the porter about. I can remember him for as long as I've been going to the Saepta," I mused. "He may be nearly as old as Gornia. It could be time we bought a new beast for ourselves."

"Thank the gods for that!" replied Paris, with feeling, before he added, "Get one that's no trouble!"

I had never bought a donkey in my life. The only things I knew were that if you got a tricky one it caused misery—and that most donkeys took delight in being full of tricks. My staff stood around watching me with cynical smiles. I decided to think about it. Finally, I announced that I wasn't allowed to make big purchases like that without permission from my husband. Their smiles broadened.

By myself I read a short note from Tiberius. He was terse, not yet ready to pour out his grief. Sister dead. Aunt heartbroken. Three little boys confused and lost. Doctor believed the foetus had been "out of place," a common cause of death in early pregnancy. Tiberius was having to organise a funeral (from which I could deduce, brother-in-law no use as usual). No need for me to come; better to look after things at home . . .

I wanted to go. I wanted to be with him. That was something else I must think about privately.

Later that evening I went along to tell Uncle Tullius he had lost his niece. He was out, so I sat down to await his return in the quiet house where Tiberius had spent his youth. I had told the staff my visit was important; I suspect a slave slipped off to find and bring Tullius. He was single-minded about his own pleasures but that night he quickly arrived home and seemed tolerant of having his social life interrupted. He pulled a face at the bad news, called for wine, even gave me some since he said I looked in need of it. I explained I had had a bad day. Tullius never asked why, and I neither knew him nor liked him well enough to discuss my affairs.

After one beaker of intense red wine, he sent me home in his personal carrying chair. I found a party wreath among the cushions, along with a strong stink of perfume. Tullius Icilius was reckoned to have disreputable tastes. I suspected once his transport returned, he would be carried back to whatever entertainment he came from earlier. But before we parted, he told me he would travel to Fidenae for Fania Faustina's funeral; if I wanted a lift in his mule cart, he would take me.

"The event will be rural," he remarked, with a shudder. "Every gruesome custom you have ever heard of. Miserable flowers, squashed berries, mounds of mouldy greenery. They are bound to display the poor corpse for all the nosy clods from miles around to view her . . . We'll have a few days to prepare ourselves. They need to get through a lot of weeping and wailing first. Don't worry, my sister-in-law will let me know when the ceremony is to be. Valeria won't pass up a chance to make it look as if I have shown disrespect by not attending. But I'll go, just to surprise her!"

I decided to take it as a sign that Uncle Tullius was warming, that he spoke so frankly to me. At the same time, I knew he was rude enough to say all this direct to Aunt Valeria or even to Tiberius. Like many such people, he made out he had no idea how crass he was—yet he knew exactly.

As if he realised I feared ten miles in a mule cart with him might be tough, he told me not to worry because he would be asleep. "I'll need to rest up ready for my usual role of upsetting people!"

I replied, as if unfazed, that I would bring a picnic for our journey.

XXIII

I had a disturbed night, with thoughts of all that had happened churning in my brain. Next morning my spirits were very low. In sadness, I wrote a letter to Tiberius, then sent off Paris with it. I had Suza prepare an overnight bag, so I was ready to go to Fidenae at short notice. While Gratus was talking to Fornix about groceries, I winked at Barley, who came with me as I slipped out of the house.

It was a grey day, no sun, though at least neither wind nor rain. Everyone I passed seemed to be talking about what they were planning at Saturnalia. It would be our first. We would be a household in mourning. I ducked my head and walked fast to avoid stressful thinking.

I crossed the Tiber again by the splintery Sublician. This bridge was a favourite with beggars, which might have made me anxious, but my surly mood obviously showed. Those who were sitting there either hid their heads or jumped up and fled. Barley wagged her tail at the ones who were pretending to be asleep. I did toss a coin to a very old woman. She cursed me. I vigorously cursed her back. She went off into panic that she had been given the evil eye. Sometimes I did not need to claim to be a druid— just as well, since I have no idea what the evil eye is or how you deploy it.

I had a plan. With no nervous escort to stop me, I marched straight to the headquarters of the Seventh. Each vigiles cohort looks after two districts, one with their main barracks, the second with a lesser presence. Siting the Seventh's main station-house over here must have seemed like throwing a military base across a river into enemy-held territory. Every night coming out on watch, the men must feel apprehensive. Nobody here would like paramilitaries, not even when they came racketing up with their horse-drawn siphon engine to put out a fire. As for knocking burglars about in these dark streets, that must always run a risk of starting a riot. In the Transtiberina, suspicion of authority was so strong you could taste it in the air.

Inside, they were safe enough. The place was heavily walled and gated. While most of them were sleeping by day, they had probably learned to ignore the smells of the obnoxious trades that were carried on in the Fourteenth and the clamour of its exotic residents.

No one answered when I knocked at the gate, though I reckoned there were personnel inside. I had the choice of looking for the day team at the nearby baths or a bar. I chose the bar, where at least they might have their clothes on. There I routed out a nest of red-tunics. My starting point is always that these ex-slaves are admirable men doing a vital job, who brave danger and like saving lives. They may be built like money chests on legs, but they have generous hearts. As usual, my approach worked, so they treated me like a favourite daughter as I pleaded for one of them to come to let me in. Those who were busy drinking called out for Arctus, who had gone upstairs with the barmaid so in this round he had no drink he would have to leave behind.

When he came down, Arctus did not have his tunic on. He was still draped with the barmaid until his mates explained what was needed, so he shook her off and was simply nude. I winced. The rest laughed. Someone threw him a counter towel, in case he met his granny in the street, after which Arctus took me to the station-house readily enough. We did not meet his gran, which was fortunate, since the modesty towel was seriously small.

The Seventh's headquarters had the usual courtyard, outdoor fountain basin, equipment room with piles of mats, pickaxes and rope buckets, shrine with imperial busts, lavatory, prisoner cell (empty with its door open), dormitories and a large pantry for ration storage. The pantry would be the key area.

The officer on duty was sitting with his cronies, who were the water-supply expert and the medic, all telling dirty stories. The office was so near the gate that they must have heard me knocking. The man in charge was unrepentant, but now I had caught him out, he wrote down details I gave him of my missing dancers. I emphasised that Primulus and Galanthus were in origin gifts from Domitian. The vigiles had a role in recapturing runaways, though I pointed out that mine had likely been scared by the murder that took place last night, so should be treated kindly. After I had passed on stories from my senator uncles about the Black Banquet, the officer warmed up slightly. He would soon be telling these tales as if he had privileged access to Palace gossip. If I ever needed future favours it might give me a slight advantage. You have to build up your contacts.

Mentioning why the young dancers might have fled gave me a reason to ask about the murder. There had been no developments, which was no surprise. Ursus, naturally, was not here. No chance of pressing him for more. Not that he would have told me.

While we were talking, I mentioned that my workmen had made an odd discovery, so were the vigiles aware of illegal activities in the Transtib that might involve scrolls? Of course not. Even so, to my surprise, another note was made, in case they came across anything like that. It would at least be a change from bath-house pilfering and purse-snatching.

Looking down my list of questions, the officer commented on my wide portfolio of interests. The Seventh are responsible not only for the Fourteenth Region but the Ninth, which includes the Saepta Julia. I mentioned that I was Falco's daughter, so he groaned and said that explained everything.

After I left, I made my way around the huge Naumachia. Although I wondered if there was anything to gain by calling at the sailors' barracks to ask about the killings, common sense set in. The barracks was a no-go area. I gave that complex a wide berth.

At our site, Larcius and the workmen had been digging. They were so proud of their finds they forgot to reprimand me for coming over unescorted. That morning they had unearthed enough scrolls to fill a barrow with grimy papyrus; Larcius was satisfied they had looked everywhere, so we now had possession of all there could be. The men would bring the new load to the house that evening. It would keep me busy, preparing a catalogue.

I complimented the team, then questioned them about everything else. No one the workmen had talked to today had been able to shed light on our two missing boys. Local gossip said that nothing more had happened about the murder either. The body must have been taken away yesterday. Serenus had nosily been to the Grove to look. If formal enquiries were still being made officially, there was no sign of it.

"I wondered if they would put up a notice asking for information from the public?"

"Oh, yes, they did that," Larcius replied, sounding caustic. "They stuck it on a tree in the Grove but the wind blew it away. Don't worry, we found it. We nailed it back up again. With proper nails this time."

"Any of the public who know anything are likely to keep away from here, though," added Trypho. "They won't see the notice."

"They wouldn't volunteer information in any case," said Serenus.

"Too dangerous," I put in, with a smile. "Tiberius Manlius wrote a request for information once. I answered it. Next thing, we were getting married."

"Not going to happen to Ursus!" the toothless Larcius supplied, in his whistly way. "Word is, he already secretly has two wives, one in the Fourteenth and another in the Ninth. Two henpecking mothers-in-law, two sets of birthdays he had better to remember or he's dead meat . . . If he ever gets transferred to a different cohort, and acquires two more, he'll probably hang himself."

If this was true, I wondered whether the stress of juggling his different lives made Ursus a candidate to be a killer himself. I did not mention it. Speculating is how rumours start. The more you were only trying to lighten your mood, the madder the nonsense that spreads.

All the same, you never know. I might try gently to find out when these murders had started and whether they occurred at all before Ursus was assigned to the Seventh Cohort . . .

As if he knew he was under discussion, at that moment the investigator Ursus hove into view. He wore the same cloak and red tunic as yesterday, with the same cool expression. Two or three disconsolate vigiles straggled behind on escort duty. They were for show. I could tell from the way they dragged their boots that they knew they had been kept from their daytime sleep but would not be asked to do much.

Ursus was putting on a brave face, though I realised he had been hobbled by the authorities. He was walking in tandem with another man, apparently discussing evidence as equals. But the person he had brought to inspect the crime scene would see the situation in a different light. I knew him. He thought himself special. In his case, it was horribly true. His presence meant that Ursus's role as key investigator had been superseded.

His name was Julius Karus. He had a black history, a creep who fixed secret executions with undue diligence, then was showered with rewards. Supposedly his current role in Rome was to head up a long-term project to tackle criminal gangs. Last I saw, he was assigned loosely to the First Cohort, taking charge of Operation Phoenix. This was intended to counter vicious gang warfare on the Esquiline and Quirinal Hills.

It ought to keep Karus busy, but the operation had gone quiet. That was not because the rival gangs had had a crisis of conscience and reformed. It was just a lull while they were racking their brains for something even more horrible to do to each other. One of the groups was led by an old man, who was dying slowly. The process had been going on for some years, but until he croaked no member of his own clan dared move and the others were waiting to see what would happen. The vigiles joked that they were sending broth to Old Rabirius to keep him alive so the streets would stay peaceful.

I could guess what had brought Karus. Cluventius and his loyal friends had already started making demands for justice for Victoria Tertia. They must have taken their complaints to someone high up; I reckoned they had loud voices too. So, while Julius Karus kicked his heels on the quiescent gangster operation, he had looked to be available for a special task. He had been sent to beef up the Seventh. Here he was in Caesar's Gardens—and he had not come to sniff flowers.

As the two officials arrived on site, out of the corner of my eye I saw Serenus pick up the barrow handles and innocently wander away out of sight with the scrolls.

XXIV

Caius Julius Karus was an equestrian, the rank Domitian now favoured to hold high administration posts. The new breed would reward him with special loyalty and keep him on the throne, however much other people feared him. Carefully placed equestrians were taking over where senators or imperial freedmen had to be reined in or, better still, sacked under a cloud. At that point, if the previous post-holders had any sense, they conveniently died.

Karus suited the current regime. His methods must have been approved, since he and the men he deployed to help him were laden with honours, though with curious silence about their citations. He now held undercover positions, whose purpose and sinister powers again were never publicly announced.

He was heavily built, though his gut looked squashy. Blue-chinned, black-hearted. He had the weight of a soldier who had served in Germany, that feast-loving province, with the stare of a man who had once served in Britain, the end of the civilised world. In most ways that didn't frighten me but my knowledge of what his career-defining mission there had been, a political execution, did make me guarded. Rome had rules but Julius Karus was permitted to ignore them.

It was possible Ursus was in tune with this political beast, though more likely he had had Karus dumped on him, in the same way Scorpus of the First had been told to give the man houseroom for Operation Phoenix. At any rate, "Hello, you're here again!" said Ursus to me, sounding unhappy. He seemed to be desperately establishing contacts so he would look like a man who knew his patch. I replied that I was supervising our workmen for my husband, as I had been intending to do yesterday when I heard about the corpse.

"This is Flavia Albia, wife to the magistrate Faustus." Ursus introduced me to Karus, who nodded.

"Karus and I have met." I tipped the wink to Ursus myself, expecting no gratitude. I have my own courtesy, based on practical considerations. Karus would move on. I might have to deal with the Seventh at any time. "I am aware of his valuable work."

I knew better than to say I had recently seen him in action. To my mind, he had no judgement. Ursus himself might have shied away from deep enquiry into the series of deaths, but he had at least carried out a faultless crime-scene inspection yesterday.

"Julius Karus has been assigned to give us new insights." Ursus braved it out.

I gave him a sympathetic smile, showing I understood the situation: "You mean, the latest victim bleated to the Prefect of Vigiles? So Karus has been sent with a big stick? Only joking!" I quipped to Karus, a man who by definition did not joke.

"Cluventius went right up to the praetor," Ursus admitted glumly. In the law and order hierarchy, that was as high as anyone could go, bar the Emperor. For self-preservation, a good praetor would always keep Domitian informed.

"He really has connections! Time for a rethink, then. Rapid response. At least now you have Karus to take the blame!"

"Always good to lumber the commissariat," agreed the vigilis, showing his feelings perhaps too openly. Ursus, with his stuck-out ears and tight habits, now had someone to resent even more, so he was making parley with me. Karus watched, excluded. We were pretending he was sharing our black humour, but we had better not antagonise him too much.

It was an interesting situation anyway, because I stood there as a lone woman, who ought to have felt threatened. But I had at my back a cluster of men holding mattocks. When I joked, my workmen chuckled. When I smiled satirically, they beamed. Serenus, who had sauntered back after concealing the barrow of scrolls, even treated us to his signature mark of appreciation: stuffed with pie from Xero's, he could fart as punctuation.

I continued to aim my remarks at Ursus. "Let me guess: has past history been hastily reviewed?"

He nodded. "We are rechecking all the old case details." At least I knew that during Ursus's time here, the clerk I saw yesterday would have made and saved basic notes. With the arrival of Karus, the old case records would have been pulled from the back of cupboards. "We shall assess similarities, looking for matches, checking any missed leads." Ursus was trying to sound efficient in front of me. Karus glared at this unprofessional level of sharing. He did all his work in secret.

I warned him easily, "Don't be tight, Karus. It's best if the public knows all this. You need to reverse the current lack of confidence. Persuade new witnesses to cooperate. Attract new tips."

Karus had listened to enough banter and he hated advice. He took over, announcing that he had come to re-interview my workmen. I knew that no one had asked them anything yet about when Victoria Tertia had died, but I spared Ursus the admission. I said they were disgusted by what had been happening so we were eager to help. I waved Karus over to them. "They will answer truthfully. I have no need to supervise."

I moved away slightly, making it plain I would not influence anything they said. I sat down on a pile of rocks, inviting Ursus to join me, though he remained stolidly standing. "Do you want to ask me whether he's good?" I muttered.

"Best not."

"All right."

After a moment he could not help himself. "You've met him before. What was your impression?"

"Deadly. He will turn up a suspect, though it may be the first person he lights upon who looks guilty. Half of Rome fits that. Then if you arrest the wrong man, the real one will brazenly carry on. He may even increase his killing rate, if he hears someone else has been given credit."

Ursus nodded warily. He stopped the conversation in case Karus glanced in our direction. We waited. Karus interrogated Larcius and the lads, which he did with more aggression than needed, just because he could. Old hands, they replied patiently. I knew they had seen and heard nothing useful on the party night.

Karus came back to Ursus, scowling. "No good. But you lost two slave-boys?" he demanded of me.

"We did. Long-haired youths who like dancing, which is not very useful in a domestic environment. We were unclear how wild the Cluventius event would be, so we took the precaution of guarding our site. The boys wanted to help. They were gifts from the Emperor to my family, after that banquet for the fallen in Dacia." I decided not to criticise Domitian's spiteful humour in front of his man. "I had given them permission to sit with the builders in case there was anything exciting to see. Of course, there wasn't."

"They ran away?"

"Simply that, perhaps. Or they might have witnessed something that terrified them. We won't know until we find them."

"You expect to? Well, that will give you something to do," Karus ground out triumphantly. "Looking for them should keep you busy and out of our inquiry."

"I shall not trouble your inquiry," I replied gently. "I never interfere." I sounded like my grandmother. Both of them. Juno.

If there was one thing that ensured I would invade their case, it was Karus telling me to keep out. As they left, I thought Ursus looked as if he realised what I was thinking. The workmen did. They were snorting behind their hands while they watched the officials depart.

I announced that, instead, now was the time for me to think more about the excavated scrolls.

XXV

I meant that.

I did surprise everyone, perhaps even myself. I picked out a sample of the material that Larcius and the men had dug up that day. They watched me park myself, all keeping an eye on where I landed, in case I attracted the predator. I wasn't worried. These horrible works were not going to absorb me so deeply I would miss him creeping up. One or two retained their wooden scroll batons. My father tells a nasty tale of a publisher who died when he was speared through the nostril into his brain by a scroll rod. A rejected writer did it . . .

I found myself a bench in feeble sunlight, where I unfolded what I could easily open of the stiff, earth-encrusted scrolls. Exploring the new material was tricky and dirty, but eventually I knew this batch included further lousy topics by Epitynchanus, though no more "fragments" of Philadespoticus. We might have more of him in the barrow, which would be a good place to leave him. There were all sorts of material, including parts of plays, history, even travelogues. I found names we had not previously come across, one of whom appeared to be a female Greek poet.

I tipped my head back, absorbing winter light, if not warmth. It felt good to be using the gardens for their intended purpose of leisure, even if this leisure was combined with work. The Emperor Vespasian famously used the Gardens of Sallust as an outdoor office, though he had slaves to run after correspondence that blew away, with tip-top Palace tray-toters to bring him snacks when reading became tedious. I bet he never had to plough through anything by Epitynchanus the damned Dialectician.

My brain said that nobody ever did. Epi and Philly struck me as doomed to be the great unread.

I expect they prided themselves on being difficult. Setting challenges for simple folk lets writers disport themselves as mighty intellects. Struggle is presented as commendable. Even intelligent readers may feel proud of suffering over unintelligible bosh . . .

Bastards.

If we could sell the previous scrolls, we could sell these. The task set by my father still applied; I would have to collect them into sets and list them. That would be best done at home, where they could all be laid out, sorted and grouped before I prepared the inventory. I carried the samples back to Larcius so his men could wheel them up the Aventine for me.

I pretended this scroll puzzle was my sole interest. For the time being, that was almost true. I felt honestly wary of the killings in the Grove.

I admit it: I was also perturbed that Julius Karus was taking an interest. I wanted to avoid him.

Ultimately, I guessed Karus had his eye on the position of Chief Spy. There already was one—there must be. In Vespasian's time the loathsome Anacrites had been inflicted upon us, after which Titus had always been close to the Praetorian Guards, who ran the secret service, so he would have had his personal appointee. Domitian was so suspicious he must have had eyes looking out for him from the moment of his accession. Whoever he was, that man managed to stay hidden. But someone was certainly drinking fine wines and collecting niche artworks in a grace-and-favour house close to the Palace, whence he could run if his master called. And that someone would have a discreet Palatine suite, where he arranged treachery and death. Did he know the envious Karus was eyeing up his post and title—not to mention his marble office?

I had been in rooms where spies ran secret agents, opened and read travellers' correspondence, pored over tip-offs from the public or just plotted against one another mercilessly, as spies do. They never named their chief. They probably plotted against him too.

So far, Karus inhabited the Castra Peregrina on the Caelian, where "scouts" from all the legions were placed to observe the Roman population.

Perhaps, I postulated wryly, somewhere in the world Julius Karus had left a civilised wife and merry children . . . No chance. He came to us direct from the legions. He arrived in Rome with no personal baggage. I thought he despised attachments. There was no room in his life for ties of affection, cultural pursuits, or flopping on a bench idly at the end of a day. For him, a bench was something to tie a suspect to, face down, while he threatened to spear them with a hot poker—and then had a soldier do it.

Once the Caesar's Gardens killer was arrested, turning him over to Karus would only be justice. Finding that person required skills Karus might not have—or maybe he did, but I had never seen them yet. Should I give him more credit? Allow him time to show his talents?

All right. Be fair to him, Albia. Let him, if he was up to the job, tackle what no one had bothered to do so far: let him catalogue all the corpses that had been found in Caesar's Gardens and the Grove, listed in date order with notes of key features. Let him create sub-groups according to the location of bodies, methods of causing death, appearance of victims and anything known of their background. Let him have that young clerk draw up an inventory of all the trophies known to have been taken. Let Julius Karus ponder how and when each of those bodies was discovered, how and where the victims might have been snatched, whether it was known they had been raped while alive, or believed they had been used sexually after death, or if any were obviously revisited during decomposition. Let him check every case for witnesses, then summon back any informants who could still be found for a new interview, which would be conducted by himself and Ursus. Or, more likely, by Karus solo.

Once he had done all that work, if I wanted to involve myself, then would be the time. I would attempt to access the documentation. (Oh, really? How, Albia darling?) Subvert Ursus so he would talk to me. Bribe the clerk to lend me the note-tablets . . .

It would take time for Karus to complete his reassessment. Meanwhile, I walked back over the river with a very different aim. I cut through the meat market, around the west end of the Palatine into the Forum, then crossed right over to the ancient street between the Curia and the Basilica Aemilia. Domitian had adapted the first stretch of this old road into the Forum Transitorium. He had built a Temple of Minerva, with an apsidal porticus at the far end that gave onto the highway: the historic Argiletum.

This street rising towards the Esquiline had a long history. It continued to teem with mixed habitation and even more mixed commerce. It had a terrible reputation for brothels, barely improved by its supposedly hosting scroll shops. In fact, there were fewer of those than people said: literature was much less in evidence than the barbers, potters, pimps and trinket-trundlers, who assailed passers-by with invitations of all kinds. This was, however, where a man in a small booth, one Donatus, had reserved for me a complete encyclopaedia that I was buying for my husband.

On our wedding day, I told Tiberius he would receive one scroll at every anniversary. There were thirty-seven in the set. This was a sure way to stop him divorcing me for years, if he wanted the whole work. Now I told the seller that, since life was short, I might start giving Tiberius a scroll at Saturnalia too, even if it brought forward the moment when he casked up the last one in his private library and could send me back to Mother.

I handed over a large sum for the next scroll. My dear husband already had the first: Pliny's Letter to Vespasian and the index. This new part covered the world, the elements and the stars. That should keep Tiberius busy.

"When is his birthday?" the scroll-seller mused, while quickly preparing my parcel, since Saturnalia was but two weeks away. He had enough fingers to figure out that piling in birthday presents as well would not only double but treble his annual sales and cash flow.

"No idea—but just for you, I will find out."

"Still good is it? The marriage?" Donatus probed.

"Yes, though still new enough for all our friends and relatives to mutter that they don't expect us to last."

"But you are in love!" he smarmed cynically.

"I am in love—and in a quandary. Donatus, my friend, I want to talk to you about philosophers."

"I need to sit down then . . . Hit me with it, Flavia Albia."

Donatus was thin, pasty, short-sighted and lacking in character, despite a life spent in the mind-enhancing world of books. He could not afford a comb for his long grey straggles of hair or a shave more than once in two weeks. He only ever had a small stock, which, like many sellers, he seemed to prefer to keep in his shop, rather than letting buyers take them. It could be why he failed to eat. My father's secretary had found him for me, though, as far as I could gather, Katutis came here on his own, not sent by Pa in the course of business. This made Donatus a neutral adviser, one with no prior obligations to the auction house.

I lobbed at him the names of Epitynchanus the Dialectician and Philadespoticus of Skopelos. He looked at me askance. "Never heard of them. Skopelos is famous for wine, not fine thinking."

I had half expected this. The only surprise was that when I had mentioned them to Tuccia in the other scroll shop she apparently knew them. "I suppose," I admitted shyly, "we are hoping that obscurity adds value?"

"Nuts!" retorted Donatus.

I tried him with another name I had come across today in the newest batch. "Didymus Dodomos?"

Donatus burst out laughing. "You are having me on!"

"You don't know this man?"

"He doesn't exist."

"He must. I have work he has written . . . Thallusa, then? A Greek lady poet?"

"Lives on an island, with her special girlfriends?"

"Lived in Arcadia, I don't know who with."

"Writes girlie sex?"

"Writes womanly stress. *Do not bring me your anxieties, take your repression from my door; I am contemplating my own troubled mind, I cannot hear your complaints any more* . . . I admit lesbian love must sell better."

"Unreachable apples and crushed hyacinths. Top topics! Where have you come across this stuff, Albia?"

"Dug it up."

"Oh, joy! Someone knew it was so bloody awful they buried it in a deep hole! Their logic is thrilling," Donatus jibed. "Such a refreshing attitude."

"Forget I asked, Donatus."

"I certainly will not do that. Flavia Albia, this is the best laugh I have had all year—and I say that in December, with Saturnalia just around the corner."

"One last question, then. If I wheeled in a pile of works of that nature, would you buy them?"

"No."

"These are rare purchases, one-offs and sought-after. No avid collectors you could tempt?"

"I don't sell to idiots." Donatus was struggling professionally, but it seemed he had his pride. If true, I respected him for it. In the end he muttered, "I'll think about it and let you know."

"That's what people generally say just to get rid of me."

He growled. "I will mention these authors of yours to my regular collectors. If anyone says anything, I can pass it on to you."

Now he had tried to get rid of me twice. I took the hint and went home.

XXVI

I spent the rest of that day at home, preparing scrolls for auction, later adding those the workmen brought. I did not enjoy this job. I overheard staff members calling me tetchy. They were wrong, though. I could be much tetchier than that.

My spirits sank lower when a slave came from Uncle Tullius. Aunt Valeria had written to him about the funeral; he was leaving for Fidenae the next morning. I confined myself to saying that Gratus would be in charge in my absence and Suza had to stay at home, since I could not face her moaning about mourners with dishevelled hair. I went to bed but slept little.

Tullius, in his mule cart, came when it was barely light, since we hoped to rattle through Rome to our northern exit while the streets were empty. Tullius always ignored the daytime wheeled-vehicle ban. Even so, he left before eager officials on the day roster started work, while the night watch would not want to delay going off duty. We escaped the city unchallenged.

We spoke little during the journey. At one point I remembered my commission for Donatus, so I asked if Tullius could tell me his nephew's birthday.

"Two days before the October Ides," he answered straight away. "You missed this year; I didn't tell you—he was still suffering after the bolt hit him. Fania's was fifteen days earlier. Their mother had believed her second child was going to be born on the same day as her first, but she came sooner." He was able to tell me without checking a calendar, a surprise. Tullius then said, after a pause, "He will grieve on her anniversary, but at least then he can lighten up for his own. If he will. He can be dark."

As he sank back into gloom, I wondered if his niece's death reminded Tullius of losing his own sister. Talk of family matters seemed out of character, yet he kept dates in his mind and thought about implications. Even so, his attending the funeral still appeared to be more stubbornness than sorrow.

Left with silence again, I pondered the odd tolerance that seemed to exist between uncle and nephew. Tiberius, I knew, had been sixteen when Tullius offered him a home. Tiberius was such a different character, serious and traditional, traits that might even have been exaggerated when he first lost his parents. By contrast, his uncle was a secretive but sociable businessman who slept with slaves, if not worse. Yet I had never heard Tiberius say a bad word about him. I guessed Tullius had never tried to change him—or vice versa. Generous acceptance on both sides. I wondered if their dissimilarity might explain why Tiberius had spent so much time on his own, reading.

Strange how sometimes you can alter your perspective, with barely a word spoken. Unusual, too, to come across someone who made no attempt to force conversation even when later we had the picnic basket out. I was happy with that.

Eventually, stiff and tired, we reached Fidenae. I had been nearby once before, with Tiberius, though we had been working on a case so could not linger. Now I was to stay at his aunt's home. When we arrived, he strode out to meet us, nodded to his uncle, then hugged me in a tight embrace.

"You needn't have come."

"I wanted to be with you."

I took him away to be private. With me, he wept, letting out his grief over Fania for the first time. Until I came, he had been keeping himself together while he consoled other people and busied himself with arrangements. I held him, saying nothing, until he stopped, left only with emptiness.

Later he wanted me to talk. It gave him new topics to think about, so I started with the story of Primulus and Galanthus. When I explained their disappearance, I had to go into the Cluventius birthday party, with its tragic outcome. Tiberius made me promise I was not investigating the deaths. I said truthfully that Julius Karus had taken over. Tiberius scratched his chin somewhat, but we avoided arguing. He knew me. He knew when he could influence me, and when not. I would not worry him with admitting my intentions, while he had too much on his mind to want a tussle he could not win.

There was plenty of other strife around us. Valeria and Tullius engaged in open hostilities. Simply related by marriage, they had nothing else in common, except their claims on Tiberius and strong distastes for one another. She was a countrywoman, he a city-dweller. She was elderly and so anxious she seemed feeble, he creaky but still a goer. They might have shared concerns for Fania's children, but Tullius openly thought that even now they were motherless, those whiny little boys were to be shunned. He had no conscience, as Valeria loved pointing out.

The funeral was next day. We all processed to a tomb that had been built adjacent to the old estate where the grandparents and parents had lived, now sold. This tomb stood beside the road, in an awkward corner of land on the boundary of the property. The usual notice gave dimensions of the plot, ground that was now sacred to those buried there, home for ever to their spirits, unencumberable by mortgage, inviolable, unsaleable. A brick wall provided protection, with a single entrance and a garden. Four or five large trees were planted in a row on the roadside, with an orchard of fruit trees and vines behind, then rows of kitchen vegetables. It was a peaceful spot. Birds flew around and sang. Roses, with one or two pale flowers braving the winter, made a sweet surround to the tomb. It was marble, the material the grandfather had imported. Inside, neat plaques commemorated family members, while a place had been marked for a new stone to be erected: Fania's.

Mourners had come from farms in the district. Tiberius announced briefly that it had been Fania Faustina's wish to lie here, near their happy childhood home, with their grandparents and parents. Nobody commented that this was odd. No one (not even Tullius) said Fania's ashes would normally have been placed in her husband's family mausoleum and only put here if they had been divorced. Naturally, we all thought it.

I met the tenant who worked the tiny market-garden. His role was to grow produce to be given to the gods in memory of the dead. When relatives came, he supplied fresh fruit and vegetables for their feast. He sold some for the tomb's upkeep. Then, if he managed to achieve a surplus, he was allowed it for his own table, or could sell it. He lived in a small building alongside. Today he helped with the funeral fire.

It was clear to me that Tiberius had arranged almost everything. Antistius spoke the formal words of farewell, but Tiberius gave his sister's eulogy. Valeria and I looked after the three boys during the ceremony. She pointed out to me a widow, whom she whispered sarcastically was a very close, long-term friend of Antistius, though not of Fania.

Tiberius confirmed this to me afterwards. He said Antistius was always over at the widow's house since, apparently, she needed continual advice on her estate. For some reason, it was beyond her to employ a farm manager. Antistius claimed he was being neighbourly.

This hardly seemed a grand romance. She was an average-looking woman, just as he was an insignificant man. She was not rich, nor were her people well thought of locally. She seemed oblivious to people's stares or had become hardened to their antipathy. She must know what Antistius was like, if only because she knew he had offended his wife with his attentions to her. Like so many relationships, it was hard to see how it had ever come about, or why they were so firmly attached to one another.

Tiberius thought Antistius would openly move in with the widow soon. I decided not to wonder what that might mean for his young sons. Someone had dressed them in mourning white for the funeral, all their new clothes slightly too large for them. Fania had always kept them in different-coloured little tunics: red, blue and green assigned to each. She said it helped with laundry. I could see that today they felt uncomfortable and strange. At one point in the funeral, the widow made a show of approaching to hug them; they were unresponsive, especially the two youngest. Aunt Valeria took them all home early.

The rest of us duly stayed until the cremation finished. This long period of waiting always has the potential to be awkward. Tiberius was strung so tight I kept him away from his brother-in-law, lest he ended up punching Antistius. Uncle Tullius did stay at the tomb to the end. He had brought a flask of expensive oil to pour upon his niece's bier; then, for all the hours necessary, he engaged with local mourners, acting for the family, even though I knew he thought of those people as clods.

Eventually, while Antistius was standing with his very close friend the widow, Tiberius and Tullius collected Fania's ashes. Together they placed her remains in an urn that Tiberius provided, then set it inside the tomb. I had never been religious, but I spent a moment thanking the spirits of his parents for Tiberius, while I made a silent promise that I would take care of him. He spent a long time inside the tomb on his own, while I waited outside for him in the quiet garden where his sister's spirit could now safely wander among those of her ancestors.

Darkness was falling as we left.

XXVII

I went home with Tullius Icilius the next day. Tiberius insisted I go. He was worried about our house and business; he put together an anxiety list for me.

He would stay in Fidenae temporarily. Now the funeral was over, he wanted to see his aged aunt more settled and to reassure his young nephews.

He devised a plan to take the boys to look at donkeys. I would incur no blame for any beast he might buy, which suited me. At the same time, the outing gave him a chance to talk to them without their father's oversight. "Discussing their feelings?" I had asked, trying to smother a dangerous thought. "Yes, nothing too awkward," replied Tiberius. He had all the sincerity of me, when promising to shun escapades he disapproved of.

His own feelings were running deep. Although he was sending me back to Rome, he could hardly bear to part from me. As I went home in the mule cart, once more mainly in silence, I reflected on how such a reticent man might seem unemotional. But I knew his pain. I grieved for him.

It seemed natural to compare the loss of Fania Faustina with that other bereavement people were enduring: Victoria Tertia. In our case, I had felt benign towards Fania, though I had never had time to get to know her. I only remembered my impatience with her for being so unhappy with Antistius yet doing nothing about it. Aunt Valeria had told me Fania had confided she was happy that Tiberius had found me. In return, I had always been glad he had a sister because it seemed to make him more humane. That was all the connection she and I ever had. Yet even for me the loss of Fania brought great sadness, and not simply because I feared huge complications would follow.

"You're quiet!" scoffed Uncle Tullius, suddenly waking. Had he deduced what had been perturbing me? It sounded like a challenge.

At first, I skirted around the obvious issue. "A winter funeral is worst to chill the spirits. All that standing out of doors among people you don't know, pretending you share something, not knowing whether to make it a social occasion or just hope to get through it . . ."

"You read the signs, then?" replied Tullius, seeing through my attempted bluff.

"Oh, I read them," I conceded. He was talking about Tiberius fretting over his sister's family.

"You'll cope, I'll say that for you . . . Did you look at the will?" he snapped abruptly.

"I didn't think it was my place."

"Aren't legacies your business?"

"Well, I try not to tangle with in-laws."

"Wise! She left a whack to Tiberius. She gave no reason, but he is her only brother. Well, he's bright enough to work it out . . . Did he say anything?"

"Tiberius? When he is ready."

"Too late by then!" grumbled Tullius.

"He won't leave me out of any decisions. He has to make up his own mind first . . . He will consult me," I assured his uncle. "You too, perhaps. Aunt Valeria has tried pressing him to move out to Fidenae—"

"That witch! I'll put a stop to it."

"No need. He knows I would divorce him! He assured me that our home and the business are in Rome. Valeria knows we can't leave. But it's obvious he won't abandon the three little orphaned ducklings. I shall help him do whatever is right." I looked Uncle Tullius straight in the eye. "He's an uncle with nephews who need help. You should understand his dilemma!"

Now it was out. For the first time ever we spoke honestly about Tullius bringing Tiberius to Rome. "Ha! I was never going to leave him with the flaky aunt. In our case, he made it easy enough. Unlike Unum,

Duo and Tres, he never whined. I had room in the house for him. It seemed a useful thing to do, and a lifeline for him. His parents had been dreamy, both of them; he needed someone realistic."

"As I heard it, you let him be."

"I let him be himself!"

Uncle Tullius firmly closed his eyes to indicate the end of the discussion.

He had no need to spell it out. Unum, Duo and Tres were Aellius, Daellius and Laellius, the always unhappy Antistii. I was deeply aware that Tiberius felt he needed to be their advocate.

I, too, closed my eyes. I dived back into the thoughts I had been having before Uncle Tullius woke.

We had our sorrows, but in the Cluventius household how much more terrible must be the effects of that hideous murder. At least Fania Faustina had died from a natural tragedy. Her doctor had told us that, once her pregnancy had gone wrong, nothing known to medicine could have saved her life. Women died from having babies. Pregnant women died all the time. For young women, a regular outcome of marriage was death.

Murder was different. Murder made it impossible for loved ones to reconcile themselves to nature's inevitability. Victoria Tertia's funeral had been held the same day as Fania's, but it brought neither peace to her soul nor respite for her family. It was no surprise to me that when I reached my home I was told that Cluventius had sent to ask if I would call on him.

XXVIII

Since Tullius had insisted on another dawn start, we had reached Rome in the late morning. Once again, he ignored the vehicle ban. It was his mule cart, so in his eyes he took precedence; he had himself taken home first, then allowed the driver to turn back down the Vicus Armilustrium to deposit me at my house. When Gratus told me about Cluventius, I sent a message to explain my circumstances, promising to come later. I managed to rest a little. After that, there was still time for me to make my visit.

It was not quite evening, which Cluventius had said would be convenient if I came home today. Bath-houses were now firing up, shops were starting to open. The Aventine was quiet because it was winter. It had almost the cool of northern Europe, though to me Rome rarely seemed as bitter as my birthplace. I was glad to be back here.

I took Suza, but I left her with the door porter. He thought his luck was in. Her heavy bust and confident manner fooled him. She saw herself as intelligent and well-groomed—a sophisticated woman. She thought him a spotty weevil. Both were exaggerations, but Suza held these views inflexibly. I knew I could trust her.

I found myself joining a family conference. It must be coming to an end, because I passed a slave taking out empty tots and snack bowls. In the manner of my father, I grabbed a sautéed date from a comport, then sauntered in as if I hadn't noticed myself doing it.

Cluventius had with him Vatia and Paecentius, his *amici*, his inner cabinet. Also present were their wives, plus his two elder children. In an apartment salon, this was a crush. Whatever debate had taken place before I joined them, everyone had fallen quiet as if exhausted.

As I had expected, Cluventius felt deeply unhappy with the authorities' desultory enquiries. Ursus and Julius Karus had attended Victoria's funeral yesterday in their official capacity, but Cluventius thought, what use was that? During the long lacuna for pyre-watching, they had reported slow progress, which they classified as normal at this stage. Ursus looked wary, like a professional liar who was not very good at it. Karus said less but implied more—came across as a better bullshitter, muttered Paecentius. Even Karus was far from suave. Cluventius had found both completely unconvincing. They had nothing to give him but refused to acknowledge their lack of progress.

After a troubled night, the family had sent for me; I could tell they had been hoping to get my husband. Vatia and Paecentius had asked around. They believed Faustus (and I, in his shadow) had relevant expertise. Scaurus, the vigiles tribune in the Fourth Cohort's Twelfth District barracks on this side of the Aventine, had told them even I would do a good job—I'd been at it since before his time, no complaints from the public . . . well, none so far. I said for a detailed reference they should ask Titus Morellus, his deputy. Morellus knew me better; he worked out of the excubitorium in my own district, the Thirteenth.

They would not bother, I could see. Research done, minds were made up. Seeing themselves as decisive men, they would decide against a second opinion. The point is to act. You don't need any muddying, with complicated new ideas.

I outlined my experience anyway. I said Faustus and I had met during the hunt for a notorious killer who had stabbed people with poisoned needles. The case had caused widespread public alarm; usefully, it was one that Cluventius and his colleagues had heard of. Faustus and I had identified the man and trapped him; Faustus, since viewed as an expert, had subsequently served as an adviser on copycat cases. I tended to work on more domestic commissions. I carried out vetting tasks, or traced people, documents or legacies. I had recently collaborated in investigating a suspicious death. I met Julius Karus on that case.

They asked what I thought of Karus. I hedged, a professional courtesy. In the case I mentioned, he had arrested the wrong man; it was me who properly solved it. But I kept his error to myself—for now.

Vatia acted as spokesman in commissioning me. I outlined my terms. A deal was struck. I was now a professional adviser to the Cluventius family.

I ran through with them what had been reported yesterday. Julius Karus was examining old cases in the way I thought he should. Nothing to argue with, nor to criticise.

"Once he completes his review of previous murders, we should see the results, if possible. That's something I can facilitate through my own official contacts . . ." Moonshine. Karus would probably say no. I'd deal with it then. "Have they found any clues to your wife's death, Cluventius?"

"They discovered her clothes." He could hardly bear to say this.

"They sent them back," Vatia said, helping him. "Romilia—my wife—has them. She will . . ." He tailed off. Quietly dispose of them, I thought.

She was staring down, not meeting eyes. Romilia struck me as a sensible woman. She would have the beautiful fabrics laundered, keep everything folded carefully, then if the family never wanted them back, she would discreetly find a good home for the finery far away, where the Cluventii would never have to see anyone else dressed in an outfit that nobody wanted to remember.

Presumably Karus and Ursus had ruled out these clothes as evidence. Myself, I would have kept them. Producing such things makes good legal theatre. One day, I hoped there would be a prosecution, where the lead barrister might ask for them . . . On the other hand, a practical lawyer might simply borrow something shimmery from his own expensive wife. Courtroom drama can be improvised.

Ooh, didn't you know that, you innocent people?

"And where were the garments found?"

"Hidden in bushes, just off a pathway, near the party."

"Was there anything else, a weapon, for instance?"

"No."

"And you have Victoria's jewellery?" I had seen her still wearing it.

"Yes." This time it was Paecentius, a wispy, raspy, abrupt man who must have been the oldest of the friends. He was not quite impatient with my questions, but wanted me to finish to avoid distress. "All returned."

"All? Did somebody check? Was everything she wore that night still there?"

"One missing piece. A necklace." Ah, *that* necklace. The killer's trophy. Its absence made it an important potential clue, yet I had to screw the detail out of them. They truly had no idea.

"I gave that to her," stressed Cluventius, more upset by what the piece represented in their lives than by the loss or its implications. "This year. For our wedding anniversary."

"Were you asked to describe it for the investigators?"

"I know what I paid for it, but could not really remember its appearance . . ."

"Oh, Father! You are such a typical man!" His elder daughter must have been left out when Cluventius talked to the vigiles. As she gently chided him now, I asked her to give me details. I did not say this was because one day it might be found in the killer's possession.

She was perhaps seventeen, the age I had been when I had started to work as an informer. Slim, modestly dressed for mourning yet today unable to leave off her gold hoop earrings. Less mature than I ever was at that age, she was nonetheless transforming under the effects of her stepmother's terrible death. Left behind to become the strong woman in the family, she would come out of this hard, cynical, solitary.

Cluvia was unsurprised that her father could remember the price of the gift, yet not what his money had bought. He had given her something similar, a less valuable item but acquired from the same jeweller at the same time. She, not Cluventius, told me the name of the jeweller. She then gave me a clear description of the missing item: "All in gold, it was a loose choker formed from small pairs of leaves, then a central pendant, hung on its fairly wide ring."

"A coin medallion?"

"No, just a smooth crescent, a lunula." Clearly Victoria Tertia had liked stylish but simple things. "Will the killer try to sell it?" asked Cluvia, darkly. I felt she realised he would more likely hoard it, his reminder of what he had done to her stepmother. I didn't want her to know he might use it to relive the crime.

"He may do. The vigiles should be asking shops to look out. My father runs an auction house. He is sometimes asked to watch for stolen items."

A cynic might wonder if Cluvia was hoping to inherit. I thought she was too sensitive; even if this necklace eventually came home, she would never be able to wear it.

We broke off our conversation because Julius Karus was announced. I realised the family council had assembled by pre-arrangement, so they could all hear his latest report. So far, he was coming daily.

Karus arrived alone. To me, it was a sign of him taking full command. Ursus had been sidelined.

In such a crowded room, my presence might have gone unremarked, but the moment Karus entered, I watched his eyes scan us while he made a mental inventory; he spotted me with raised brows.

Mildly embarrassed, Vatia explained that they had called me in as a consultant. None of them had ever been in a situation like this. Karus merely nodded. He was too clever to object. I sat quiet, not wanting to antagonise him.

There was little to add to yesterday's account. Despite great public sympathy, there had been a very poor response to appeals for information. Examination of old cases continued. So far it had yielded nothing, but no such consolidation had ever been done before, so it had to be useful. Karus was sure his work would eventually lead to the killer.

"I want him found. I want him stopped. I want him punished!" Cluventius insisted.

"We all do, sir," replied Karus, mildly enough.

Cluventius then eagerly told him they could now describe the missing necklace. Karus looked suitably pleased; he made notes. I spotted that, like me, he made no mention of trophies. He claimed notifying goldsmiths and pawnbrokers would be standard routine. Ursus, he said, could get on to that. The fact that Victoria's other jewellery had been found on her body confirmed that the attack was not about robbery.

"That is no consolation to the victim's family," I chided. No need to stress that rape and death had been planned. He pursed his lips; I was warning him to stop, starting my work for them.

I was right. They were upset. The young girl got up from her seat, pressing knuckles to her mouth, and swiftly left the room.

I followed. She was leaning against a wall immediately outside in the corridor, sobbing. I held her while she wept, the way that only two days ago I had nursed my own husband through grief. Cluvia was thin, slight, vulnerable and, to me, unbearably young.

When she was calmer, she told me she had been due to marry. The man's family had now unexpectedly backed out. They could not even wait for a better time but had informed her father at his wife's funeral yesterday. They pretended they were only delaying while the family recovered, but Cluvia understood they would never resume negotiations. She half understood why, though even she thought the speed of their reaction had been insensitive.

I told her it was no surprise to me. This was a common response to tragedy. The Cluventii would be tainted. True friends, like Vatia and Paecentius, would not flinch, but other people would shy away, bolting from a situation they found embarrassing and awkward. "You will all be flabbergasted by who drops you socially—but also by who never wavers. I suppose you liked your intended fiancé. But don't think about him, Cluvia. You are better off without these people—and best that you found out now."

She nodded. She was sensible for her age—many girls are, despite public perceptions. She would have to shoulder too much responsibility. Ahead of her, this young girl had fears and disappointments, plus a great deal of weeping.

One of her terrors came from knowing what had been done to Victoria Tertia. I told Cluvia gently that, although she had been hearing much about similar attacks in and around the Grove of the Caesars, in general such crimes were rare.

"It could have been me!"

"It could have been anyone, Cluvia. It's a cliché to say that your stepmother had the bad luck to be in the wrong place at the wrong time—but that is the truth. This was a random, opportunistic attack, made possible simply because the poor woman wanted a quiet moment. A few beats of time when she left the party, and either she would never have been spotted or else there might have been some disturbance that put him off."

It made me angry.

"Don't dwell on this," I advised Cluvia. "Don't let it spoil the rest of your life. Love her and remember her. Love your father, be kind to your siblings, especially the little ones. But then, promise me, you will still live."

The young girl gave me a straight stare. She mopped her eyes and pulled back her slim shoulders. "I shall try. She was a good woman, Flavia Albia. That is what she would have wanted for me."

I might have been even more moved on her behalf, but then Julius Karus came out into the corridor, staring at us curiously. Others followed. The meeting was now breaking up. It was time to leave.

XXIX

Soon I was seething: when he found I had no transport, Karus decided it was wrong for me to walk home alone so he would come with me. I had Suza. Suza didn't count.

Being escorted by Domitian's hitman had all the thrill of seeing an escaped lion eat your pet rabbit. He stomped along, a big military man, whose constant glancing around showed him to be more nervous in a city environment than I was. You need to stroll quickly and quietly, aiming to slide past trouble before it notices you coming. Then you must listen out in case anyone runs up behind.

"I am here to look after her!" Suza had loudly assured him. It was good enough for me. With her have-a-go attitude, muggers would be quickly scared off.

Karus did not talk to maids. He would not even acknowledge that she had spoken. *How rude!* Suza was obviously thinking. While she mentally tried to phrase a put-down, I noticed a nice bangle in a shop display, but decided against window-shopping. I would note where it was and maybe come back alone. A woman with a strange man cannot show any interest in such things, in case he thinks she expects him to buy it for her, which can only mean *he* will expect a return.

What a horrible thought.

His motive for the escort duty was a twisted need to find out about my commission. As we walked, he began probing crudely. "So how are you seeing your role in all this, Flavia?"

"I have no intention of stepping on your toes, Julius Karus," I murmured, playing it sweet. "As you will understand, these people feel they are floundering out of their depth. It's natural they have made official complaints, which had nothing to do with me, incidentally; I had not been commissioned then. I shall advise them on what is appropriate. Perhaps I can curb their agitation, leaving you and Ursus to get on with the investigation."

Karus gave me a sideways look, as if he feared I was being satirical. I wrapped my stole around my head, while I kept walking.

"They are desperate for answers," Karus acknowledged.

"Of course. What is your opinion?" I asked, starting my own digging. "Will this man be caught?"

"Such individuals are always catchable."

"Not in their minds," I answered sadly. "The longer they get away with it, the more confident they feel, the more arrogant they are."

"Untouchable, they believe," Karus agreed. "But that is when they make mistakes."

He was right, yet how many more women had to be attacked before this killer made a fatal error? Since he was now talking, I slowed my steps discreetly to allow more time. We had already come across the Aventine tops almost as far as the vigiles headquarters, so I was sheering off to the left. Once we reached the Temple of Diana Aventina, we would be in Lesser Laurel Street where I would be home.

I paused as if subconsciously watching a delivery of wine to a cookhouse, then waited for a laden mule to pass in front of me. "I presume it is correct that killings have been happening for years? Have you any idea how long?"

"Fifteen, could even be twenty," he conceded, though it was like pulling fingernails.

"And it's definitely the same man? How many other victims?"

Karus shrugged, trying not to give too much away.

"I imagine record-keeping by the Seventh Cohort has always been deplorable?" I was wooing him, suggesting he had found himself landed in a hopeless situation where, due to others' incompetence, vital information was simply unavailable to him. "Be fair, though. They don't have the manpower, or the supervision, let alone enough support from higher up.

I take it none of them can be the killer? Their basic term of service is only six years."

"Right," agreed Karus. "Some have done more, but not long enough to interest me. Ursus has been with the Seventh for four years." So Karus had run personnel checks. I wondered if Ursus knew that.

"Then have they any ideas about this killer?"

"Ursus is sure it's a sailor."

"Evidence?"

"Only that the area is full of them. He's wrong," announced Karus. "The timeline goes back much too far—any sailor would have been re-deployed." Military life was his field, so I was willing to accept what he said.

"What would be the average posting, then, Karus?"

"In the army, it could be twenty-five years in, normally, two to four provinces. I'll have to check about the navy, but it won't be longer."

"There are only two navies. Ravenna and Misenum. We can leave out the Classis Britannica, I dare say. Isn't it Ravenna they draw the crews from for the amphitheatre shades?"

"My point is," Karus put me straight, "that sail-riggers who come here for arena duty would not be allowed a shore posting for longer than a year or two. Too cushy. Drag them back to a floating job, before they learn to like it too much. No, Ursus insists on talking to the commander of the marine barracks. He can do that all he wants, but it is not one of them."

"What about their commander? How long has he served there? A rogue chief of staff has been known, though usually the worst they do is put on a dress and ludicrous rouge, then fornicate with scrubbers in bath-houses."

"They all hate the post." Karus remained unsmiling. "None of them ever lasts long before requesting a move."

"No allure in Rome?" I bet he was wrong—I bet they all had mis-tresses. "All right, life in a big barracks in the Transtiberina cannot be glamorous. So, we're back with the vigiles' normal circle of suspects. Their day-to-day problems in handling it. Realisation that cases were connected will have been slow in coming. And, of course, as more bodies were found, it must have been too easy to dismiss them as prostitutes, women who to many people do not matter." I sensed a twitch. "Were they?" I slid in quickly. "Were they in fact all prostitutes?"

Karus was finally coerced. "One was a schoolgirl," he confided. That seemed to count; it really bothered him. He mentioned others: "A flower-shop keeper, who sounds to have been a decent woman. Quite a few where no one knows anything about them, so I expect you would say, Flavia Albia, better not to make judgements just because this pervert killed them."

"Yes," I confirmed. He was accusing me of harbouring liberal opinions, which his master Domitian despised, so he was bound to hate it too. But I kept my tone level: "I do say that. Even low-grade working girls are human, surely? I suppose there are high-class courtesans in Rome, drifting around in translucent silks, or money-counting brothel madams who intend to retire to massive villas, and who will do so if they aren't carried off by disease. But the kind of woman who gets herself assaulted by a punter in a public garden, when she has no protection, not even from a pimp, now *she* will be doing it for the money in the meanest sense, Karus. She is a woman alone or hitched to a useless man. She does the deed behind a pavilion or under a bush for a few scraps of food to put on the table, invariably for her children. She will never be rich. She's close to destitute. She will not live long, even without a pervert strangling her so he can watch her die."

"Well!" said Karus. He did not disagree, but my passion had put a breach between us: too kind-hearted, Flavia Albia. Girlie talk that a man on a mission was not swayed by.

"You know you have to stop this," I declared.

"I know I do. I will."

So that was him: practical, half reasonable, utterly arrogant. An agent with no time for failure—and no concept that failure could happen to him.

I knew enough to realise that that might be just what was wanted: he might have the right determination finally to catch this killer. He wanted the kudos; perhaps, for career reasons, he needed it. That could be why, when we reached my house, I allowed myself to thank the hit-man for escorting me by inviting him in for a nightcap. Even Karus flashed a look of surprise.

If old Grey Eyes, my husband, had been there, he would have been curious to meet this man. He wasn't, but Gratus would handle the situation. Nothing awkward would arise. In any case, as soon as the front doors opened, it was clear this was a home full of people, people who were being treated to genial entertainment.

There were oil lamps and even braziers, due to the time of year. Our courtyard was alive with sound and movement. "Ah, that's nice—a harpist and his band of musicians come sometimes to play for my husband!"

This harpist, a superb citharode, was very famous indeed. Yet if Karus had ever heard of him, he gave no sign of recognition.

That told me something else: Karus worked only in straight lines. A clue had to turn up where he expected it. For him, links were always joined on a single plain. He was going to miss a chance here.

As we made Karus welcome, I explained that the Fabulous Stertinius had entertained guests at our wedding. On the same day, my husband had been struck by lightning—which Karus also seemed not to know. Either he had not read my security file (every informer has one) or it was badly out of date. I did not expect this hard man to have gone to the Forum to peruse the *Daily Gazette* society column. Still, his barber ought to have bored him with our story . . .

Stertinius had been touched that the accident happened after he had played. Now he regularly visited us, so his beautiful music assuaged the mental and physical pain Tiberius suffered after being felled by Jupiter's bolt. The musicians always made it a social occasion, an improvised practice session, in return for which we fed them. They thought our house a civilised bolthole, one of few they visited from choice. We were proud of that.

Now, since I had brought a visitor, the musicians stopped jamming and moved aside, sitting discreetly in a corner while Fornix brought them a meal. I was starving, but I signalled that I would wait until the agent left. Gratus served Karus one cup of wine, then took the flagon away. I had water.

Talking to Karus socially was one-way traffic. Able only to discuss his work, he was soon favouring me with his theories on murder. He had fixed ideas, no surprise. I could have said in advance what they were: "With men, it's all about power—inflicting rape, terror, pain and, the ultimate thrill, death. This is very different from a woman who kills. For a woman, it's always because they say they are doing good. They even seem to persuade themselves of it—that they are nurturing sickly victims who need help, even if the so-called help means putting them out of their misery. Women generally kill the old, babies, the sick. If they do have a real motive, it's simple: they kill for money."

I had never been convinced by this. I'd known of too many women who had killed off their husbands just to get rid of them. Tonight, however, I kept quiet. Karus did not want to hear my thoughts. "They may be feeling insecure—relatives have died, or they are being divorced so they feel vulnerable and need a financial cushion. Of course, women very rarely kill—"

At that I snapped. "Face it, man. Women do. Female murderers are just better at it. Women are much cleverer, so nobody spots what they are doing. You think that they don't exist only because they are never found out."

That was it for Karus. He rose to go. The Emperor's hitman had good enough manners not to hang around arguing with a woman in her own home. Or, more likely, I was too fierce for him.

As he passed the table where I had laid out the unearthed scrolls in their various sets, he looked at them with mild curiosity.

"Don't ask!" I exclaimed fervently.

Julius Karus was not up to much as a spy. He went on his way with his military tread, after not asking.

Once he had left, Gratus murmured to me, "I held back refreshments. He looked as if his favourite finger food is iron nails! Do you want a proper drink now?"

"Juno, yes, please!"

I rushed over to Stertinius. He and the band pushed aside their food bowls immediately, welcoming me into their group. I told them to continue eating, as I would be doing myself. They asked after Tiberius—but

I said it was me who needed to talk to them tonight, and it had nothing to do with their stylish arpeggios.

Karus had failed to make an important connection. Once he had annoyed me with his dogmatic theories, I saw no reason to point out what he had missed. The Fabulous Stertinius had been the hired entertainer at the Cluventius birthday party. No one takes much notice of the musicians, but their eyes are everywhere.

Karus could have interviewed key witnesses tonight. Now I would do it. Far be it from me to engage in a contest with the agent over gathering information—yet I would take advantage of this opportunity.

XXX

As I sat down with them, the lyre-player had reached for his instrument, greeting me with an exquisite slither of notes. The flautist and drummer both smiled through their moustaches, while they bowed over the low server around which they had been sitting to eat. All the long-haired group wore their usual exotic robes in vibrant colours with wide, contrasting borders, long-sleeved like eastern viziers' nightgowns. These were to show white-tunicked Rome that they were artistes, who didn't give a damn. I noticed they could afford better hem embroidery than I ever had.

Fornix himself brought me a bowl of food. Gratus poured his magical mulsum for everyone, although the musicians stopped his hand when their tots were only half full. It might have been politeness. More likely, their professional approach made them cautious. Their attitude to life was pure. To them, befuddlement would harm their playing.

Night had closed in. It was just about mild enough to stay sitting out, so Gratus quietly lit more lamps. Once they had finished eating, the players' hands strayed back to their instruments. Our conversation was punctuated by short splashes of melody and beat.

"Hiring you to play seems to attract disasters!" I said ruefully to Stertinius, telling him I knew they had performed at the Transtiberina party. "I need to ask what you all saw at the Cluventius bash. The family have hired me to give them professional advice. Do you mind?"

They did not mind, especially since they knew me; they were intrigued that I might be taking an interest.

The terrible event had shocked them. Stertinius, whose fees were astronomical, even said that after Victoria Tertia was killed he considered waiving the recital charge. However, he usually asked for payment in advance, to avoid being tangled in rich people's business practice (that is, don't pay until they have to, and if they can, don't pay ever). This precaution, he admitted wryly, now spared him a moral dilemma.

As an entertainer who enjoyed his fame, Stertinius had become heavy from good living. He must be forty, or even forty-five. His wiry hair had thinned, while his hands looked to be on the verge of becoming arthritic. That would be a disaster. I knew that while playing to soothe Tiberius he had shared his own fears for the future.

I guessed that with most clients he would remain aloof, though with us he talked, which he did with much intelligence. The thin wind-player and bandy-legged drummer generally pretended they were exiles from colourful homelands, so had no Latin. Even if this were true, I knew they observed and listened. Both had bright beady eyes, which missed little: if anyone made a decent joke, you could see them laughing at it.

They would give me the tenor of that party. I could trust their version. They had had the best possible inside view. "I know you can't have seen the attack in the Grove but tell me about earlier. Let me reassure you, the net will be wide, but I don't count you as suspects."

Stertinius thanked me drily for that. He then gave me a picture of the evening, which he described as well-organised and respectable, though he was satirical about that. But he summed up their audience as pleasant to play for—a rare treat at private functions.

Stertinius had found Cluventius rough and ready, as might be expected of a man whose life had been spent among large draught animals. "With a few measures inside him, he was bellowing and braying himself. When he and his pals cheered at the end of our set, I knew how Orpheus felt playing to animals . . . yet theirs was honest pleasure."

He called Victoria Tertia a lovely person—though he did describe her keeping the caterers on a tight rein. "If anyone wiped a drip off a spout with a finger, she made them fetch a clean jug. She was on to it instantly."

"You too?" I queried, smiling.

"We never need supervision, dear lady! Apart from Fluentius." Fluentius was the wind-player, primarily a flautist though he carried other instruments—single and double pipes in different sizes and even a large set of panpipes; he seemed proficient on them all. "We had to watch him flirting with the young daughter."

"No, it was all right," claimed Fluentius, lazily. "I told her straight she could trust me, though I was taken. But if I didn't already have five other girlfriends, she would be the one."

"And how did Cluvia respond?" I asked. "She's very sweet, and at the time her engagement was close to being finalised. Some young cad in the import-export trade, from what she told me."

Fluentius rolled his eyes. "Yes, he was there. Pretty at a distance, but looked a loser to me. My bet is he will let her down."

"He already has," I revealed sadly. "They've backed out, because a family in distress after a murder makes 'nice' people flee."

Fluentius said he would send Cluvia flowers. I told him not to. The last thing Cluventius needed was a daughter running off with a rapscallion from the performing arts. Besides, Fluentius shouldn't put his five other girlfriends' noses out of joint.

"They are used to it!" scoffed Stertinius, calling time on the repartee. "Tell us what else you need from us, Flavia Albia."

I explained that my first thought, before I'd known the specifics of the crime, had been to blame the husband for his wife's disappearance. Stertinius confirmed that they had seemed perfectly happy together. The musicians knew when Victoria had left for a breather, because it was just after she had made sure the caterers brought refreshments for them.

"Did she tell you it was all a bit much for her?"

"No, but we could see she was tiring. She seemed to be a quiet woman, one who wears herself out looking after people around her. She said she'd be back in a moment if we needed anything. Cluventius was still throwing himself into it. Very loud. Hugely convivial. A time-of-his-life host."

I shuddered. "Exhausting!"

"Oh, he wanted to celebrate and why not? It was a really good party."

"And you can confirm he was there at the time his wife must have been murdered."

"Unfortunately, yes. We had completed our main session, the recital we were hired for. After we closed, we dallied for a bite to eat. The lady was so kind to us, we thought we would play another set as thanks. I went and offered to Cluventius—so that was when he started looking around to tell his wife. Then he realised she had gone. The poor man, he immediately felt guilty about not missing her sooner—he erupted."

"Did it strike people immediately that something must be wrong?"

"Yes, because she had mentioned stepping aside but only to catch her breath—and that was quite a while before."

"How long, Stertinius?"

"As long as it took for me and the boys to eat, then Pamphyllus to stuff in seconds."

"Quite long!" the drummer confirmed sweetly. Pamphyllus was not tall, but huge-bellied and always frank about his enormous takeaway. "Then I had to spend a few moments washing it all down."

"You know his 'few moments' of quaffing," Fluentius reminded me. I did. Although the others were abstemious, Pamphyllus liked a beaker after their main set.

"They knew something had befallen Victoria, out on her own in the dark," I mused. "They realised she had been gone much too long. They were all a bit merry by then but had to do something about it. They started the search quite urgently?"

"Straight off," confirmed Stertinius.

"Well organised?"

"Surprisingly so. We joined in for a time. As long as we could. We had a concert the next day, so finally we had to slip away and leave them to it. Anyway, Cluventius had called in people. There seemed to be enough of them. We made enquiries afterwards, so we heard what had happened. Terrible. Absolutely awful. That poor woman."

I explained that it was not the first time; the pervert had taken many previous victims. "Had you ever heard of similar occurring?"

Stertinius shook his head gravely. "No—but we'd never played Caesar's Gardens before. Wrong side of the river. I hate the Transtiberina. It stinks of tanneries and fried fish. Then, if the client's security is less than tight, sailors push their way into the recital. We only agreed because Cluventius knew we had done a musical soirée for the Empress recently, in her own gardens further along. No one says no to Domitia Longina. Not if they like life. So that was a precedent. We were trapped."

I smiled. "I expect the Cluventii had to pay accordingly!"

"But of course! Am I not the Fabulous Stertinius? I set my rates accordingly. As your mother knows." It was Mother who hired him to play at my wedding.

"She told me she wangled a discount."

"I always let them think that," grinned the great musician. His hands passed over his lyre strings expressively. "Mind you, in your mother's case she was charming. I might have weakened."

I smiled again. "Ah, she is the Fabulous Helena Justina!"

"Exactly."

We talked some more about the party, though with little more to add. They had taken more notice of the guests than many guests took of them. They told a story expressively. I could smell the roses and taste the roasts, hear the rise and fall of cheery voices—yet my gaze still could not reach beyond the edge of the entertainment, to see what had happened to Victoria Tertia on that lonely path in the dark.

Expecting nothing, I did ask if the musicians had seen anything of my dancing boys. To my surprise, they had. During the main recital, Primulus and Galanthus, shameless pair, had sneakily slunk their way in. Once they began dancing, stewards fast manoeuvred them out.

"Unsuitable body movements!"

"That's them. I'm afraid they have only mastered one style: imperial lewd." I outlined how they had come to us. Stertinius had not played at the Black Banquet; music to accompany that tense event had been provided by professional funeral players. A "threnody combo," Stertinius scoffed and, in his opinion, a poor one, not the best death ensemble that could have been chosen.

Returning to the dancers, I said I hoped they had their clothes on.

"Bum-starver tunics and altar-boy amulets," confirmed Pamphyllus.

"Gongs on thongs? Yes, I was aware of the amulets, though I tried not to look. I thought they were bound to be engraved with saucy seduction scenes, like rent-boys' lamps . . . Oh, I'm saddened, Stertinius. I intended to offer that pair a good home, then see what they made of it. The lads seem to have run away that night, but if they encountered the killer, they might just have been petrified. I want to find anyone who saw them after they were chucked out of the party."

The musicians could not help. We would all have thought no more about it—until suddenly Fluentius recalled that as the musicians were making their way home they had heard distant screams. "Sorry, I forgot all about it. We knew it could not be Victoria Tertia because it did not sound like a woman. Too squeaky. Not even a whore being beaten by a sailor, we thought. Younger. Children, maybe. Messing about. It sounded like nippers playing frighten-yourself-silly games, long after they should have been in bed."

Whoever it had been, the sounds had come from the other direction. The musicians were halfway to the Sublician Bridge; they had had no incentive to turn back. It was late, wintry, dark, out in the open. Noises carried a long distance. By the time they could have reached the scene, anything alarming would have been over. They reckoned whoever they had heard might have been as far away as the Porta Portuensis on the district boundary.

If it really was Primulus and Galanthus who were squealing, we had little hope of finding them. The vigiles would not operate beyond the city gate without good reason. They could, and if they were following runaway slaves who were likely to bring in a reward, they might be bothered. Otherwise, if the boys had gone that far, they were on their own now.

XXXI

It had been a long day and I was ready for my bed. The musicians sat on in the courtyard, as they often did. They would quietly play on for their own pleasure and practice, until they rolled themselves up in their robes where they were, sinking into sleep as the oil lamps died. In the morning they would all be gone.

The night was still young. Gratus and Fornix were relaxing outside, listening to the music. Just when I was about to go upstairs, a late visitor arrived. Gratus went to the door. I waited to see who it was, in case of some crisis.

To my surprise, it was Donatus, the scroll-seller, bringing a parcel that contained my next encyclopaedia present for Tiberius. "I came to meet my reader!"

"You're out of luck." I explained why Tiberius was in Fidenae, although meeting him was an excuse, really: Donatus was more eager to look at my scrolls.

"I promised to think about them."

"You promised. I thought you were shooing me out of your shop."

He peered around, spotted the table covered with scroll sets, and went straight over there. Unlike Julius Karus, he immediately began to poke through them. "I would never buy these! They look like old onion skins."

I joined him, agreeing they were filthy. "There are no complete sets. Some of the poor tattered things are just bitty extracts."

"And yet somehow they always retain the precious papyrus sheet that names the so-called author!" Donatus marvelled bitterly as he continued looking. He was quite violent with the rolls, shaking them so the remaining dirt flew out, then throwing them open right to the far ends. He pulled at rods and waggled loose pieces, grabbed a lamp and scrutinised title sheets. "Nothing here is by that well-known writer Anonymous, the invisible sage of nowhere."

I saw his point. Even so, I felt obliged to argue on behalf of my treasures. "Maybe whoever last owned them just threw anonymous material away."

"Or wiped his bum?"

"Well, kindled a bonfire. They were found in a garden."

"If we were in Egypt, they'd be used as mummy wrappings . . . but we're not, are we?"

"Are they any use, Donatus?"

"They are utter rubbish, if you ask me."

"I did ask you."

"Well, that was very sensible, Albia. You came to the one honest scroll-seller in Rome. I, unlike all the other bastards, will tell you what these items are—and why, even though their contents are complete dross, they could have value."

"Thank you."

"My pleasure."

"Tell me, then. This is what I wanted."

"At Donatus and Xerxes, we aim to please."

"Xerxes? I've never seen any sign of him."

"Pure invention. A partnership sounds more reliable than a one-man outfit. It sounds as if when one seller is less than helpful, or has gone off and closed the shop for a week, the customer can complain to the other. Punters are so easily fooled. But you don't need Xerxes. I can give you the lowdown."

"So, honest partner-inventor?"

"So, that lyre-player and his band have got drinks," said Donatus. "Can I have one?"

I saw Gratus rear elegantly to his feet, going for the flagon. Donatus looked around my gathering, which now even included Suza and the dog. Suza did not want to miss anything. Barley had come to investigate; bored by what was going on, she clambered slowly into her kennel, turning around to look out at us. She managed to indicate how patient she was with us, dragging on after sensible dogs went to sleep. I was on her side. I felt ready to drop.

"You are out late," I hinted, while we waited for Gratus. Donatus replied it was early for him; he would probably go around a few bars after we kicked him out. "Probably" sounded like a firm decision. I mentioned my exhausting day. He said he was sorry to keep me up—clearly not planning to leave yet.

As a good informer, I braced myself. You never send them away. Either they never come back again, or they lose any will to cooperate.

Once powered with mulsum, Donatus said immediately, "Your scrolls are forgeries."

That told me.

His new attitude tonight was impressive. He still had the stringy hair and languorous expression, yet he had sharpened up. Since I visited the shop, he had done much more than I expected. He had asked among his clients, he said, one collector in particular. Sure of his ground, Donatus spoke firmly. It seemed odd to receive a tight, factual lecture from him. Although he would always look the kind of unwashed obsessive who would offer barmy theories, as weird as his own shop customers, suddenly he made sense.

"Say again where you found them." I did so. Donatus squared up to it: "I think I know what's going on. The usual way to age papyrus involves burying it in casks of grain, which will work its way in nicely among the whole roll and stain it. Something else has happened with your little cache because if you unravel these, as I did, the far end is still cleaner than the start. I expect you noticed?" I cannot say I had. But I was no expert; that was why I went to him. "Otherwise people use 'cedar baths.' I found that in Pliny—"

"You've been reading my reserved scrolls?" I experienced a twinge of outrage. I felt as if someone had grabbed a new acquisition of mine, and started it before I had had a chance to.

"Books should be read. I think Pliny is wrong—he's just done his usual thing of passing on some tale a correspondent told him without testing it. Cedar is wood. It would be hell to get enough juice for some kind of 'bath.' I do sometimes use walnuts to darken repairs, but only on small areas. Legitimately, of course."

"You can buy cedar oil," I countered. "It's used on furniture and floors. It's good against moths."

"Why does this household need an encyclopaedia? . . . Yes," Donatus agreed grudgingly. "It's the main pesticide for protecting scrolls, but used very thinly . . ." Under challenge, he was losing interest.

"Why were my scrolls buried in the ground?"

"Someone has been experimenting. They hope the earth will stain them, so they look like antiques."

"Why bury them in the Grove of the Caesars specifically?"

"Good question, Flavia Albia. Out of the way, presumably. Someone who doesn't have land of their own? That's most people! In Rome, who owns gardens? Did you mention a cave?"

"Man-made. Represents a ghastly grotto. Pile of rocks. We are dismantling it to rebuild with an imperial nymphaeum."

"Your turning up there is someone's hard luck, perhaps—or perhaps not."

"Why?"

Donatus took a long swig, emptying his beaker. He was hoping for a refill. I pretended to be so excited I overlooked this yearning. Gratus still had the flagon by him but had closed his eyes as if absorbed in the delights of music. Donatus stopped hoping, being even more keen to impress me: "If you are passing off new finds of scrolls as ancient, Albia, they have to look right. What's written must be scrawled on the correct material for the time and seem to be suitably aged since then. The lettering and dialect must match whatever would have been used by that author, not to mention the content. His style, his sphere of interest." That matched the kind of comment Tuccia had made when I showed her the scrolls. "But crucially," Donatus added, "you must come up with a believable context for your find. You must show that your fakes came to light *now* for a reason. A tomb collapses through neglect or is struck by lightning. A flood washes material out. An earthquake throws up long-missing treasure."

"Might someone have known the plans to excavate the grotto?"

"Could be. But I suspect that they chose the cave only because it was so isolated. Otherwise, they would have needed to be on the spot just when you dug, if they were to exploit the 'discovery.' More likely this was just an experiment. Not very successful, because their burial hole was obviously damp."

I nodded. "Stagnant puddles. I find the grotto creepy."

"The presence of water could speed up the ageing process," mused Donatus, rather taken with this idea, "but if left too long, scrolls start to rot. You can see where it has happened. It makes them unreadable in places—though admittedly they do look authentically old as a result. My fear would be that if they dry out now, they will fall to pieces." I thought, Better sell them on fast, then! "The only good thing—going back to your cave, Albia—is that any fakers can now claim it was your building work that brought them to light."

"Wrong, unlucky fakers! I have got them, so any claims will be made by me. Anyway, there's a big flaw. That cave is man-made, in the time of Augustus. Epitynchanus and Philadespoticus hail from the School of Miletus, hundreds of years ago."

"Ah, the crucial error! Detail. This is *so* often where forgers go wrong!" Donatus was enjoying himself being snide. "Such people think they have it nailed. Good craftsmanship. *Excellent* scholarship. But they become over-confident, so a vital historical element is wrong. Their story breaks down. *The cave wasn't built*— I love it!"

We fell silent. Gratus saw I was happy to continue the conversation, so he came and poured more drink. I declined.

"All right," I said. "I am being an auctioneer's daughter: what is your provenance for this kind of forgery? Who says literary counterfeiting takes place?"

Donatus let out a hollow laugh. "History says so, for one thing. The best literary fraud I know began with the tumbledown tomb of a certain Dictys, a minor figure in the Trojan War. His burial place fell to pieces. In the rubble was a memoir he had written about his personal experiences. Unfortunately, he was a latecomer to the war, so he made out he had collected further stories from Odysseus when he ran across him."

"His memoirs were 'found' at the ruined tomb the way we found our scrolls?"

"Allegedly. They were brought to Nero. According to different stories, they were translated from an archaic language into a more modern version, either before they were brought to Rome or afterwards on Nero's orders. The need for translation gave authenticity, though of course it meant the resultant copy was no longer ancient. Nero handed out big finders' fees all round, because he was delighted to be able to promulgate this genuine story of what happened at Troy. People have a real wish for knowledge."

"But?" I sensed a contradiction coming.

"Apart from, was it really the tomb of Dictys and was a real epic found in it? Plus various textual curiosities, I believe? . . . Flavia Albia, what is the most famous trait of Homer's Odysseus?"

"There are so many . . . Clever, stubborn, full of hubris, complicated. Wily, untrustworthy—he lies, cheats and steals. Odysseus the Liar." I chortled quietly. "I'm with you. It sounds like a forger is tipping the wink."

"Astute woman! Honest forger, too. But would people notice whatever he was slyly telling them . . . ?"

"Verdict?"

"No verdict. The stuff vanished into an imperial library and it all died down quietly. What saved a big scandal is that nothing was being sold on the market. No one has any reason to publicly challenge Dictys's brand-new, somewhat belated so-called autobiography."

"Well, memoirs are generally ghosted, Donatus. People who have adventures are full of themselves, but that makes them rubbish writers. Was it a good read?" I asked. If Tiberius were here, that would be his question.

"No idea. I only sell stuff, I don't have to read it. If it caught on at the time, it was a fad, one of those cascades where ignorant people think they want to read the latest sensation simply because everyone else has. We shift a lot of copies that way, so as dealers we never point out what crap it is. Most buyers never open the thing, or they give up at the first papyrus join."

"Meanwhile people lie around at dinner parties claiming the stuff is wonderful . . . Bestsellers—the most unread books in the world." I smiled. As I waved an arm over the table of scrolls, I could feel myself frowning. "Here is the crunch: if I try to sell these grub-infested items, will there be a public challenge?"

Donatus looked at me sadly. "I doubt that. You will offer them through your father, I presume? Falco, if he's careful, will catalogue them as 'believed to be counterfeit.' Is he an honest auctioneer?"

I pulled a face. If such a person existed, then my father was. "He says so. Will he be able to sell them?"

"Of course!" exclaimed Donatus, as if speaking to an idiot. "Double the price—with added value for mysterious origins and notoriety."

XXXII

So my scrolls were condemned as fakes.

I knew something of counterfeiting from the auction house. There we encountered it mainly with statuary. When I had first started going to the Saepta Julia to help out, I was taught two rules. First, there are five big names in Greek sculpture: Myron, Phidias, Polyclitus, Praxitiles and Lysippus. Any piece that came in as one of those was definitely *not* by them. Not a big-bottomed Venus, a dying Gaul, a Boy taking a Thorn out of his Foot (whether left foot or right), a discus-thrower or two nude men with cloaks over their arms, brandishing daggers and earnest expressions, who were being called the Tyrannicides.

I was warned that there were tyrant-killers from more than one Greek city, though all have the same foot-forward pose and there are always two. This is why Rome has Brutus and Cassius, yet the other sixty Liberators are ignored. "You cannot have," my father declared once, "Brutus, Cassius and Ignoticus, their best friend from school. However much Ignoticus loathes dictators, he would make it one too many and would ruin everything." ("Yes, but," I said, "you know there are sixty and I can even name some."

"Go and annoy your mother," answered my father.)

Second rule: some statues are labelled, generally on their base. This is always helpful. It is intended to attract buyers' interest, which it normally does. However, anyone can carve any name on a plinth, at any time in its history. The inscription you are looking at was probably chiselled last week. Falco knows a man who will do it for the price of a good fish-supper—though of course neither my father nor even his father before him (Geminus, the outright rogue) would ever be involved in such an enhancement.

According to them, that is.

One way to make sure a pedestal label is right is to ascertain that the lettering is of the period when the statue was made, using your knowledge of archaic alphabets (every auctioneer has this knowledge, apparently, though I was never shown the lists of letters); also, it must be in the right local dialect. Doubt will never stop an auctioneer pointing out the plinth label, though there are set phrases for implying caution. "We can only offer guidance, without guarantees. We can find nothing against it. You must make up your own minds, perhaps taking expert advice. It says, 'Falsus made me'—and it is perfectly possible that Falsus actually did."

A phrase my father finds useful in the context of proof is "Corinthian Doric." Occasionally, when deeply moved by the exquisite perfection of a piece, Falco even refers to that extremely rare variant, "Corinthian Doric Ionic."

Copies can be made for several reasons, not only the obvious one of fraud. True, a sculptor may make out that a piece of his own work is by a better-known man, in order to disguise its mediocrity and get paid more. Or, since a beautiful original can have only one owner, people may commission copies out of pure delight in its elegance.

This has advantages. If the original is ever lost, damaged, destroyed by earthquake, fire or flood, or sunk in a shipwreck while being foolishly transported to Italy from Greece, at least copies still exist and hack carvers in Campania can run you up another based on a copy.

In addition, a new version can be requested in the right size to fit its planned location—something that is beloved of designers, both interior and exterior. Awkward niche? Get yourself a scaled-down Athena Parthenos, two foot three with helmet. Don't forget to allow for a base. As you were: call it two foot one.

Donatus reminded me that, alongside the growth of art galleries where real and doubtful statues thronged, Rome had acquired a rash of libraries. Some monumental porticos were designed to house both statuary and literature. The grandest had both a Greek and Latin Library, as at Vespasian's Temple of Peace. Even our current emperor, Domitian, not known for cultural pursuits (apart from poetry competitions, which for me don't count), was sending out emissaries through the civilised world to copy scrolls in order to replenish libraries that had been destroyed by fire. This would counter-balance the scrolls he had burned in the Forum because they were written by radical intellectuals who railed against one-man rule. We were to have all the knowledge in the world—unless it was anti-imperial.

Munificence is how emperors hope to make the public love them. Private men had also created libraries, in order to show off their personal taste, appreciation of the arts and, let's face it, wealth. Ex–provincial governors with years of service abroad would come home crammed with love for exotic cultures. The less moral ones brought booty to prove their enthusiasm for the lands they had plundered. Even since plundering had gone out of fashion after one or two famous court cases, private collecting had flourished. Retired imperial freedmen had to spend their bribes and pensions somehow. Senators wanted to beautify their villas more extravagantly than their peers, so they looked like bigger men. Men, or occasionally women, even built libraries from a genuine love of literature.

This had led to what Donatus called bibliomania. Possessing literature for study was no longer enough. The goal, as with the monumental libraries at Alexandria and Pergamon, was to acquire all the literature in the world and stuff it into your book cupboards. A private individual of worth had to have shelves groaning with rare works, works his friends might never have heard of, works they would marvel at, drooling with jealousy, whenever he showed off his collection. People were purchasing ghastly scrolls they would never read, simply in order to own more than anyone else.

This thirst for rare works had become quite refined. Collectors wanted to boast *they* had the only existing copy of some ancient piece that was significant in intellectual thought or, worse, they wanted an autographed manuscript that a well-known author had personally owned.

They were desperate for scribbled annotations by Thucydides, a ring-mark where Sophocles had stood his wine cup, a bent stylus and the oil lamp Homer wrote by. (Oh dear, how irritating: Homer was blind, so better call it Aristotle's.)

Donatus said if maniac collectors made a mistake, they were never going to admit it after they had paid an exorbitant price. Doubtful scrolls managed to slip onto the market unchallenged. Other men, darker minds with murkier motives, enjoyed the thrill of owning unique scrolls secretly, gloating over their possessions in locked rooms that no one else ever entered, hoarding treasures no one even knew existed. These secretive types were exactly what forgers were looking for because whatever they bought would be hidden away, never subjected to critical scrutiny.

"So where is this leading?" I asked, after Donatus described this background. "Bibliomania has created the environment for fraud. Are these scrolls of mine, you think, part of a deviant trade?"

"I know they are."

"Is it widespread? Does it affect all kinds of writing?"

"There are rich pickings for fakers, and the best of them have mastered everything: history, philosophy, poetry, drama, memoirs—intriguing memoirs, memoirs that should never have been written, hideous memoirs no one in his right mind wants to read. The older and more obscure the better."

I was ready to believe it. "So Epitynchanus and Philadespoticus would be good choices to forge because, like Dictys, whose tomb allegedly threw up memoirs, they are so little known. The materialist philosophers lived a very long time ago. No one even remembers who they are, so their scrolls are less likely to be challenged?"

"True."

"So we end up that these scrolls of mine, roughed up and coloured by burial in the ground, are still likely to find buyers?"

"Absolutely. First off, they do look like the real thing. Forgers are the most knowledgeable people in the book trade, Albia. These are very convincing—at least at the dirty end. If the burial experiment had worked better, they might be perfect. Of course, I know what your profession is, so take my advice. If you have decided to find your counterfeiters and bring them to justice, you must search for people who really know their stuff. There is excellent craftsmanship in the hardware of your battered scrolls—indeed, there has been expert battering. They are damaged in ways that would really have happened over many years. And then some-body went to great trouble to invent the contents."

"It's garbage," I said frankly. "Who writes garbage?"

"Most authors." Increasingly, I liked his attitude.

"But who *reads* garbage?" I persisted.

"The bloody public!" Donatus was earnest, not letting out a smile. "Nobody has to read your scrolls, Albia. These will be rare things, items to be caressed and treasured. Exquisite antiquities that collectors' friends don't have. They were deliberately made, quite recently, that I guarantee. Made for the bibliomania market."

I rounded on him. "How can you guarantee it? Donatus, you have been making enquiries among your contacts. What did you find out that's relevant? Stop holding back, man. Tell me the full truth."

We danced the dance informers must endure. He writhed. I pushed. He looked vague, pretended not to understand—and then he told me.

After I visited his shop, something I had said to him resonated. About a year ago, there had been rumours of a scandal. A long-time collector, a sensible, knowledgeable man, whom Donatus would not name to me because he said the man was famously secretive (plus Donatus sold him scrolls occasionally), had been on the verge of buying a newly discovered manuscript of stunning rarity. Then came a buzz in the trade that the sale had gone wrong. At the last minute the buyer had withdrawn in acrimonious circumstances. The scroll's veracity was called into question on expert advice. It had been offered to him by a highly regarded dealer of many years' standing, which made it worse. The dealer then main-tained he had been taken in too. There was talk of a compensation claim, but it came to nothing when, sadly, the dealer passed away—

"Because of this dispute?"

"No, it seemed to be normal illness. Mind you, the trouble won't have helped."

"And what made you think of this when I came to see you? Anything particular?"

"A name you mentioned. The expert declared the supposed author of the disputed scroll was entirely invented. Never existed. A complete wrong 'un."

Please, I thought, do not let this be Epitynchanus or Philadespoticus. Their work was awful, but I had become poignantly attached to them. Epi and Philly were mine now. For one thing, I must be the first person for hundreds of years who had read their stuff. Well, the first person since the forgers, if my supposed materialists were not real.

The fraud might never have come to light, said Donatus, but the forgers had chosen a ridiculous name. They gave their author a birthplace, biographical notes and a list of his (supposed) other works on the title page, in the manner of Calimachus's *Pinakes* at Alexandria.

"Hades, that means nothing!" I burst out scoffing. "Even my pa is in the *Pinakes*, listed for some daft play he once wrote." And his poems. We never talk about the poems.

The scholarly expert, a specialist in the School of Miletus, easily discounted the ancient author's background as a spoof. The scholar could distinguish between the writings of Thales, Anaximander and Anaximenes on the basis of a few phrases, he could talk for hours about their metaphysical naturalism and, most importantly, he knew who had taught whom in their circle, plus who had become a follower of the Milesian School in later centuries. He had never once come across the alleged author of the problem scroll. He declared him to be a dastardly fiction and his supposed work to be pastiche. The buyer was furious; he lined up a judge to adjudicate and compensate, but after the dealer died the scroll could not even be found by his heirs so there was no case to answer.

I gulped. "I need to know: who was the fictitious author?"

"Well, I can't believe you were fooled, Flavia Albia. It was Didymus Dodomos, the Dodecanese Doctrinalist."

I had to admit this had a loud ring of untruth.

XXXIII

Donatus left, finally off bar-crawling. I noticed my steward and cook slipped out to join him. They were entitled. Neither answered to me. Gratus might be a freedman, but he was not mine. Fornix appeared to be freeborn. They were at liberty to go out; my only regret was remembering how when I was younger I would have gone with them. Now, I was so whacked I had to be steered upstairs by my maid.

In bed, my head spun. At first my brain churned with tumbling questions. I might have to go back to Donatus tomorrow, preferably while he had a hangover and might answer meekly. For now, I wanted to consider the implications for myself.

Was the Doctrinalist truly dodgy? Having glanced at the fragment Larcius and the men had dug up, I could well believe that the one true thing about Didymus Dodomos was that he was contrived. If *he* was an invention, what of the rest, Epitynchanus and Philadespoticus, or the forlorn female poet Thallusa?

> *So when you say you love me,*
> *I ask for definitions,*
> *Then when you try to give them,*
> *I challenge your traditions . . .*

Thallusa had promise. Thallusa must be the product of true imagination, coupled with genuine knowledge of unhinged, unrequited, rather youthful love. Thallusa could once have been me.

Often, of course, that is why we read. To find ourselves. To exclaim, *Yes, yes, that is exactly it!* This author really knows . . .

It was an attractive thought that even if the scrolls were blatantly put together for criminal profit, it could still be exploited by the Didius auction house. We would have to catalogue them honestly, but the beneficiaries would be Tiberius and me, as finders . . . One big feast for the workmen, in return for handing over the scrolls, then off to the reading-couch supplier for us—with no need to hold back on bronze fittings!

I was learning that, even though I came from a remote province and had been adopted by strangers, I was the true child of a Roman family business. It gave me a warm feeling. Perhaps it was the warm feeling you experience when you have wet yourself, but never mind. Natural accident. Nobody minds, darling. Don't worry.

I did want to find out who was behind the fraud. My professional curiosity throbbed. Who had made these scrolls? Who had dreamed up the experiment of burying them? Who had written the mad words of the awful pseudo-philosophers? And did the perpetrators realise their artefacts had been found by others? Or would they still go back to collect their hoaxes? Whether they did or not, if I put the scrolls into auction, which must involve advertisement, how would the fraudsters react to me having them? They could not come forward to claim them, especially once we had labelled the scrolls "as seen: assessed as counterfeit."

I wondered what the legal situation was. Apparently, no one had yet been asked to buy these things as genuine, so no one had been defrauded. The pseudo-philosophers could never be charged with plagiarism, even if it turned out that their ideas were taken from real ancient authors. I had a feeling that when you're dead you can't sue. Or be sued. This is presumably definite if you'd never lived in the first place. Even so, as I lay awake, disturbed by wild turns of the brain, I imagined—or invented—a hack lawyer who might specialise in litigation on behalf of the deceased, and who might be induced to try his hand with the non-existent . . .

Back to reality. Much careful work had gone into those scrolls. Exposing them publicly might ditch their makers' hopes for fakes of this type, making collectors more wary. And if the forgers learned that I had dug up and kept their product, would it be dangerous for me?

Would it avoid trouble if I tried to find a buyer behind the scenes? This might bring a lower price than the auction estimate, but would a private sale be safer? Even if that person later sold them on, with or without an honest description, the trail would become murky . . .

I was thinking like a criminal. It showed that the line between straight- and double-dealing was as thin in the auction world as everyone believes.

Details about the original failed sale struck me as familiar. I knew one possible source for the scrolls. Donatus had refused to name the man who had nearly bought the so-called work of Didymus. He had never even told me which dealer was offering the forged scroll. But I knew of one who had died about a year ago, of a supposed natural disease, and who had been very highly regarded. Back into my head came Mysticus. Back, too, came Tuccia, who now owned his business. I could hear in my head how she had cheerily cried out to her staff: "*Someone found some buried scrolls!*" It had sounded like a warning for them to be discreet. If they had already encountered fakes, that made sense. If they themselves had produced them, it made even more. Had my buried scrolls originated in that shop?

Tuccia and her staff had pretended to me that they thought those scrolls were genuine. She had spoken of Epitynchanus and Philadespoticus as authors whose work she knew, knew so well she had discussed their beliefs in detail. Perhaps she had been lying through her teeth—or was she innocent, and had she read through a lot of fake scrolls without realising? One thing was sure: when the old man holding the gluepot for mending scrolls had cried, "*Go on, Tuccia! This is a previously unknown work!*" I had thought it seemed like teasing even at the time. Maybe now I understood.

That day in their workshop, I could have been standing in the very place where the scrolls were put together. Had the workers been tenderly gluing other fakes to bury? Had those skilled people at the Mysticus scroll shop written the wizened Greek and Latin letters I had struggled to decipher on the filthy papyrus I now had downstairs? Had they ripped sections to look like wear and tear, then attempted to stain everything with false antiquity by burying the collection at the sacred Grove? If I had allowed Tuccia to keep the first batch we found, as she had wanted, would she later have conveniently "lost" them? And if she believed I had identified her workshop as the source of fakes, what would she do about it?

I became drowsy, thinking wryly of the irony that my husband was so anxious I might take risks while investigating murders, while all the time I had unwittingly discovered a crime that looked more innocent. But it wasn't; there was money in fraud. I was even proposing to profit myself from the unearthed artefacts. That would dangerously aggrieve the people who had created them. They might want to silence me. The silencing process could be just as dangerous as getting in the way of a serial killer. Tuccia might be a fatal enemy.

More troubled than I had expected to be, eventually I dozed. I had occupied this bed alone for years, yet after a few months of knowing Tiberius, his absence was almost unbearable.

I heard the music downstairs come to a close. Later I heard Gratus and Fornix crashing home, the worse for wear. Drax, the yard watchdog, barked at them; Barley, on the floor in my room, only stirred irritably. I lay with one arm across the space where Tiberius ought to be, as at last I sank fully into sleep.

XXXIV

Every informer knows you can wake up on a hundred mornings ready for your trade, yet nobody wants you. On the one day you are desperate for a lie-in, some idiot will disturb your peace. If your luck is worse than average it will be Sosthenes, a fountain-designer, who insists that your staff drag you out of bed, a time-consumer who loves to talk, a no-hoper who has so few commissions he need not rush away, a fright who fibs that he won't keep you long so you can wait for your breakfast until he has left (he has already had his own, so he's all right; he recommends a snack bar that you know is rubbish).

"We met!" he cried triumphantly. "I am the special water-supply adviser to the Seventh Cohort of Vigiles."

"I wouldn't boast of that on the Aventine. The Seventh's name is mud here."

Although he worked with the Seventh, so must have seen them in action, he looked surprised.

Sparsus, the apprentice, had been sent to show this pain to the house. Even Sparsus had the sense to stick the man in our courtyard, then run. Gratus said he had been told to fetch a bucket of steam, with a lid to make sure that he lost none of it on his way back to the site.

"Does that young man have no common sense, madam?"

"Yes, but he leaves it safe at home under his pillow, in case somebody steals it."

Gratus laughed. I knew he liked working at our house.

———

When it came to designing fountains, Sosthenes was top notch. He told me so. There was no other evidence.

I decided I had better take an interest because Tiberius would, since Tiberius loved waterworks. Sosthenes was in line to create the nymphaeum at the Grove, so he was a contact to be nurtured by our firm.

Somehow I squeezed in a question. "Are you an architect?" This was the one professional my husband would hate. All builders think architects are nuts.

"I have architectural knowledge," hedged the visitor. Got it. He never finished the training. "My sphere is ephemerals: statuary, hydraulics, mosaics, high-class marble work. All naturals for a nymphaeum."

He had been promised the commission, for what that was worth. Had he tendered? No, the new-build programmers were not bothering with the formal submission process. Oh, really? That told me six other designers were probably being led on in the same way; quite likely none of them would be awarded the work. Some bureaucrat had told this dreamer he was first choice, on which flimsy basis Sosthenes was deep in preliminary drawings, site surveys and estimates. Chance was, he would never even be paid for his time.

The figures were looking good, he claimed, though I felt sceptical after he mentioned they had been put together by Spendo, the dwarf with a face like molten rock who, according to our clerk of works, produced prices so high that clients' eyes watered. So the nymphaeum might be too expensive to build—or at least expensive enough for the decision to be tangled in bureaucracy where delay is often drawn out into permanence. From what I knew about imperial projects, they had oodles of money but no ethics; just when a professional believed they would be using him, someone changed their mind and everything was cancelled. Since the altered mind might belong to our emperor, only the brave complained. They probably ended up building public toilets in provincial towns.

Being drowsy still, I let Sosthenes talk. For a deadbeat entrepreneur, he was full of theories. A tricky one was that Tiberius had said he fancied a fountain in our courtyard. "Good choice!" cried Sosthenes. "Good stuff! Good spot!"

Of his own accord he had out a folding rule and was measuring a wall. I mentioned that if he put his folly there he must move the dog kennel. He approached it. Barley, who in reality preferred to sleep in our bed, growled at him from the courtyard steps. "Good dog!" pleaded Sosthenes. She growled louder.

"We do not have a water connection," I demurred. That ought to fix him. "We have to send a slave out with buckets to collect all our supplies. Tiberius Manlius knows we cannot have a home fountain."

"No problem," claimed the designer, becoming bold. "You can be fixed up with a link. The Aqua Appia comes in at the end of the Clivus Publicius, but it is too low for your purposes. Not to worry. The Aventine boasts a siphonised branch of the Aqua Marcia, the coldest and clearest water in Rome. Tell Tiberius Manlius to order the pipes, then I shall organise the job. I know all the aqueduct-works boys—they will bump you up the queue if it's for me."

"Good idea!" It really was—like most things you instinctively try to avoid. At the moment Dromo was supposed to be our water-carrier, which made our supply erratic. "But we cannot afford your fantastic font right now." I spoke with my usual determination. To Sosthenes, clients were reeds who would bend to his current, even though it was hardly surging. This was the first time he had met me. An education. "Is that why Larcius sent you up here? To nobble us with a niche? I do not think so!"

I was right. Larcius had more sense. Suddenly I was back in command of my home. After much blather, the designer accepted I was serious: no sparkling wall fountain. None, despite his claim that my husband had approved the idea.

I said I would talk to Tiberius, implying he would end up crushed by wifely power. Only he and I knew it was not my style.

Sosthenes came clean. Larcius had sent him as a witness. The designer had had a sighting of my lost dancing boys.

On the afternoon after Victoria Tertia was murdered, Sosthenes and Spendo had gone to the Grove for Spendo to measure up and price Sosthenes' working drawings for the hypothetical nymphaeum. To their surprise, Larcius and the men were absent. They subsequently learned that this was because I had instructed the men to leave the site that day while things settled down following the death. I had brought them back over the river to work at Fullo's Nook.

"Is that," asked Sosthenes, hopefully, "a bar with scope for water features?"

"No. No space, and after paying us for his worktops, Fullo will have no cash. Get on with your story."

Although the grotto site was closed, Sosthenes and Spendo had climbed over the barriers then clambered about, making notes. While they were there, my two dancers turned up. The two professionals spoke only to one lad; for some reason the other was being carried around by his brother.

"What was wrong with him?"

"They never said."

"Did you ask?"

"No, I wasn't particularly interested."

Assuming these lads had no business at the building site, Sosthenes told them to leave. He claimed he had "politely shooed them away," though I gained the impression he was more aggressive. Designers are not tough, but the boys would have been unused even to wimps telling them to clear off.

"Did they ask for Larcius?"

"Not by name. The one who talked merely asked me where the builders were. He sounded curious. He never said the two of them had any connection with you."

"Had they been hurt?"

"Not obviously. They looked like a couple of long-haired urchins, up to no good. The floppy one might have been in a fight, I suppose. The other was just shifty."

"See any wounds?"

"No, but they seemed whacked."

"Scared?"

"Could be. Very unhappy. They were looking over their shoulders as if someone might be coming after them—little thieves who had been caught in the act, we thought. I didn't want them pinching anything from the nymphaeum site."

I remembered that the workmen had taken away all their tools. But maintaining site security meant preventing loafers hanging around, so I said nothing.

"When Spendo came over, they were scared of him all right!" exclaimed Sosthenes. "One look, and they fled fast enough."

"Yes, I gather he is unusual . . . Where did they go? Which direction?"

"Back the way they came, I think."

"Which was?"

"Through the gardens."

"Sublician Bridge direction? Towards the Naumachia? Portuensis Gate?"

"I couldn't tell. I didn't care really, so long as they left."

I thanked him for coming to tell me, but I prepared to dismiss him.

The only good thing to come out of this story was that why ever they had gone missing, Primulus and Galanthus had at least tried to come back. Alone in the Transtiberina, the inexperienced boys would not know their way home to the Aventine. They had tried to find the builders, but when that failed, they could have wandered off anywhere. At least on the day after the murder they were still alive.

"Larcius gave me a message for you," Sosthenes ended. Was it an apology for sending him? No chance. "He says better not go over to the Grove again. That pervert who keeps nabbing women, he did another last night."

XXXV

Warning me off had fixed it: I was going to the Grove.

I skipped breakfast. While I was putting on walking shoes, Sparsus came back to the house, needing further instructions about the "bucket of steam" he was supposed to obtain. I explained. I was kind about it. Well, fairly. It was time he started thinking twice before accepting ridiculous errands.

At least I could brush off objections from the others by saying I had him as my escort. Also, as we headed over to the Transtiberina, I could pick his brains. I hoped this vague young man had brought them with him today.

"What's happened, Sparsus? The fountain-fiddler said there's been another murder."

"Yes, the Pest has only gone and killed another one!" Sparsus was glum, wanting to feel excited, yet depressed by such terrible things happening so near to their site.

"Tell me, please."

"We only heard from a pedlar who came by to sell us flatbreads. They found another corpse in Caesar's Gardens."

"Who found her? When? Who was she? What had happened to her . . . ?"

"Hold on, Albia! I only know what the bread man said, and he was mostly 'Do you want chickpea spread or honey?' Some gardeners found a dead body. It's over in the main part of Caesar's Gardens because the vigiles are there, a lot of them this time. They have a space roped off. Running about like daft red rabbits. Larcius told us to keep out of the way."

"Good thing." It sounded as if Julius Karus was involved. More men. Crime-scene protection. Pointless agitation. Trampling evidence. Anyone who showed any interest would put themselves in line to be his suspect. I knew how his mind worked. "If they come across to question you, be helpful. If it happened last night, you were at home on this side of the river, so they shouldn't bother you as witnesses." I phrased it carefully. Best not to pre-empt Karus playing the idiot and harassing them. However, I did not want him trying to pin any deaths on my men. "You've nothing to tell them, Sparsus, so just be patient with their little games. Otherwise, stay out of their hair, let them get on with it."

"Are *you* going to stay out of the vigiles' hair?" Young Sparsus was beginning to show signs of the satire the others possessed.

"No," I confessed. I added coldly, "Because this is my job, Sparsus."

I did not tell him that sometimes my work felt about as useful as being sent to a hardware shop for a bucket of steam.

He would not have picked up the joke. He still dimly thought such a bucket could be had, only he hadn't managed yet to find the right tool shop.

Soon after we entered the formal gardens, we located the find scene. I sent Sparsus to the building site. By myself I walked quietly up to the roped-off area, where I stood in silence, close to the vigiles who were guarding it. I had given these grim-faced hunks a nod. They even responded though they, too, made no comment. I watched as a covered trestle was carried towards us, then placed on a cart and removed by a small guard party. It was an open-sided cart that seemed already to contain buckets of something. As they came by us, I almost requested a sight of the body. But there was no point. I knew what would have been done to the woman. I felt too sick on her behalf to stare at her remains.

The cordon stayed in place. Within it, I could see other men, bent over, scrutinising soil, plants, foliage around the bases of minor statuary. While they searched among clipped box and along earthen paths, I did nothing until eventually I made out Karus. Very politely, I asked the vigiles if I might go and speak to him. At once, they lifted up their rope for me.

It struck me that I had not mentioned who I was or how I had an interest, yet I felt they knew.

I might have expected Karus to have given orders: *If that interfering woman turns up, keep her out.* I certainly thought he would himself rebuff me. He must have had a theory: keep them guessing—if they believe they know the rules, change the rules. So he let me come right up to where he was standing with another man, whom I had not seen before.

This was where the body must have been found. A low fence with criss-crossed diagonal slats ran alongside the path; a stretch had been pulled open to access flattened foliage where the dead woman must have been lying. Behind the fence was the normal arrangement of small ornamental trees set among a variety of shrubs, with plants that would be starred with flowers in a warmer season. Due to the time of year, everything was bare. Normally birds would be everywhere. None came today.

Julius Karus stood with his arms folded, watching moodily as the vigiles kept searching. His companion looked nervous; perhaps he was edgy because of Karus. Intelligent, then.

I nodded, a grim greeting. Karus slightly nodded back. The stranger only stared, wondering about me, yet apparently lost in his own awkwardness at having to be here. I waited for them to speak first. The silence was heavy, joyless and sombre.

I had come in a cloak so I wrapped myself deeper in its folds. In the end I had to break the spell: "I assume it's another the same?"

Having made me speak first, Karus released the story easily enough. "Two."

"What?"

He relished my surprise. "One fresh today, the other only scattered bones." The bones must have been in those buckets I saw on the cart.

They knew who the first victim was. Karus told me the gardeners had been ordered to conduct a full search after a woman had come to the station-house last night to report a friend missing. She had heard about

Victoria Tertia, so was anxious, especially as she had to confess that her friend, who was younger and had two children, had come out after dark to earn coppers as a prostitute. Normally this witness would have been sent away to wait longer before bothering the vigiles, but Karus rightly jumped on it.

He must have been at the station-house. As soon as the woman came in, he took over. By sunrise he had the entire gardens staff out walking in lines on a grid pattern. When they had first started, there must have been a good chance he would catch the killer unawares while he was still involved with the victim. But Karus had been unlucky. There were no sightings.

The man standing with him was the superintendent of Caesar's Gardens and the Grove. Berytus by name, he was older, not far from the end of his administrative career. A sagging, thread-veined face, with heavily pouched eyes. Extremely uncomfortable at this scene.

Some of his staff had discovered a woman's corpse not long after they had begun their search that morning. Almost simultaneously others nearby came across skeletal remains. A decomposed body had once been buried at the back of an arbour, but due to the winter dieback of foliage, weathered bones could be seen, partly exposed by animals.

A long-ago attempt had been made to hide the older corpse. The new one had been left at this spot last night, where anyone strolling on the path might glance over the border fence and see her.

"Unfinished business!" said Karus, with lip-smacking relish. I could tell he enjoyed shocking the superintendent. "The perp meant to play with her before he finished." He let the other man work out what that could mean, if he could in fact imagine that such things happened.

"Was this one posed?" I asked, remaining expressionless.

"No. But naked. The men are hunting for her clothes."

While the superintendent brooded miserably, Karus and I discussed the situation as professionals. We presumed the killer's intention had been to move his dead victim away from the path before he had finished with her, probably to shift her from Caesar's Gardens into the sacred Grove where there was more cover; he may have meant to do so in daylight, had the presence of searchers not stopped him.

"Did the people who found her know her?" Both men looked surprised at my question. I managed not to sigh. "If this woman regularly came here for her trade, surely the gardeners might recognise her?" Berytus confirmed they did, which was how the vigiles knew this was the missing woman. The group who had found her were now in shock. It was not the first time corpses had been found by gardeners, though, not by a long way.

I glanced at Karus. Sometimes the person who claims to have discovered a murder is secretly the killer. Karus shook his head slightly, so he knew this too; he was warning me to say nothing in front of our companion. I duly kept quiet. Besides, gardeners had been set the task of searching this morning, so that seemed to rule out the killer-discoverer theory.

From his behaviour, I reckoned Berytus might never have seen any of the previous corpses. He knew about them but had always avoided viewing the remains. Karus presumably had made him come out in person to this one. The man had been left deeply troubled. He did not say so, but I knew he would never forget what he had seen now. He made a trite remark about how terrible the situation was, filling time so he could stop thinking about it.

"How long have you been in post?" I asked him.

"Three years." His gaze flickered, as it struck him why I had asked. "I was at the Emperor's villa in Alba Longa before." The citadel. It was said that our brooding tyrant's hideaway had beautiful garden terraces.

I didn't bother to look at Karus, though I sensed he was also noting this timescale: too short. Not Berytus, then.

Karus asked bluntly, "How many staff on your complement have worked here longer than ten years?"

"Surely you don't think it could have been one of them? Oh, I suppose you must consider all possibilities . . . About half. They tend to be either long-term hands who have been here all their lives, or much younger, mere apprentices."

"Forget the apprentices. Give me a list of the rest."

"Well, yes, I can do that . . . It's a joke, of course, that we train them but they are immediately moved to other sites."

"Typical," said Karus, but coolly, like someone who had no experience of that. From what I knew, he always kept a close bevy of loyal men. He hailed from Spain, Tarraconensis. Don't blame me for knowing; when he first started throwing his weight about, it was my husband who had looked him up. His main command, the troops who helped on the British expedition that had made Karus's career, was a cohort of Asturians—more Spaniards. He had men of his own in Rome; I had seen them and hated their attitude. Karus was the kind of agent who would accept a special assignment on condition that he brought his own trusted team. It was arrogant, but his kind somehow obtain approval for whatever they want.

"Any of your staff you would suggest particularly as perverts?" he asked bluntly. "What about those who found today's corpse?"

"Oh!" A nervy squeak. "Well, Blandus and his group may be the longest-serving in the gardens, though I can't say I have had concerns of that kind about them . . . All the hardy perennials are grim-looking specimens. Not many smiles, not given to cheeriness. I put it down to bad backs and hitting their heads on tree branches. I can place Blandus first on the list for you . . . This is all so horrible!" Unused to such scenes and frightened, the superintendent kept exclaiming how ghastly the situation was. "What kind of person can do such things to another human being?"

"I believe murder gets easier after the first time," I told him bleakly, hoping he would shut up. This was no place for innocents, or not unless they held their peace. Those of us who understood were heavy with our own unspoken response.

"Your answer is he's a person who enjoys doing it!" grated Karus.

The unnecessary put-down only agitated Berytus more. "I still cannot believe anybody would! Why hasn't he been found? How can this beast be roaming the gardens, yet no one ever spots him?"

I could have left Karus to deal with it, but I saw he was ready to lash out. I weighed in with a measured explanation: "It's simple, sir. Because he does not look or behave like a beast. When he is found, this will be the most ordinary man. Everyone will be amazed. Of course, he has also to look like someone who has a proper reason to be here. People must pass him yet not give him a second glance."

Berytus settled somewhat, in the face of my quiet certainty. "You know what he is like?"

"I can prophesy."

"So, who is he?"

"Not young, because we know he has been doing this for fifteen or twenty years. He must have been an adult, or nearly so, when he started. Not too old either, though. He has to be fit, strong enough to subdue victims however hard they fight for their lives—although he has learned to overpower them very quickly."

"Why does he do it?"

"He may have had disappointments in his early life. He may blame others, especially women."

"What else do you know?"

"He is probably married, has a job, maybe children."

"Oh, surely not! You don't think so?" the shocked superintendent demanded of Karus, who did not respond, though neither did he argue against me.

I continued my ideas. Professionally, it was useful to sum up now. "This killer is competent, well-organised, intelligent. Although he lacks a conscience or human feelings, particularly towards women, in his daily life he hides that. But he has no regard for his victims. Even if he gives himself some reason why they need to die, he is completely unfeeling towards them. To him, the women he snatches are just things, things to be used for his pleasure."

"Pieces of meat," put in Karus.

"Yet," I told Berytus who, of course, was looking appalled again, "you will find this strange. His wife will never see him in that way. Does she know what he does? She may suspect, but even if we catch him she will never acknowledge his guilt. He must almost have two personalities. I'd say he is regarded by his community as hard-working, pleasant, a fellow who will do anything for anyone."

"She cannot be right!" Berytus appealed again to Karus.

Karus surprised me. "I think she is. This individual has been in the Transtiberina for decades. As far as we know, no suspicion has ever attached to him. He blends in. We have appealed for suggestions of his identity, even promising anonymity, but nobody has come forward."

"No one at all?"

"Well, we've had a few mad ideas that were easily discounted."

They had probably received more loopy reports than he suggested. When my uncle was with the Fourth Cohort, Lucius Petronius used to rant about crackpot theorists. Karus clearly knew most tips would be irrelevant, spiteful or purely unhinged. All the same, having to look into the suggestions tied up the vigiles. The very ordinariness of the man involved made every allegation a potential clue. In an inquiry like this, even unlikely pointers must be checked, in case.

There was no reason for me to stay. I asked Karus to let me know if he found anything. So far, neither the recent victim's property nor anything that could relate to the much older bones had turned up. I then requested details of the friend who last night had reported the latest missing woman. To my surprise, Karus told me.

I confirmed honestly that I intended to interview this witness. Apparently, she had been so fraught last night that he could extract little. Now he must reckon maybe she would talk to me.

Later, I said, I would inform my client Cluventius about the new discoveries. We should hope he did not hear of them from elsewhere. It would serve no purpose if he rushed off in high agitation to the praetor again.

"You're doing a good job with him!" answered Karus. His praise, I thought, was tongue-in-cheek.

XXXVI

The woman who had reported her friend missing lived in a one-room rental in a quarter inhabited by waterfront workers. Here were the dangerous glass and pottery kilns, watermills on the Janiculan slopes and brick factories on the Vatican. Tanners, fish-pickle suppliers, metal-beaters, dye-brewers and other antisocial small businesses had been shifted to the Transtiberina out of the luckier districts of Rome. People of influence lived centrally, whereas here there were only the poor, foreigners, and others with no political voice.

Here, too, lived thin women, old before their time, who struggled to earn a tiny income from selling themselves. Many of the men they went with were brutish. Most of the women died young. They expected they would succumb to battery, disease or pure exhaustion, though at least they would make it into their twenties or thirties. The one taken last night had had her thread snipped at nineteen. Even at that age, she had two children, by different fathers, neither of whom were around. I heard the infants grizzling from the bed, as I interviewed her friend.

This older woman maintained she had been like a mother to the victim, though they were neighbours, not relatives. She was of an earlier generation, yet I suspected she still occasionally worked in the same trade. She might well have introduced the younger one to this hard method of survival. Her appearance was as the other must have been in life: hollow-cheeked, scrawny, an unhealthy colour. She looked as if she drank, or worse, if ever she could afford it. And as if she would drink, or worse, in preference to eating or sleeping.

She told me they had heard what had happened to Victoria Tertia.

Their attitude had been *He is at it again; watch out*. Most did not stop working. Prostitutes in the district were being as careful as they could, but they had to live. When the young woman, whose name was Satia, had decided she had no choice but to go out to Caesar's Gardens last evening, she left her children in her neighbour's care, saying she would collect them by midnight, sooner if she managed to find a customer and earn something. She was a good mother. That was why she had had to venture out in the first place, because they were all starving. On previous occasions she had always returned when she had promised. When she failed to reappear yesterday, it meant serious trouble had befallen her.

Satia had no pimp. She was not that type. Neither did she have a close friend with whom she could go out in a pair, watching out for one another, as some girls managed to do. Caesar's Gardens was her usual walking ground. She never went up by the Naumachia: it wasn't a nice place.

Originally, Satia's family were immigrants, though none but her survived. She looked foreign. She could have been beautiful, but misery had worn her down. She had grown up half starved and remained so all her life. There was nothing of her. In fact, she was so slight that anyone could have subdued her physically—though a man from the vigiles, who came to say they had found her, had told her neighbour that Satia had fought hard to survive.

Her missing clothes had been nothing but rags. She had no jewellery to speak of, only a tiny wire bracelet that someone had given her when she was a child. As an adult, her arms were so thin she could still wear it.

Nobody knew what would happen to her orphaned infants. The neighbour promised me she would look after them for the time being. She seemed so willing to hang on to them that I knew she planned to sell the poor mites into slavery. Whatever pittance she got for them would be used up within a week.

That was how it had been in the Transtiberina for years. Again and again, women like Satia had been abused and killed. Few people would miss them when they disappeared—sometimes they were never missed at all. Either way, no one thought that anything could or would be done about it. Until now, nobody had cared.

XXXVII

My mood was doleful when I emerged outside. There, for some odd reason, the Transtiberina seemed more normal than usual. I passed through streets with better shops. I even found the famous area where an oddly placed group of businesses sold high-quality furniture. Embittered by this contrast with the sad world I had left behind, I did not pause to look. Tiberius and I had discussed having a citronwood table when we could afford it, but right now I had no interest in researching fancy goods.

I wished he would come home. With my mind trammelled in the troubles of this district, I pushed aside the longing. I almost blamed myself for having a life. Normality. Security. Husband. Home. People. Enough money to live . . .

I walked slowly back to the gardens. I had been told that the group who had found Satia's body had been taken off the search and sent to recover. I went to the huddle of hutments that the superintendent had pointed out.

Inside the gardeners' hedged compound, Berytus had a cottagey office, prettified with a border of shrubs but so tiny it contained only a worktable and a cupboard. I looked inside, but he must still have been stuck with Karus. I found a stable, barely hanging together, for the pony that dragged away rubbish to dump in the countryside; I had seen the rough-coated, sturdy creature, barely able to haul his overloaded cart, especially after Larcius and company had added building rubble to it.

Equipment stores leaned askew as if homemade. Haphazardly positioned between them were compost bins, piles of rotting prunings, a collection of battered trolleys and carts. A manure heap steamed. Log piles teetered. An area was dug, a nursery for young plants, though at this time of year only a few miniature cuttings struggled among hardy weeds. A couple of statues loitered; a muscle-bound nude man looked as if he was waiting for a war to come along, while a half-size young goddess in not-quite-white marble looked over her shoulder at her bottom as if wondering who had smacked it so often that it was grimier than the rest of her.

From the lack of accommodation, I gathered the staff in theory lived elsewhere, though I thought it quite likely they could stay surreptitiously overnight in their sheds. A pipe from the Alsietina brought them water, which poured endlessly into an overflowing basin beside which stood rusty buckets. I could see nothing that looked like human sanitary provision.

In an outside grassy area stood benches and other outdoor furniture, borrowed from the public gardens; this was where staff must gather for rest and refreshment. At a licheny goat-legged table, four men were waiting to be sent home or given new instructions. All looked hardy, suntanned, wearing short-sleeved brown tunics that had seen years of life but not many launderings, all sporting scratches and bruises from their work. One was clearly senior, in charge, another a lad. Even before I arrived, they were barely talking, still stunned by discovering the corpse. The lad, a presumed apprentice, was most shocked, visibly tear-stained and shivering.

I sat down with them, then introduced myself. I said I was working alongside Julius Karus, which implied he and I were collaborating. If he disagreed, let him put them right.

Though I addressed myself to the senior, I recognised one of the others. First, I reminded that one of how we had met briefly, when I was lost while looking for our building site. As before, he was polite, almost too much so; I felt the humility was feigned and he was laughing up his ragged sleeve. He hoped I had found the right place. I confirmed it, thanking him for his directions. His name was Rullius.

Blandus took over, making it plain he was the man I was supposed to talk to. While he held forth, no one else got a word in. We began gradually, taking time to get used to one another. He, too, appeared sceptical of a woman, though he let me ask my questions, to which he responded, even though he was such a slow conversationalist that the hard work felt like digging up weeds with deep taproots.

"I met your superintendent." Out of my direct vision, I thought a couple of the other men exchanged satirical glances. It might have been dislike of their supremo, or something else. "Berytus tells me your team is the longest-serving?"

"We've done some time here, that's correct," confirmed Blandus.

"So, you have prior experience of these deaths?"

Blandus agreed that there had been bodies before. It went back many years. Sometimes gardeners had found them. Or it might have been members of the public. With the public, they generally reported their discovery to the gardeners, so summoning the vigiles was up to them. They called them in to avoid trouble later. Besides, the red-tunics would take away the remains. I probed, but Blandus would not be drawn much on his opinion of the Seventh, though he did say drily that they were a fire brigade, so if they ever found anyone to arrest they would just throw a bucket of water over him. Once bodies had been removed, for the gardeners that was the end of it—until the next time.

"It seems most of the victims were working girls," I said. "Satia certainly came here for that reason last night. A witness told me. Apparently you knew her?"

"We knew who she was. We had seen her." Blandus seemed to become more aggressive.

"Spoken?"

"We don't have time to speak to people." This was untrue: I had seen gardeners leaning on spades or brooms on plenty of occasions. They clustered to natter over piles of leaves more often than I ever saw them sweeping those piles together. Gardens are not only made for strollers to engage in high-minded reflection; they are places of low-grade communion. Gossip is easier than weeding.

"You knew what she was called?"

"I suppose."

"I suggest, without judgement, some workers might have known this poor girl and—I dare say—some of the others who died, through using their professional services?"

Blandus, now definitely defensive, would not say. He could be as coy as he liked: I firmly believed some garden staff would have engaged with the women who patrolled the garden walks, and I bet they didn't wait for dusk to fall. Probably all of them paid for a trick from time to time. "All right. What do you think about them coming here to work?"

"It's harmless," said Blandus, still aggressive. "It's nature, isn't it?"

"When women are desperate . . . My next question is obvious, so I apologise. The vigiles must have asked it, but has anyone who works in the gardens or in the Grove of the Caesars ever noticed someone who could be the man who does this?"

"Oh, yes. The firemen always ask!" Blandus made himself sound like an extremely patient country-dweller being generous to a numbskull townee. "Have we ever seen anyone acting suspiciously? Hanging around unnaturally? Bothering women?"

"No?" I kept my cool.

"No!" The men let out laughs at being asked yet again. I sensed they all thought that the women who died were not worth investigation time.

"Well, thank you."

"And if we do," Blandus carried on, regurgitating what must be their constant assurance to the Seventh, "we have to run along like good boys and hand in the information at the station-house. We'll give it to bloody Ursus."

"Who will stuff it in his old tips cupboard!" chimed Rullius, letting his contempt show as he suddenly spoke up.

"We call him the Pest," Blandus told me, taking over again. "That man who takes the women. Whoever he is. A nasty pest."

"Pest doesn't sound nasty enough," I suggested.

"Then you've never had sooty mould or lily beetles! If I ever catch him, I'll squash him under my boot, like the big slug he is."

He made a mime of doing it. The action was so vivid I could hear the squelch.

———

I fell quiet, wondering what else I could possibly ask. There was no point querying if they ever found jewellery, meaning the trophy pieces that were taken from dead victims. These workers were paid a trifle. Anything of value that turned up on a path or in a fountain bowl would be considered theirs by right. They might possibly share profits among themselves, though I doubted that. Seated here, they formed a group, yet any man who found something would turn it into cash secretly, I suspected.

Rullius, the polite one, leaned in closer than I liked. "I heard you were interested in some writing things that were found." I distanced myself physically and simply nodded. "I saw some people who came and buried those."

"Oh?" The puzzle of the scrolls had faded to insignificance today, but I made myself show interest in what Rullius was saying. "When was that?"

"Couple of months back."

"Know them?"

"No."

"What did they look like?"

"A man and a woman. I took notice because they had a big spade with them."

"Can you describe them?"

"Too far away. I thought at first they were going to the old cave to have it off. Obviously," he told me, with the humility I found two-faced, "we have to stop lewd acts in the sacred precincts of the Grove."

"Too right! We have proper gazebos for bunk-ups!" His unnamed colleague, who had not spoken before, was their rude joker, it seemed. "Adultery arbours. With beautiful views—for us to watch what happens inside!"

"Lovers don't usually bring a big spade!" scoffed Rullius, ignoring him.

"People do come to steal plants," Blandus weighed in and told me, as if trying to control his men. "We have to watch out for anyone who turns up equipped for taking our shrubs and trees. Settle down, lads," he warned directly. "The lady doesn't want to hear any dirty talk." Though he said this, I could see they were jeering at my supposed primness, all of them, including him.

I could have lived without hearing about buried scrolls too. But I was stuck with it. "So, this couple you saw were not having a tryst, but digging holes among the rocks, Rullius? I presume it happened before my men took control of the site."

"Before, yes. I went over to look at what they had been up to, after they went off again. I dug up what they left behind. When I saw what it was, I just put it all back. I thought they were getting rid of some old rubbish. Or leaving a votive offering to the spirits of the Grove," added Rullius in a tone that mocked religion. He was a cool one.

"Assuming wood nymphs like to read," I countered, in the same spirit, though I was feeling drab. I could not imagine a dryad enjoying a quick flip through Philadespoticus of Skopelos, even on a quiet day for tree-haunting. "If you do ever see them and their spade again—"

"Run to the station-house and tell bloody Ursus!" muttered Blandus.

If these men realised they might be murder suspects, they were not trying very hard to look innocent. Apart from the silent apprentice, three were old enough to qualify. One aggressive, one lewd, one disrespectful to women: any of those characteristics would fit the perpetrator. Did they know how I was thinking? It seemed none of them cared.

Karus and Ursus, and even I, had assumed there was only one killer. What if more were involved? Sometimes or always? Or if he really did act alone, yet the rest knew who he was? Suppose, because he was one of their own, they had covered up for him all these years—suppose they were still protecting him now?

I wouldn't employ these men to prune my courtyard roses. Perhaps all staff in the gardens were equally unlikeable. Or perhaps I was being prejudiced and so failed to relate to them. Perhaps *they* refused to connect with *me*. They could be too stupid, or too ingrained with unhelpfulness, to see that it would be better to cooperate with me than to wait until Julius Karus jumped all over them.

I changed the subject. I reminded them about Primulus and Galanthus, asking them to look out for my two lost boys. They all nodded solemnly. Gardeners had been previously asked this; had seen the notices my workmen had put up on my instruction. The men here showed little interest, though Rullius gravely assured me they were trying hard to find the missing ones.

They struck me as untrustworthy, but it could simply have been that they lived in isolation out of doors, with little social interface. They were used to people ignoring them. They had come to resent that. In return they cut themselves off from normal communication.

Only as I made my way home did I wonder if introducing that talk of the scrolls had been a tactical distraction.

XXXVIII

I crossed the river so I could go to see Cluventius. He took the news of the latest death and discovery of bones spikily, as if the increasing body count was a further offence against him. Since the known victim was a working girl, he seemed less concerned about Satia than he might have been. Social prejudice never fails. I assured him investigations were in hand, with Karus using due diligence.

Client report done, I was free. I had really wanted to go back up the Aventine because it was about time for Paris to come from Fidenae. As I entered the house, he was tying up the donkey in the yard. Paris himself could be heard through the open yard door, crossly yelling at Patchy, then Patchy furiously braying back. Fornix trotted out from the kitchen corridor to assist.

Leaving the cook to it, Paris stormed into the main courtyard. "He's all right, but he has to stay there longer. His aunt got sick. The nippers keep snivelling; he worries about them. There's a letter, when that mad creature lets me get at the pack on him." Fornix had already stopped Patchy treading around in circles, quietened him, and was unstrapping baggage. "He sent back Dromo," added Paris to me, his tone rich with meaning.

"Dromo! Come out! Have you been driving your master crazy?"

The reluctant figure of Dromo sidled around the frame of the yard door. There was little of his clever-slave act in evidence. For Tiberius to blow up at him was highly unusual, a sign of my husband's state of mind. Dromo hung his scurfy head while he gruffly admitted that they were "not seeing eye to eye at the moment."

I was angry. "It's your job to see things the way your master does! Who is looking after him without you?" Tiberius would look after himself. That was not the point. With his family worries, he needed support.

"Where are those horrible dancing boys?" demanded Dromo, who could very easily pretend to lose the thread of a conversation. I rarely thought he changed the subject on purpose; he was not that bright.

"Not here. Don't ask where, because we don't know."

Dromo had his mouth open to ask me anyway, but my expression stopped him. "What am I supposed to do around here without my master?"

"Keep well out of my way, I would suggest!"

I felt like someone in a comedy, taking the frantic-housewife part. At any moment, someone would rush in to say my husband had been captured by pirates while trying to dodge a brothel madam whose daughter was in love with him. If I was lucky, a handsome soldier would be after me—though, more likely, he wanted my big chest of treasure and, anyway, he would turn out to be my long-lost love child . . .

Watching me irritably handle the situation were three other people. My maid, Suza, had taken it upon herself to bring out all my jewellery so she could "polish things." Cobnuts. That meant try on pieces. She must have found out where I hid the key. Helping her brazenly explore my collection was my cousin Marcia. I glared; they pointedly avoided notice.

Slightly aloof and not fingering necklaces sat Tuccia, the scroll-shop owner. At least when Suza had emptied my jewellery box onto the small table, she must have cleared away the scroll collection first. Either that or Gratus had whipped them out of sight.

"Suza! I hate people playing with my stuff. Put everything back and take my box upstairs again. Marcia, you can unhook my best Etruscan earrings right now and help her. If you came for a chat, just occupy yourself and I'll be with you as soon as possible. Tuccia, this is a surprise! What can I do for you?"

A sensitive woman might have asked whether this was a bad time.

I plumped down on the stone bench. Barley took a nervous look at me, then slunk into her kennel. At my signal, Tuccia pulled her seat nearer, though not too near.

For a trip out, she had dressed herself in an unbleached long tunic with cherry-red cord bands and a sludge-green stole, which had, fortunately, almost all faded to anonymity. She wore a hat. It appeared to have been made by a couch-upholsterer, in mustard cloth, dotted like measles, on a padded bandeau at the front. All her hair must have been roughly clustered inside it, apart from two quite tightly rolled little ringlets in front of her ears. Her manner was a matching mix of moods. She was bright yet wary today, firm yet indecisive. I had liked her last time; I was suspicious of her now.

"I had to come!"

"Really?"

"Somebody said you investigate things." Was this alarming to her?

"I help solve problems."

"I heard you found some other scrolls."

"Yes, and I've learned a lot about them." I was really wound up, no chance of holding back. "This bunch includes Didymus Dodomos, for instance, a complete fantasy. Now don't tell me you read him, Tuccia, along with Epitynchanus and the other idiot!"

She hung her head. "Oh, Juno," she murmured, as open as you like. "You must think it was our workshop that produced the Didymus fraud."

I did, but I had expected I would struggle to make her acknowledge their involvement, not for her to point it out herself. I was not yet ready to show any leniency. I didn't only disapprove of forgery, it made me angry. My father would say punters' greed encourages deception, yet I reckoned sometimes innocents were exploited. "Your repair people have all the skills—plus I heard them joke about buried scrolls."

Tuccia leaned forward, full of earnest appeal. "You have to believe me, the problem with the difficult scroll was before my time."

I was meeting a lot of sincere people today. Professionalism took over. I grilled her as firmly as I would any suspect. "The controversy only involved Mysticus, then?"

"Yes, but he certainly had not had the scroll made. He was taken in by the fake himself. He was very experienced, yet he thought it looked properly authentic."

"His customer was sure Mysticus was implicated. The word in the trade is that he accused Mysticus of deliberate deception. It was going to court?"

"Yes, to be honest, there was some talk of that."

To me, Tuccia did not seem sufficiently perturbed, so I asked, "Is litigation common in the world of book-collecting?"

"Oh, no, it never happens."

I remembered what Donatus had told me about collectors: that could be because they were so secretive. They would flinch from challenging. Going to law would expose too much idiocy.

"Where did that scroll come from in the first place, according to you? How did Mysticus acquire it?"

"He bought it. I know he did."

"Previous owner?"

"I never heard. But he obtained it in good faith." Good faith and bad judgement!

"Do you think Mysticus was so upset by the confrontation with his customer it might have affected his health?"

Tuccia looked surprised but seized on it. "Well, that could be so. Yes, indeed! He was very ill around that time, and then he died. He could have been affected by worry."

Indeed, I thought—but by the worry that he was found out. "Stress is a wonderful thing!"

"Oh, don't!" Tuccia's expression changed slightly. She leaned forwards and asked, almost in an undertone, "Somebody told me you investigate crimes, like your father, Falco?"

She had already asked me this and seemed obsessed by my occupation. I realised I had not mentioned it when we met before. Was that what had brought her scurrying here today? "Sometimes I do."

Now Tuccia pleaded, to a degree that I found overdone: "Albia, please understand. You have to!"

I wanted to hear the story. I cocked my head. "So, what's to understand?"

"Let me tell you."

"You do that!" I sat and waited, wearing the face that my family call Albia's Medusa Mask.

Tuccia clasped and unclasped her hands, like a pent-up child waiting for a present. "Oh, Albia! What have you heard about the Didymus scroll? Has Marcus Ovidius been talking to you?"

"Ovidius?"

"The collector who nearly bought it."

"On my list to interview!" He would be, if I could trace him, now she had revealed his name. "He brought in an expert for a scholarly opinion, I believe?"

"As I wasn't involved at the time, I don't really know," Tuccia answered, once again distancing herself from the old scandal. I watched her: she was wearing that slightly troubled, almost puzzled face, yet on another level she was not exactly quelled. She was still able to come out with the kind of jokey insight I might use myself: "Mysticus had to pay his own expert to give counter-arguments. You know how it is in that situation, Albia. My expert witness says black, your scholar says white, and anyone could call in a third who will review what both his colleagues have decreed, then say there is much to be said on both sides and he will call it grey."

I had to admit this is always the trouble with experts. Peer review has all the strength of slopping wet clay. More tolerantly, I suggested, "In the auction house, we reckon you have to use your own intuition. First instincts are generally correct."

Tuccia sighed. "Unfortunately, for once, Mysticus's instinct let him down. It seems I am stuck with the results," she complained. No charges had been levelled at her, so she was unnecessarily sorry for herself.

"Perhaps Mysticus was already sickening," I offered, now being as fair as I could. "He lost his sharpness because of illness, perhaps."

"I'd like to think there was an explanation."

She could not know what Donatus had told me last night, so I asked innocently, "Had suspicious scrolls turned up before in the trade? Was forgery a known problem?"

"No, I think that was why Mysticus was unprepared. He had never encountered anything like that before." If true, he must never have heard about the Dictys memoirs of the Trojan War, with wily Odysseus glossing the script for added value: the story Donatus had told me. If that happened in Nero's time, Mysticus was a dealer then and should have been aware of it.

"What happened to the contentious scroll? Where is it?"

Tuccia looked blank. "I'm afraid I have no idea."

"Please ask your staff. Have a good look in the shop in case Mysticus left it there. I would very much like to see it." Something told me that was asking a lot. The suspect scroll would not resurface.

Tuccia quickly worked out why I wanted it. "You think because you have another fragment that mentions Didymus Dodomos, they must both have been produced—"

"By the same forger," I concurred easily. "If this author really is a modern invention, that would point to the rest being suspect."

"Oh!" Tuccia went pink, perhaps with excitement. "Will it help you find the people responsible, Albia?"

"The criminals?" I deliberately called them that. "I doubt it," I thought best to say. "These scroll-producers seem extremely clever. They leave no clues as to their identity. I imagine they are proud of their concealment processes. Mind you," I added inconsequentially, "I do have a witness who once watched them digging at the Grove of the Caesars."

Wide-eyed, Tuccia squealed, "Ooh! Caught in the act. So, does that mean your witness will be able to identify them? Who was it?"

"Best not to say," I murmured, not least because I regarded the witness, Rullius, as suspicious himself. Never mind protecting my sources; if he was telling the truth about the two diggers, I did not want anybody getting to Rullius to pay him off. "Remember, your shop is somewhat suspect!" I aimed at Tuccia, though without direct evidence I was not threatening her too heavily. She giggled, seeming to find this a game. I wanted to snap her out of that. "You need to be careful, it seems to me."

"Oh, get away! It is not us." She appeared to think she and I were giggling together, the way we had done the first time we met. She had not noticed my attitude had changed. Tuccia heaved a mighty sigh. "Oh, Albia, I wish I had your job. It must be so interesting!"

"What about yours?" I returned, genuinely curious. "You work with literature; you love to read. You meet a variety of people, you have challenges daily. You are a woman in charge. I get the impression you were thrilled to have taken over the shop. Weren't you glad to inherit from Mysticus?"

"Oh, yes," Tuccia admitted. "I cannot deny that. The circumstances were sad, but I wanted it more than anything. I love being the owner—I love finding works for customers. I even love commerce. Some dealers shy away from that, but I revel in both buying and selling. And, of course, people will always want books. I am now secure for life."

"Nothing beats security," I agreed. "Mind you, if you think my life looks exciting you need to know we informers traditionally deplore our precarious income, our dubious clients and the wild uncertainty of our survival!"

I excused myself, went to use the facilities, washed my face, holding the linen towel to my skin with closed eyes, then came out to ask Gratus to bring refreshments.

"More relaxed now, are we, madam?"

"Cheeky!" In fact, I found talking to Tuccia draining. We could have had a lot in common, but she was as slippery as wet seaweed. Something about her made it now impossible to take her at face value—and that meant I could no longer like her.

Tuccia and I shared a slipware saucer of small almond cakes while sipping mint tea. Over in a corner, Suza and Marcia had equipped themselves with cushions, the fancy ones that I liked to keep out of the sun; they were lolling with a platter of treats while they waited for me to be available. Fornix kept carrying out a selection of herb drinks for the shameless sunbathers to try. I shifted position on my bench, so I need not see them.

Two painters who had taken to working here strolled through the courtyard. Since I had paused with my mouth full, they broke in to say they had heard mention of black and white, so I had better understand that if I wanted a decoration scheme with a black salon and matching white one, which was up-to-date sharp fashion, it came very expensive. I told them off for listening in, so they wandered back to the upstairs balcony where they made as much racket as possible.

Gratus came and cleared, taking away the dish of fancies even though there were two left. He also carried off our cups, without offering refills.

"You wanted the other cakes, didn't you?" Tuccia asked, nodding after the steward.

I smiled gently, though I disliked the way she must have been watching me. That kind of close observation was supposed to be my job.

"So, are you planning to investigate the scroll-forgers?" she quizzed me.

"Probably not." I gave her a straight look. "Not free right now. I am very busy on another case for a paying client. I don't have the resources for two searches. Besides, not much point, is there? Where's anyone to hire me? The scrolls I found were never offered for sale. If there has been no material loss, an informer has no one to prosecute."

"Oh!" Tuccia considered this, her mouth a tiny pinched roundel in her always slightly immature face. "Do you take people to court, Albia?"

"I have done." I had to use a male intermediary, which was a pain. I preferred other types of work.

"So, what will you do with the scrolls, Albia?" Tuccia asked obsessively.

"The scrolls? Sell them at auction, clearly labelled as unreliable."

She twinkled mischievously. "So, you have no qualms about benefiting from something that was created with fraudulent intent?"

I twinkled back, though it was my turn to scrutinise her. Pale skin, small nose and chin, somehow untouched by real life—or unresponsive to it. "No qualms at all. We found them. Nobody will come forward to claim them; they can't do so without admitting guilt. And so," I added sweetly, "I may as well benefit myself!"

At that point, a messenger came to our house from Cluventius. He had people with him who knew something about the garden killings. Tuccia took it as a chance to leave, seeming relieved to escape. I told my cousin Marcia that if she wanted to talk she had better come along with me.

XXXIX

Marcia was the daughter of my father's older brother, a soldier who had died before she was born. Her mother, the fabled Marina, who still survived, had been extremely beautiful. She was bright enough to have latched on to the Didius family with never-failing pincers, pleading for money. Cruelly for both, Marina was now losing her grip on reality.

Marcia, a looker herself, had recently escaped her home responsibilities via a fast-paced love affair with a man called Corellius. He worked for the Palace's secret service; he ran a diplomatic house where he spied on visiting ambassadors. Marcia had joined him "to help with housekeeping." Her mother was cared for by a nurse; I suspected my father paid for it. Marina was no trouble so long as the nurse kept the door locked so she could not wander off.

But as swiftly as Marcia and Corellius had fallen for each other, their affair had disintegrated. Now he had been abruptly posted abroad. Marcia thought he might have asked for the move. She had had to leave their diplomatic quarters.

"That's a shame." I had thought they were good together. "Will he come back?"

"He might." Marcia was pretending to brush this off, though, like all unhappy lovers, she was absorbed in her shattered relationship. "I simply cannot go back to the apartment with Mother."

"So where, then?" I asked, with foreboding.

"Your house? I need a lot of space where I can stomp around cursing him."

We had space. "We have no beds." We had a few.

"I can help you shop for furniture." This was like having an extra sister. "Albia, don't make me live at home. She was driving me nuts and it's just too sad to watch as she deteriorates. She drinks. She smells. She keeps getting out and bothering strange men."

"Your mother always bothered strange men."

"Yes, but in the old days they liked it."

"How long has Corellius gone away for?"

"A month."

That was not too bad, I told myself.

As we walked, I outlined my two casework problems. These should take anyone's mind off a broken heart. "They could be linked," suggested Marcia, easily hooked in. "The scroll-forger may be the Pest. Every time he goes to bury a load of phoney literature, he grabs a woman."

"Too many flaws." I rejected it. "A witness saw a man and a woman burying the scrolls. But that was recent; the killer has been operating for years. According to Tuccia, fakes never happened before, not until Mysticus was fooled."

"She lies," declared Marcia. A woman of rapid judgements—but I had worked with her before, often startled by her astuteness. Occasionally it would be suggested that Uncle Festus might not really have been her father, only for Marcia to say something needle-sharp, which proved she was one of the quick-witted Didii. She also had the madcap dark curls and raunchy humour. She was theirs all right.

"You took against Tuccia?"

My cousin sniffed, an oratorical ploy. "I'm surprised you can be fooled by a mould-coloured stole and a spotty snood. Don't annoy that one; I bet she broods. Get on her wrong side and months later, she'll put a dead rat under your mattress."

"I tend to agree!"

"Do you really think she forged those scrolls, Albia?"

"Conceivably. First, she has the right staff to make the goods and second, she herself has studied enough to produce the creative writing. I believe she would actively enjoy the task."

"I can't stand her," declared Marcia. "That hideous 'Poor little me, what do I know? I wasn't there in those days' act, when she's as quick as mercury."

I chuckled. "You were listening, then?"

"Flavia Albia, I have no interest in your pitiful earrings collection or in palling up with your maid. She's just a dim girl from the coast with a big bust and mediocre ideas."

"You are so rude!" I had always loved Cousin Marcia—precisely for that reason.

"It's a knack. Of course I was listening! Tuccia came to find out what you know. I was on to her. You and I can work together against her, can't we? So is it settled that I'm staying?"

I said Marcia could live at our house if she didn't whine about losing Corellius and as long as she helped with my work.

"Oh, I will! I need to haul you out of Tuccia's clutches. Face it, Albia, you wanted to be giggly with her because you don't have any female friends. Any woman who runs her own business appeals to you, however big a crook she is. Well, now you have me instead."

"Thank you, darling," I said meekly. "But you are staff, Marciana. I am in charge. Don't push it."

She snorted.

At the Cluventius apartment we were to meet two witnesses. First, we faced the usual situation where my client, though a tragic recent widower, immediately noticed that my chaperone-cum-assistant was a very striking woman. Then his adult son, though barely past puberty, came in and stared. Finally, the male party in the new witness duo had a good look at Marcia too.

Men are not simply attracted to beauty. They sniff out character; they cannot cope when they get it, but the allure is there. Marcia was super-intelligent, highly demanding of her partners, and stroppy with absolutely everyone. In addition, she went to boxing lessons. One wrong move, she could break teeth. This was not immediately obvious to the men who noticed her good looks, but some later found out. That was fun.

Luckily, Marcia, bereft of Corellius, never registered today's droolers. They could moon all they wanted: she was in her own world. Her lover not only had an intriguing past, an exciting role as a spy for the Empire and even an interesting limp, he could also price wet fish and mend shutters. I understood why she was smitten, for these useful traits are what a woman needs. Marcia's indifference to anybody else would probably continue for at least a week.

So, to work.

Cluventius allowed me to interview the witnesses in private in a small room at his apartment. They were the husband and mother of a previous victim of the Caesar's Gardens killer. She, Methe, had disappeared five years ago. They had never found out what happened although, because of the other victims, they had guessed. Knowing about Victoria Tertia, this pair had come today to express fellow-feeling for the family. Cluventius might have felt more bemused than grateful, but he had kept them there, saying they ought to talk to me; he made them wait until I came. After greeting Marcia and me, he left us alone to talk.

The couple said Methe had been a wonderful girl, loving, hard-working, good-tempered and, according to them, beautiful. Marcia and I took that to mean she had a good nature and they had forgotten any faults.

The husband admitted, not too shame-faced, that Methe used to go out to earn a few coppers when his income as a freelance carrier was not making ends meet; he had his own cart but needed to hire a mule to pull it. Her mother had come to live with them: another mouth to feed. He knew what his wife did on those nights. He said he had never liked it, but what else could they do? One night, she just never returned.

The husband had let the mother-in-law stay on afterwards, so he was not all bad. Hardly bad at all, by most standards.

The couple hoped the newfound bones might be their missing one. Karus, they told me, had found details of Methe's loss in case-notes so that morning he had come to them at home to discuss the find. At least he was following up on old reports—and doing it effectively, it seemed. He asked questions about Methe's height and build, whether she had had all her teeth or had ever suffered broken bones, even whether she was pregnant when she disappeared. He was going to let her relations know if anything in his investigation identified her.

"This is good, isn't it?" her mother pleaded. "It may help us learn what happened to her."

"It may." I was guarded. I knew how many other victims there had been. "Did he ask whether Methe wore jewellery?"

"No, he didn't."

"Well, tell us, then." Marcia, an abrasive assistant, came across as so crisp she was like laundry left in the sun too long. "What did she have on that day?"

I had seen a lot of this with the Didii. Love was always shattering their worlds. Then they were bad-tempered. Unaware of the reason, our witnesses seemed to take Marcia's grouchiness as efficiency. By comparison, I must have seemed too soft to be any use.

Methe, they said, would have been wearing her snake bangle. They described it as like thousands of other snake bangles, a double coil of cheap metal around the wrist, originally with two tiny chips of glass glitter as eyes. If anyone ever found it, Methe's Cleopatra snake would be as horrid as all the rest in Rome, except hers had one of its eyes missing.

"We still miss her so much," her mother mourned. It sounded like a much-told tale, yet no less moving for that. Even Marcia fell quiet and tenderly took the poor woman's hand.

Years of grief showed in her lined face. Although the pair had spoken of hungry lives, she was heavily rounded, a woman who spent most of her day sitting, unhealthily immobile, while she fretted over her lost daughter. "We think about her all the time, wondering what could have happened to her. Every day I have a little talk to her, as if she was with me. Not knowing the truth is the hardest part. I want to find her and fetch her back."

Her son-in-law nodded. He spoke little but hung his head with a pained expression as if on the verge of tears. This did not come across as false; he was sincerely at a loss as to how to show his pain to other people or internally cope with it.

I let them talk about the day Methe went missing. They spoke vividly of their fears that they might never know what she had had to endure or where her body lay. I promised that everything possible was being done, with revived interest from the vigiles. Karus, the specialist agent, had been assigned for extra muscle, while I too would monitor what happened.

Afterwards, as Marcia and I walked home together, my cousin was quiet for some time. Finally, she piped up, "We have to do something. We need to try to lure this man out. He will have seen you in the gardens, but he won't know me, or won't know that I am connected to you. I ought to go and walk about there, when it's getting dark."

"Absolutely not!" I said.

Marcia supposed she would end up doing it anyway. She was quite surprised, not at me saying no so fast, but that I kept saying no and I meant it.

XL

The use of a decoy had been discussed in my family on other occasions. It had been considered during investigations my father or I had run as informers, or when my uncle was investigating officially. We never did it. The idea was always rejected as too dangerous. Far too many things could go wrong: either the female lure might not be able to fight off the criminal or the observers who were supposed to keep her safe might fail to intervene in time. The villain could never be relied on to turn up where the decoy was or, if he did, he would spot the set-up and retreat.

"I can be careful, Albia."

"You won't have to. You are not to do it."

"How the hell shall we catch him then?"

"Meticulous casework."

"Oh, right! Like that agent asking whether Methe had all her teeth left and was she pregnant?"

"Karus is awful, but not an idiot." I was forced to defend him, since I knew his reasoning. "Listen, I couldn't tell her mother and husband he asked those questions because he is now in a position to count the teeth that are grinning out of a festering skull they dug up this morning. Maybe there were tiny little bones from a foetus inside that skeleton, like another corpse I once investigated. I couldn't say that, Marcia Didia—nor tell them how today I saw what might have been their own darling, collected up by the vigiles then stuck in a big old dung bucket on a filthy cart."

Marcia quietened down. Even so, she muttered, "I still think I should do it."

My father, with whom she had always been a favourite, would kill me if I let her.

Still combative, we kept walking along the Vicus Armilustrium in silence. Then a male voice behind us called our names. Perhaps tense after discussing the decoy idea, we turned more nervously than usual. But it was Methe's husband.

His name, we knew, was Seius. In his thirties, half bald already, all stubble and wheeze. His bulky mother-in-law was too slow, so he came hurrying after us alone. Standing outside a trinket shop, he explained: after we had left, he and she had had a conversation, concluding there was information he ought to pass on.

It was not about Methe. "You put up a notice?" He told us that he always looked at communiqués fixed to trees, in case they related to his lost wife. He had seen Karus's appeal for information, but he wanted to discuss my own small poster about our missing boys. To my annoyance he told me it was no longer there. "The gardeners take them down."

I stiffened. "Are you sure it is gardeners?"

"Seen it happen."

"Any particular gardener?"

"I couldn't say."

That was a pity.

I asked what was bothering him. Seius looked awkward, then said there was a problem. Keeping calm, I said, "Tell me what." Marcia assured him I could be very understanding. I tried to look like someone with that quality, though it's one of many that I scorn.

Seius, it seemed, was sometimes given piecework when Caesar's Gardens produced more waste than the gardeners' own beaten-up pony could haul away. I admitted I was aware that heavy loads of rubble from dismantling the old cave had been added by our men. Seius had helped remove this. Now that he said so, I thought I remembered Larcius mentioning him.

"Nothing wrong with you helping out, surely?" demanded Marcia.

He was still reluctant, but confessed he knew someone who wanted the larger pieces of stone. Apparently, the friend gave small payments to Seius. This private arrangement now embarrassed him. I saw no reason to object. I already knew that scavengers had been rifling through our rubbish piles, with Larcius willing to let them. It was only rock. It had no resale value for us.

Once we were clear on that, Seius relaxed and told me that while he had been ferrying our refuse, he had come across Primulus and Galanthus in Caesar's Gardens. One was limping, while he hauled along his brother, in an even worse condition. They looked so pathetic he gave them a lift on his cart, out through the Portuensis Gate on the far side of the Transtiberina, then a short way down the road towards Portus. When he stopped to offload, they disappeared. If I wanted to come across the river, he could show me where.

We went, of course. First Seius picked up his cart, along with his mother-in-law, patiently seated in it. Marcia and I let her stay alongside Seius on the driving seat, while we sat on the back with our legs swinging. In theory it was easier than walking, though by the end we had stopped laughing. We were hurled about like badly tied-down cargo.

At one point, on the other side and near some riverbank warehouses, Seius dropped off his mother-in-law so she could go home. We passed out under the Portuensis Gate. I started to feel apprehensive because I knew this road divided about a mile beyond the city, with one branch heading off into quite hilly, empty country. We had made no attempt to find out how far we were to be taken. I even muttered to my cousin that we were like a couple of daft girls, blithely allowing ourselves to be hijacked by someone who might intend us harm.

"*But he seemed so nice!*" lisped Marcia. "*We never thought he could be like that!*"

We had told no one where we were going, or with whom. Only Seius and his mother-in-law knew. She was an unknown quantity, but definitely owed him favours. Would that include ignoring a habit of preying on women? As the cart rattled on, I miserably cursed myself as gullible, while I wondered if Seius, with his convenient work as a carrier, might be the killer . . .

This is the curse of long-term violence. It causes loss of trust in society.

It impacts on freedom of movement, particularly women's. Perfectly decent people come under wrongful suspicion when they try to help others. Perfectly sensible people are gripped by unnecessary fear.

As we rode out, I realised how much land Julius Caesar must have owned. His Transtiberina gardens covered a large acreage within the modern city boundary, yet they extended out beyond the gate, too, along the road to Portus. I had never really considered this previously. When my family went to the coast we generally used the left-bank route, on the Via Ostiensis. Yet here we were, still among extensive beds and features, once owned by the mighty Julius—therefore still tended by official gardeners.

When at last we reached what Seius said was our destination, Marcia and I were so stiff, we could barely climb down. Seius had behaved politely throughout. I no longer feared for our safety, although I did suspect this might have been a wasted journey.

The Via Portuensis, like all major routes out of the city, has tombs stationed along it. Seius had brought us to where his mate, the one who wanted the stones, was building a wall around a garden at a mausoleum. The place had some similarity to the family tomb at Fidenae where we had placed the ashes of Tiberius's sister. This was built as a small columbarium that must contain a couple of short rows of niches for urns of ashes, maybe two rows of five each side. It was designed like a miniature temple, with a triangular pediment over the lowish doorway. Adjacent was a kitchen garden, and pear, cherry and walnut trees. A blackbird warbled his territorial challenge from somewhere high up. The tomb guardian was creating a dry-stone wall to mark out the boundary. We were told he intended to inhabit the wall with land snails, an extra food source.

He went into a huddle with Seius, both clearly still nervous that we knew they had taken the site material. Marcia went across to reassure them we had no interest in old rocks. I heard the friend tell her he had seen nothing of our runaways. Presumably they had jumped off the cart unnoticed, so they must have travelled on farther down the road. But he never saw them and had not heard any mention from neighbours.

We had come the distance so I looked around anyway. It was me, therefore, who investigated a little toolshed. I could see only spades, hoes and shears, though at the back was a low pile of sacking. Something else dramatically caught my attention. Large numbers of flies were zooming about. There was a gruesome smell. The tomb guardian, busy with his wall and so not using his gardening tools, must have missed the fact that recently his shed had had occupants.

"Primulus," I murmured into the warm, humming darkness. At the thought they were ever here, I went into shock. I recognised that sickly odour. We were about to uncover horror. "Galanthus. It's me, Flavia Albia."

I thought calling was pointless. Then I saw a slight movement; my heart throbbed with panic. Someone whimpered. Afraid of entering the shed, I shouted to the others to help me.

Under the sacks were both my missing boys. Galanthus was brought out first. Seius gently pulled him from the shed. He was filthy, starved, terrified, unable to stand, unable to speak coherently. He began spilling tears as he was laid on the ground outside, shielding his eyes from the light.

Inside the shed, I heard the tomb guardian exclaim. Gingerly he towed something out, using a sack. We all recoiled. Primulus was dead. He might already have been dead when Galanthus was first seen carrying him around.

For four days, Galanthus had been crying here, alone in the dark with the corpse.

XLI

G alanthus, you are safe. It's all over. We are here. We have come to take you home."

"No one bad will hurt you." Marcia understood, even though she might not realise the significance of the deep mark on the boy's neck, where I knew someone must have wrenched away his amulet. "He cannot harm you. We won't let him."

The boys must have met the killer. He had grabbed them. He presumably intended to kill them; he had certainly taken trophies. He must have been responsible for Primulus eventually dying, even though for some reason he had let them escape. Galanthus was too traumatised to tell us.

The men reacted faster than I expected. I did not have to ask for help. Perhaps the loss of Methe gave them a greater feeling for the boys' plight, but they were basically good people. Having known trouble themselves, they did not hesitate.

Two things were decided. Galanthus became highly agitated when he thought he might have to go back through Caesar's Gardens on the cart. Seius would find someone known to him who ferried goods across the river; they would take Galanthus home by boat instead. Seius hurried off to organise this.

While he was gone, the guardian offered to me that, if he was paid a small amount to cover fuel, he would cremate the body here. He would find a niche for Primulus within this garden tomb. I had come out with money; I gave him all I had, promising more.

I made a quick scan of the body, which was already decomposing.

The dead boy was still clothed but he, too, had lost his amulet. I could not tell whatever else had been done to him.

On the whole I am not squeamish. It was horrible even to look at the corpse. The distinct smell of human putrefaction is unforgettable; to have known the deceased makes you gag even more. The horror would stay with me.

While his brother's pyre was being built, we did our best to save the survivor. Galanthus was stripped of his own stinking garments, wrapped in an old man-sized tunic, then carried by Seius to the wharf. Among the many laden riverboats that are towed up from the coast, smaller vessels nip like flies. Gigs surged under oar. Sail-rigged shallops dragged in endless tacks under the infinitesimal Tiber breezes. Seius had brought us to a man with a small dinghy. He stepped aboard, still carrying the boy. Marcia clambered in with them.

I waved them off, urging them to hurry, then stayed to see the pathetic corpse of Primulus start on its final journey. Sweet herbs from the garden were strewn on the small funeral pyre. The guardian brought me winter flowers to lay beside the body. For the second time in less than a week I stood listening to the crackle of a funeral fire, lost in drear thoughts.

The dancing boys looked about twelve, so Primulus had still been a child. Others had corrupted him in the past, but I took responsibility now. I had barely known him, yet my sadness began with what any good mistress would feel for her slave, dying so young and so terribly. From my own past life as a street child arose deep pity for his fears and his lack of love. I grieved that I had not been able to provide him with better.

I stayed until the flames died. The tomb guardian found me an old terracotta pot. It had a rough surface and a large chip out of the rim but was suitable. I collected the few ashes into this simple container. We placed the pot in an unused compartment inside the tomb. I was told that the family who had built it were generous; nobody would object to their ancestors being joined by one more sad little spirit.

I promised to have a plaque made: "To Primulus from his brother Galanthus." This presumed that his brother survived.

———

It was the end of the day. The guardian drove me to where Seius lived near the city gate, in order to return the cart for him. He offered to escort me on my way, but he had done enough. I bade him farewell. Then I was by myself at last.

My journey home would be on foot. I had to go to the Sublician Bridge, crossing Caesar's Gardens first. No one else was about. I was on my own. Larcius and the men would have left for home, unaware I was in the area. Twilight was gathering.

It became difficult to see very far. If anyone was lurking behind arbours or trees, I would not detect his presence until he chose to step out. Birds had stopped singing; there were no hunting owls. I found my way along dark, silent paths where most people would have been deeply apprehensive.

I felt no fear that evening. I walked steadily, my head bare and all my senses alert. I was watching, listening, aware of every breeze or twitch of a leaf; I might have caught even the faint throb of a moth's wings. My jaw set and my heart was on fire.

It might have been stupid to walk alone but I made my own safety. I walked with a purpose that would have been a warning not to interfere with me.

Let him come. Such men are cowards. They rely on surprise and violence. They find their power in fear. Seeking vulnerable victims, this man would not touch me.

I was ready, though. If the pervert had been brave enough to strike, I was so angry about my boys, I would have taken him on. And I believe I would have killed him.

XLII

He might have been there. I never saw him. Quite right, you abomi-nation: don't risk it.

I crossed back on the narrow Sublician Bridge, fighting for space with pack animals. I found Serenus waiting for me at the Aventine end. After Marcia had reached home and told of our adventure, he had come out with a lantern. As soon as we met, he called up a commercial chair, so I was able to have my weary bones carried up the steep slope to our street. All around I heard people behaving crazily as they convinced themselves, far too early, that Saturnalia had begun.

Once home, I hurried indoors. The ground floor was lit to welcome me. Gratus appeared, finger to lips. He pointed to a corner of the court-yard where, in the glow of an oil lamp, I saw an unexpected sight. Curled up on what I recognised as Dromo's sleep-mat I made out our rescued boy. Someone had him wrapped in a blanket. In front of him squatted Dromo. He had a bowl in one hand, from which he was feeding Galan-thus with broth off a small spoon, a mouthful at a time, making him wait between each one. His gestures were as firm as those of a parental bird poking food into a chick's beak.

"The lad was starved almost to death," Gratus murmured. "Fornix gave him soup, he wolfed it, but after so long unfed, it exploded out of him. Dromo decided of his own accord to fetch a bucket. He got him washed and even cut his hair. Now he has taken over. For some reason the boy lets him."

I nodded, less amazed. This was why Tiberius never got rid of

Dromo: on the verge of driving us completely wild, that daft lump would occasionally startle us with his soft heart. He was a few years older than Galanthus, giving him senior's rights. And anyone helpless would make him passionate on their behalf. I had seen it before when he was moved by a tragic story. People are complex, so why not slaves too?

I sat in the courtyard, resting. It was peaceful for once. Marcia had gone out. After she delivered Galanthus, she had taken it upon herself to remove the scrolls, transferring them to my parents' house ready for Father to auction them. Suza, my maid, Marcia's new friend, had gone along to help. I had no energy to worry about them being out at night. In any case, Mother might make them stay over.

Eventually Galanthus fell asleep. Dromo came across to me with the soup bowl. Barley walked up to look at him appealingly, but once she saw Dromo diving in she knew better than to wait. "I had better eat this up. We don't want waste."

"No! Well done, Dromo. You are looking after the poor lad so kindly." Dromo was lapping noisily. "Has he said anything about what happened to him?"

"He just shivers. Something has driven him crazy."

"Yes, something horrible must have happened. When he settles, he may talk to you. He is very, very frightened, but you seem to have won his trust."

"It's up to me, then!" Dromo had his mix of self-assurance and complacency.

"Yes, it may well be. I want to catch whoever did this. Anything you can gently find out from him may help me."

"This is important."

"Extremely important. Don't bombard him with questions, just encourage him to tell you what he remembers. See if you can tice out his terrible adventure."

"Like when you ask people questions?"

"Yes, Dromo."

Dromo liked that.

"Where has the other one gone?" he demanded abruptly.

No one had told him yet. I decided to be straight. "This is not nice,

I'm afraid. Primulus is dead, Dromo. The reason I came home later than the others is that I made sure he had a funeral."

"Was he murdered?"

"Yes, I believe he was."

"Did Galanthus kill him?"

What?

"No, I am sure he did not. From what I can tell, Galanthus was attacked too, though not hurt so badly. He tried to rescue his brother, but he could not save him."

"He's got a huge lump on the back of his head," Dromo told me suddenly. His pudgy face was serious. All this mattered to him, particularly his own role in it. "I saw the lump when I was washing his hair. Part was bleeding because of washing him, but I wasn't rough."

"No, of course."

"I'm a good body slave. I know how to do cleaning. I had to—the condition he was in was disgusting. Fornix gave me some stuff to put on the cut. That stopped it."

Dromo handed me the empty bowl and well-licked spoon. "I've finished. Now I shall go over there and stay by him. You'd better not need me for anything else. I need to watch whether he's all right. If he wakes up frightened, I can tell him not to be."

"You are such a good person. I shall tell your master all you have done. He will be very proud of you."

"Yes, I expect he will. Oh—I remember something. When I found that lump on his head, I asked how he got it. He only cried out, 'The man!' Then he went all sobbing and scared again."

"That's the kind of detail I'd like you to prise out, if you can, Dromo. Can you try getting him to say what man it was?"

"I expect I can do that."

"Do your best. Galanthus is on your mat, I see. Do you want me to find you another one?"

"No, thank you. I'll just squash on there with him. Then it will be easier to look after him if he's crying."

So, Dromo returned to his charge. Barley, who must be a kind-hearted dog, went over and lay down with them.

I went to the kitchen, where Gratus and Fornix fussed over me. I was ready to have other people take command, though I wished it was Tiberius.

That night I left my bedroom door open onto the upper balcony. I could only sleep lightly. From time to time I heard Galanthus start awake and begin mithering. Dromo would talk to him. As I listened to make sure I wasn't needed, his dull voice and his banal observations sounded comforting.

Gratus had a room on the other side of the balcony; at one point I heard a creak from the folding door, as if he, too, was monitoring the scene below. He normally put out all the lamps, to save oil and prevent fires. Tonight he had left a small one down there with them. So, for the first time after his ordeal, Galanthus was neither alone nor in the dark.

XLIII

Dromo did well. He looked after that traumatised lad as if a baby had been left with him. He could be heard like a grave little girl, muttering privately as she acted out domestic scenes with her precious doll. Galanthus was washed, combed, dressed in a patched tunic that Gratus found, fed his breakfast, given water. Most importantly, he was talked to. Intermittently, he seemed to answer.

The lads stayed in their corner, only moving when Dromo deemed it time to lead his charge to the latrine. Their voices were too low to hear. I left them to it. Even when Marcia came home, she stood back.

"Two days!" she announced.

"To what?"

"Selling your fake scrolls."

"Do I care?"

"You will, when I tell you Falco's auction estimates. Apparently the Didymus will get a huge boost from his previous notoriety, while nothing by Philadespoticus has ever appeared on sale before, so that's a fantastic draw."

I snorted. "I think we know why! He is rubbish."

"Exclusive and sought-after, that well-known dud category. Your mad father has convinced himself that works by well-known forgers sell for much more than the best originals. People love crime. He wants to invent a name for the faker, build him up, attract public awareness by saying his scrolls are contemporary masterpieces, antiques of the future. I concede that two days will be tight to achieve this fantasy. He's going to say, '*Look around today. Who is keenly watching progress on these lots? Perhaps the brilliant mind that created these exquisite scrolls is present in this portico . . .*' The best thing, Albia darling, will be if you can find the crook, have him sued for squillions and make him a celebrity."

"Added value." I knew how my father's mind worked. "Watch him go: '*I am seeking high hundreds here. Start me at a thousand, if you please!*' He's had me doing it on the podium before now."

"Me too. You know, he thinks a woman taking the sale enhances the bids. Will you go to the scroll auction?"

"Looks like I'll be too busy finding this murderer." To me, that was a damn sight more important.

Marcia shrugged. "By the by, Falco is saying 'he' for the famous faker, even though you and I think 'she.' He doesn't want it to be Tuccia. Forgery from a woman means less profit."

"I don't see why!"

"Oh, don't be stubborn, Albia. *Why* doesn't matter. Face up. Men make all the judgements. Men want men."

"You mean men have the cash? There is no reason at all why a woman cannot possess her own money, then use it for fine-art collecting. A woman may buy scrolls—either for her fancy library or, if she is really daring, so she can read them."

"Cynic."

"A woman can have taste and critical values."

"But this is Rome," my cousin argued. She managed not to say that I came from a dead-end province, therefore had no idea. "Men form the opinions, especially daft ones. If someone buys your scrolls *because* they are fakes," said Marcia, "that idiot will be male, believe me. A pompous, conniving, thinks-he's-artistic male snob who follows all the other sheep when buying."

"Some men are decent!" I argued back. Even if a woman had really created the scrolls, I said she would be somebody who understood male buyers. Marcia did not disagree with that.

"Albia, I'm going to visit the Writers' Guild to see if they have any-one who might be capable of plagiarising philosophy."

"They don't. Only no-hopers and has-beens bother with the Guild.

They'll either run away, scared witless because you're female, or leer and grope you. Do what you want."

We stopped wrangling. Marcia posed herself with her head covered, enjoying how miserable she was, crazily yearning for her lover. She did not even know where Corellius had gone. If he really was trying to dodge her, I suggested the escapee had kept quiet about his destination because otherwise she would pack a bag and follow him. That went down well.

I skulked off to my room, where I wrote a sad letter to my husband.

Around mid-morning, Dromo barged in to declaim that, due to his skill as an interviewer, Galanthus had told him everything.

"Everything" turned out to be little more than the sequence I had guessed, yet better than nothing.

On the night of the Cluventius party, the two boys had tried to gate-crash. After they were swiftly expelled, they hung around within ear-shot of the music. They continued to entertain themselves with moves they knew. Any watching pervert would have seen them: two louche, long-haired, unsettlingly beautiful young boys, sinuously dancing.

They hid when they saw Victoria Tertia. They watched a man stalk her, rush her and grab her. In horror, they watched everything he did to her. Dromo was embarrassed to say; I told him to skip it.

They knew who Victoria was because they had seen her at her hus-band's party. While the killer went deep into the trees, they were too scared to move, only discussing in whispers what they ought to do; they had had such a rollicking from the ushers they dared not return to report what they had seen.

When the man came back from depositing the body, he must have returned very quietly. They never heard him. He hit them both with something heavy, something like a boulder. Galanthus passed out. When he came round, bloodied, he saw the man trying to strangle Primulus.

Galanthus threw himself on the man, biting and kicking him. As dancers they were quite athletic, so somehow he and Primulus, who was just about alive, fought off their attacker. They must have shocked him into loosening his hold, unable to control two of them simultaneously. They managed to escape into the dark.

They heard him blundering about, trying to find them. They hid in undergrowth all night. Primulus was in a bad condition; he could barely breathe.

Next day, Primulus's condition deteriorated. Galanthus carried him. He saw the vigiles but was afraid to approach them. He managed to find our site, but Larcius was missing and two strange men angrily sent him away. Terrified that the killer was in the gardens still looking for them, they wandered until Seius came past them in his cart. He let them ride along. When he stopped, Galanthus hauled his brother off the cart, found the tomb guardian's shed, secretly crept in and hid.

His brother never spoke again. Galanthus thought he had died the first night. He then did not know what to do, whom to trust, or whether the terrible man who had attacked them would follow and find them. He thought that he, too, would die. Even now that he was back with us, Galanthus was terrified the man would come for him.

"Will he?" Dromo asked me apprehensively.

I said that we must keep Galanthus safe. Even if I could catch the man, the poor boy would remain afraid for the rest of his life. The nightmares might fade slowly, but his terror would not leave him. The man had taken the boys' amulets, which seemed to make Galanthus, and also Dromo, feel he had acquired a permanent hold over them. Galanthus thought he was coming to finish what he had started. That might be true; I knew the killer would want to silence his surviving witness.

After discussion with Marcia, I decided what to do. Paris had left for Fidenae, but I sent my intelligent steward and burly cook as bodyguards. Wrapped up so he looked like a delivery sack, Galanthus was put on Dromo's handcart then wheeled down the hill to my parents' house. Marcia went to explain. My mother would take care of the boy. Feed him, soothe him, have her doctor look at his head, assess him mentally.

"She'll say, 'Another of Albia's strays!' like she did when she came here one day and met Suza," Dromo informed me. "Can I stay there too and be looked after?"

"No. You must come straight back and lurk around here."

"Why? Am I pretending to be him?"

Marcia gave me a tart look. "*Decoy!*" Yes, I would be using Dromo, making him bait, just as I had said we would never do because it was too dangerous. To most people one slave is indistinguishable from another. If the man came looking, he might suppose we had the right boy at the house. All we had to do was keep the door locked. Dromo would be safe. "Well, he's just a slave, isn't he, Albia!" my cousin sniffed.

"He is our slave and we shall protect him." I hoped that was true.

I was anxious for Galanthus, too. Another thing I now had to decide might force me to put him in the way of the authorities. It was: would I tell Julius Karus we had found our missing runaway—and that he was a key witness?

XLIV

I would have to tell Karus. I could see no other way forward.

The problem with Galanthus being a slave was that the law would distrust his evidence. To be used in a court, anything he said would have to be extracted formally under torture. This is a stupid aspect of procedure, which guarantees that slaves say what people want to hear. Because of it, they are often too scared to come forward with evidence in the first place.

I would never subject Galanthus to that. I would have objected even before the killer had put him in his current state. He was too young, and now too fragile, to withstand the hostile legal process. Even if the killer thought no slave would be used to testify, he would have one fear: he could not stop the rest of us acting on anything the boy remembered.

That, however, was limited to how the attacker had behaved. Although Galanthus had seen what was done to Victoria Tertia and the attack on his brother, I knew he was unable to identify the man responsible. It had been dark. He could give me no physical description; he had never seen a face. The man had never spoken. All Galanthus could say was that the killer was strong. His actions were swift and vicious. When he was chasing the boys, he was agile and determined. They had been very lucky to escape, because he knew his way around Caesar's Gardens and the Grove much better than they did. That in itself told us something about him.

Since Paris had left with my letter to Tiberius, Gratus took a message from me to the Seventh Cohort's station-house. Karus was out, so Ursus intercepted Gratus. It was Ursus that Gratus brought back with him.

The inquiry chief was chipper. He had pre-empted the despised imperial agent, gaining a meaty clue to follow up by himself. Of course he demanded to see Galanthus, but I managed to avoid that. I said the boy was too traumatised; he might clam up completely if faced with a scary official. The shaven-headed, big-eared Ursus, with his plodding feet and well-picked teeth, did not scare me, yet to a whimpering lad he would represent the oppressive side of life. For one thing, Ursus really liked the idea that people feared him.

He surveyed the house, gazing all around from our courtyard. "Nice place! How many families live here?" He assumed rooms and suites were rented out.

"Just one," I said. He whistled. "Plus a tribe of builders." The two painters were staring down from the balcony, as visual proof. Being nosy saved them having to paint. "And hangers-on." Marcia and Suza were giving each other manicures. They waved sweetly.

Who likes people to think they live extravagantly? I moved on swiftly to work.

Ursus had not brought his clerk. He scribbled notes for himself. "This is one of those lads you put up notices about?"

"Yes, when they first went missing. I understand our appeals have been taken down. By gardeners, said my witness." Ursus looked up from his note-tablet. "I suppose," I suggested slowly, "their story will be that they remove advertising for tidiness. I dare say bill-posting is not allowed." Ursus said nothing. Still, he sucked his lips as if in thought. I left him to absorb the point.

I described the killer's attacks and mentioned he had taken the lads' amulets. I had never looked at them closely, but Ursus, no jewellery specialist, was happy just to jot down "two neck charms." If trophies were ever discovered, there would be time enough to persuade Galanthus to identify the boys' property.

"Having these items back would do us," Ursus reassured me. "We wouldn't need your boy in court."

"He is not going to be put there. I say that right now. And no one gets to torture him."

"I can live with that, Flavia. You'll have to vouch for what he says." Ursus paused. "That is, I'll need your head of household. Where is he, incidentally?"

"Away. Family business. He has the wild idea it's safe to leave me here in charge. I'm sure you could put him straight on that madness!"

"Well, you seem to be managing all right on your own, Flavia," Ursus crushed me with patronising false praise. "Those painters could do with a boot up the arse, though. What do they think they are here for?"

"I believe they are discussing the philosophy of colour while a dado dries."

Ursus grunted. "He's an aedile, isn't he? The householder?"

"Until New Year. Then he reverts to ordinary hen-pecked husband . . . Let's get on, shall we?"

I wanted to discuss my theory about the killer living and working close to his field of action.

"Interesting. I can go along with that. Don't tell bloody Karus, because of the Naumachia. Karus is convinced this individual is a sailor . . ." Actually, Karus had claimed to me that this idea obsessed Ursus. I glimpsed tensions I could play on. Station-house investigator is a lonely job. Ursus might talk to me because he had to be aloof with his men: I did not look to him for promotion and he did not need me for support. I encouraged him to carry on decrying Karus: "He's had me looking at the salts for days."

"Pointless! You must be going crazy with it."

"Right. Then he decided it could be one of the ambient snack-sellers. Turned out they are more transient than anyone thinks. But every time I came up with a suspicious stuffed-vine-leaf vendor, he was just standing in for a cousin with a bad knee, normally lives in the Campagna and is shit useless for the case. His cousin's done the job since he was fifteen, but he's only eighteen now."

"Shitty ditto! Fast turnover?"

"You might imagine sausage-sellers are solid tykes who have done the job for ever."

"But they come and go?"

"Flit around like sand flies. Never in one place. My theory is they make so much money at it, they slide away on holiday and never come back."

Ursus and I were friends now. He was telling me jokes. Worse luck, they were as lousy as those your best buddy knows, the ones he regurgitates after too many drinks. At least your pal can burp amusingly. Ursus was too clean-cut and disciplined. He would rather give himself a hernia holding it in.

"I would expect gardens, and especially sacred groves, to be packed with deviants, Ursus?"

"Alibis. Deviants are clever. They always have someone to vouch that at any relevant time they were screwing a rent-boy, or drunk in a gutter, or locked up for pinching loincloths off washing lines. Either that, or someone gives me good gen about a character who behaves weirdly, only I then extract the awkward fact that he dropped dead three years ago."

"Don't you hate awkward facts?" I murmured.

Ursus careered on. "Next, old Karus persuaded himself it must be someone who uses Caesar's Gardens as his outdoor office. So why would he be there in the dark, which is when these bints are bumped off? Besides, can I find a man who has sat on a bench reading for the past two decades? Of course I can't. For one thing, anyone who tried it would have been mossed over long ago. Even statues don't stick around that long—they get nabbed by lovely homeowners for their peristyles." Ursus let his eyes wander around our home again. Fortunately, we had no statues. "Where did you get that bloody big urn with the octopus?" He had passed it in our atrium.

"Wedding present. So," I said, sticking to the task in hand, "everyone acknowledges that the killer knows the area, but I am not sure we have given that enough attention. He must live and work nearby. My uncle, ex–Fourth Cohort, had a theory about multiple murders. He'd draw an arc on a map, including all known disposal sites. Nine times in ten, the killer turned out to live within walking distance."

Ursus nodded. "Standard. You can see why. This sick bastard is constantly in the district and nobody queries him. He feels secure. He can scout for new victims, then jump back home fast after he does the foul deed. If we ever arrive to ask questions, he points to his dear old mother, who sweetly swears he's been there all the time with her. Sometimes if she's daft enough, she actually believes what she's saying."

"Then while sonny stays at home with Mother, says my uncle Petronius darkly, he can watch the local forces who are out trying to catch him."

"Oh, yes, this bug has got his eye on us!" Ursus sounded bleak. Pessimism was his favourite act. "He thinks we are going nowhere. He believes himself much cleverer than us. Too clever to be caught. He's probably working up to doing another woman right now, just to show everybody and himself that he is invincible."

"And isn't he?" I could be morose myself. Informers, on bad days, are the worst pessimists. We have a lot of bad days.

"No, he's bloody not. His time has come. I'm going to get him now," declared the Seventh's man. He dropped his voice. "If only so I can stuff bloody Karus!"

Ironically, that might be how this was solved. I had wondered if Karus would manage it—but perhaps it would be the other way around. The vigiles, who had never yet stirred themselves to take out this killer, might be driven into positive action by jealousy: jealousy of the incomer, the official favourite, the Palace scrutineer. To them, Julius Karus was a lousy imposition. He had no experience of day-to-day law enforcement. Until recently, he had never been to Rome—let alone lived with it year after year, learning all this city's grubby criminality, its stinking social perversions, its dreary, petty, uncontrollable theft and its vicious professional underworld.

The vigiles, if they chose to stand up for themselves, could master Karus. To catch the kind of individual we had at Caesar's Gardens, doing his foul deeds and dumping remains in the sacred Grove, required a specialism the red-tunics had neglected, yet they did own it. Now they would finish, do what was needed. Finally. Not to save women. Not to give survivors vengeance. Not even to impose justice on the man. But purely to stuff Karus.

"If this killer is really a bold one," I suggested, "he's probably had a drink with some of your lads."

Ursus did not take that amiss. "Trust me, I've got them looking out for anyone who asks too many questions about the case."

"I wonder if he has tried making friends with Karus?"

"Would he? Is he totally deranged?"

"No, perhaps not that unhinged."

"So—this lad of yours, who has gone all timid," Ursus mused. "Where have you got him?"

"Safe. But I won't tell anybody where."

"Fair enough." Finalising, Ursus flipped through his tablet pages. "So, you say Galanthus was hit on the head and he bled profusely?" This was unexpected. He took good notes.

"Yes, the clots were so bad, we had to cut off his hair."

"Something to go on," Ursus shared with me. "We may find the implement, and sonny may not have washed it."

With a smile, I told him he was thinking like Karus.

Without one, he told me what I could do with that statement.

I grinned and apologised.

He grinned back. He closed his tablet set. "So! Who do you think he is, Flavia Albia?"

I had firmed up a theory. "I think he is one of the gardeners. What about you?"

Ursus flexed his shoulders. Crunch time. He was open with me: "It is a grub from the gardens. I agree with that. I'm going to line them all up and take a proper look at them."

I decided to give him everything that might be useful: "From the little I have seen, the gardeners all have nasty tendencies, so the criminal could be any of them. Their superintendent is ineffectual and his workforce are crude. But," I said, "Galanthus said something about their escape. He went for the man, Ursus. If you come across the killer, look for distinguishing marks. They all carry scratches and casual wounds from their occupation. But if you can get to him soon enough, the one Galanthus fought off will have specific scars."

Ursus was sharp. When I first recited what the boy had said about his adventure, Ursus had paid attention. "Say no more, Flavia! I'll be going after the individual who has human bite marks."

XLV

Before he left, Ursus told me his plan. First, he would let out news in Caesar's Gardens that I had recovered a runaway, who was talking. "If I tell the super 'in confidence,' then on past form that cracked old cove will tell all his staff. The Pest will know. I'm going to send you a man. He'll stay here. Keep your doors and windows locked, then my man will jump on anyone who turns up looking for the squealer." He supplied me with what passed for a grin. "I'll see if I've got a man who can paint."

"Oh, thank you!"

"This place needs some attention." I so love visitors who criticise my home. "I hear you took on that Sosthenes, the waterworks designer."

"Who told you so?"

"Station-house gossip. He supposedly maintains our supply lines and cleans our big fountain. We'd rather do it ourselves, but they make us use Public Works."

"Is he any good? Or is that just what he tells everyone?"

"He can unblock a pipe. Well, he can hit it with a mallet and see what happens. If things are slack we watch him at work—it's a good laugh. You're having a tap on the Aqua Marcia."

"I am if I agree to it."

"Oh, I think Sosthenes has already had trenches dug. Lovely quality, the Marcia. Crystal. The Fourth up here are bloody lucky to be washing smuts off in that. And another thing," he mentioned, as unperturbed as if he was inspecting my fire buckets and knew I had to endure his spiel, "if ever you want another of those big octopus pots, I know someone who can knock one up for you. No one will ever believe it only came from his workshop yesterday."

Our *pithos,* with its smiley, writhing sea creature, was a fifteen-thousand-year-old masterpiece from ancient Crete, made by a fun-loving civilisation that no longer existed. A dear friend gave us the present so we didn't want to double up. Who needs to be obligated to the vigiles, anyway?

"Some big city houses have his stuff, and I believe his prices are reasonable." So, not only scrolls were being faked? Rome had craftsmen churning out "historic Greek artefacts' on a daily basis? I was too cynical to feel surprise.

"A pair would be more valuable, you know."

I was an auctioneer's daughter: I knew. I was sick of Ursus. I stood up to show him out. The man was so helpful, on so many fronts, I thought he would never take the hint and leave.

Despite my gritted teeth I thanked him, saying I would take his potter friend's name because my father might use his expertise. An auction house can never have too many contacts who know how to invisibly mend a cracked vase of enormous antiquity. Pa likes experts who can stick handles back on. Or make fine replacements. Handles to go with pots, or pots for handles. The words "work has been done to it" are the most regularly used by auctioneers, especially when dodging queries.

"I'll keep in touch, Flavia."

"Call me Albia." Call me by my proper name, you irritating deadbeat— or I'll kick you into the street without opening the door first.

"It has been very enjoyable talking to you." Ursus must have had a mother who taught him manners. Maybe the Seventh Cohort had acquired polish since the days when my relations all loathed them.

"I hope it's been a relief for you to get away from Karus. Maybe," I ventured, "if you do find a suspect, I could sit in on your interview?"

"No chance!"

Wrong, then. The Seventh had not changed. They were irretrievable, unhelpful donkey turds and always would be.

I bet he would have stolen my octopus pot, if he had had a handcart with him.

He winked. "Get those lead pipes ordered up so your hole in the road is backfilled before some citizen falls into it!"

Yes, there it was outside: a really dangerous deep hole. Sosthenes had dug us a trench. Tiberius Manlius was having a water feature. Dear gods, I hoped his sister's will had bequeathed us enough funds for it.

Note to self: ask Larcius who Tiberius likes to use as a pipe-supplier.

My cousin had gone out. She had taken my maid. As a lodger, Marcia Didia was unspeakable. No wonder Corellius had dumped her. She had only been here a day but was driving me wild with her impertinence. A broken heart was no excuse.

The girls came home to tell me they had been to the Temple of Minerva-on-the-Aventine, that holy dive where craft clubs congregate to pool funeral funds, hold rowdy banquets and get sick-in-the-street drunk. Most notorious was the Poets' Guild, now the incorporated Failed Authors' Conglomerate. No aristocratic authors who would become known to history were members. Rich patrons kept good authors in dinners and Sabine farms; decent writers didn't need a club of obnoxious peers. The temple mob was as awful as you'd expect from men who consistently fail to get their work published. I knew that. It was why I had not bothered to go.

Despite my warnings, Marcia had been surprised to find the scribblers she encountered all denied knowledge of forged scrolls, before offering wine to her and trying to look down her tunic. She would learn.

"How many received your super-trained uppercut?"

Marcia shuddered. "*So-o* ghastly! I couldn't find the energy to thrash them. Suza stood on the foot of one." Suza smiled sweetly, reminiscing. "He'll have broken toes. We told him to see it as research. The pain should help him write laments. *Where do you get your ideas from? Angry women.*"

So much for the scribblers. The would-bes had never heard of Epitynchanus or Philadespoticus. Only the poetess Thallusa had aroused any interest. This, we women at home agreed, was due to Sappho. She had ensured all female poets are seen as rampant lesbians, which the totally masculine Writers' Guild found thrilling. But none of them had ghost-written her supposed work. The old boys went gooey at the suggestion.

The Didymus Dodomos controversy was known to one of them, said Marcia. His doctor had forbidden him to drink wine, so he was half sober rather than three-quarters drunk like the rest. He knew Mysticus had been fooled by the fake scroll: he remembered that a man called Ovidius had almost bought it from him—and usefully, because the scribbler had tried to sell his own work to Ovidius, he knew where the litigious buyer lived.

"Is he really litigious, Marcia, or was it a one-off?"

"He tried to sue his barber once, for a bout of ringworm."

"Get anywhere?"

"Free shaves for a month as compensation."

"Oh, he's good!"

"I decided to come home and tell you, Albia. I told Suza we'd better not go without you."

They were right. I wanted to investigate this man myself, although I could not manage it any time soon. I had to berate Sosthenes for pre-empting me on the fountain, tell Larcius to order lead pipes since we were having a water supply whatever I said, sort out the self-willed painters, instruct Gratus that we were about to have vigiles protection and he, too, must look out for a pervert who might break in, hunting for Galanthus. Then write a letter to Tiberius, describing my day. Make it funny enough to lighten his sad heart, while not too detailed so he acquired new worries.

When the vigilis Ursus sent us from the Seventh arrived, Suza had whacked him with a besom before he had been in the house half an hour, but he bore her no ill will for it. He was built like a pigpen and, by their standards, taciturn. "This is nice! My chief said I'd like guarding you folk. I see you're having a wall fountain."

He reckoned his presence was now unnecessary. Julius Karus had arrested the Pest. "Sure it's the right man?" I was sceptical.

"Karus says so!" The vigilis spoke sourly. Then he winked. "Ursus thought you would be interested, Flavia. Knock three times and he'll let you into the station-house."

"What an offer!"

"If you're going to be living in her house, I advise you to call her Albia," commented Marcia. He looked surprised. Then he perked up as if he had just noticed my cousin was a beauty. I sighed.

Karus had put his suspect in isolation for a few hours to make him sweat. That never works. Later that afternoon, he intended to make the killer confess. I could observe his interrogation technique for myself, if I could get over the river by the time he started.

XLVI

There was a buzz at the station-house. This is bound to happen when a culprit is finally arrested for a notorious, decades-long series of crimes. Vigiles who would normally have slept during daylight hours had decided it was vital to untangle ropes in the yard. A few did not bother pretending to be busy, but stood around with their arms folded, just watching.

The suspect was called Quietus. This fact was not extracted by Karus, who had yet to appear. Having arrested his man and sent him in, he was still out looking for evidence—his idea of a good task sequence. The name had been asked by Ursus, so the clerk could complete today's arrest list. Ursus liked neat records. He and I stood surveying the man from the doorway of a holding-cell, while we agreed that Quietus was a nice peaceful name for a gardener.

I had met him before. It was no surprise.

This man had been in the group who had found Satia's body yesterday; he was the one who had boasted of spying on lovers when they were canoodling in arbours. That fitted. He certainly could be a killing pervert. But he would not be the only gardener who snooped on people *in flagrante*; I reckoned they all did it. His habit was indicative only. To me, not proof. But the special agent wanted easy answers.

Julius Karus arrived. He rattled the gates, then swept in with a small knot of his own men. He had about six today. The First Vardullorans, given the honorific title of Faithful Asturians, had been the governor's bodyguard in Britain when he was killed, presumably by Karus, on the Emperor's orders. These tough boys were then batch-granted citizenship, a rare treat. Any were free to follow Karus if the assignment as his hit-squad appealed.

The Varduli were a tribe in an area near the Atlantic coast of Spain; my husband was a rarity who had diligently looked them up. They were short, thickset men, unsmiling, who spoke only to each other and only in their own language.

As Karus approached the holding-cell, Quietus became anything but peaceful. He kicked off, causing uproar. Perhaps he had heard that when an officer goes into a cell with a suspect and closes the door, what happens will be uncivilised. He was expecting broken ribs.

Oddly enough, Karus responded. He snarled that he would talk to the necrophiliac swine outside, then. Let the process be public. I thought he wanted to show off to the Seventh or even, if he had noticed my presence, to me. Karus would be brutal. I wasn't expecting acumen and talent.

An Asturian dragged Quietus out through the portico and threw him onto a tiny low stool. Karus had a chair, which he used as a prop more often than a seat. Normally in Rome, you stand, I sit; this is the sign of my breeding and authority, compared to which you are dirt. You are the captive, doomed; I am the general, glorious. However, Karus preferred to loom over his suspect to dominate him.

In the one-sleeved brown tunic I had seen before, Quietus had rope-bound hands and was now barefoot. There were no signs that he had been knocked about already; he must know it could still happen. He had a long, narrow face, as if his antecedents had come from eastern Europe, but he spoke in the thick Rome dialect used by the lowest class. Leaving him to stew had not quelled him, and he failed to use the time to prepare a believable defence. But he wasn't bright; all he had to say was that he hadn't done it, which he kept doing even though no one had asked him yet. Even if true, that would never be enough.

Karus snapped orders to clear the yard. The Seventh's men sloped to their sleep cubicles, though left the doors wide open. Ursus and I went up the stone steps with them, remaining outside as observers on the second-floor walk-around. The Asturians stationed themselves in the exercise yard; they stayed very still, so all attention focused on their chief. Karus was protected, though everything about him said he could carry out his own thrashings.

Tackling a violent criminal with threats of equal violence might make sense to Karus, but I thought if Quietus was the Pest, it would be too familiar. He would know all about fear being in the mind.

"I am Julius Karus. I shall be asking you about the killing of women and boys in Caesar's Gardens." He hurled something onto the ground between them. "This is the billhook you were found mending today."

Leaning over the balcony rail, I could see it was a sharp blade, shorter and stouter than a sickle, with a vicious curved end. The garden variety was similar to many tools used in agriculture, or even the grappling hooks deployed in fires by the vigiles. This blade was still attached to its handle, where two metal flaps were folded to grip the wood, but the shaft itself was split, so badly it had snapped. Clean splinters indicated the break was recent.

Karus leaned in close. "You were covering up what it had been used for. I know, and you know, how the tool was broken." He ladled on more details: "You smashed it over the heads of the two dancing boys. There's blood here. It's their blood."

"It's mine!" protested Quietus, managing to stay fairly calm. "I got cut when the billhook broke on me."

"Don't talk!"

My uncle, Lucius Petronius, had taught me a few things about interviews. Aggression worsens your odds. It is hard enough to tell whether the suspect—or innocent witness—is tense because they really are a villain who needs to out-step you, or whether they are clean, but terrified of your accusations. Petro liked to be firm, yet to seem understanding and patient; he aimed to make them settle down, so they were more likely to tell him the truth.

Standards, as he loved to tell us bitterly, had slipped since Petro's day. "I'll tell you what happened," Karus declared. He was certain. His straight aim was to make the suspect agree with him. "I know what you are like, Quietus. The superintendent has been telling me all about you."

"He's an old idiot—"

"Silence! Berytus says you have worked in the gardens and the Grove of the Caesars for as long as bodies have been found. There are records. And you're filthy-minded, Quietus. What you enjoy isn't weeding or planting, it's sneaking up to watch couples engaged in copulation. When you get down on your knees, it's to spy on them through knotholes. You go with the whores who come to the gardens, or when you are not fornicating yourself, you watch what they do with other men. This unhealthy interest in grubby acts makes you my prime suspect."

Quietus protested. "I could never do those things he does."

"Don't deny the evidence."

I glanced at Ursus. As "evidence" the billhook proved nothing. In any case, Galanthus had said the boys were hit with something very heavy, which to me sounded different. Ursus kept his eye on the yard, but his face tightened as if he had bitten a gooseberry.

"You helped find that woman's body yesterday—I say, you knew she was there. You put her there."

"What? You're lying." Quietus echoed our thoughts. "You've got nothing on me! Go and stuff yourself up a centaur's arse, Karus."

Colourful imagery had no effect on Karus. "Do you want to tell me why you do it?"

"I never did anything!"

"Who, then? Are you telling me somebody else does it?" Quietus opened his mouth but had no answer. Karus now spoke to him more conversationally. "No. You can't suggest anyone else. It's you. You snatch them, you knock them cold to control them, you rape them, then you strangle them. They die, at some point. You want to watch that. That arouses you, doesn't it? Then you like to leave them dead in the open, so you come back to their cold bodies. Dead women can't argue. That gets your juices going. Once they decay too much, even for you, you dig a hole and pop them in it. But when you think they might be found before that, you lay out their bodies in positions that will shock the finders. I find this disgusting, but I will listen if you want to explain why you do it."

Quietus said nothing. Even from upstairs we could see him licking his lips nervously. He had a sheen of apprehension. Karus took the suspect's anxiety for guilt.

He was on the prowl as he started off again: "All right, I'll suggest some reasons for you. Perhaps women have treated you so badly that you hate them. Or perhaps wise ones never want anything to do with you, so your only recourse is to grab one and force her. Which is it, Quietus? You're damaged and punishing, or you're naturally vile to those you hate? I think most likely it is not your fault. You were hurt by a woman, early on in your life—is that it? You never stood a chance of being normal? Which do you say, though? What makes a man like you commit such crimes?"

"There's nothing wrong with me and I never did it."

"Now don't just say that. Choose a reason!"

Quietus was clever enough to see where this could lead. "Oh, I get it. You make me choose, so you can call that my admission?"

"I don't need your admission," Karus replied confidently. "I have enough evidence. You're damned."

At this point he picked up his chair, as if he was going to smash it down on the suspect. The back legs screeched on the roughly paved yard as it was lifted. Quietus flinched. Karus put down the chair again. Then he moved in much closer, increasing the prisoner's agitation.

"This has been happening for years and I'm looking for an explanation. One idea I have is that you blame the victims. What are these women, most of them?" Karus demanded. He moved about, walking to and fro in restless bursts, then leaned over the chair back. "Prostitutes. Bad creatures. You go with them, you spy on them with their customers, but to you they are vermin. They use men's needs, they prey on men, they get money for doing it. You'll say you want to clear them out of the gardens, especially the sacred Grove. That's a special place. Honorific. It should never be invaded by these women—and the boys, of course. They were as bad. Filthy dancers. Insects like them should be stamped on—isn't that what you think, Quietus?"

"I don't like them," Quietus let himself admit.

Karus was on it: "That's it! Now we're talking. You hate the whores."

"Not hate—"

"You hate them." Karus was having no dissent. Quietus reacted by trying to stand up. Karus roughly pushed him back on the stool. "Don't try it!" He signalled to his men. None of them moved. Karus did not need support. All stubble and bullying, he was heavy, a lifelong soldier. In confrontation he had a calm that implied he could break a man's neck without thinking about it. He throbbed with barely hidden power.

Quietus lifted his bound hands to his forehead as if wanting to flatten his hair, then dropped them impotently. He must feel that he stood no chance.

"Admit it—tell me how you hate the whores!"

"Yes—"

"You want to wipe them all out!"

"No—"

"That's it! Throw him back in the cell." As his squad moved to the prisoner, Karus looked up to us. "I'm finished! This is the Caesar's Gardens killer. He's filth. A pustule. A fungus growing on society. He won't need a trial. Send him to the praetor, for transmission to the lions."

XLVII

K arus took his crew off for a drink to celebrate. Ursus and I stayed put. We stared down at the empty yard. We had no sense of triumph.

Eventually I asked, "Might I have a go with him?"

Ursus shrugged. "What's to lose?"

We walked down the steps together. A couple of vigiles appeared, as if to check whether he wanted anything. The rest stayed in their cubicles. They are rough but Karus's bullying had been too much. The atmosphere was deeply subdued.

"I'll have to be with you," said Ursus. "Security."

"That's fine. Glad to share ideas, if you have any." He offered none.

With a jerk of his head, Ursus signalled he wanted a word before I started. He strode over to the huge octagonal fountain bowl where the vigiles filled their fire-fighting siphon and buckets. There he plunged in both hands to wash himself, as if cleansing away moral filth. It was anyone's guess whether his decency was offended by Quietus or by Karus.

Ursus washed with vigour. He was like an enormous dog, shaking himself energetically, splashing anyone in reach. I waited until the wild torrents subsided, then scooped water onto my face more daintily. We both had our backs to the cells, though Quietus could probably not see us.

"What's special about the group he belongs to?" I wondered, almost to myself. "It could have been any of the garden staff. True, they found Satia, and the superintendent put them top of his list as suspicious. Now Karus has convinced himself that the billhook is a clue. I discount it. Galanthus speaks of something much heavier."

"Plus," Ursus now told me, "one of my men found a rock in the woods that could have blood on it. We can't be certain."

"But all the more reason to accept that Quietus was simply mending the tool . . . Three men in that group led by Blandus are old enough to be the Pest. Are you going to bring the others in?"

"No point." Ursus was blunt. "They will all blame one another."

I agreed. We could waste time and drive ourselves nuts with those raddled satyrs. I had a better idea. I told Ursus to have the apprentice fetched instead. "Not here to the station-house—he'll be terrified. Let him come to that bar your men drink at."

"Get him drunk to see if he'll crack?"

"Well, we can make out it's an informal chat, not an interview."

"Is he bright?"

"I would say he keeps his eyes open."

Ursus sent a man.

Since we had Quietus, we might as well extract what we could from him while the boy was being fetched and Karus was off the premises. I walked to the door of the holding-cell, which stood open. Quietus was sitting on the ground; there was no furniture. He looked up, more arrogant than a man in his position ought to be, more truculent than many would be after Karus's grilling.

He was perfectly ordinary. No one would take him for a monster; he was hardly handsome yet had no hideous features. Hundreds of thousands of workmen in Rome, slaves and free, looked similar.

"Yes, now comes the soft session!" My idea was to win his trust, although I found that an unpleasant prospect. "I'd like you to come outside again, please, so we can discuss your predicament."

Without waiting for a surly answer, I walked back across the portico corridor, out into the exercise yard. It was cold; I huddled in my cloak. Ursus followed with Quietus. Ursus made a gesture for me to take the chair, though I had already done so. It was mine because I was an aedile's wife—but we informers have our ways. Forget the position of command. Whenever there's a chance, we rest our legs.

Quietus was shoved back down onto the low stool, while Ursus stood nearby, feet planted, thumbs in his broad belt.

I spoke to the suspect conversationally. I never shouted, talked over him, or even stopped him denying guilt.

"My name is Flavia Albia. We met the other day. I want information; I am not here to judge you."

"I've done nothing!"

"Noted. What I would like is to explore whether the evidence really points to you, or if you can add to what is known. The reason you have been arrested was explained by Julius Karus. He thinks you have a suspicious interest in women, and you were caught mending an implement that has blood on it. I want to discuss specifics, especially other evidence."

Quietus was sneering, probably at being questioned by a woman.

"It is in your interests to help."

"Why should I?"

"Because they will kill you," I said baldly. I could hear Uncle Petro saying, "Don't use threats unless you can back them up," but with Karus involved there was no more to lose. "Do you want a terrifying punishment for something you have not done? Tell me about the billhook. Where were you, when Karus found you mending it?"

"By the sheds. Our compound, where you saw us."

"It was not at one of the victims' burial sites?"

"No."

"Or anywhere near them?"

"No."

"Where had the damage to this tool occurred?"

"Digging in a flowerbed. Not where we found that body, it was another assignment afterwards. Work goes on."

"And when the handle broke?"

"I was jabbing at a big old root. The billhook snapped and it sprang up at me."

"You were cut, you say? Can you show us?"

He held out his hairy arm, pulling off a rag to demonstrate a dirty, jagged-edged wound, several inches long, still wet where the blood seeped.

This had clearly occurred today. If it was not properly cleaned and dressed it would go septic. Ursus examined the arm, wrenching up the man's elbow, then checked the billhook. Blood on it had dried.

"Looks recent," I deduced. "Primulus and Galanthus were attacked six days ago. If the tool was used since, the blood would be gone." Ursus nodded. "The superintendent can confirm the assignment to the flower-bed, if necessary." At this he nodded again.

While he had hold of the suspect's arm, Ursus carried out an experiment. Calling for a volunteer, he had Quietus's hands unbound, then made him take hold of this vigilis, as if attempting to strangle him. "Don't grip. If I hear my man so much as gasp, it will be you who dies!" Out came his rule, to measure the hand-spread in the same way as he had on the body of Victoria Tertia. Ursus shook his head. "Lucky for you, you have small paws for a man. This might even dissuade Karus from holding you—but don't bank on it. He doesn't believe in science." Suddenly he gave another order: "Strip him!"

Vigiles came and wrenched off the gardener's tunic. It was not purely demeaning; it allowed Ursus to scrutinise him all over. "No bite marks!" he said to me, in a low voice. "It's not him."

Addressing Quietus myself as he struggled back into the garment, I played it frank. "Well, you look to be in the clear. But you should know my runaway boys have been found. That's why we are looking for human bite marks."

"Are they dead?"

"Assume not. The killer hit them—maybe not with your tool, but if they were hit with a rock instead, you still can't prove it wasn't you, can you?" Quietus seemed to take it in. I changed tack, hoping he was ready to cooperate. "Now tell me about Satia's corpse," I said. "The group of you who found her yesterday morning, how come you were there? Were you working in that area normally?"

"Yes. We're on winter maintenance. Clearing debris. Picking leaf litter. Aerating the soil for early bulbs when they nose through. But we had been ordered to look for a woman."

"A search party? Who gave you the orders?"

"The Super. Karus had ordered him."

"Just to be sure, who are we discussing? This was you, with Blandus in charge, plus Rullius and a young lad? Were you all close together?"

"We hadn't started. We found the dead woman as soon as we walked up the path."

"Did you all spot her at once, or did one point her out?"

"Someone pointed."

"Who?"

"Can't remember."

"Try, please. Was it you?"

Quietus made out it was a strain, but he conceded what had happened: "Not me. Rullius had leaned over the fencing. At the same time Blandus let out, *'Bollocks, we've got one!'* A dead body," added Quietus, unnecessarily enjoying it. I made sure I showed no reaction. "We knew the Pest had been at his old tricks again."

"Had you yourself ever found one of these bodies before?"

"No."

"What about the others?"

"Probably. The boy threw up. It must have been his first. We get enough of the women dumped on us. I don't know."

"Really? Don't you ever talk about it?"

"No. We all want to forget." I looked sceptical; his attitude did not ring true. Quietus reconsidered his answer. "All right. Blandus had found bones before." I felt now he was attempting to implicate Blandus. "I know, because he always tells apprentices if they come across remains to run and fetch him."

"What—he *likes* bones?"

"His wife's got a big dog!" joked Quietus, again hoping to offend me.

Unimpressed, I simply asked, "You mean they tell Blandus so he can bring in the vigiles?"

"We always bring the firemen in." Quietus wanted to establish that they behaved correctly. By now he was not resentful. I was picking through facts. He was answering.

That did not mean he was unmoved. Sometimes a suspect savours attention, but this one was more stressed than he wanted to show. Underneath, Karus had shaken him. I felt Quietus now saw talking to me as his only chance. In his mind he could hear the arena lions roar. "We always follow routine," he insisted, after I remained silent.

I glanced up, pretending to check with Ursus. He gave a faint nod. I wondered if he knew that the gardeners said he just threw reports into a cupboard, ignoring them.

"Where were you," I then asked Quietus lightly, "the night before? Before Satia, the last victim, was found dead?"

For the first time, I saw him hesitate. "You'll take it wrong." His dialect was thicker than ever; I had to strain to work it out.

"No, I told you: I don't judge. Come on. What were you doing? Where did you spend the evening and where did you sleep?" He would not answer, so I told him a story myself, again speaking unexcitedly: "I had a look around your compound, the day I met your group." At that, he looked up, indignant. Ursus made a one-fingered gesture for him to stay put, although Quietus never actually moved. "I reckon some of you sleep there. Tell me the truth, Quietus. You should do, because Ursus here will now send somebody to look."

Ursus did signal to one of his men.

"We are going to find out," I told the gnarled, long-faced suspect. "We'll find signs of whoever has been sleeping there—and if it is you, we shall find your trophies."

"What trophies? I don't know what you're talking about!" This seemed genuine; Quietus's face even registered horror, as if he thought I might mean body parts.

Ursus put on the big sad smile of an enquirer who knows when somebody is lying. I kept going steadily. "Who slept in the compound two nights ago? Tell me."

When Quietus remained stubbornly silent, Ursus finally stepped in. "Are you married?" he demanded.

"No." The sudden new tack drew an answer.

"Ever been?"

"No."

"Can't afford it? Or just don't want to?"

"No point, is there? I can get what I want without the hassle."

"Where do you live, then? You do live somewhere!"

Quietus knew Ursus could find out, even if it took him time. "Some nights I sleep in the work compound. No one ever said I couldn't. I don't have to pay room rent."

"Anyone else do that?"

"Some of them. Sometimes."

"Which others?" demanded Ursus. Quietus shrugged unhelpfully.

Re-entering the conversation, I ticked off possibilities: "Your apprentice?"

Quietus was not going to shake me off, so he admitted, "He stays with his parents. He's just a lad."

"The rest of your team? What about Blandus and Rullius? Are they married?"

"Both. Rullius never stays over, he goes home. He has a nice family."

"Nice families are never nice," Ursus commented despondently, as if privately to me. "But they are bound to be nice enough to vouch for him." He turned back to Quietus. "Your team-leader—Blandus?"

"Blandus and his woman are not getting on."

"Not getting on? What is their problem?"

"Quarrelling."

"What about?"

"Life. Stress. His hours. Him not handing over enough of his pay. What he says about her mother. What she thinks of him. Especially that."

"Oh, nothing unusual! Tell us again," said Ursus, taking over once more and putting on pressure. "Which of you, your team, slept out in Caesar's Gardens on the night Satia was killed?"

Quietus applied a helpful expression. "I was in the stable. Blandus is our team-leader, so he has the luxury; he kips in the Super's office."

"Does Berytus know?"

"Berytus knows nothing about anything! It's temporary, Blandus says."

"How long has he been doing this?"

"Past six months."

"If Blandus has quarrelled with his wife for six months, does that mean he goes with prostitutes?"

"I shouldn't think so!" Quietus took pleasure in telling us. "One of the things they fight about is how Blandus can't manage it, these days."

He seemed to think that was an alibi for the team-leader. Ursus and I glanced at each other, knowing it could mean that in order to perform Blandus needed stimuli—rape and murder, for example.

XLVIII

A vigiles bar tends to be large, poorly lit and full of empty flagons. The men there are good-humoured, because they have gone off duty. They sit talking amiably about wrestlers or their children, except when they have just attended a large fire, one with casualties. At such times they are silent. They drink hard and use bad language, while sudden fights may flare, spilling out into the street. These are soon over. Best to walk by. Best to let them recover. Theirs is a hard job. They cope in their own ways.

The gardeners' apprentice was already sitting with them. Kind-hearted, they had placed a food bowl and beaker in front of him. He was so shy he only toyed.

Ursus and I walked in casually. He went to order. I sat on a bench beside the lad, hoping a bite might be brought for me. It was. Globuli. Fried curd-cheese balls. I hate them.

"Thanks!"

"You're an informer. Bound to be on the cadge. Dish of the day, and as it's afternoon now, three for the price of one."

"That's better than the Stargazer where I live." We appeared to be currently in a saloon called Aphrodite's Arse. The picture was so faded someone had written it, to remind them where they were. "The Stargazer offers one bowl for the price of three."

The globuli were elderly by this stage. Time does not improve fried cheese. Covering up the cheesey roundelos with sprigs of parsley had disguised the damage, but I pulled off the greenery. I also hate limp parsley.

Food chatter was our strategy for softening up the lad. "I met you, didn't I? What's your name?"

"Gaius."

Ursus and I shared a glance. No Roman only supplies his praenomen. Total inexperience. Gaius had barely stopped drinking mother's milk. Every time anything was said, embarrassed colour flooded his skin, not just his face but his neck and thin bare arms.

"We want to have a quick chat," I said, smiling. Ursus echoed my smile, though his was more worrying. "It's nothing to worry about. That's why we thought we'd meet you here, not at the station-house."

Oddly avuncular, Ursus chipped in: "Gaius looks as if he'd enjoy seeing inside a fire-house. I bet you'd like a go on a siphon-engine, wouldn't you?" Gaius, who worked with three men like mushroomy tree stumps, looked as if he realised this would never happen.

I let time pass, gnawing globuli. My jaw was barely up to it. No point telling Ursus that informers on the cadge want soft gourmet rissoles in a perfectly balanced three-pepper sauce, with a side plate of asparagus. At the Aphrodite, rissoles were off. I knew not to embarrass myself by asking.

"How long have you worked at Caesar's Gardens, Gaius?" Less than a year. Always on the same team? No, the Super moved apprentices around; he thought they would learn different skills from different people, though the men all seemed to know the same things. How was he, the superintendent? A nice man, said Gaius.

Ursus chuckled. "I've heard him called an idiot!"

"Actually, Berytus is very kind and knowledgeable." After slapping down Ursus unexpectedly, the lad was off, an enthusiast: "He was at Alba Longa, in the Emperor's long terraces at his citadel. Lucky man! That must have been wonderful. Then he was brought to Rome, to help with the sunken garden at the Palace, but it didn't work out, so he was moved again."

"Why didn't it work?" asked Ursus, as if he wondered whether residents complained that the man was a pervert.

"His style is rather traditional. Imperial designers want innovation.

Imported plants. Contemporary layouts. Caesar's Gardens suits him because things are kept the way they have always been."

"Does he get along with his staff?"

"I think he prefers plants. I'm the same. He says if you put them in with tenderness they will give you back tenfold."

"Unlike people!" I commented. Gaius smiled, but was blushing more than ever.

There had been no sign of any passion for greenery when I spoke to the team before. As far as I remembered, Gaius had not even spoken. At the time, I put it down to his shock about Satia's corpse. Now I wondered if he always kept quiet with the older men, rather than standing up to their hidebound attitudes. "You enjoy your work?" He nodded. "How do you find the other gardeners?"

"Oh, they are all right."

"They look rough to me," said Ursus. "I'd say they were skivers and lecherous toads. Have they made you go with them to learn what to do with women?"

Gaius writhed with awkwardness, but he answered calmly, "Yes, but I already knew what to do. After the first time, they stopped nagging on about it. Then I just avoided the subject."

"Who nagged you?" Ursus carried on. He spoke as if it wasn't important, though I knew what he was doing. "One of them or all of them?"

"Quietus mostly. He took me."

"To a brothel?"

"To a woman in the gardens."

"Rural! You know we've got Quietus locked up at the station-house?"

Gaius looked nervous in a way we had not seen before. "Because of the billhook?" he quavered.

Ursus let his questions roll out steadily, with a low level of excitement. "Did that tool really break today?"

"Yes."

"He was mending it?"

"He is our tool-mender."

"That figures then . . . You know we found those missing boys?"

"Yes, it's the talk of everywhere—someone had smashed their heads in, hadn't they?"

I pushed away my bowl. I had done all I could with the globuli. "Gaius, you wouldn't want to suffer what was done to those boys. I won't even tell you about it."

Eyes wide, he whispered, "Are they dead?"

"Some things are worse." I let him take that in. "So, Gaius, if you know anything, you ought to talk to us. Tell me about the night when that woman Satia died. Gardeners were sleeping at your compound. I'm sure you know about it, so you need to tell us who."

Gaius did not want to. We waited, but he refused to give. Ursus and I turned to one another. We held a short conversation together, letting the lad listen.

"He's frightened."

"He would be. Who can blame him?"

"He thinks telling us could lead to trouble for him."

"He's right. He has to work with them."

"Can we keep him safe?"

"We can."

"We could take him out of the group—say he has had a breakdown."

"Because of what he saw, the corpse. It's feasible."

"I would have him at my house, but you know the position. If the Pest, as they call him, comes looking for my boys . . . Well, you know. Does the Seventh have a safe house?"

"We can look after him."

"Where? At the station-house? What about Julius Karus?"

"I won't tell Karus."

"And you've got your suspect in the cells."

"Quietus will be leaving as soon as Karus does the paperwork. Don't worry your head, Flavia. Our lads will take good care of Gaius." Ursus turned back to the apprentice. "Lots of fire-fighting tools to play with—and our tribune is very sensitive. He would love to have someone who knows what he's doing to plant up window-boxes."

I kept my face straight at this prospect. I would balk at the Seventh "taking good care" of me . . . Still, I was not a lad. The worst they could do was take him to a whore to lose his virginity—again.

Ursus took over my food bowl; he picked at my leavings of globuli fastidiously, masticating with his perfect teeth. "You ask him again about the night in question, Flavia."

So the task was mine. I squeezed out from Gaius what he knew: when Satia died in Caesar's Gardens, he himself had gone home earlier. He lived with grandparents, not parents as Quietus had said. Quietus and Blandus had both stayed behind at their compound. Quietus always camped with the pony, while more recently Blandus had bunked down in the office.

"Rullius?"

"He goes home."

"Where does he live?"

"Across the river."

"And next morning," I suggested, "who decided where your team would work?"

"The Super. We weren't gardening, though. He told us we had to look for the woman."

"Did any of the men object to the area chosen for you to search? Anybody restive? Anyone think you ought to work somewhere else?"

The young man's face clouded. He had worked out that I wondered whether one of his colleagues had known in advance that a corpse was there. He flushed again, then burst out anxiously, "Everyone knew we were going to find something awful. All the staff had been told we had to search for a missing woman, who was probably dead. We were assigned areas and sent to them at first light. Nobody had a choice. That agent—"

"Karus?"

"He had come to say how it must be done."

I knew all this was true. "All right. Now think back. Can you remember, Gaius, the night of the big birthday party, when Victoria Tertia was murdered? Did Blandus and Quietus sleep in the compound then, too?"

"Yes, they did." The lad was bright enough to see the implications, which clearly unsettled him. "I know they were in the gardens early next day, during that big commotion about her going missing. They helped people look for her . . . Oh, I don't like having to talk about this!"

Gaius abruptly snuffled into his hands, wiping his eyes. If a suspect had started to cry during an interrogation, Ursus and I would suppose he was feeling sorry for himself because he had done it. Not this one.

Still, I would not be soft: "Gaius, you don't need to cry. But I feel you haven't told me everything." He seemed past cooperating. Still I tried to squeeze more out of him. I suggested everyone at Caesar's Gardens suspected who the killer was, yet nobody ever said anything. "It's going to be the last person imaginable," I mused. "In the end, though, we shall find some clue and pick him up. Time is running out for him. It's inevitable. Then, when the vigiles arrest him, everyone who knows this man will refuse to believe that it's him."

I had spoken as if I had a clear idea who it was. I must have sounded more convinced than I felt.

Lured into sharing, Gaius at last decided to unburden. Almost apologetically, he told us something new. What he said concerned Rullius, the third gardener he worked with.

Rullius, Gaius wanted us to believe, was a nice man. Everyone liked him. He worked hard, he was helpful to everyone, he even volunteered to look after the sanctuary of Hercules in Caesar's Gardens. He had a wife and children. He lived with them across the Tiber, just past the Trigeminal Gate. Every night he called out, "I'm off, then!" as he headed away. He crossed on the Sublician Bridge, coming back to the Transtiberina with the pack animals at first light next day.

This seemed to clear Rullius of guilt. He was never in the gardens or the Grove after dark, when bad things happened. At least, that was what everyone thought—but, said our young witness quietly, it was not entirely true. One evening, before our workmen began their demolition task, Gaius had been on his own in the Grove, looking at the big trees. He loved trees. He loved the ancient peace in that sacred forest.

After Rullius was supposed to have left for home that night, Gaius saw him, still in the Grove. He was going to the slimy grotto. Something about him prevented Gaius calling out. He watched as Rullius went into the old cave. Although Gaius stayed looking at plane trees for a long time, Rullius never came out again.

It grew dark. Gaius had to go home to his grandparents. But he felt Rullius had entered the cave with an air of purpose so, until Larcius and the workmen dismantled the rocks, Gaius believed the other man sometimes used to sleep there.

XLIX

Ursus called over a man to take the apprentice to the Seventh's head-quarters. I saw a wink and overheard instructions for keeping him hidden from Karus. It was time for us to move.

Fastidious as ever, the investigating officer removed strands of parsley from between his teeth, using a double-ended toothpick-cum-ear-scoop from the pouch on his belt where he kept his ruler. Unsurprisingly, I could see he had a knife-with-a-spoon too.

"You have a knack," he said, between expert picking. "I might never have got that out of him. Good for you." His praise surprised me. Still, I knew who would claim full credit. My contribution would be ignored in reports. "I like your style, Flavia. This new lead may have broken the case."

It was a very small lead. "He lurks," I disagreed. "When he can't be bothered walking home across the river, or when his wife has her mother staying, or the children keep nagging for new toys, Rullius stays out and lurks. That proves nothing."

"It's a lead," insisted Ursus. "Now, we ought to have a look at those gardeners, shouldn't we? Karus has been pottering about, but we can do it properly. And I want to inspect this grotto in the forest. You'd better show me."

Privately I cursed. I had, of course, intended looking by myself.

We stood up to go. As we walked through the district before we headed towards the Grove of the Caesars, Ursus broke more news: he had received a catch-me-if-you-can letter. It had been thrown over the station-house gates last night. The troops found it that morning before I arrived.

"Addressed to you?"

"Yes. If it's really from the killer, this is personal. *'Ursus, greetings! You are doing very badly with me, I must say. Your new friend has not helped you get any nearer. I had to take another one out of action to remind you.'* Bad writing. Bad spelling. But you get the point . . . This *could* be him—or it could be a mindless creep in the community with time on his hands."

"Unsigned, I take it?"

"Oh, he knows his own nickname. I bet he's proud to have one. Such criminals see a label as validation. *'Just nudging—from your respectful friend the Pest.'* Annoying turd!"

"Would you say direct contact is rare in these cases?" I was thinking I must ask Uncle Petro about his experience.

"No. But I'd say it's a trial," Ursus growled. "I haven't got time for such nonsense."

We talked about having to investigate the note, a distraction from the real search. Other investigators, Ursus grumbled, might let themselves become sidetracked by such apparently compelling evidence. To him, it would be wasting endless effort.

"You believe it's a hoax?" I asked him.

"Open mind."

"Pursuing it, though?"

"Incontrovertibly!" Ursus assured me in a hollow voice, his form of satire. "This is of 'utmost importance,' in the good old phrase—so I'll give it to Julius Karus! He can keep it tucked in his loincloth so he can wave it at witnesses."

I grimaced.

I was about to grimace much more. To reach the grove from the bar near the Via Aurelia, we had to pass the Naumachia. The fastest way was right up close at the end that faced the river, on the encircling pathway where snack and trinket booths would be set up outside on public occasions. I had avoided this area until now.

With Ursus beside me, I had no qualms about randy sailors. However, a commotion was occurring that did cause concern. As we reached the massive oval structure, one of the vigiles came running towards us. He stopped and exclaimed with relief when he saw Ursus. Breathlessly he explained: a man covered with blood had been seen dragging a woman into the Naumachia. He was shouting, she was screaming. Terrified witnesses reported he had a knife to her throat.

"Sounds like a domestic," I said. "Some wife has burned his meal again." More likely he was a brute, she had said she was leaving him and taking the children, he refused, and now the obsessional idiot intended to kill all his family. "I'll go on," I attempted, since I thought it a coincidence, and nothing to do with the gardens killer. If so, it would give me a chance to explore without hassle. "I can start at the Grove by myself, Ursus. I'll leave you to deal with this nutter."

"Not so fast, Flavia! We do have a man who talks them down when they are jumping off a roof—I would let them jump, but pulling them back saves a mess on the pavement. Sadly, he's not been at work for weeks, due to his bunions. You are going to come with me and use your magic touch—calming a maniac who is making wild threats should be right up your street."

Oh, Juno.

"Karus is there," said the vigilis. "People are saying it's the Pest."

"Not his style!" I gasped, running. Karus. That was all we needed.

"She's right," Ursus grunted, more out of condition than he would admit. "We looked at two decades of old crimes, and in all the reports, the Pest never used a knife once."

The vigilis, strong and healthy, kept trotting comfortably alongside us. "Well, this fellow has grabbed one from somewhere—and apparently it's an enormous blade."

Letter to Manlius Faustus: Sir, we regret to inform you that in the course of a brave action, selflessly attempting to save others, your wife met with a tragic accident . . .

L

Leaden grey, the huge basin reflected almost the entire winter sky. However deep it was, the undrinkable waters from the Alsietina aqueduct kept permanently churning in from Etruria to top it up. The filler pipe was thirty feet in diameter. Even after they fed off it to irrigate local gardens, huge quantities of water torrented in.

It is often claimed that the Flavian Amphitheatre is the largest ever, a new wonder of the modern world. Fortunately, I had a brother aged twelve who loved correcting people. Postumus had spent time with his birth-mother at a nearby arena, so this flooded basin ended up in the spidery note-tablets where he obsessively collected knowledge. Largest ever? Postumus knew: "The new amphitheatre in the Forum is six hundred and forty feet long *times* five hundred and twenty-eight feet wide, while the Naumachia of Augustus in the Transtiberina—I certainly *don't* mean his other naumachia in the Field of Mars, by the way—is, as that emperor tells us in his helpful inscription *Things What I Have Done*, one thousand eight hundred feet long *times* one thousand two hundred feet wide. Indeed it is—"

"Twice as big, darling." Get your facts straight, gullible tourists.

Olympus! Eighteen hundred by twelve hundred feet made, as Ursus muttered, a bloody big pond. I had vaguely been aware of the monument's exterior size on occasions when I had had to walk around it. Once through the entrance, it was breathtaking. From inside, it was like staring across a huge flooded marsh. The surface rippled sluggishly beneath the wind. Odd coots and mallards treated it as an isolated lake.

Out here, on the edge of Rome, without the crowds it had been built for, this was a lonely, mournful place.

The impression of remoteness was heightened because during long periods of neglect seagulls had come up from the coast, taken the high walls for beautifully faced cliffs, and nested there. They stared down malevolently, like omens of the underworld. Occasionally a huge bird would sweep past us at speed, full of threat.

Some banked seats had human occupants. Dear gods, whatever was about to happen here would have an audience. Sailors based in the barracks had heard of goings-on. They had rushed to see, and were catcalling the parties involved, though I was confused as to whether they meant she should hang on for rescue, or he should get on and kill her. There was no time to wonder; it was crisis point.

The man with the knife had gone on board a ship. To have any chance of reaching him, we would have to find another on the far side. That meant jogging all around the interior on a decrepit walkway. It was risky. The planks sagged in sodden decay under us. Everything needed maintenance, because nowadays naval displays took place on the Field of Mars or in the much superior Flavian Amphitheatre. Those venues were conveniently central, and the Flavian basin could be filled and emptied in less than an hour, a crowd-pleaser.

Vigiles, who had been called by the public, reported to Ursus while they ran with us around the basin. A distressing story emerged. It must have started while Ursus and I interviewed Quietus, then talked to Gaius, with trouble erupting after Karus had left the station-house. Keen to prove his theory about Quietus, he must have brought himself back to the gardens. The woman who was now being held captive had been visiting her brother, who worked in the ship sheds by the Naumachia. A man had learned that she, his wife, was having an affair—using the sheds as a love nest. The discovery had happened when Karus's men, searching Caesar's Gardens, found messages between the lovers.

"What—were they buried?" I had visions of more scrolls.

"No, they were hidden under plant lists in the superintendent's office."

"He's not the crazed husband?" I gasped.

"No, he was the lover."

"Holy muses! *Berytus?* Who's the husband?"

"The man with the knife? A gardener. One of his staff."

This just got more and more unbelievable. "How did he find out?"

"Karus named the lovers."

"Karus!" snorted Ursus. As he ran faster in disgust, his plodding feet threatened to sink through the rotten boards of a waterlogged part of the walkway. "Bloody Karus! What did he do?"

His man smirked. Karus, the "special agent," was thought far from special by all of the regular cohort. "His stupid troops had brought the love letters out of the office. They lolled on some seats and were reading out details, laughing their heads off. The ship sheds were mentioned, there was stuff about assignations, the lovers used 'visits to her brother' as a code. It was heartfelt—there was even poetry." The Asturians must have done this where I had sat myself, talking to the gardeners. "Karus came along after extracting his confession from Quietus."

Ursus humphed.

"Karus snatched a letter, read out some of it, then came to the end with the woman's loving signature."

"He never said her name?"

"He did. This is Karus. 'Your darling Alina, pining for you, sweet Berytus,' he read. Then, for the poor sod of a husband, that was it. He works in the gardens. He was listening in."

"If he is a gardener," I asked, trying again to identify him, "what is he called?"

"Blandus."

"Oh, shit!" said Ursus. Mentally I echoed him.

The next part was ghastly. Not only had Blandus learned his wife was cheating, the revelation had been in public, at his place of work. The Seventh had one of his team in custody and the apprentice helping with enquiries, but Rullius was there. Blandus must have been mortified. And there was worse. Alina's lover was the man in charge, his chief: the gardens superintendent.

At first no one noticed how badly Blandus reacted. He said nothing; he seemed stunned. Then even his colleagues, who might have been in the know all along, were too late to hold on to him as he went for the superintendent. Unsuspecting, Berytus was felled. While he lay helpless on the ground, the maddened husband put the blade of a spade on him. He rammed his foot down hard as if he was splitting apart perennials, through the man's neck.

Before anyone else could react to this horrific act, he had fled. Covered with blood, Blandus had hared off across the gardens to the Naumachia, where the errant wife, who liked "seeing her brother," was waiting for her lover.

"What about him? Berytus?"

"Dead. Head half off. Catastrophic blood loss. No chance."

We reached the far end of the basin. A pier ran out over the water, where ships could moor so combatants in shows could be marched on board. A lopsided old trireme could be seen some way offshore, going around in wayward circles. We were told it was rowed by sailors, after Blandus threatened to kill his woman in front of them unless they took him out. Another, significantly low in the water, was very slowly following them. This, we were told, contained Karus and the Asturians.

"I hope he drowns!" groaned Ursus. A third boat, much smaller, was being prepared for us. Brilliant.

I took stock. Naumachiae were created for all sorts of water spectacles. You could show sea gods cavorting with their weed-draped wives, or trained animals plunging about in spray, but the best shows were mock sea battles. Then the water would be packed with triremes, so many big ships that they could barely manoeuvre on the lake. The point was not to watch them in motion, but to see them crunch and ram each other, then know men on board were dying. Augustus boasted in the *Res Gestae,* his summary of his reign, that his show hosted thirty full-size vessels. Three thousand men had been afloat, in addition to the rowers.

When Titus inaugurated the amphitheatre, he had presented another event here, then so had Domitian, even though he hated to follow Titus. Ancient maritime battles were restaged, with participants dressed in exotic clothes and armour. These were tremendous occasions: uproar from the banks of seats, the clash of oars, the ringing of trumpets. Then the screams. Screams because all the participants were criminals, taking part as punishment. They drowned. That was the intention. People loved it.

Our boat was ready.

I felt deeply conscious that this entertainment space and all its equipment were being decommissioned. Domitian was digging out his own naumachia basin farther north on the right bank, and this big beast had begun dying around us. The surrounding district was being built upon. The naumachia structure had been left to crumble; any ships that could operate properly had been carried off elsewhere. The sheds where the lovers had met still existed, but the few last craft were ramshackle. Someone kept them afloat: if there is water, with boats, there will always be men offering to take the public out. Historians never mention this. In fact, news only spreads by word of mouth, because who wants the Palace getting wind? Bureaucrats will stop it, or at least regulate fares and impose stupid safety rules.

No rules applied at the Naumachia of Augustus when I had to go on it in a four-oared bumboat that lurched so badly it took on water while still moored. A British coracle would have been more secure. I did not bother asking if this interesting skiff was clinker-built. Them telling me it was not a skiff but a wherry would have wasted time we did not have. It was to be rowed by vigiles, though a sailor helped me on.

"Watch those hands, barnacle!" ordered Ursus. "She's a married lady." We had come so far in our relationship that he had turned jovial. Too jovial for me. "You are our mascot, Flavia, our little flying goddess Fortune."

"Albia."

"Never. You will always be Flavia to us."

He clambered aboard after me, nearly capsizing the boat. I was given a bailing ladle: always a bad omen.

Next thing, we were out on the water. As a pleasure trip, this was low on relaxation. The boat was so leaky it could barely make progress. The vigiles were ill-coordinated rowers, Ursus a disoriented cox.

Our task was to come near to the ship that contained the hostage, without being sunk by the other, manned by Karus and his team. These leftover vessels were not stage replicas but genuine triremes, if not full size, then close. My brother, the fact-lover, would have told me how many oars, how many extra men they could carry, what speed, what weight, how the toothed jaws on the prow worked in battle, et cetera. I did not care. The two ships were huge. Rowed well, they could dart across the lake as smoothly as gadflies; steered with skill, they could turn full length with a supple slide, like water snakes. They were built to destroy other craft. We were a fragile craft dithering in their way. The triremes on the lake today were neither rowed nor ruddered competently. Our position was extremely dangerous.

"Oh, shit!" repeated Ursus. Rubbing one sticky-out ear, he added that he hoped I could swim because he could not, so he needed me to rescue him if he fell in. Keeping him in suspense, I went on bailing.

The vigiles proved to be adequate scullers. We decided not to reinforce Karus but head directly for the ship with Blandus. We managed to reach it. This one had not decayed too badly so rode high, though unevenly. I had enough battleship lore (from my brother) to know triremes are made of light woods that absorb a lot of water, so they need to be beached every night to dry off. Someone must have been taking care of this one, possibly hauling it into one of those ship sheds where our lovers liked to meet. Some of its oars were out of commission. On our side, near one of the steering rudders on the stern, we found a gap where our small boat could creep right up to the peeling hull. At least we did not have to face the crazy painted eyes at the front or risk the water-level bronze-clad jaws swiping us into oblivion.

For some reason, those aboard had stopped rowing. The great ship had slowed gracefully, so now it slopped on the lake, as close to motionless as it would ever be without dropping anchor. We were aware that if Blandus told the sailors to continue, the trireme could move off again at any moment. Our bumboat would probably capsize.

Nobody spoke. One of the vigiles signalled silently to a rope ladder that hung down the side. As the great ship rocked, this device swung uninvitingly. The vigiles are experts with ladders, which are part of their firefighting kit. They use wooden ones with good fixed rungs. None wanted to tackle this.

Ursus should have led the way. Sadly, he was a green-featured unfortunate who found himself stricken with queasiness even on an inland lake with unruffled waves. He gripped the side, his attention on one thing only. Any moment now, Ursus would throw up.

I sighed.

A girl has to do what a girl has to do. I stood upright, carefully so the wallowing bumboat did not roll so much that it sank. I grasped the ropes with both hands, waited for the moment when we rocked in towards the trireme, stepped up, then somehow began climbing.

LI

Perhaps I should have mentioned: my first husband was an ex-marine. Marry twice. Marry often. It widens your range of learned skills.

I won't say it was easy. The worst thing, as I set off on this madcap task, was knowing there were five shocked but fascinated men below, all looking up my skirt. I heard a male voice exclaim, "Shit, Flavia! Come back. You can't do that!"

I am not daft. I knew I could.

My heart was beating from terror, as much as from the exertion needed. Still, my brain kept hearing Lentullus, laughing and gently chiding: "That's it! Keep going, chick. You'd better not stop or you'll be stuck." I now thought that was probably correct. If I stopped, I was done for. My strength would fail. I would fall off. "Come on!" his lovely ghost told me. "You can do it." I could still picture us, acting like idiots in the old courtyard at Fountain Court, when it was still a laundry, so the proprietor was yelling at us not to dirty the wet linen. Him on the balcony telling me how, me climbing. We were in love. We were young. We could do anything.

To him, teaching me how to shin up a rope ladder had been huge fun. To me as I struggled upwards now, what had seemed feasible at eighteen was much more difficult ten years later. In another decade, I would never even try it. By about halfway, I wished I had not started. Three-quarters, and I realised I had a problem. To accommodate the two top rows of oars, the ship flared out. Looking up, with my arms and legs giving way on me, I knew I had no chance of climbing past that overhang. I was aware of people shouting. It might even have been encouragement. All I could think now was that I would never get aboard from this ladder. I could not even reach the top.

LII

Sailors pulled me in. Of course. Sailors have keen antennae for approaching women. They want to ogle mermaids, ignore sirens, worship mothers, or sidle up with invitations if it is anything else in a skirt.

Reaching hands grasped the rope ladder. They pulled the entire thing higher, grabbed onto me, then hauled me in over the rail. When I fell down, they picked me up again. When I stumbled, they stood me more firmly on the worm-eaten planks that passed for a deck. There were smiles in all directions. Why had so many people been speaking of the Transtiberina nautical presence as a nuisance? These were kindly, public-spirited, almost polite men. They straightened my clothing for me so I hardly felt assaulted at all.

They must have thrown the rope ladder back down. Activity resumed behind me, as the vigiles began coming up from the bumboat. Without waiting, I went to address the problem we had come for.

Blandus had retreated to a small cabin at the back (stern, thank you, Postumus) that must be intended for a trierarch. He had blocked the opening with a spar, but it made a feeble barricade. Although someone had said originally that Blandus was shouting while his wife screamed, by now it was the other way around; she was doing the shouting—wincingly personal abuse—while he screamed in uncoordinated anguish. He was very heavily bloodstained from the waist down. Since there were no obvious wounds on the couple, the gore must all have pumped from Berytus as he died.

I saw no hope of a good end to this. Even if I calmed their hysteria, I would be unable to make any promises. Blandus was doomed and knew it. He might claim that killing his wife's lover in the heat of discovery was his male right. That was enough for Rome to exonerate an emperor who stabbed a rival under some crackpot delusion, but a gardener would be granted less grace. For a start, he had not found the lovers entwined in bed, which was the traditional criterion for a reprieve. Besides, the victim was a senior official, who had worked directly for Domitian. Blandus had dealt his own supervisor a horrendous death.

To top it all, his crime besmirched a sacred grove, one dedicated to members of the imperial family. Sacrilege. Double sacrilege. Under Domitian, no mercy for either. Tyrants always make much of honouring the gods and respecting the past. They will belong to the past themselves one day—and Domitian had convinced himself he was already godlike.

My only hope was to rescue the woman, if I could. That Blandus had not yet killed her, despite a lengthy stand-off, suggested his heart might not be in this. I had hoped the weapon had been exaggerated too. When the public say a lunatic has a large knife, it often turns up smaller. Not here. After leaving a spade stuck in Berytus, Blandus had snatched up the tool the gardeners used to saw through sturdy tree branches. You could see they kept it very sharp. He no longer pressed its ugly edge to his wife's throat, but he was still gripping the device intently. I would not want him waving it too near anyone, especially me.

I went as close as I dared, then started to talk. Tiring, the two parties at least stopped their shouts and screams.

Alina was squatting on her heels, elbows on her knees, tangled dark head in her hands, lost in despair at today's events, as if simply waiting for whatever happened next. She expected nothing good. She was about my age, barefoot, bare-armed, wearing only a ginger-coloured long tunic, with little jewellery; if she had had a stole, she must have dropped it in the tussle at the ship shed. She presumably knew it was her lover's blood all over her husband, and that Berytus had to have died.

Mentally, I was scrambling together what I knew about Blandus: disparaging to women, always said Berytus was an idiot, despised the vigiles, sneered at authority in general, had already been sleeping out because of marital problems, had a damning suggestion of impotence . . . If they had children, no one had mentioned them. For their sake, I hoped not.

His wife, though as normal as a sack of greens, was younger. That made her significantly younger than her lover. Was Berytus a father figure? Did he buy gifts? Or could he use advanced love-making techniques? I had only seen him shocked and dithering after Satia was found, but to others he had had more depth of character. He had been too hidebound for the innovative imperial court, yet the apprentice Gaius had admired his knowledge of plants. On the verge of retirement, yes, but not decrepit. To Alina, he would have been a man of authority, more important than her husband, much more interesting. She sent him poetry. He kept her letters. Perhaps theirs was not an affair of sly couplings in the back of a ship shed, but true love.

In which case, no wonder her husband had run amok when he found out.

Help me, gods, all you grand, dispassionate, pantheon gods of Rome and you rough-cloaked little divinities of Britain. I can do this only if Blandus persuades himself he wants me to end the hostage-taking. I need Alina to keep quiet, I need Blandus to listen, I need to be in control. I must find words, the right words even for a man towards whom I feel no sympathy, words to convince him that if I tell him to surrender, he can agree to it . . .

I started to talk. It felt as if I was there arguing with them for a long time. That may have been an illusion. I became aware that the sailors and vigiles settled quietly, letting me try whatever I could. I thought one or two were watching Blandus closely, in case he lashed out. If he had done, none were near enough to help me.

I do believe I was succeeding. The distraught man was listening. Sometimes he even growled a response. At least he now placed the pruning saw on the deck. It lay there, too close to him and too far from me for retrieval. He looked ready to grab it again at any moment. I did not bother asking him to hand it over.

Blandus was down on his heels behind the weapon, in the same attitude as his wife. Elbows on bloody knees. Head in his hands. Side by side, they looked very much like people who had shared a life, who were still linked in their damaged way. Only that terrible blood, staining his legs and boots, soaking his tunic, said their marriage was over.

He was agreeing; he would free his wife. Even though I had done my best, it came as a surprise. In these situations, you say what you must. You try to sound honest, but I am not sure I myself believed my own calming words.

"All right. Let's be sensible and put an end to this." I still spoke in a level voice, actively supportive. I had even stepped forward, offering a hand. I was going to help Blandus to his feet, lead him away from Alina, let someone else snatch the weapon, hope there would be no nonsense. I knew he would be arrested, though we had not said so.

Everyone on board began to prepare for the moment. The sailors were even quietly moving to their rowing stations. We reckoned without Karus.

The second trireme must have been circling closer, with its occupants straining to work out what was happening on board ours. It had crept right up, while all our attention was on the captor and hostage. Thwarted by lack of information, Karus grew impatient.

I heard a shout. Everyone heard. Karus gave a loud yell; he named Blandus, bawling that he was coming to get him.

More happened. Our ship shuddered as if bucking in a whirlpool. With a loud, groaning scrape, the other trireme passed by, right up against us. Planking screeched. A series of hard blows jarred us. People staggered. This trireme was shoved awkwardly sideways, its high prow swinging outwards. As the second ship collided, I heard oars snap. Sailors yelled. Our trireme continued moving on, badly nudged but righting itself and still afloat.

Had Karus thought Blandus was getting away? Had he tried to disable us to stop him? He would never admit a mistake; he would call it an accident. Whatever it was, he bungled the manoeuvre.

My brother, the couch tactician, would say that once you decide against ramming head on, which does carry risks, you can take another trireme by approaching at the stern, their vulnerable end; then you pull in your own oars and rake past, smashing all their blades to leave them helpless. You bend your own undamaged oars again, to tread up alongside them. Before their rowers can move, your hoplites scramble over for a bloodbath.

The Asturians had sailors to help them, but if the sailors warned Karus, he ignored it. Their oars were out, so the collision smashed them. With our vessel at rest temporarily, ours had been shipped. Fortunate. Damage was minimal.

Their ship had suffered. With their blades gone along one side, they had been taking in water. Either they were holed, or simply poorly caulked and leaky, but with sudden intensity, the lake came washing in. Our sailors started jeering, matched by derisive applause from the distant Naumachia audience. Ours took their stations. We moved away towards the landing stage, leaving the other ship squat in the water, its bronzed ram virtually nose-down in the lake. With the basin unused for shows, the water level was not high and hidden debris from long-ago fights must still have rested on the bottom. The Karus trireme settled. From the far banks of seats, we heard cheers and foot-drumming.

On board our ship there was a new crisis. The surprise of the crash tipped Blandus over the edge again. He leaped up, dragged his pruner hard across Alina's neck, left her collapsing on the deck. He stabbed at himself, an inadequate gesture with a tool meant for sawing, then staggered to the side, climbed the rail, and threw himself into the lake, shouting that he had killed Alina and would drown himself.

I reached his wife but she expired at my feet. There was no struggle; I heard a small sigh of resignation. Alina, having lost both her lover and her husband, surrendered herself to Fate.

While other people rushed to her, I ran to the rail. Below in the silted water, I saw a new boat: a little skiff was tossing against the trireme. Standing up, a youngish boatman wielded a long oar. He must have known about Berytus and now Alina. Not offering rescue, he was pushing Blandus down again and again, every time he resurfaced. He finally forced Blandus under the water, using all his strength to make sure he could never come up. I guessed he had rowed out from the ship sheds. I guessed he was Alina's brother.

Informers are free to choose how they pursue justice. As he looked up and saw me, I raised a palm briefly. Then I turned away.

LIII

Small boats aplenty had appeared. They could pick up survivors from the foundered ship. It was too much to hope they would abandon Karus. He and the Asturians ought to be safe: they should have learned to swim in the army.

Ursus, still green, had also looked over the rail. Hugging myself to control my shock, I suggested that was the brother. "Well, murder belongs in the family," was his bleak comment. Without stopping to watch, he gave orders for our trireme to be rowed back to shore.

I am tough but I was trembling. Once we reached the wooden pier, I feared that my legs would give way and topple me into the water as we disembarked. My plight was noticed. A member of the vigiles walked backwards all the way down the gangplank, holding out his big hands for me to grasp so I could walk off safely. They do this in fires, of course. Leading scared women along wobbly planks is everyday work for them. If they take to you, they don't even manhandle you.

I kissed his cheek for this. The Fourth Cohort would have been outraged by such a gesture to the bastard Seventh, but I make my own rules.

I have never seen a man blush so badly. He recovered when his grinning colleagues pointed out that their chief was still vomiting, even now he was back on land.

Ursus rallied. "Flavia Albia, I'd heard about you, but I didn't believe the stories. It's one big adventure after another when you are around!"

I smiled weakly.

I wanted to go home. No chance. Ursus was determined we should complete our interrupted mission to the grotto cave. We chose not to stay to see Karus netted and landed.

I did glance behind once. Where the clash of triremes had occurred, I saw a lone skiff still stationary on the lake, as if its now-seated rower was on watch to ensure Blandus never resurfaced. It would not happen. Unless his gases brought him up, he would stay down there, his body drifting along the sludgy bottom, among abandoned wreckage and the lost bones of drowned combatants from old maritime spectacles.

The Naumachia seats had emptied of spectators. The lake basin was placid. Its greyness mirrored the winter sky as it returned to supporting only coots and mallards.

Walking in silence, Ursus and I went over to the gardeners' compound. He had to conduct a scene-of-crime visit after Berytus's murder. The deceased was a public official. Bureaucracy has its regulations. The Treasury could not simply drop a supervisor-grade soul from the Leisure Amenities payroll; there must be a full manpower report before another time-server could be assigned as his replacement. Someone would be given temporary promotion to cover. Due to the sensational circumstances, there might need to be a public statement. An unlucky lackey would have to inform Domitian.

Meanwhile the corpse remained, lying on the ground, though with a covering groundsheet. Ursus bent to lift a corner. Still queasy, he signed that this was a bad idea. "Don't look, Flavia! He's nearly in two bits." He had no need to warn me. I had seen the blood on Blandus. I averted my gaze even from the murder weapon, which was lying alongside. It was a long-handled foot spade, shod with a tapered iron piece. "We'll take that. Nobody wants darling daffodils being planted with a shovel that has killed a man."

Ursus wiped the blood off the blade on a topiary hedge. This was an elegant demi-lune of well-clipped low box, fringing oleanders. His men muttered jokes that rain would soon wash the twigs clean. In any case, blood was a good fertiliser . . .

Ursus made them gather up the note-tablets the Asturians had left scattered on those tables where the gardeners liked to sit. He said it would be indecent to have the dead lovers' sweet talk passed around any more. I asked what he would do with the letters from Alina to Berytus. Ursus gave them to me, on the understanding that, even if I read them first, I would make sure they were destroyed.

I put them in my satchel for now, but I wanted to read them. As we walked over to the grotto, I told Ursus I had a professional interest. I was mildly intrigued. It struck me that even if a gardener's wife was basically literate, her reading and writing skills would not normally extend to writing love poems, or even quoting them. Alina would have gone to a professional letter-writer. Plenty of those existed; in hard times, I had even done such work myself. Because of the fake philosophers, I had a current interest in commercial ghostwriting.

Ursus said he was glad someone cared. He would leave all that nonsense to me.

When we approached my husband's building site, we could see it would not delay us long. Nothing was there. We had no cave to search. The old grotto had been reduced to a bare space among the forest trees. Ursus had brought a couple of vigiles, who walked around aimlessly, as if they thought slimy green rocks and puddles might suddenly pop up, like primeval dragon's teeth.

Every stone had gone, leaving flat, tidy ground. Sparsus was giving it a final brush over with a besom while his elders ate their last picnic and watched him at work. Trypho, no longer spooked by creepy feelings, was looking cheerful.

"Flavia, you don't hang around!" marvelled Ursus.

Even I was impressed. "It was payment by the job. The sooner we finish, the bigger the profit margin. When our team tackles a big pile of rocks, believe me, it vanishes."

Larcius and the men had already packed up. All their tools, even their site barricades, were loaded onto barrows and the sack-trolley, ready to move out; had I not arrived, they would have been away.

If new trees were planted, nobody would ever know that the gloomy cave had ever existed. If Sosthenes ever got approval for a nymphaeum, he had a perfect virgin site.

Unfortunately, that meant no clues to our killer. Ursus cursed. He had lost any evidence that Rullius or anybody else had ever used the place, with anything a killer might have hidden in it. I knew he had been hoping to find the trophies taken from dead women.

I took my usual upturned bucket to sit on, then let him deal with this. After what we had just been through, or in deference to my heady mascot status, his grilling of my workforce was fairly polite. As always, I told Larcius to answer his questions fully. Behind the vigiles' backs, Serenus was winking at me. I glowered, to show I meant it.

Larcius confirmed what he had once told me: on taking possession of the site, the workmen had found unpleasant relics of human occupation. At the time they had thought the leftover trash meant use by lovers or adventurous young people. The grotto was sited too far into the Grove for criminal activity. Larcius had not even gained the impression anyone homeless lived there.

"Did a gardener called Rullius ever come along to see what you were up to?"

"No, sir."

"Do you know who I mean?"

"No. What does he look like?"

"Ordinary!"

"No one really bothered us once we started."

"But somebody had definitely been here before?"

Larcius answered patiently, as if telling a member of the public that he did know how to dig a hole: "We found rubbish, food evidence, though not in great quantities, plus—if you will pardon the expression—human shit. Just enough for us to be careful where we put our feet until we had cleared up."

"Find any bones?" asked Ursus. "I don't mean from a rack of lamb. Skulls, pelvises or long shanks. Remains of female skeletons?"

"No, sir."

Larcius glanced at me. The sharp-sighted Ursus jumped in to ask why he was looking at Flavia. I answered: "We found an odd bunch of buried scrolls. It is no secret. I mentioned it at your station-house. Your officer-of-the-day took a written report."

"It's official, then!" Ursus nodded, satisfied. I could not tell whether he had seen that report: knowing the Seventh, probably not. It would have ended up in a rubbish pail, or at least in their infamous case-notes cupboard.

"Yes, and it's why I am interested in ghostwriters."

He rolled his eyes. "Pegasus the flying pony! So, what's happened about this little mystery, Flavia?"

"Nothing. No one ever came forward to claim the scrolls. We don't know why they were buried. They were barely passable as reading matter. I read them myself, because I like a challenge, though I found them grim. I am having them sold at an auction." Tomorrow, but Ursus had no need to know that. As forgeries, the scrolls had enough notoriety, without vigiles turning up at the sale so bidders nervously melted away. My father would tell me never to bring officials in. I was supposed to know auction etiquette.

"But nothing else ever got dug up? . . . The main excitement would be," Ursus summed up to Larcius, "if you had found a box, a bag, or similar container, stuffed with odd bits of women's jewellery. A lot of it would be cheap trash. Bangles. Chains. Earrings. Amulets . . . If you found anything like that, there's no comeback, I just need to have it. It's my one missing link to the pervert who takes all those floozies. Never mind if it's sold, pawned, or donated to your cuties—"

"No," broke in Larcius. He was a good clerk of works, which meant he knew his business and rejected nagging.

"Nothing at all?" For once Ursus sounded desperate.

"Nothing!" I broke in, before one of the men whacked him. Violence had been dealt out enough today. "They would have given it to me. Ursus, please stop messing about."

I had had enough. This had been a tiring day, wearing and tragic. We had wasted effort on a minor suspect, a dire personality but he looked wrongly implicated, while the real person of interest must be laughing. My fear was that all the attention given to the tragic love triangle would make the killer jealous. He would feel driven to attack a new victim, to claw back his own celebrity. Thanks to Blandus, another woman would be raped and killed in the Grove, as a gesture.

Something in me snapped. "I cannot keep doing this. The vigiles have gone astray and I see no hope of anything changing."

Ursus raised an eyebrow, giving me his "annoying woman" expression. *"Astray?"*

"For heaven's sake! Why did you ever settle on the Blandus group as suspects? Because the superintendent fingered them. Why did Berytus do that? Now we know. It had nothing to do with the killings. He hoped you would arrest Blandus, leaving Berytus a clear way to Alina. Due to Karus, you took in Quietus instead, so now three people are dead, yet you have come nowhere near the killer."

Ursus had the grace to show he took my point. Being from the vigiles, and the terrible Seventh, he would only say, "Settle down, Flavia! Anyone would think you were walking away from the job."

"I am. This inquiry is all yours. I won't be associated with the wreckage. Somewhere there must be evidence, clues you have repeatedly not found. Quietus is a dud. Berytus lied about Blandus. There is no convincing suspect, but *you* have the personnel list, *you* have the old case notes, *you* even have a special agent drafted in—for what that's worth. Ursus, I'm going to inform my client his fears are correct. The vigiles cannot do the job."

"Ah, be fair!"

"I have been fair long enough. You have the manpower and you claim to have the expertise—so you damn well get on and catch this man!"

Ursus muttered to Larcius, "Must be the wrong time of the month. Take her home, will you?"

Larcius knew better than to agree with that lousy time-of-the-month hypothesis, in case I really erupted. But he signalled in silence that he and the workmen were ready to escort me.

I was having none of it. "Keep away from me, all of you!"

I set off for home by myself. Being men, they all cringed and let me go.

———

Gardens are good places for solitude. The Grove of the Caesars, so dark and hemmed in, often seemed deserted and ominous, but the wide walks and tended beds beyond the old stand of forest trees offered peace and healing.

Healing and peace were not what I wanted, however.

LIV

Home. It felt as if I had been away for days.

When I came in, works I had never approved were waiting to jar me. A long uneven hump ran across the courtyard, improperly levelled after being backfilled; the fountain designer had brought in a water trench. It was not where I would have agreed to have it. Sosthenes had marked out his feature halfway along a wall, on a sight line through the atrium from the front doors: boringly conventional. In front of it, the two painters stood, while they discussed how they could paint a false garden either side. Very in vogue, they claimed. Very trite to me. Barley was sitting there with her back to me, inspecting the wall with the painters. Disloyal hound.

A bright new standpipe post attached to this wall must support water delivery; it could have been placed much closer to the kitchen. I watched Dromo turning on the metal tap. When no water came out, he turned it off, looking puzzled. He waited a moment, then turned it on again hopefully.

"Dromo! Give up. Sosthenes has not yet connected the supply."

The slave abandoned the attempt, turning himself around to scowl. "About time!" he greeted me.

"I had to do my work. Was I needed?"

"I'll say!"

"Have you had an adventure?" I could see he had. Dromo was full of pent-up excitement, with something to tell me. Knowing him, I would not want to hear it, but I had to.

"Guess what! A man walked in when you were out."

Apprehension. "Not into our house?"

264

"Right in. Sosthenes had left the doors open because he came to do his trench. They'd all gone away to buy stuff, leaving the doors like that. Anyone could just come in. Gratus and Fornix were out shopping. Marcia and Suza went to see a man—I think it was the one you told them not to visit. I was all on my own," Dromo complained.

"Where was the vigilis who was sent to look after us?"

"He went off with Marcia and Suza because they are so attractive they need an escort everywhere. In case."

"In case of what? They're tough enough." He left the house he came to guard? That was the Seventh all over. "Well, I'm sure you coped. What did you do, Dromo?"

"I was in charge of the whole place, so I jumped up and I called out, 'Ho there! What are you doing in our house, stranger?' He said he was looking for a boy. I said, 'I am the only boy here. I am Dromo and if you don't get out of here at once, I'll give you a thrashing with my cudgel.' He didn't know I've lost it somewhere. This man looked at me, smiling horribly. He seemed to be thinking what he could do to me, but he turned around and walked out. When Sosthenes and his workmen came back, I gave them a good talking-to about leaving the doors open."

My mouth fell open. I closed it.

Dromo lowered his voice, sounding nervous. "Was that man looking for the dancer?"

"Sounds so."

"I was brave, then!"

"Yes, you were brave to stand up to him. You didn't tell him about Galanthus?"

"I certainly did not."

The thought of Dromo encountering the Pest, right in our house, made me go cold.

"Good boy. Dromo, your seeing this person in daylight could be important. Will you describe him for me?"

"Easy." Dromo shrugged, convinced he was good at description. "He was nothing. Just ordinary."

As I'd thought. I had always said he would be like that. It is always the trouble with serial killers. They look like everybody else.

LV

Having dropped my main inquiry, I was stuck with fake philosophy. After a fitful night's sleep, I rose next morning, thinking I would ease my mind by losing myself in the scroll sale.

Marcia brought word up from my parents' house that there had been "a lot of interest" in my scrolls. Mentioning pre-sale interest is an auctioneer's way of prophesying gains. If they claim to have quiet confidence, that is shorthand for "Get the drinks in."

Falco had in fact sent for an amphora. Though he had not gone so far as to summon the legendary Faustian Falernian from our maritime villa near Ostia, he had collected a very drinkable Alban from Grandfather's old house on the Janiculan. It was too soon to be stocking up for Saturnalia. Pa reckoned nectar would be needed tonight.

I was nearly late. Idiocies held me up. First, when the fountain team appeared that morning, I had to deal with Sosthenes. Otherwise he would go ahead and we would be stuck for ever with a feature we would hate.

"If we accept your fountain—for which, incidentally, you have provided no specification, no drawings and no estimate, so take note: I've never agreed anything—here's my condition. I want it on the other wall."

Sosthenes said he would prepare a variation order. I snapped: nuts, I wasn't the soft-hearted vigiles, having their supply maintained at public cost, I was a contractor's wife. He knew what he could do with his talk of variations (which generally the client has to pay for). "Listen up, man. What I just said is your client brief. So, you will move that water pipe, at your cost, because you installed it without asking."

"You were not here."

"No excuse. And, Sosthenes, I want my courtyard left level this time."

He burbled about sight lines, as they do.

"Forget that. In this house, we don't give a stuff for people at the door. The only ones who matter will be having dinner with us. That will take place in our designated dining room, which is *there*." I pointed. It was an empty room, but Tiberius had frequently spoken of its future with vision. "Our friends will be gazing out from their couches, looking across the courtyard with delight to our fountain which, do not argue with me, is going to be *there*!"

Sosthenes caved in, but I heard him asking Gratus whether I had had some bad experience yesterday.

Next I had to interrogate dear Cousin Marcia about what she had been up to in my absence. After she had made a play for ignorance of why ever I could possibly be asking such a question, she admitted she had gone out with Suza, trying to visit Ovidius, the litigious scroll collector.

"I told you not to."

"Oh, I thought you didn't mean it. Never mind, he refused to see us. His slaves say he is a complete recluse."

"Don't try again."

"No, Albia."

"I mean that." I was hoping that, recluse or not, Marcus Ovidius would appear at the auction to bid on some scrolls. Assuming I ever got there, someone might point him out to me.

"Oh, you are *so* grumpy. How does Tiberius Manlius ever put up with you?"

I was missing Tiberius. Also, my conscience was pricking. I felt bad that we were selling these items, which he had never even seen—and selling them in his name, because his workmen had discovered them. Advice from the Didius auction house had been that to offer them as "pre-owned by a magistrate" would lend enough authority; they had a loose definition of provenance.

Finally, I had my own professional tasks; I had to cross to the Rau-dusculana Gate area (the wrong direction from the auction) in order to report to my client, Cluventius. Calmer now, I would omit how I had raged at Ursus yesterday about lack of progress, and my threat to abandon the case.

Ursus or Karus had already been to tell the Cluventii that if they had heard of any Transtiberina excitements yesterday it had been an unrelated domestic incident. This had been accepted. I was able to confirm firsthand what it had been about.

Unfortunately, there was a reason why the Blandus love triangle barely disturbed my client. When I said the vigiles were holding a suspect, Quietus, although I had doubts it could ever stick, Cluventius reacted with a dire announcement: "Oh, no! They have the case wrapped up. Julius Karus told me himself: Quietus made a full confession to him, last night."

This was bad, yet no surprise. I replied quietly that if the suspect's admission was true, I was very glad to hear it.

Perhaps my feelings showed. To me, there was only one way Karus could have extracted this from Quietus: he had beaten him up. That meant this "confession," though legally it would be deemed safe, solved nothing. The Pest would live on and keep killing.

To my surprise, Cluventius did not accept the Karus version. He agreed: "Yes, it stinks. I would like you to continue your own enquiries."

He was a sharp man. He wanted the truth, for his wife's sake. He could not be satisfied with the agent's easy answers.

There was still no need to mention how yesterday I had felt I was struggling so much against ineffectiveness that I had wanted out. Cluventius was my client; I liked him, his family and friends. Today I was ready to stick with them. I answered that I would need to tread very carefully—but until true justice had been done, I would keep investigating. Like Cluventius, I wanted to prove what had really happened. I wanted the real killer caught.

"Are you sure, Flavia Albia?" Our professional relationship had swung around to the point where the client was worrying on my behalf. Smiling, I reassured him.

On past experience, no one would let me see Quietus again; he would be a broken man. Officially, battering him would never be regarded as wrong, yet the physical results would stay hidden. The tortured man would only emerge from the station-house when he went to die. He would barely be able to totter across the arena when they pushed him out to meet his fate.

Even if at that point he retracted, the Roman crowd would only erupt with jeers. Plenty of criminals crossed the sand for their meeting with the beasts while tied to low, wheeled platforms; often it was not due to their reluctance, but to too many broken bones. It was too late to plead innocence. That only made a convict's sins seem worse; he was still brazenly lying, even after he had been condemned by our peerless legal system. Such a degenerate must be completely without conscience.

Meanwhile, in the Transtiberina the real killer, still free, would sooner or later persecute more victims. Caesar's Gardens would never be safe. The sacred Grove of Gaius and Lucius would be despoiled with yet more sacrilege.

Sometimes the best action is to ignore a problem temporarily. While I thought about what to do next for Cluventius, I took a few hours of respite at the sale of the buried scrolls.

LVI

S malls" day at the Saepta Julia. It was raining. The sale had been moved from the huge open-air courtyard into a corner under a colonnade, blocking passers-by. As they had to step out into the weather, they cursed loudly. The shops on that corner could not be easily accessed, so their owners were glaring out balefully. Even the walk-about snack-sellers looked depressed.

Staff had set out the usual mismatched stools and chairs that were awaiting sale on a furniture day. Wise punters had brought their own cushions. Everyone sensible had a cloak, while dodgy ones hid their faces under hats. Most of any auction audience can be classified as shifty. Of course, people say the auctioneers are worse.

It was the end of the year. Romans were deep in preparation for Saturnalia. While their enforced jollity did involve wondering what the heck they could give as a present to their awkward Auntie Livia, few would choose something to read. Her sight had gone, but that wasn't the problem. Whatever you pick out for a grumpy old relative, she is bound to complain she has already read that one. So, it would be bath oil as usual.

My father was selling someone's library. He had cracked the Auntie Livia joke as part of his cheery patter, but it had not helped. The library had belonged to a man, now deceased, who had had every scroll he possessed re-copied neatly by one scribe, then he kept them all in matching scroll boxes, fastidiously labelled on identical tags. He had owned a collection of glorious world literature, but it now looked boring.

Homer and Aristotle failed to reach their reserves. Fortunately, a small group of adventure novels livened things up, a common result of abduction by pirates or a visit to the moon. A flurry of interest in travel-ogues was followed by a deep trough of near rejection for comedic plays (Roman based on Greek), then a surge of bids for original Greek trag-edies; one lot included what my father described, po-faced, as suppos-edly a piece of wick from Aeschylus's oil lamp. "As is. *Caveat emptor,* as the proverb has it. No returns. Who's read *The Oresteia*? Oh, we've got some clever ones in! All the parts, was it? Aeschylus, smart fellow, was the first writer to realise that if you write a trilogy, you will sell three times as much. But we only have one piece of his wick! Start me at a thousand . . ."

Surprisingly, Father had five proxy bids on his book. Then more peo-ple in the colonnade vied fiercely. Some were dealers. This was what they had come for. The price went up like a comet, until that wizened bit of lambswool alone turned the library sale into a dazzler for the late own-er's daughters. At the end, everyone applauded. Although it was only mid-morning, Father took the sellers to lunch. They would be paying. Falco would not reappear.

Gornia took over the gavel. He now sold a mixed batch of pendants, styli, strigils medals, and strange bits of military equipment. The bygones went for coppers, though coppers mount up. Then he offered a batch of lecture notes of Quintilian, the rhetoric teacher; these were in fact notes taken by someone in the audience at public lectures that Quintilian had given before he retired last year. That meant they were unreliable; moreover, Quintilian had complained. "The great man has very sweetly declared he assumes stealing his intellectual property is done out of af-fection for him. Now is your chance to acquire some fine material from the official tutor to the Emperor's young heirs, sadly not autographed . . ." No, Quintilian would rather have sued for breach of copyright, but too many notes of his lectures had made it into the wide world.

Gornia rattled through at speed, not because he used the "auction-eer's chant" method to add urgency, but because his bladder wouldn't last it out. We reached my scrolls, but he had to go. After he nipped off for relief, my cousin Cornelius, one of dopey Aunt Allia's almost as dopey children, took over. I'd known him since he was eleven. He was now in his early twenties but unchanged: large, chubby, taciturn, with uncombed dark curls. Primarily a loner, he had a shy manner, though he knew what to do on the podium. Given a list of my scrolls, with descriptions, Cornelius worked through them even though, as I remembered, he was barely literate. He would have been coached in advance, helped by his excellent memory. People who cannot read or write, or not well, develop much practical intelligence, because they have to.

I could have taken the gavel, but I really wanted to observe the audience. While Marcia demonstrated the lots, pointing to scrolls with antics that increasingly annoyed me, I acted as bid-catcher, collecting each final price in a note-tablet, with the name of its buyer. That meant they had to tell me who they were. I had the list of absentees' bids as well. All useful.

Prior advertising ensured we had drawn serious buyers. They were already keyed up after the library sale. Some, I knew, had been sent invitations, after names were suggested to Father by Tuccia from the Mysticus shop and other contacts. My man Donatus attended. Tuccia was missing, though I did recognise one of her staff, Tartus, the man with the pointed nose, like a triangle, whom I had talked to about Mysticus. Earlier, during the library sale, Donatus told me who some other interested parties were; he said we had not lured out Marcus Ovidius. We did have a couple of fervent collectors, plus agents who would act for people who could not, or did not want to, attend in person. Too shy to come, too secretive or, as Father hoped, too filthy rich.

There was a distinct change in atmosphere once we reached the buried scrolls. Men who had been biding their time sat up. Snack-sellers drifted off to try their luck around the jewellery stores because no one would be wanting a lukewarm sausage here.

On the podium, Cornelius began: "We follow with a number of scrolls of unknown provenance, offered today by a serving aedile, Tiberius Manlius Faustus. A well-respected man. I have to say that as he married my cousin . . ." Mild laughter. Cornelius could handle the crowd. "You may have heard he was struck by lightning for daring to have her . . ." Louder laughter. "Sorry, Albia!" I brandished a fist, so my bangles rattled. Guffaws. This crowd was easily entertained.

"Get on with it!"

"We are able to offer various scrolls with an ancient appearance, though we have been unable to verify their history. Buyers must make their own judgement. Usual terms will apply." Marcia waved a document that was supposed to be our conditions of sale, though it looked as if it had been used to wrap butchers' bones. "Our reader has put them into sets, although in some cases no author can be assigned."

First offered were a few scrolls or fragments that had had no title page. I had devised brief notes to identify these: "Extract from play, with accusatory Chorus"; "Cosmology, abstruse"; "Nutty theories"; "Recipe for game pie, not tested." Even part-works and odd papyrus sheets were snapped up. Dealers bid relentlessly, but Donatus had told me they had clients with no critical discernment; they were just desperate for rare works to let people show off.

Cornelius made a joke that we ought to have donated the recipe scrap to Xero's pie shop. People seemed to know what he meant. Xero's has a reputation.

Now came accredited works. Fierce rivalry between two private collectors, plus Tartus from the Mysticus shop, drove up prices; Tartus must have been trusted with a substantial bag of denarii. Despite being dubious, with their authors unclassified in reliable catalogues and their papyrus perhaps too recent, Epitynchanus the Dialectician and Philadespoticus of Skopelos became hot stuff. Bibliomaniacs craved these things. Philadespoticus, with his single fragment, caused a frenzy. The three-cornered fight became so tense, Cornelius started to look nervous. He had one bidder whose way was to loll on the sidelines as if taking no interest; then, just when the gavel was about to fall, he would nod. A second man stayed head down over a note-tablet; immediately the first had bid, still without looking up he waved a higher figure. Tartus from the scroll shop leaned on a pillar. He looked as if the situation was a big joke—yet, with perfect timing, he coughed at Cornelius and acquired what he wanted. It was Tartus who bagged the Philadespoticus. The man who waved looked ready to disembowel him with a scroll rod.

If the Mysticus shop was the source of the fakes, I could not see why Tartus had bid. The only possibility was that after Philly's fragment had acquired a new history of sale by us, Tuccia could now offer it around for an even higher price. Our auction house was helping to make pieces more desirable. In future, the buried scrolls would be as "previously sold by the Didii," actually gaining respectability from us . . . Mind you, nobody would ever say, "Albia, daughter of Marcus Didius, has read them and she reckons these are crap."

The fragment of Didymus Dodomos had been withdrawn from sale. Marcia had told me my father had decided that, in view of the previous incident, with the Dodecanese Doctrinalist nearly landing himself in court, we would not risk it. The fragment was still listed, however. People who might be interested would see we had it.

I had a last-minute change of mind about Thallusa, the Greek poet. I noticed Donatus was after her half-damaged scroll, but I liked her work too much; I decided to keep it. At my signal, Cornelius looked quizzical, then declared a no-sale. With the Didius auction house, that meant no commission but it was allowed: the Didii are not shysters. Not to relatives. All right, but only occasionally.

We did well. I could say more, but auctioneers don't boast. You are supposed to pretend you look after everyone, buyers and sellers equally. You disclaim any interest in money. Never, says the code, show delight in your premiums.

I hung around while payment and collection occurred. Cornelius bought up any leftovers from wandering sausage-sellers for him and the staff. We bribed the shop-owner whose premises had been blocked by our sale. A few unsold items were carried upstairs to the office, where tomorrow Father would curse them, using foul language if he was still hungover from his lunch today.

I nobbled Marcia. "I've been thinking. Go back and talk to your friends at the Writers' Guild. See what they know about letter-writers, in case we can identify which one Alina used."

"Isn't everyone dead in the love triangle?"

"So the writers will thank you for bringing salacious gossip about that."

"Selling gossip's your profession, is it, Albia?"

"Just try. They are writers. Wear a low-necked tunic. Now get out of my way. I want to tell Gornia you were hopeless at demonstrating."

Marcia squealed, but Gornia agreed with my assessment of how she had shown the lots. I said if he could cope with a dancing boy, Galanthus might be suitable. He could make very elegant gestures, and he might see working at the Saepta as a safe haven. The old porter promised that the boy would be treated kindly. I would ask Galanthus whether he fancied a new life in antiques.

During the final stages, one dealer wanted a word with me. He was middle-aged, with dry, crinkled hair. I had seen him buy very decisively from the library collection earlier today, then bid more selectively on our scrolls. When he talked he made short, chopping movements with both hands. What he talked to me about was Didymus Dodomos.

"I act as agent for a collector who likes to stay out of the public eye."

"Do I gather he wanted the Didymus?"

"I am to ask you about its provenance."

"The scrolls were found all together in a hoard. There is no history."

"May I look at your fragment?"

"Yes. Can I ask you why?"

"Could I take it away?"

"No. Come clean. What is your interest?"

"The man I represent . . ." He paused, making it significant. ". . . he is Marcus Ovidius."

I sighed. "I see. Ovidius wants to compare my scruffy piece with the scroll he once nearly bought from Mysticus?" Now that I had examined so many new "old" scrolls, I would like to compare them myself. Were they produced in the same workshop? If so, was it here in Rome? Had I even been there? "What has happened, may I ask, to the controversial scroll?"

The agent's hands flew out, open-fingered. "It was lodged with a third party during negotiations." He snapped his hands together again.

I was thoughtful. "After Mysticus died, it just stayed there?"

"Marcus Ovidius will retrieve it, if you will agree to set the scroll and your fragment side by side."

I took a swift decision. "Yes, I can agree to that, but skip any third parties. Tell Ovidius I shall bring my fragment to his house, if he will be there in person with the scroll. Since Ovidius never bought it, I presume it still really belongs to the Mysticus shop." According to the new owner, she did not know where the scroll now was. "So, I insist we invite her, Tuccia, to be in attendance."

The agent looked surprised but made no objections. He said he would set up a conference and let me know when. In conversation, he told me that the attraction of Didymus Dodomos was that he wrote in praise of gardens, a passion with his client. "If you go to the house, make sure that Marcus Ovidius lets you see his beautiful garden room."

The agent signed off on the items he had purchased. Marcia took the money. When I checked afterwards, I still could not tell his name; his signature was scrawled illegibly.

LVII

By the time the sale ended, the rain had slackened off. I started for home. Down came more rain. I had gone too far to turn back to the Saepta; I had passed Pompey's Porticus and was rounding the Circus Flaminius. I scuttled for shelter into the Porticus of Octavia where there happened to be a library, one I sometimes used.

With nothing particular to look up, I got into conversation with the librarian. He lacked the skills to escape me. Buoyed by successful commerce, I was in a silly mood. "Are you familiar with Obfusculans the Obscure? They call him a deconstructuralist. I dipped into his wonderful commentary on *Aesop's Fables*—his analysis of why the hare ought to have beaten the tortoise really hit the spot. In general, I disagree with every line he writes—it is *so-o* stimulating!"

On his dignity as chief of a prime library, the man had so little sense of humour he failed to spot satire. "Ought we to try to obtain this work? The Emperor, as no doubt you are aware, wishes to have copies made of all works that are not currently held in Rome."

"You could certainly stuff Obfusculans into any space where Domitian has cleared out philosophy. The Emperor burning scrolls must put you in a moral quandary."

"No comment!" By this point the librarian, who was very old, twigged that I was merely hiding from bad weather. He told me to stop larking or leave, so as it was still torrenting down outside I made a real enquiry: "Have you anything by Epitynchanus?"

The librarian slowly searched records. "No."

"Philadespoticus?"

"No."

"Didymus Dodomos?"

He bridled. "Absolutely not! I am surprised at you, Flavia Albia. I would have expected you to know that author, so-called, is notorious."

"Under a cloud?"

"Supposing he ever existed. Which I *doubt*," he snarled, as if for failure to exist a man should be prosecuted. "Our holdings include no disreputable confections."

I bet they did. "Forget him, then. How about a Greek lady poet called Thallusa? Anything here of hers?"

To my amazement, more slow-paced perusal of records produced news that the Library of Octavia did own a slim scroll. "Please may I look at it?"

"No. It has been borrowed."

"Due back when?"

"We do not impose timescales."

"How long has it been out?"

"Let me see . . . over a year."

"Juno! You operate a real trust system."

"Our readers are men of probity."

"No penalties?"

"That would not be in our spirit of learning and enquiry."

"No, but it might bring your items back. Could you issue a reminder, in order to retrieve it for me?" No, they could not, even though it was obvious their dozy reader had forgotten what he had. "Oh, please! Thallusa seems to have slipped down the back of his couch. Nudge him, or you'll lose her." Recent events made me think that the existence of this scroll would enhance the commercial value of the torn and grubby Thallusa I possessed. Greed and bibliomania were catching. "As a matter of interest, can you say how you acquired your slim scroll?"

More shuffling, now through different records. Then the old one pronounced proudly, "It was a gift to the library."

"From whom? If it is not a secret."

"Oh, donors are always willing to be known, Flavia Albia. Otherwise, why do it?"

"Generosity. Reverence for the gods. Bad conscience—or just having a clear-out. Who was he, your big-hearted benefactor?"

"More often our donors are women, Flavia Albia."

"Of course. More generosity, better at clear-outs. Was this one female?"

"No. The acquisition was from a man, a professional dealer who sometimes hunts down rare works for us. He keeps a little shop in the Argiletum, so in most cases we buy from him, but he very kindly opted to make over this particular scroll without charge."

"Thallusa is a no-good for his profit margins?" I had forgotten jokes were a waste of effort. "Does he have a name?"

"Donatus."

Well, tickle me up with a centaur's tail.

Keeping a neutral expression, I said that since I knew Donatus, as soon as the skies cleared I might pop along to ask whether he had a second copy of his Thallusa scroll. A passing assistant overheard. He opened a cupboard, out fell a mess of aide-memoires, from which he was able to say that their copy had in fact been returned to the library. It was sitting in a basket, waiting to be re-shelved. He naughtily let slip that it had been in the basket for six months.

I asked for it. The librarian declined. Since the slip for return had not yet been filed, I would have to wait.

"You really mean you don't let women take things home."

"Not as a rule. But your husband is a magistrate so we could put it in his name."

"Not today, though?"

"Once our staff can allocate some of their valuable time to catching up on returns."

This was an old, traditional library, created in honour of the sober-natured sister of the tight-arsed Augustus: the sister Mark Antony had wed and dumped. Clearly Octavia's staff had not updated their systems for a hundred years. I knew better than to argue. But before anyone stopped me, I picked up the scroll of poetry, went to a reading table and unrolled it.

The helpful assistant came along, fussily slipping his returns note inside, for action later. "It had been out on loan to Berytus, the gardens expert."

I whispered, "Just as well he had brought it back—Berytus died yesterday!"

The assistant shuddered. "That would have been hell! We can never get our scrolls back after a death." A slave of indeterminate age but stubborn independence, he knew how to turn his back on the old librarian's disapproval. He dropped onto a stool for a muted gossip. "Berytus often used to come down to the library when he worked at the Palace. We saw much less of him after he moved to the Transtiberina. What did he die of, Albia—a bad case of blight, or nibbled by vine weevils?"

"He was pruned rather horribly." I knew this assistant, who was friendlier than the management, so I outlined what had happened yesterday. He winced, even though I left out a lot of gore. I mentioned that Berytus and his girlfriend had shared a love for poetry. "She couldn't borrow from here herself, but I suppose there was nothing to stop him, a trusted reader, lending her items taken out in his name?"

The assistant mimed horror. Then he said complacently, no, Berytus could pass whatever he chose to whomever he liked, so long as eventually he returned things. "In good condition."

"You check?"

"Our 'trusted readers' tend to be doddery old codgers. They are inclined to leave half-chewed bread-rolls as place-markers."

"Despite their confusion, I bet they pick out the cold meat from the rolls first?"

"Flavia Albia, you are a wise woman!"

"Well read," I boasted. "Got it from Obfusculans the Obscure. All the deconstructuralists are very sound on old men's habits—being ancient themselves."

The slim Thallusa looked in good repair, and much cleaner than the part-work of hers from the buried collection. It looked too new to be an original that had survived hundreds of years. Whoever had scribed it had the same handwriting as that used on the Thallusa papyrus we'd dug up; since I had that with me from the auction, I was able to lay them side by side to check.

Where are you now, unreachable Hyacinthus?
Is it Elysium, or Stygian Hades?
Where have you landed,
So lucid and candid
(so delicate-handed!),
O Hyacinthus!

I did not care when these poems were written, by whom or whether with criminal intent. I enjoyed them. I would have bought Thallusa straight from a shop as a contemporary publication, with no farcical pretence that I was being offered a rare old discovery. She spoke to me.

I had a thought. Perhaps not all the buried scrolls were counterfeit. Thallusa and others could be real authors. Philadespoticus and company might be inventions, but modern scrolls could have been put through an ageing process simply because the copies looked too new. Someone wanted to cash in on the crazy collecting market.

Was Thallusa's opus genuinely written hundreds of years ago by a Greek woman who ate honey in Arcadia and lived with a flock of goats? And was public disinterest in Greek ladies' poems why Donatus could not sell the scroll, so had given it to the library?

I was not the only reader Thallusa appealed to. I remembered that Ursus had given me Alina's letters yesterday; I was still carrying them around in my satchel. After glancing out at the weather, I remained in the library to read those too.

Actually, the handwriting of Alina's hired scribe had a familiar roll to it, though I could not identify why.

This was a sad experience. Date-wise, the letters had become jumbled. Poor Berytus had probably kept them neatly, but Karus and the Asturians had chucked them from hand to hand without mercy. Even so, I pieced together the story of a developing love affair. At first, the couple had tried to resist their adulterous attraction—*the wisest words I'll ever say: did wisdom, then, drive you away? (Thallusa.)* Dissatisfaction with her marriage had soon brought Alina round. She and Berytus had talked about flowers, they discussed poems, they met in the ship shed for passionate love-making, with the connivance of her easy-going brother.

I could not tell how they had imagined this would end. I found no sign that either of them ever attempted to make it permanent though nor was either avoiding the idea. Rome allows divorce. Alina could have left Blandus; perhaps she was frightened of him. Berytus appeared to have no competing commitments, although he might have feared that luring away a staff member's young wife would not go down well with his superiors. Handled discreetly, they could have managed. On the evidence of the letters, their attachment was deep; as much as love ever endures, theirs seemed capable of lasting.

I spent an hour lost in Alina's yearning, until I could no longer bear the chord it struck with a time years ago when I myself had been heartbroken over an unattainable man. Perhaps the saddest thing for me was that I no longer cared for him in the same way or thought of him at all unless we met. Now I was broody for a husband with business in another town, but the ache was mild; he would be coming home soon. These days I read love poetry in a different way, though I still remembered the dark days:

> One day I'll find a warmer place,
> Where I can wear a braver face:
> Till then, although I love you,
> I have nothing to atone:
> For there's no crime yet called living, honey,
> No crime yet called giving.
> And the only time that you can say I wasted
> Was my own . . . (Flavia Albia)

Alina, too, found love and enjoyed her affair. Her later letters were happy ones. She never seemed apprehensive. Once committed, she wrote to Berytus very strongly. Consummation works wonders. Good sex is magic.

Sometimes she mentioned her daily life. One event caught my attention. She had had to miss an assignation with Berytus when Blandus obliged her to go out with other people.

I told you I might have to be socialising with those people. I do not like that man he works with, though everybody else seems to. They admire him giving his time at the shrine. I think he looks at people oddly. His wife seems very distant. She never allows a word against him, though I have seen him treat her rudely, not letting her be friendly with others . . .

Alina did not name the man.

I gave in the slim scroll and packed my satchel, bidding the staff farewell. Outside in the colonnade, I stood for a moment, letting my mind clear. "Where do you get your ideas from?" must be one of the most frequently asked questions by members of the non-creative public, especially those who believe they could do your job. They hate the answer: "From doing nothing."

All day you have been labouring. You are not work-shy; your production is excellent. Then comes the moment when you close the stylus box, set aside the waxed tablets, bathe, eat, see your family, settle yourself for sleep. You have moved into the other sections of your life. Despite domestic pressures, you relax. Then your brain takes over, working by itself. Ideas are not deliberately formed. They come from the absence of thought.

So, as I stared vacantly out from the porticus, I braced myself for the gloomy wet streets again, readying myself to dodge drips from overhangs. Everywhere was damp. Occasional passers-by were hunched, as if it might suddenly start raining again. Then here it came: the gripping idea I had to follow up . . . *a nice man. Everyone liked him. He worked hard, he was helpful to everyone, he even volunteered to look after the sanctuary of Hercules in Caesar's Gardens. He had a wife and children* . . .

Rullius. Rullius, in the words of the apprentice, Gaius. Gaius who once saw that man go into the cave in the grotto and felt so unsettled he had to tell me.

. . . *this will be the most ordinary man* . . . *I'd say he is regarded by his community as hard-working, pleasant, a fellow who will do anything for anyone* . . .

Me. My assessment of the man they called the Pest.

In the hunt for the killer, general attention had glanced at Rullius, then moved away again. But now, as I stared at the gleaming rain-black wet street that curved around the Theatre of Marcellus, my attention fixed on him.

They admire him giving his time at the shrine . . .

I knew now. I needed to tell Ursus to search the sanctuary of Hercules.

LVIII

Once more it had stopped raining, though the air was heavy with moisture, suggesting another downpour could be imminent. Underfoot was treacherous, so slippery on the ancient pavements I had to take care. Head down, I watched how my feet trod, in case I slid.

This detour of mine was probably crazy. To reach home as I had originally intended, I would have walked along the curve of the river on the Embankment, through the meat market, passing the Pons Sublicius on the way. I could have visited my parents, knowing that if Father had returned from his long lunch, he would happily celebrate today's auction success. Mother would be pleased to see me, mildly deploring him. Or I could plod straight home, huddled in my cloak, hoping to find Paris with a letter from Tiberius. I had things to do, things of my own, things that would not risk the ignominy I would face instead if I was making a professional misjudgement.

For an informer it was a classic risk. I never hesitated. I walked as fast as possible around the Theatre of Marcellus on its northern side. This brought me to Tiber Island, shaped like a moored ship in the middle of the river, the "island between the two bridges." For once I crossed there. I went over both bridges, the Fabricius and the Cestius, with the sanctuary of the healing god Aesculapeus between them. Gaining the Via Aurelia in the Transtiberina, I headed for the station-house of the Seventh Cohort.

The gates were locked, but for me someone opened up a crack. I asked for Ursus, who sniffed out my mood immediately. "Hello, hello! What have you found, Flavia?"

"I have worked it out. I believe it is Rullius. He may have used the grotto for some foul purpose, but I don't think he hid his trophies there. Even if he did, he has obviously had to move them. There's another place he goes. I want to search the sanctuary where he volunteers."

Ursus made no jokes about how I had stormed off yesterday, neither did I bother to apologise. That was gone. I had my big new idea, and with it a request. He went along with it, gathering his cloak. "Please come too. I want a witness. Anyway, I feel anxious."

"Of course you do, Flavia. That's an after-hours haunt of gladiators," agreed Ursus. "I'll go. Unless you need a thrill, why don't you wait here?"

"No chance! Gladiators are darlings, and I shall have you to guard me."

We looked at the map on the office wall. We identified the sanctuary. "It's out-of-city," Ursus complained. "It won't have been searched."

"That's why the Pest can risk it. Don't tell me your mother warned you never to go beyond the city walls else the bears will eat you. I know the rules. You can go through the gate so long as something connects with crime in Rome."

"Bugger the rules, I'll go if I want . . . It's getting dark. We'll have to nick the tribune's mule. I won't bother to ask him—he can find out when he wants to go home. I'll ride. Hop up behind me if you want a quick lift."

He nicked the mule, which seemed to know him. I hopped up behind. We set off together, me gripping his wide belt and trying not to let his night-stick poke me in the kidneys. I had heard him giving orders; soon this sanctuary would be flooded with vigiles, though it would take them longer to arrive, as they would be walking. Anyone who spotted Rullius in Caesar's Gardens was to sit on a bench as if awaiting an assignation and mark him. "No need to actually get your willy out and play with yourself," Ursus instructed easily. "Just look as if you're doing it."

We rode almost as far as the garden tomb where I had found Galanthus. Most of Julius Caesar's walks, statues and pavilions were gone now, but traces of the old gracious garden layout remained. Public moves to repopulate the riverbank would eventually bring big wharf and warehouse complexes, but had begun quietly with permitting religious shrines.

Hercules, according to Roman mythology, had a connection with Rome. In his tenth labour, he stole the cattle of Geryon, which he drove all across Italy, bringing them to the Aventine. Some were rustled by the filthy monster Cacus, that charmer after whom shit is nicknamed. Hercules slew Cacus in his disgusting cave under the Palatine, starting our fine tradition of good city public health. In gratitude we had temples to Hercules everywhere, including my favourite, the little round gem in the meat market. Meanwhile his status as a human who became a god and ascended to the stars made him a protector of emperors, with their own celestial aspirations. But if gladiators had built him a shrine, that was because he was a big, strong fellow, who could overpower anything.

We trotted down parallel with the river, then through the Portuensis Gate. Syrians and Judaeans lived here and were buried in their own cemeteries. Officially outwith the city boundary, they had created shrines to various foreign gods, especially patrons of commerce and guardians of travel. At the first milestone stood the Temple of Fors Fortuna, goddess of Fate, a fickle dispenser of luck. Turning off the road there, we came to the remains of ancient quarrying for tufa and a vineyard. Here was Hercules in a rustic sanctuary. Hercules Cubans: Hercules having a nice rest on a couch.

Two statues left us in no doubt. In the larger, the demigod was seated. Carved into a rocky outcrop, there was also an aedicular shrine, in the form of a rectangular niche, framed with columns and graced with a pediment, containing a pictorial scene. There, the powerful figure of Hercules reclined on a flat-topped rock with a three-legged serving table in front of him. So muscle-bound that he looked stony himself, head back, the demigod appeared to have already quaffed from the cup in his right hand, yet he kept the other on his club.

Not all sanctuaries contain temples. This was a peaceful retreat with informal facilities. Hercules never needed to preside in a grand colonnaded edifice, on a hilltop acropolis. Here he was, having a break from his travels and labours, surrounded by greenery. Other divinities shared his space among the lovely trees and shrubs: Jupiter, Minerva, Venus,

Bacchus, with some of their dedicated busts in red-painted natural stone, others in marble. There were the usual miniature statuettes deposited by the faithful, plus a long flat table for offerings. A private individual had donated two small altars. Stone furniture showed that people came here for outdoor dining, honouring their dead or simply meeting in professional societies under the guise of funeral clubs.

It was all guarded by a sanctuary crone. A typical bent nosy-noddle, clad in black, she sidled about, eyeing visitors as if they had come to steal cakes off the altars, while eagerly cupping a clawed hand for tips. There were no cakes, so I bet she kept alive by eating them. Ursus seemed wary of her; he must have encountered half-mad, half-mendicant old bats before. With the light fading, we had no time for niceties. "Don't give me any trouble, Grandma!" he commanded. This passed for finesse with the Seventh.

I could see the crone believed her religious devotion made her the equal of anyone. Before she sounded off at him in screechy indignation, I quietly soothed her: "Ignore him. He's just anxious, and a man. I warn you, there are more coming. We apologise for invading. Information suggests that Hercules Cubans has been used by a criminal for hideous profanity."

"Not in *my* shrine!" bleated the guardian. She was going to be wrong about that.

I looked around. A neat boundary of plants marked out the sacred area. All temples in Rome had trees—symmetrical rose bushes, oleanders, olives, plane trees—softening them. Here were myrtles, figs and nuts. People always think of temples as isolated marble monuments, with grand steps, tall columns, friezes and huge pedimented porches. But even in those, their surroundings are always pleasant places for reflection; this simple shrine reflected that. Hercules Cubans lived in a small garden. Someone worked hard to keep it neat for him. All the foliage was trimmed, clipped and tidy. Bushes were round. Trees stood straight; twigs had been tipped to thicken them. Paths had manicured edges. No moss crept onto stonework.

"Your shrine is beautifully kept. Tell me who looks after the grounds, please."

"One of the gardeners comes to tidy round for us."

"One in particular?"

"Rullius."

"Has he been doing this for a long time?"

"We have known him for years."

"He does a good job. A nice man?"

"So lovely. Everyone thinks he is wonderful." I glanced at Ursus. He acknowledged my unspoken comment. The crone saw us. She fluttered, as if hints of the man's real nature might sometimes have worried her, though she said nothing. Whatever Rullius was accused of, she planned to stand up for him. Whatever we claimed he was, she would say we were making a crazy mistake.

"I would like to hear exactly what your gardener does, please. Describe his routine when he comes."

She gave me a look as if I was crazy, but she went through it: he would arrive, weed the ornamental beds, hack out brambles, prune bushes, deadhead, deal with ants, sweep paths. He brought his own tools, the ones he used in his day job. He took them away again afterwards.

"Does he keep anything here?" The crone looked bemused. They are always good at that. "Any tools or personal possessions? I suppose after he finishes," I guessed, "he has a bite to eat?"

"He makes a little offering to the god." The crone gave me a weary look. "This is a place," she spelled out, "where people come to honour friendly spirits. The college of charioteers meets here regularly."

"Their funeral club?" I was not surprised. We were out on a road from the city, so necropolis burials would be common. Associated gatherings would happen. Ursus had thought it was gladiators, and he might be right, but chariot drivers fitted. As benefactors, they would have disposable wealth too. "Rullius is a loner?" I pressed on stubbornly. "He never meets people? He shares his thoughts with Hercules in private? Does he do that out here by the altars?"

When the crone did not answer, Ursus pressed her: "If a funeral club meets, they must have a place to gather." Silence. That convinced us. "Come on, Grandma, their rites may be secret, but not where they sit down together to dine."

"The marble cave," she reluctantly admitted.

The carved niche where Hercules reclined turned out to be on one outer wall of a room dug into the rock behind. The devotion hall was so discreet, it felt as if it was deliberately buried. The crone let us in. It was like being underground. Pitch black. We could see nothing.

Ursus sent her to fetch light. With tremulous hands, she lit a single minute oil lamp; these shrine ghouls are always frugal. Immediately walls loomed with a subtle gleam. Despite the rural exterior of the sanctuary, this must have been an expensive indoor room. We gained no real impression of size. Our tiny light barely lit a single pace in any direction, though we glimpsed multi-coloured marble on floor and walls. Heads of charioteers on flat-backed pillars, like garden herms, emerged out of the darkness to look calmly at us as we gingerly walked about. The drivers' circus faction must have paid for all this. They would hold club gatherings, reclining for cult feasts indoors when they were not dining al fresco. They, of course, would bring torches.

"Rullius comes here." Ursus spoke heavily, not even a question: he knew—and he knew why. He was wincing, the way I once saw him wince at Victoria Tertia's body. "Dear gods."

From near the door, the crone's voice wavered. She clearly had no idea why Rullius liked it here. "I let him in when he finishes. He takes a few moments quietly, all by himself."

"Very pious! Alone with his memories . . ." Reliving crimes. Memories of rape and murder. Ursus could hardly bear to think of it. "Does he keep any property in here?"

The crone grew more nervous. She fidgeted, trying to stop our questions. "He leaves a few bits and bobs with me. I always give his things to him when he comes inside for a rest."

"He is never resting . . . Show me his stuff!" growled Ursus.

I said more quietly, "Show us, please, Gran."

So she went back to her hut, while the vigilis and I stood in silence in the vaulted funeral room, almost in darkness. We were thinking about what we might discover. Our mood was dark. The chamber was not oppressive in itself; the busts of charioteers had friendly faces. Only the thought of the depraved behaviour that had probably happened here caused an eerie atmosphere for us.

The woman brought a sack. Ursus weighed it with one hand, then muttered and led us outside again. We approached the flat table for offerings. At this point, his vigiles team began to arrive. We had formal witnesses. They had brought torches so, as the dusk deepened, whatever we brought out was illuminated by the quiet flicker of torchlight, objects displayed in a centre of winter darkness that made this feel like a ritual. We were not giving offerings to the gods, however, but taking something back into our world.

First came a bag with dice and gaming counters; nothing untoward. The old shrine guardian fussily explained the gardener liked to play against himself for relaxation. Next, a personal multi-tool, which a man could use for trimming his nails or cutting up an apple for a snack. An old hat. A bent chisel. "See, it's just a man's stuff!"

"And this?"

Finally, the horror: from the bottom of the sack, Ursus pulled out a locked wooden box. From the start, he must have felt it was there, but he left it to last. He had a sense of theatre. This was what we were looking for.

Seizing the chisel, Ursus was able to knock off the lock. The crone squealed. She fell silent once the lid came up. At that point, even she must have realised what the supposedly likeable gardener had been doing over the years.

Glinting in the light of an oil lamp, we saw a tangle of jewellery. Right on top lay a snake bangle: a double turn of cheap metal, the usual mad expression, once equipped with tiny red glass eyes—one of which had long been missing.

"Methe!" I never met her, but I knew enough about her, her permanently grieving mother and her decent husband; I was on the verge of tears.

Very controlled, Ursus tipped the box. A river of sad possessions ran across the offerings table. With a palm, he stopped any that rattled too near the edge. He started counting the pieces, but gave up, covering his mouth with one hand as if to hold back curses. There might have been as many as a hundred. Most were painfully cheap. Chains, earrings, pendants and bracelets finally reappeared while we witnesses stared with heart-broken sympathy. All the women who had lost them were being remembered. These belongings, torn from them during terrible deaths, at last spoke for what had happened.

Barely able to touch anything, I did what I had to. First, I separated out Methe's snake bangle.

"Pull out what you can identify," said Ursus, his voice hoarse. "You can return them."

"Evidence?"

"He is not going to argue. I am not going to let him."

I picked out the two amulets my dancing boys had used to wear, then the gold ornament on an expensive chain that must have belonged to Victoria Tertia. I could not find the thin wire bangle Satia's neighbour had described because too many were similar. Some of these personal things, like some women's bodies, would never be identified. Some remains would stay anonymous even though the women's jewellery was found. Some owners were lost for ever.

I had no need to ask Ursus what would happen next. The shrine guardian was taken into custody to be questioned, and to prevent her being tempted to send unwanted messages. The sanctuary was placed under vigiles guard. Any of the public who had gathered on the perimeter were dispersed. Then the inquiry chief, with a small detachment of vigiles and me in attendance, set off to bring in his man.

LIX

There might have been a problem. Vigiles who had walked across the gardens reported that, once dusk had fallen, the gardeners had packed up for the night. Rullius had gone home.

We knew that he lived over the river, near the Trigeminal Gate. To my surprise, Ursus had already identified where. For some time, he had been having likely suspects watched. Rullius was one.

"Head of my list." That could be bluff. I was not arguing.

"Did you tell Karus?"

"Am I a babe in the cradle?"

The possible problem was that a short stretch on the left bank of the Tiber was traditionally disputed territory among the vigiles. Three districts coincided. Three cohorts pretended to haggle over who should patrol there: the Seventh coming down from the Campus Martius, the Sixth coming in from the Palatine and Circus Max, and even my home group, the Fourth, sometimes, if they wandered down from the Aventine and felt like causing an inter-faction rumpus. In fact, there was no doubt the Trigeminal Gate stood in the Eleventh District. The gate and its porticus, plus the riverbank temples and meat market, were therefore assigned to the Sixth Cohort. The Seventh's patch ended at the Theatre of Marcellus. So Ursus had no jurisdiction.

He maintained that before we left the station-house he asked his tribune to liaise. Possibly he had. At any rate, the Seventh were making a quick foray purely to lift a suspect. It was in a huge case, a case for which they had done the legwork and possessed the background notes, a case no other cohort could desire to take over—even at this final juncture, when medals might be earned.

"In and out, before anyone knows we've been," Ursus ordered. He had no intention of being thwarted. This investigation had caused him so much grief and he was determined to gain credit. In and out it was to be, or even quicker than that.

"So now do we inform Karus?" I asked mischievously, as we arrived outside the building.

"No, he's buggered off back to his special assignment, thank you, blessed gods."

"And how will that affect Quietus?"

"Don't ask. I'll sort it somehow, depending on how badly the Asturians smashed him up . . . Come on, Flavia. Let's go in before this individual looks out of a window and sees us."

It was an average apartment in an average block. Families would feel crowded, single people oppressed by those families. Too small, too noisy, too hot in summer—like anywhere in Rome. This counted as decent. No one around here would believe their tenement housed a major long-term perpetrator of disgusting crimes. It seemed a place for nothing worse than pilfering and cheating. Incest, perhaps, but always kept nicely behind closed doors. The worst things around here would be smells from the meat market, a rat problem near the corn dole station, and fevers if the river flooded.

Nevertheless, it was where that ordinary man Rullius lived.

"He's at home."

"The wife?"

"Her too."

"Children? How many?"

"Four, we counted. Around five, seven, and nine, plus a baby. Three went out to play, half an hour ago."

"Find them. Keep them somewhere else."

"How, boss?"

"How do I know? Give them juice. Buy apples. Play bounce-the-ball."

I hoped their mother had not told them never to accept an apple from a strange man. Surely even a serial killer's wife would do that? The man on watch told us the children looked well-kept and healthy. When their father was at home, he came out into the street with them sometimes, for games. From what was said, I gathered Rullius had been under surveillance for much longer than today. Ursus knew his job.

"How many exits from the apartment?"

"Just the one. They all lead off the stairs. He's on the fourth floor."

There was a plan. Ursus intended to avoid a stand-off, or shouting, struggling, attempts at escape. Most of all, if the public got wind of what was happening and came out to defend Rullius, he did not want a riot.

I met the wife. When she answered the door to a polite knock, I was pushed forward to speak to her. She was small, mousy, so expressionless she seemed to have no character. Even so, she bridled while she claimed roundly that we must be mistaken: her husband could not have done anything to bring the vigiles.

I could never decide whether she knew everything but would not face the truth, whether she had no idea and would never believe it, or whether all along she had been aware and accepted or ignored what was being done. If he was a classic killer, she was a classic killer's wife. It would be easy to suppose he controlled her.

"I suppose you will say he was with you?" asked Ursus. Although she looked as if she would never say boo, not even to a rat on the baby's cradle, the wife snapped out angrily that he was. "I haven't told you when," Ursus pointed out quietly. He made a gesture for her to stand aside. One of his troops took hold of her arms, in case she kicked off.

"Some men are vile," I said, as I went past. "You picked one."

The truth was, Rullius had probably picked her. He would have chosen her carefully as cover for what he really wanted to do.

Ursus and a few of us went into the apartment.

The formal arrest was utterly mundane. Indoors, Rullius was eating. When he saw Ursus, he at once stood up, though neither threatening nor trying to escape. "Red-tunics! Here you are," he said, as if friends had arrived to collect him for a visit to festival Games. "I wondered when you'd come." He sounded as if he would just pick up a cloak before leaving.

That was it. He submitted quietly. In and out. No struggle, no riot.

There were bruises on him that might have been from bite marks, though probably too old now for a definite identification. I noticed Ursus looking at the size of his hands, though he did not bother to measure them.

Rullius never denied what he had done. He accepted that his time was up. He would never give any details; he would never show where more bodies were; he never named further victims he had killed. But he always agreed that he was the Pest.

I know Ursus believed Rullius felt relieved to be taken so he could finish killing. I never thought that. Had we not picked him up, he would have continued until he was prevented by age or his own death. What he did to women was so much his nature that there was no cure and no retirement. He saw nothing wrong in his actions. He felt no shame. He was proud to have done it so many times before anyone had stopped him.

Outside in the street, the Seventh's tribune had arrived. A heavy ex-centurion, he stood opposite, observing but not participating—as they do. If anything went wrong, it would not be his fault. With him was a similar hard-bitten tribune, from the Sixth, so due liaison must have taken place. The two men talked quietly to one another, not speaking to anybody else. They looked to be discussing their children's education or what they had done on holiday.

The tribune told Ursus he was claiming his mule back, so the inquiry chief would have to walk. That suited him. Ursus would march with the tight detachment that took their prisoner back across the Pons Sublicius. He would not be satisfied until that man was inside the Transtiberina station-house, safely chained in a cell. Action then would be routine. All the case notes would be bundled to send to the praetor, Rome's senior law-giver; he would sign off with "guilty: no trial needed" and a free ticket to the amphitheatre. But Ursus muttered he was going to have a big hook screwed into the ceiling and leave a piece of rope with Rullius in the holding-cell.

"I'll mention you in reports, Flavia."

"Albia."

"You'll always be Flavia to us, girl! Our mascot, like a little winged Victory up on a plinth."

By tomorrow they would have forgotten. They reckoned they had solved this case. I was an informer; I knew how procedure worked.

LX

It was really dark now, with a strong sense of winter gripping the city. No more rain had fallen. Dim lights appeared at food shops, looking muzzy in the damp atmosphere. The streets remained quiet, but with occasional revellers starting Saturnalia too early; they whooped loudly to annoy and frighten people. Treading quickly in the shadows, I managed to avoid having them run at me.

I went straight up the Aventine to Prisca's bath-house. I spent a long time strigilling, as if I had to scrape away my investigation, like physical filth. Afterwards, with my washed hair soaking up scented oil in a hot towel, I lay on a slab in the massage room, merely resting.

Prisca came in. "Caught the Pest yet?" she carolled, expecting a negative.

"Yes. Arrested this evening."

"Well done you, you marvel!" She paused, ever shrewd. "Never mind now. Come in tomorrow, my love, and tell me the delicious details then." She patted me once and left. I liked Prisca. She could see when her customers were desperate for recovery time. She was my kind of businesswoman. She sent me a free pastry, plus a kind message that she had despatched a runner to tell my household I would be arriving home soon.

I did pop in at home, since I was passing. I told Gratus I had a vital client visit before dinner.

Paris was back. "Tiberius Manlius will be coming home tomorrow."

"And?" I sensed more.

"And he can tell you himself."

"Is there a letter?"

"No. He will speak to you when he comes."

To tell me what? Nothing good, or he would have written it.

Sosthenes was fussing. He had built our fountain, though I could not inspect it because of the formwork; concrete needed to set. "A wonderful, waterproof material, Flavia Albia, adaptable, easy to use, cheap, plastic, permanent, seamless—"

"Sosthenes, I keep reminding you, I am a contractor's wife. I know the Seven Virtues of Concrete." I had cut him off at six. Don't ask me for the last. "Show me tomorrow."

Tomorrow was shaping up to be a busy day.

Cousin Marcia had gone back to the Saepta Julia to take Patchy, the intransigent donkey, finally home to Gornia. She was hoping the porters would be celebrating their good auction with a bonfire and a merry fry-up in the big Saepta courtyard. Marcia intended to drink herself silly so she could forget Corellius. She was set on seducing some rich goldsmith from the Saepta arcades.

Rescuing her from whatever situation she got into could be another task for me tomorrow.

All I would want to do was spend time with my returning husband.

At least I managed my client report. I brought Cluventius up to date as soon as possible. With no Patchy, I was forced to walk.

"A man has been arrested." I took his hand and folded into it his late wife's beautiful gold chain and pendant. "I assume this is something you recognise." He had not been able to describe this when requested to give details, but he knew Victoria's missing jewellery when he saw it. He wept. Being tired out by that time, I wept briefly myself. It must have done us both good.

We talked quietly about the outcome. Nothing could bring Victoria

Tertia back, or eliminate the memory of her corpse lying in the Grove that day, but Cluventius had shed his terrible urge to rave at Fate and blame the authorities. Everything that should have been done had been. No other women would be attacked by Rullius. The Grove of the Caesars had received its last desecrated corpse. Allowing my client to leave his rage behind was the critical part of my job; at last I felt good.

I let him decide if he wanted to attend when Rullius went to his death, whether the convicted man was to be eaten by lions or forced to fight as a gladiator. I never go to such events.

The family would recover to some degree. The youngest children might forget, or merely remain subdued. Cluventius's elder son would go into the family business, seeming to shrug off the tragedy in time, though of course he was marked for ever, as his father also would be. I heard later from other sources that the daughter found respite in music; Cluvia, apparently, began attending a lot of concerts.

I would be paid. I hardly liked to take money for this, but I had been professional for too long to go soft. You do the work; you earn the fee. I had promised the family to make sure the truth was uncovered, as it had been. Perhaps Ursus with his surveillance team could have solved the case eventually, but I had pointed the way to the sanctuary of Hercules. I made Cluventius aware of that, though with a light touch. He understood.

He escorted me to his door in person. I asked him to have a slave call for a hired chair as I was exhausted. Engeles, whom I had met the day Victoria was found, went to get out their own. While we waited, I made a joke about Patchy being so awkward, smiling over my dread of trying to buy a new donkey for us. Cluventius, who had worked with pack animals all his life, laughed. He said he would find me one. "Not too young nor too old. A beast of all burdens for light home use? Good with children?"

I drew in a long breath. "Yes, probably."

"Leave it with me, Flavia Albia."

The chair came. I climbed in. As Engeles and the other bearer turned for home, I let myself assume my long day was done at last. All my experience let me down. I should have known never to fall for that nonsense.

LXI

Never work with family. My cousin Marcia would have to go. She was still out on the gad at the Saepta so I couldn't tell her.

I had a memory of telling Marcia to go back to the Temple of Minerva, to ask the Writers' Guild for details of hacks who composed letters for people. I did not expect that, while I was busy, Marcia Didia would fly off madly to follow up on it. Or that she would find the man. If I, with my wealth of experience, had asked the dreary Guild to suggest a contact, they would have produced either nothing or a possibles list as long as a tragic play.

What she had done was to trip up at Minerva Aventina, flirt, flollop her figure enticingly, extract a few suggestions, then unerringly pick out the correct scroll shop to descend upon. When I saw who had now come to see her, I knew why. Marcia was determined to implicate someone she loathed: Tuccia. This is no way to conduct business as an informer. You have to be impartial or your case goes bendy.

Not Marcia. On her way down to the Saepta, she had stopped at the shop. There she had left a message with a couple of slaves who had never seen her before, so when the amanuensis came back from an errand, they sent him up to an address none had recognised. Marcia was still out, of course. I had to deal with it. Now the scribe was trapped in my courtyard by Gratus, who quickly explained as he dumped the witness on me.

I was surprised he was from the Mysticus workshop, though not as surprised as the slave. If he had known, it was unlikely he would have come.

"Flavia Albia!" He was a repairer, the silent young man I had seen hunched at a bench, copying in lost papyrus sections. In a week of ordinary-looking people, this was an ordinary-looking slave. He had long hair and a short, patched tunic, no distinguishing features, not much hope or joy.

While I was there the other day, he had never joined in with the conversation, though I reckoned he had been well aware of the others joshing Tuccia. "I was told somebody wanted to know about some letters I wrote for a woman called Alina."

"They do," I said, trying to fuel interest. "If I'd known where you worked, I could have asked Tartus to tell you—I saw him today at the auction." The response to that was wary, which at last piqued my interest. I dropped onto my dolphin-ended bench, ready to endure this task.

"You seem apprehensive. Don't the others know you carry out work on the side?" They probably did, but he looked vague about it; any money he earned ought to belong to the shop, specifically to Tuccia, who owned him. Some people would have let him take on outside jobs; she, I suspected, would be a mean owner. She was enjoying her new life too much. For me, it was promising if he resented her.

"You can talk to me in confidence," I assured him gently. "I am sorry if my cousin has exposed you in some way. At least you still came to see us, for which I thank you. What is your name?"

"Diocles."

"Tell me about working for Alina, please."

Diocles had heard what had happened to his one-time customer, so even before I started, he knew everyone was dead with no risk of comeback. Many people would think there was no point in my asking. None of the parties were clients of mine. The only crime was adultery, which some see as a sport.

He had liked Alina, and was sorry she had died, especially in such a terrible way. He was upset enough to open up. Alert to the slave's unease, and perhaps to my increased interest, Gratus brought him a beaker of mulsum. The steward then sat with us, watching and encouraging Diocles.

The slave told a simple tale of a woman from a poor background who had never been to school, but who in adult life had acquired a lover who taught her to read. She could write a little too, thanks to Berytus, though she was still unsure of herself with composition. She came to Diocles instead. Berytus had been given his name by someone who owed him a favour for providing advice about plants.

Berytus had had Alina use a collection of poems for reading practice; whenever she wanted to write to him, she would suggest quotations. The lovers were particularly taken by a conceit they found somewhere of Cupid watering plants from an amphora; clearly the god of love looking after plants tenderly was made for them. Diocles thought it all rather sweet.

While he sipped his mulsum, Diocles suddenly said, "When I saw you, I thought it was a trick. I thought you had got me here to your house so you could ask me about those scrolls from the Grove."

I looked at him, full of innocence. "Goodness. I never thought of it! But while you are here, if there is anything you can tell me, I would love to hear it."

Now he was sorry he had spoken. He downed his drink as if he was intending to leave. Gratus swiftly gave him more mulsum.

"Alina seems to have loved those poems by Thallusa," I said. "To be honest, I had been thinking Thallusa was invented by someone."

"Oh, no!" exclaimed Diocles. "She's real enough."

I jumped on that. "Some other authors in my scrolls might not be?" He turned shy. I cursed internally. My rule for interrogation is to prepare as much as I can. Here, I had not even expected him, let alone that he would talk about the buried scrolls. "To be honest with you, Diocles, I know much of what we discovered at the Grove of the Caesars is fictitious. I had reached a conclusion that the scrolls were produced quite recently at your shop. If your expertise is copying, have you yourself ever been involved in producing new works?"

"No," he said.

"But you do not deny their origin is the Mysticus shop?"

"I know nothing about what they get up to." He was digging himself into a hole, because he still implied the fraud went on there.

"Of course," I mused, "this all started when Mysticus had a complaint about the Didymus Dodomos scroll when he offered it to Marcus Ovidius. It was about gardens, I believe. Lovely subject!"

"We never wrote that scroll," Diocles burst out. As he fell deeper into his hole, he became more and more unhappy. "Mysticus bought it from someone. Another dealer."

"Really!" I kept playing innocent. "All right, I accept Mysticus bought the Didymus scroll, so someone else must have faked it. But afterwards, this is what I think: that first counterfeit scroll gave people at your shop the idea to produce more. Tuccia says the Ovidius controversy happened before her time—but did she want to make more fakes? Everyone says Mysticus was very honest. My guess therefore is that he wanted nothing to do with any cheating, but after he died, once she possessed the shop, it was Tuccia who started to produce other scrolls. New owner, new régime."

Diocles answered darkly, "A lot of things changed at the scroll shop after Mysticus died!"

"Like?"

He was deeply unhappy. "Not for me to say."

"Oh, go on!" I said, with a fey giggle. I could have been Tuccia herself.

Diocles stood up. He was leaving—but would he drop a crucial hint before he fled? "I like to keep my nose clean," he said. "I only ever once wrote out one new fragment for them, which was the Philadespoticus. I mend things by recopying missing bits, but that's all above board. I didn't want to do the fakes."

"You are a slave. Could they compel you?"

"If they wanted, but they were afraid I might be so upset that I'd go and snitch to someone. So, they leave me alone. And I'm sorry, Flavia Albia, but I can't talk to you no more."

I let him go. I try never to get slaves into trouble; their lives can be hard enough.

I believed there was truth in what he had said. He had explained why the supposed "Philadespoticus of Skopelos" had only a fragment in the buried collection. He had confirmed, in effect, that the buried scrolls had originated with Tuccia and others of her staff. Presumably today Tuccia sent Tartus to buy some back at the auction because it might disguise the fact that she had produced them in the first place. They had put a lot of work in and she might believe there was still profit to be made. Once the heat died down, Tuccia and those of her staff who were willing might produce even more scrolls. Maybe she would have fun inventing even more terrible authors.

I liked the fact that Diocles believed Thallusa was a real poet.

LXII

I slept. It was bliss. I only awoke because of noises in a nearby room. Gratus had decided to clear out the painters and their equipment so it could be a bedroom, as intended. Paris was helping him. Dromo was watching. The painters were on the opposite side of the balcony, for once not quarrelling with each other. They were plotting how to quarrel with Gratus and Paris.

I dressed without aid, since Suza was downstairs hearing from Marcia about her adventures at the Saepta last night. Neither took any notice when I appeared, so after my breakfast, I found my messages left on a tray by Gratus, read them and picked out an address from one. I left that note displayed for Gratus to know where I was. Then, without saying anything to anyone, I picked up something I needed and took the dog for a walk.

I passed Sosthenes. He was coming on site with his workmen and what appeared to be sacks of mosaic tesserae. "Flavia Albia! Blue or green for preference?"

"Turquoise."

"Where are you going?"

"To see a man about a scroll."

Barley wagged her tail.

I had the Didymus Dodomos fragment in my satchel, and the address of the secretive Marcus Ovidius learned by heart.

LXIII

The garden room of Marcus Ovidius was truly beautiful. One of his
slaves took me, then left me to marvel while he told his master I was
there. I could happily have waited for hours.

You came in through a single small door. Light was supplied from
above, though it was muted. Once closed, everything including the door
was painted—painted so exquisitely it looked like a real garden. The
mural ran around the corners and over the ceiling. Trees seemed to sway
gently. Birds looked ready to take wing as they raised their beaks from
trickling fountains, looking up to butterflies alighting on fronds. You
could almost smell the roses and violets.

And yet it was not meant to be real. You could acknowledge playful
visual deception. You felt contained within a grove, yet knew you were
standing on a marble floor indoors. The sky was a frieze; the ceiling dangled golden boughs yet was coffered plaster, so clearly not sky. You gazed
at a dark dado, painted with criss-crossing reed fences to enclose the
garden on the walls, an inviting representation, yet you could not enter.
You were meant simply to admire. You could sit or stand in the room,
sheltered from weather, private from people, cut off from the sounds and
stresses of real life, losing all sense of time. Trees, shrubs and flowers in
delicate pale blues, bright greens and yellows soothed you. Fruit, flowers and even the fencing were picked out in flecks of contrasting gold,
like sparkles. There were repeats and regularity, yet each plant, insect
or bird was sufficiently different for new delightful discoveries wherever
you looked.

I had seen frescos with enchanting panoramas of fantasy buildings set in imaginary landscapes. I had heard of a room like this one in the private villa of an empress. I am afraid my first reaction was that of wife: I was glad my husband was not here or he would have bankrupted us, wanting one. Holy horticulture, I wanted one myself.

That, of course, was the point. The motive for Marcus Ovidius's eager collecting was for other people to know what he had. He yearned for the world to envy him.

When the slave came for me and took me to his master, there was nothing about Ovidius to suggest his reputation as a recluse. Dammit, he *had* been at the auction. (Why had Donatus said otherwise?) I immediately recognised him—not always bidding himself, presumably because his agent had been there. He had bought things, though I could not remember what; when he settled up, he must have used an alias. People did that. The auction world was full of secrecy, often pointless. Ovidius had presumably left his agent to get what he really coveted, though later it had seemed to be the agent's idea to set up this meeting.

Marcus Ovidius was not long past fifty. His features were nothing special. Clean-shaven, he reeked of an expensive skin lotion. He had a crease-free white tunic and several cameo rings, plus a vivid belief in his own fine mind. He must possess money, probably inherited: his house was an enormous property on the right bank of the river, where anyone else would have built a large warehouse and profited. Tiberius, with a storage business in his family, would have groaned that the home was a waste of access to the river. I thought the area was too busy for leisurely enjoyment of a domestic property, even one that was provided with elegant grounds.

Ovidius wanted to start. His agent had not yet turned up and neither had Tuccia, though he assured me he had invited her, as I had stipulated. I was early. Ovidius did not object; he was desperate to compare the Didymus scroll with my Didymus fragment. No need for anyone else to get in the way. We laid out the documents and began without them.

They were in Latin, and not written by the same hand. That was not significant: even so they could have originated with the same author.

The style definitely matched. In both, the author spoke passionately of gardens and the joy they could give, yet he was intensely practical. He discussed the layout of terraces and walks, the virtues of topiary where wild nature was tamed, a striking variety of plants. He went into minute detail on how to propagate by sowing seeds, grafting or rooting cuttings.

"Not hoary philosophy, like some other scrolls I found buried," I said. "It seems to have been written by someone with deep knowledge of growing things. I believe you used an expert to evaluate your potential scroll? Nobody seems to remember who it was, but would he be able to comment on comparing the texts?"

"I was my own expert," said Ovidius, surprising me. "I study widely. I have immense experience of textual evaluation." I would not want to be sued by this self-assured pompous man; he was bound to act in court on his own behalf—and to do it tiresomely. My uncles, who practise law, say "presenting his own defence" is guaranteed to make them abandon a case.

"You had almost accepted the scroll as genuine?"

"Influenced by Mysticus. He believed in it. He was generally trustworthy—though one must always take one's own precautions. I had wanted to buy something on the idealistic Greek 'paradise' concept, but I came to the conclusion this work is a Roman cultivation handbook, with no history I valued. Solid stuff—not ancient. The author has literary merit, though he is no Theophrastus or Xenophon. A close reading suggests that, whoever he is, basic information had been supplied to him by a skilled gardener for . . ." He paused.

"Enhancing?" I suggested. "Fancifying?"

"Quite. Adding more elegant turns of phrase . . . As the purchaser, it was not for me. I am all for intertextuality, Flavia Albia, but I desired a thesis on the ideal of a walled enclosure, an exquisite plot that contains and inspires peace, prosperity and plenty. Food for the soul, not 'How I prefer to graft cherry trees.' You may disagree, but I had my agenda. Mysticus knew that. When I decided he was passing off an ancient author, that settled it."

"Had you gone to Mysticus asking him to find something?"

"No, my agent alerted me that he might have this."

"But you had bought from Mysticus previously?"

"Oh, yes. He had a great knowledge and was personally popular."

"You trusted his judgement?"

"Completely."

"Had you ever come across the writer Didymus Dodomos before?"

"No."

"Had Mysticus?"

"He said not."

"That made the material more desirable, to you as a collector . . . Is it possible that this scroll was deliberately put together in order to appeal to you?"

"If so, then it is not simple fraud, but a fraud aimed at me personally! And at least they could have written what I wanted!" His self-concern was alienating. Probably better if he stayed a recluse.

"So has today's comparison of the two pieces satisfied your concerns, Marcus Ovidius?"

"The same person concocted both, no doubt about that."

"If I proved it was deliberate fraud, would you want to take it further?"

He looked vague. "I decided against before. One never wishes to look too easily fooled . . . Still, what shall I do?" Ovidius mused. "I might even buy the scroll after all. What about your fragment, Flavia Albia? Will you sell it? Will you sell it to me?"

I had no intention of letting him have it. "I shall keep it. It has a useful section on pomegranates, which I want to grow in my peristyle." I made sure I picked it up; I tucked it safely into my satchel. "Your agent seems to have let us down today. Of course, he may have to answer the demands of other clients. I saw him buy items for you yesterday, even though you were present."

"Incognito produces a better price for me. I am so well-known."

"Have you worked with the same agent a lot?"

"Some years. He is much more than an agent; he is very widely read and has a good intellect. He understands what I am looking for. That was why he pointed me to Mysticus for my Didymus scroll." I found it typical that Ovidius called it "my" even though he had never owned it. I was amused he spoke so highly of the man who had nudged him towards a fraud.

"I never caught his name," I said. "Your agent?"

"Xerxes."

I felt my eyebrows shoot skywards. "The sleeping partner of Donatus?"

"I wouldn't call him a sleeping partner. They work closely all the time."

I had been led to believe Xerxes was an invention. Now it seemed he was real and active—and involved with the first fraudulent scroll.

"Did you ever know," I asked narrowly, "how Mysticus had acquired that scroll?"

Ovidius looked surprised I had asked. "That was no secret. It was how Xerxes knew of its existence—Mysticus first had it from Donatus."

By this point nothing surprised me. I was buying my husband's encyclopaedia from a two-timing double-dealing scroll rat.

LXIV

Since our business was concluded, I flattered Ovidius, begging him to show me his garden room again. It was just as beautiful the second time. Using my husband's building firm as an excuse, I screwed out of him the name of the artist who had designed and painted it. Of course, we would never be able to afford anything like it. Still, you can dream. I knew if Tiberius had been there, he would have collected the contact details, just in case they came in handy.

To walk back across the Tiber, I took the Pons Aemilius, the big old stone bridge below Tiber Island. Instead of turning right for home, I went left, down the Vicus Jugarius into the Forum, across to the Argiletum, then straight to Donatus's lock-up. He was there. So, looking surprised, was Ovidius's agent, the supposedly invented partner, Xerxes.

"Xerxes! He does exist," I said to Donatus, as if he might not have been aware of it. "So here you are, mysterious Xerxes!"

"I didn't think I would be needed," Xerxes explained brazenly, while Donatus had the grace to look sheepish.

"Right. Marcus Ovidius and I managed to have a very successful meeting without you or Tuccia." Perhaps the two men were apprehensive, though they were braving it out. I leaned on the shop counter, straightening bangles: an old trick, but it makes people nervous sometimes. "Now I've had a walk across the river with time to assess what I learned from him. How dubiously intertwined scroll-dealing is! How sickeningly devious are scroll-sellers!"

They laughed it off. Donatus had recovered his dash. "The collectors won't ever talk to each other—but we dealers are one big happy club."

"I see what you are, Donatus. It's not pretty. One of you invents an author and creates a scroll; he fudges the issue by selling it on, your dodgy partner points a client to it, and if everything should go skew-whiff because the client smells a rat, that scroll has been fitted out with too murky a history for anything bad to happen for you pair. Its fudged chain of ownership will keep you out of trouble."

"'Invents an author?'" Donatus quoted back at me sweetly. Never trust a man whose hair broadcasts that he does not own a comb.

I smiled. "You and Berytus. It's a pity he's dead—not only because I can't ask him about your collaboration on gardening but that poor man wrote a damned good handbook, from which he himself should have benefited. Instead, 'Didymus Dodomos' is discredited and scandalous, while the only people who gain from the superintendent's vast knowledge are underhand, unethical shysters. All of you. Even Mysticus, 'trustworthy' though he was supposed to be, manages to escape blame—but only through inconveniently dying." I took a deep breath as a new thought reached my indignant brain. "And there's a question!"

Donatus and Xerxes applied expressions of puzzlement. Their acting was as fake as their literary credibility.

"Suppose," I suggested, "Mysticus was genuinely honest. A good man, as everybody said. Suppose he realised you and Berytus had deliberately faked Didymus, so he was about to expose you. He might have felt he had no choice, with Ovidius threatening to sue him. He was a fit man, not old, had a family, was used to working in the Vicus Tuscus in all weathers—yet he died. That illness of his sounds suspicious. Donatus and Xerxes, should I be wondering whether Mysticus died of unnatural causes? If so, was it down to you two? He put you under threat—so did you help him into Hades?"

I caught them on the hop. They had thought only that they faced a tricky argument about their fake scroll. I realised I did not care about that, nor the others. My concern was protecting human beings or, if I was too late to save their lives, finding them justice.

"If you want, go into your shop and confer about how to stop me exposing you."

"You wouldn't!"

"I am an informer. That is what I do."

Letting them discuss it was generous, though not too unsafe, since I had been in the shop enough times to know there was no back exit for escape. They did step away, heads together. I watched them consider my accusation: Donatus, still unkempt and possibly unwashed, Xerxes with his abrupt, chopping hands as they talked. Leaning on the counter, I linked my own hands together on my waist girdle. I waited, gazing at the sky, as if with a sudden interest in winter clouds.

They sidled back.

"Was the Mysticus death suspicious?" I demanded.

"It looked that way." Donatus was happy to make the accusation.

"But it wasn't us," his partner pleaded.

"No." I was cool with them, but fair. "I believe you. But if somebody removed Mysticus, the question is, who benefited? Who wanted his business? Didn't I hear from someone that Mysticus was married with family?" Glaucus had said it, right at the beginning.

"Wife and young children," Xerxes confirmed.

"Why didn't they inherit? What happened to them?"

This time it was Donatus who knew: "There were two little ones. They died in similar circumstances to Mysticus. Very soon afterwards. Same kind of illness. Never recovered. Afterwards his missus just disappeared."

"Did a doctor look after the sick?"

"Probably not. Tuccia helped the family. She nursed them."

"Very conscientiously?" I asked, very drily. The two men considered what I meant.

"And who would benefit from removing that family?"

"Tuccia," they chorused.

I straightened, preparing myself. "I was talking to a law-and-order agent, who reckons that when women kill they fool themselves it is out of pity. Women are nurses and nurturers, so if someone is suffering, they want to take away their pain. But Karus, my contact, was cynical. He believes 'I wanted to help them' is a lying excuse. He says when women murder others, it is always for financial gain."

"Gaining a shop, for instance!" Xerxes contributed.

Donatus, keenly accusing her, gave me details: how Tuccia first appeared as a relative, helping out in the scroll shop. Very soon Mysticus was ill. Tuccia insisted on nursing him, as she did later for the two small children. She sat with the patients day and night; nothing was too much trouble for her. None survived. Tuccia seemed sad, yet somehow untouched by the tragedies. She took on a bigger role in the scrolls business. She had appeared to be extremely kind to the invalids—while, as Donatus suggested, giving them the wrong medicine. No one had suspicions—or none they could prove.

"And what about the wife?" I asked. "The dead children's poor mother? Tuccia once told me the bereaved woman 'quietly disappeared,' so we could suppose she was too upset to stay after she had lost Mysticus and her babies. Or was she afraid she would be the next victim? Tuccia suggested she went home to her own people. Apparently, she was from the country?"

Xerxes jumped on that. "Rubbish! Callista was a Transtiberina girl, through and through a city woman. If she's gone to her family, they live near the Via Aurelia."

"Oh!" I knew a man who could find her, then. "Of course," I argued, "Tuccia may turn and place blame on her. She may say guilt and fear of discovery were why Callista went into hiding. Have there been any other mysterious deaths close to Tuccia?"

Xerxes shook his head, but again it was Donatus who knew the gossip. "Oh, hers is such a sad story, Albia! She had a mother she looked after, but her mother died during an illness."

"That fits!" snapped Xerxes.

"A sister," added Donatus, drolly. "And even the sister's baby."

"Brother-in-law?" I demanded.

"He'd run off with a fishwife. But that meant there was no one left behind to ask awkward questions."

"Was Mysticus alive at the time? What did he think?"

"The situation bothered him. He felt very unhappy," said Donatus. "I had a drink with him one evening, which is how I know all this. He told me Tuccia seemed to be strangely unlucky. He wasn't going to say anything, though, because what had happened to her relations looked quite ordinary. He was letting her work in the shop because he felt so sorry for her. Next thing, he was gone himself, the two poor little babies died, his wife not there—and suddenly we had Tuccia running his business."

"A lucky break—or planned? Was she left it in a will?"

"She just sort of took over. Someone had to run the place, and Callista was nowhere in evidence, so it ended up being hers."

"The staff treat her contemptuously. They dislike what happened."

"They don't like *her*! But they are slaves," said Xerxes, the agent and realist. "She's taken charge. They have to get along with her."

I threw in the other complaint against Tuccia: "Then your escapade with Didymus gave her the idea of profit in fakes. Well done for that! She started to use the slaves' expertise to make more, and she tried burying them for an aged appearance. A woman and man were spotted in the Grove of the Caesars with a spade . . ."

"Tuccia with Tartus," suggested Xerxes.

"Maybe. Once that happened, her staff were complicit. She might have kept them sweet by promising cash?"

"Slaves," repeated Xerxes. "They would go along with anything, if Tuccia gave them money." He was quiet for a moment. "She seems to have been very clever."

"Oh, she is," I told them both. Grimly, I summed up: "She has murdered a number of people without anybody noticing. She has set herself up financially, with a life she adores. But what she can be most proud of, thanks to your original idea and the enduring greed of bibliophiles, are her wondrous creations: Epitynchanus the Dialectician and Philadespoticus of Skopelos."

Xerxes murmured blithely that he particularly liked Philadespoticus; he had bought that solo fragment yesterday on behalf of Marcus Ovidius.

LXV

I struck a shameful bargain, of which I am proud. I would never proceed against this amoral pair for their Didymus Dodomos fraud, so long as they sold Tiberius's encyclopaedia to me at special rates: two scrolls for the price of one. As an auctioneer's daughter, I insisted on written terms. They had to sign an affidavit, even though they claimed a scroll-dealer's word was his bond and a simple handshake was traditional. I said cheating seemed even more conventional; I had their signatures witnessed at the apothecary's booth opposite. He was Egyptian, so literate in seven languages. Or so he told me.

I asked if they had invented Thallusa; they denied it. Donatus claimed that if anyone wanted to invent a poet, they would never choose a woman; there was no money in female poets, not even graphic lesbians. He said he had donated the scroll to the Porticus of Octavia after the old librarian became awkward about his connection with the Didymus scandal, threatening to end their rare-works purchases.

They asked what I intended to do about Tuccia. They imagined I would challenge her, question her, try to persuade her to confess. I saw no hope in that, even though I now believed she had killed people, while persuading herself and everyone else that her patients needed "help to sleep" or "relief from pain." And Karus was right: she had murdered for gain. Nobody had noticed what she was doing, which fitted my theory that women get away with murder because they are too clever to be spotted. But, then, I also thought such women are too clever ever to admit their crimes.

Tuccia would deny it all. Illness is easily explained away. Only one person might have witnessed all that had happened to the family. But if we could find that woman, she might be prepared to talk.

I went to see Ursus.

He was pleased, once he felt sure I had not come to claim credit for his capture of the Pest.

"No, I'm going to make your career, Ursus. Listen to me and you could end up nailing two multiple murderers in a week."

"I'm interested!"

"This is a woman."

"The Seventh are not prejudiced. We will arrest anyone."

"And you so often do . . . The murderer will never admit what she has done, but someone lives in your district who must have watched how she went about it. This witness can tell the full story and it's in her interests to do it. So, if you are persuasive . . ."

"Does a dog lick its vomit?"

"Ursus, I think this poor soul has run away to hide here in terror. She fears becoming the next victim. Find a scared woman who lost her husband and two dear little children, who is living near the Via Aurelia. You should be able to do that; it's the really big road, right outside your station-house." He grimaced at my cheek. "The murderer is Tuccia, the witness is named Callista. Her dead husband was Mysticus, a scroll-seller."

"You do love scrolls!"

"I have an enquiring mind."

"You could do this, Flavia."

"My household is going to need my attention."

"I can find her," claimed Ursus, grandly, "so long as she's never gone out on her own in the evening, and got herself grabbed and murdered in the Grove."

I reckoned she would stay indoors a lot. All he had to do was track her down. Then he must persuade Callista that, even if she talked to him, she would be safe.

"Flavia," answered Ursus, "any woman is safe with the Seventh Cohort. Are you coming for a drink with us?"

"How rash would that be? No, thank you. My husband is coming back today, so I am going straight home, like a good wife. Just one more thing. I assume Callista will be concerned about justice for her husband and her innocent children—but do tell her that once Tuccia is formally condemned, she, as the widow of Mysticus, will automatically own the scroll shop."

It would be a neat irony if a woman who killed for financial gain was finally informed upon by another woman, to acquire the same inheritance.

LXVI

Home.

A donkey I had never seen before was drinking all the water from the new fountain. Twinkling with polychrome mosaics, it made a superfine trough for this big beast. Dromo and Suza were attempting to entice it away, though they jumped back in alarm every time it turned its heavy head to look at them. Barley was barking a sustained challenge.

Elaborate scents came from the kitchen area. I could hear Gratus making a to-do with what sounded like our entire wedding crockery.

Fornix came out, apron-wrapped. He started to lead the reluctant donkey towards the builders' yard. Larcius and the workmen decided to come to inspect the fountain, after which they covered it up while everything finished setting. Paris appeared and shouted at me that Uncle Tullius would be coming for dinner.

Marcia was reading a letter, which she hurled aside with a wild shriek. "Corellius has explained everything! He thought I would worry if I knew he was having medical attention. He went to have a special surgeon amputate his damaged leg—then a prosthetic limb fitted!"

"Of course. A false leg! I am surprised, my dear, you never thought of that."

"You'll miss me if I rush off to him!"

"So true, darling."

Everyone dived back into whatever they had been absorbed in, while I sat temporarily on the dolphin bench. As I reached home, I had spotted an interesting large wagon, apparently laden with furniture, lumbering in from the opposite direction. I was ready the moment that Barley stopped barking. She turned towards the atrium, the end of her tail twitching. Like me, she had heard the familiar key turn in the lock.

"It's Master, Barley!"

The dog moved her tail three inches in each direction. I stood up.

Barren,
The shell-hollow
Of my life
Without you . . .

Tiberius Manlius entered quietly. As the master returning, he gazed around in a rapid summary of what was going on. Romantics might imagine that, after two weeks away, he would come to kiss his wife. Not this one.

"What's under the hootch?" he asked, gesturing towards the tarred pall that covered my new building project.

"Don't look," I said. "We think a rat is living there. Besides, the concrete has to set."

That didn't stop him. You know how it is. Somebody tells you not to go to a grotto, so straight away you head over there and start poking around. At least I had let Sosthenes provide a gorgeous shell-lined apse with glass-cube mosaics, plus a fine marble basin. Tiberius would have to concede this was better than green slime. He noticed at once that they had run out of scallops near the bottom edge. But the waterproof concrete, with its classic seven virtues, had set well.

"Nice job."

"I did my best," I said levelly. "Any boys we allow to play in it can have miniature triremes. They can hold mock-naval battles in their own little naumachia."

Our eyes met. "I'll just go to fetch something," Tiberius said, turning off towards the atrium. "If that's all right?"

"You know it's all right." He paused for a moment, assessing my reaction. What was coming would be tricky. I made sure I was inscrutable.

When he came back, he was carrying the three-year-old. The five-year-old was beside him, clinging to his knee. He had put them back in coloured tunics, the way their mother always did, Daellius in blue and Laellius in green; at least they looked more comfortable than the last time I'd seen them, trussed in white at her funeral.

They were both crying. I found out later they had been travel-sick in the swaying wagon. They were tired by the journey to Rome and terrified. They had been here before, but then they had witnessed their uncle being struck by lightning, with everybody panicking. Their mother had been in deep distress over their father's bad behaviour; now she was dead, while he must have given up on them. Their brother had presumably chosen to stay with Antistius, but these two had come with their serious uncle to their scary aunt. Some would say that was brave of them.

My husband was pleading, though he had no need. There he was, with his grey eyes, warmth of heart, easy attitude. Upon his arrival, for me the troubled world had stilled. Tiberius Manlius was mine and they were his, so they were mine too. A ready-made family. Lucky me.

Silence had fallen. All our household stood in the courtyard around us, watching. With foreknowledge from Paris, they were agog to see what I would do.

I knew. No child in my house would ever have to feel as I did as a lost waif in Londinium. Mother would be proud. I went straight over to Tiberius and his nephews, stooped, picked up the second one myself, then wrapped my arms around all three. Since my husband had not thought of kissing me, I gently kissed him. "Welcome home," I said. "Welcome, to you all."

The little boys' first names were Gaius and Lucius, like the princes, the two princes who were commemorated in the Grove of the Caesars.

Appendix

You think that by buying up all the best books you can lay your hands on, you will pass for a man of literary tastes: not a bit of it; you are merely exposing your own ignorance of literature. Why, you cannot even buy the right things: any casual recommendation is enough to guide your choice; you are as clay in the hands of the unscrupulous amateur, and as good as cash down to any dealer. How are you to know the difference between genuine old books that are worth money, and trash whose only merit is that it is falling to pieces?

You will go on buying books that you cannot use—to the amusement of educated men, who derive profit not from the price of a book, nor from its handsome appearance, but from the sense and sound of its contents.

Lucian of Samosata,
remarks addressed to an illiterate book collector

Epitynchanus the Dialectician, "the Controversialist," and Philadespoticus of Skopelos are today virtually unknown. Concerned scholars have voiced the hope that when scrolls from the Villa of the Papyri in Herculaneum can be unravelled with modern technology, works from these intriguing philosophers, followers of the ancient School of Miletus, will emerge among those that the villa owner chose to leave behind in a heap of rejects when Mount Vesuvius erupted. Until then, no writings that can safely be attributed to Epitynchanus or Philadespoticus survive. Even details of their lives are sparse.

There is no record of Didymus Dodomos, who rates not even a Wiki stub.

Of the Arcadian poetess Thallusa, little remains. A widely discredited suggestion has been made that it was in scraps of her work that Samuel Pepys wrapped his Stilton cheese when he buried it to escape the 1666 Great Fire of London. This claim was put forward by Mimsy Bloggins, a romantic novelist. Generally derided, Bloggins appeared in a television documentary, passionately advocating her theory, which gained a following in social media. During the late 1980s and 1990s, Bloggins continued to further her idea through personal appearances on C-list chat shows. She also self-published a five-novel saga envisioning the life of the Stilton cheese while in the custody of Pepys. The original documentary is occasionally shown at 4 a.m. on TV channels at the end of the regular spectrum.

Another claim made by Bloggins is that four lines of Thallusan verse cited by Flavia Albia form a precursor to "Identity Crisis Blues," a satirical rock anthem celebrating the introversion, confusion and mental unhappiness of university students in the late 1960s; no copies are officially known to have surfaced.[*][†]

Obfusculans the Obscure is too obscure even for modern scholars to write PhDs about him.[‡]

---

[*] The author of *The Grove of the Caesars* has seen this poem. *Davis, 2019.*
[†] And she can sing it. *Ibid.*
[‡] I bet some idiot academic will try. *Ibid (unattributed)*